Praise for Paul Park and the Novels of Roumania

"Paul Park is one of the most gifted and subtle story writers I know."
—Jonathan Lethem

"Complex, ambitious, lively, engrossing, and entirely original . . . If you like the work of Philip Pullman, Gene Wolfe, or Ursula Le Guin, you ought to be reading Paul Park, too."
—Kelly Link

"Deft, inventive, and intelligent, *The White Tyger* opens a window onto a world where imagination rules. This is as deeply pleasurable to read as Madeleine L'Engle's *A Wrinkle in Time* or Philip Pullman's His Dark Materials trilogy."
—Andrea Barrett, author of *Ship Fever*

"These books are dangerous and as glittering as amber and bloodstone and, yes, tourmaline. An embarrassment of riches—the Baroness is one of the great characters of fiction. Like Miyazaki or Pullman, Park is not afraid to write real risk and beauty."
—Maureen McHugh, author of *Mothers and Other Monsters*

"Readers can revel in every twist of the Baroness's descent into madness. . . . This is another interesting addition to the series."
—*Starlog* on *The White Tyger*

"This volume offers a lot of intriguing, exciting matter for our appreciation. . . . The villain has grown so monstrously alluring that the temptation to let him or her take over is enormous and hard to resist. But what a detailed, microscopic, insightful, unforgettable portrait Park presents!"
—Scifi.com on *The White Tyger*

"All the best writers are explorers. Only a few are discoverers. Paul Park is one of those rare talents in SF, like Gene Wolfe or William Gibson, who have opened entire new

worlds, hitherto unimagined and, indeed, unimaginable. Is it any wonder that his fellow writers are among his most eager readers?"
—Terry Bisson

"The plot is enthralling, the prose is graceful and clear, the themes important and intelligently handled. But it's the characters who kept me reading late into the night, each of them vivid, faceted, and utterly real in a world in which reality is mutable."
—Delia Sherman on *The Tourmaline*

"Paul Park knows fairy tales, contemporary and classic fantasy, and literary science fiction, and he borrows tropes from all these genres. . . . At times, though, it's bound to remind you of the Harry Potter books, Philip Pullman's novels about Lyra Belacqua, and even Gene Wolfe's recent *The Knight* and *The Wizard*, as well as such older classics as *The Wizard of Oz*, Joan Aiken's Dido Twite chronicles, and even Philip K. Dick's classic *The Man in the High Castle*. But then all these works draw from the same well of fantasy, the same pool of dreams and nightmares."
—*The Washington Post Book World* on
A Princess of Roumania

"Complex, elusive, haunting, written in a transparent prose that slips you from one world to another with prestidigitous ease, *A Princess of Roumania* is a quietly and profoundly original novel. To compare Paul Park with Philip Pullman or John Crowley gives a hint of the kind of satisfaction his fiction provides."
—Ursula K. Le Guin on *A Princess of Roumania*

THE WHITE TYGER

ALSO BY PAUL PARK

*A Princess of Roumania**

*The Tourmaline**

*The Hidden World**†

Soldiers of Paradise

Sugar Rain

The Cult of Loving Kindness

*Celestis**

The Gospel of Corax

Three Marys

If Lions Could Speak and Other Stories

No Traveller Returns

*Denotes a Tor Book
†Forthcoming

THE WHITE TYGER

Paul Park

A TOM DOHERTY ASSOCIATES BOOK
NEW YORK

THE WHITE TYGER

A Tor Book
Published by Tom Doherty Associates, LLC
175 Fifth Avenue
New York, NY 10010

www.tor.com

ISBN-13: 978-0-7653-5434-1
ISBN-10: 0-7653-5434-9

First Edition: January 2007
First Mass Market Edition: February 2008

Printed in the United States of America

0 9 8 7 6 5 4 3 2 1

FOR LUCIUS LIONEL, MY SON

THE WHITE TYGER

Communication with the Dead

1 A Radioactive Incident

SHE LAY DOZING in a bed of pine needles in the Mogosoaia woods, wrapped in a gray shawl against the chilly summer night. In her hand was a letter from her aunt Aegypta, gone now five years. *Ma petite chère . . .*

Waiting for darkness, surrounded by enemies, she lay on the west bank of the Colentina River in a stand of old trees, nineteen kilometers northwest of Snagov Portal, the tram line, and the broken wall of Bucharest.

But in her dreams she was far away. Miranda had discovered—or was it a coincidence?—that if she closed her eyes like this, with the onionskin pages of her aunt's final letter clasped between her fingers, images would come to her in the moment before sleep, images that were new to her, though on waking she could recognize them as memories.

At that instant she imagined her seventh birthday party, which she had celebrated in Mamaia by the seaside. English fashion, her aunt had arranged a picnic on the sand dunes with the servants' children, and there had been small cakes and ices. The Chevalier de Graz had stood above them, guarding against an accident or an assault, though he was dressed in his best uniform and ornamental braid.

NOW ALSO HE stood watching her, twelve or even seventeen years later, scruffy and disheveled but still vigilant. In his left hand he held her father's pistol. His right hand ached from his wound. He was looking toward the river and the ford, where under moonlight they would learn if they'd escaped their pursuers' net. There was nothing for him to do but wait and watch till then, and take a confused comfort in Miranda's presence. Bending down in the uncertain light, de Graz could just make out the small French words under her thumb: *... si vous êtes comme je crois ... If you are as I think a princess of Roumania ...*

A lock of her dark hair had fallen over her face. She mumbled something. The letter slipped from her fingers and fell open. But de Graz was more interested in studying her cheek and lips, feeling the tug of small emotions he didn't understand.

He would have scorned to read further even if he'd been curious, even if he'd been able to decipher in the half-light Aegypta Schenck von Schenck's tiny handwriting. Casting his mind forward into the next hour, biting his lips with a nervousness that nevertheless contained an admixture of wordless joy, he would not have had the patience for an abstract argument of any kind: *My dear niece, by this time you must suspect that there is more to the world than the evidence of your senses. By this time you might picture to yourself our globe with its little circle of illumination, a circle with its center in Great Roumania, and showing at the limit of its bright circumference the nations of Africa and Asia, and to the west the North American wilderness, dark and trackless beyond the Henry Hudson River. Closer to home we find the Byzantine Turks, and Russia, and the German Republic with its tributary states. We find barbaric Italy and unpopulated France, and Iberia behind the curtain of ice mountains. In the North Sea there are the submerged remnants of the British Islands, a proud nation once.*

You know all this. It is what everyone knows, every shopkeeper and office clerk. I want to bring you news of another country just as real as these, but it is nevertheless hidden or secret, a landscape of the heart, you might call it, or of dreams, but whose influence can be seen in every natural phenomenon. This is a country that the dead can visit and not only the dead. My dear, though in the ordinary world you must sometimes feel feeble and alone, please take consolation in imagining yourself a personage of terrible importance in this secret country, if you are as I think a princess of Roumania. I mean if you can find the strength to do what's right, or even if you can't.

You must suspect all this already. Everyone suspects it. Not to suspect it would make life intolerable. But faith is one thing, action is another, and science is a third. Now I must explain to you that access to this hidden world can be achieved in several ways which vulgar people might call conjuring, a word I despise because of its implication of fakery and fraud. Because of it, many intelligent persons cannot even reach out their hands to touch the strands we others grope for blindly, the nets that make a pattern for the universe, and that constrain the many-colored incidents of our experience like a school of brainless fish. . . .

IN MOGOSOAIA THE sun was setting. But earlier that day, two men had stood on a work site near the town of Chiselet on the Bulgarian frontier. "Intelligent persons," in the words of Aegypta Schenck, they would have rejected with contempt the entire contents of her letter, dismissing it as criminal superstition. But their agreement on these matters had not helped them to explain the facts at hand. Surveying the wreck of the Hephaestion, the night train from Constantinople to Bucharest, they were full of doubt, dissatisfied with their own opinions and each other's.

The passenger compartments had tumbled off the high embankment. Three cars lay on their sides. Roumanian work crews, pressed into service from the town, labored with dour resentment under their German overseers. They had not yet managed to repair the tracks. For the time being, all trains had been rerouted to the old line through Calarasi.

The Hephaestion had driven over a mine that had blown up the baggage car. Pushed in front of the engine as a precaution, it had exploded and burned. Nothing much was left of it now. This was due not so much to the power of the mine as to the effect of the ordnance that had been packed inside the car, contravening international and local regulations.

"Many things . . . are not good," said Joachim Beck.

Dispatched as a consultant by the German embassy, he combined several useful areas of expertise. A medical doctor and a professor of industrial design, he nevertheless spoke Roumanian like a three-year-old. This was especially galling to Radu Luckacz, who was fluent in all central European languages. To labor in this unproductive way, to ignore all Luckacz's attempts to answer him in his own language, was obviously a form of condescension. The other possibility—that the doctor was playing some kind of doughy, Teutonic practical joke—Luckacz had examined briefly and then discarded. There was nothing in the German's cold fat features to suggest a sense of humor.

And of course the circumstances were quite serious. There appeared to be some sort of epidemic in the town. Whether it had been caused by exposure to a biological, chemical, or radioactive contaminant, or was unconnected to the accident—none of that was sure. The work crews, however, had been recruited under duress. The men wore gauze masks over their faces, and so far none of them had gotten sick. Since the previous day, German cavalry were stationed in the town.

Now the German doctor and the Roumanian police chief walked along the berm under the embankment, a quarter kilometer from the wreck. Several lead canisters had been laid out in a line beside a bush. They were evidence of the forbidden cargo and had broken open during the explosion; they were empty now. They had contained African pitchblende or radium. Luckacz was unsure of the details, which had not been shared with him.

"This, you hide—pah! Herr General . . ."

Luckacz gritted his teeth. It was only because he knew in advance what the man was trying to say that he was able to understand him. Communication was not meant to function in this way. At this rate Luckacz would be competent to host an emissary from Borneo or Hindustan. Interpreters would not be necessary!

". . . Herr General . . ."

Antonescu, Luckacz almost said. And it was true what Beck was toiling to explain. His enormous bald white forehead was lumpy with effort, but Luckacz had gone on ahead: It was true he'd tried to keep the news of the accident from the German authorities, but that was more of an official reflex than any kind of subterfuge—this was an internal police matter, after all. It had been General Antonescu, as part of his terms of surrender, who had personally delivered one of the lead canisters to the German headquarters in Transylvania.

"But . . . this is nothing . . . pah!" said Dr. Beck.

With the toe of his brown leather boot, he prodded at the row of blackened metal tubes under the bush. What did he mean? No, Luckacz could guess: He meant the risk of contamination from this incident was not significant in his opinion. After all, the pockets of his brown raincoat bulged with dosimeters and radiation tubes, none of which he had bothered to consult.

Luckacz, though, was far more nervous, and he winced to see the broken canisters shift under the doctor's toe, as if an oily, snakelike poison could still seep from them. He resented how, for appearance's sake, he had to walk along with his hands in his pockets as if unconcerned, conversing (if it could be called that) with this idiotic German. When Radu Luckacz had responded to the wreck, the first thing he had done was to cordon off this entire area.

"But this is . . . bad . . . ."

So which was it? Nothing? Bad? Luckacz turned toward the doctor as he labored to speak, imagining for a moment he could pry open with his fingers the fellow's thick red lips, perhaps insert a gloved hand into his mouth and extract some kind of slippery meaning—this was an important subject, after all! What did the Baroness Ceausescu call these Germans? Potato-eating fools, she said.

No, it was not productive to think of Dr. Beck as a potato-eating fool. The man was an eminent professor at the University of Heidelberg. Luckacz was fortunate to have the benefit of his expertise, no matter how much he felt like seizing him by his cravat or pounding him on the head.

"But I must insist to you that Antonescu was the source of this accident. Only the fact that he was in possession of one specimen of these lead tubes has proved this—two hundred kilometers away! These are his partisans who have exploded this train, and it is similar to many of their activities since the conclusion of the old regime—I don't know how familiar you are with this kind of politics. But Antonescu was the virtual chief of state under the Empress Valeria, deposed five years ago and now deceased, thank all the gods. But Antonescu is a potent enemy of the current government. . . ."

Luckacz let his voice trail away. How ugly it sounded, even to himself! Harsh, nasal, Hungarian-accented, the words pedantic and awkward—this was not his natal language either, after all.

The doctor raised his fat hand. Luckacz wondered what percentage of his speech the man could understand. And his head very much resembled a potato after it has been scraped clean. Doubtless the bulges and depressions would have interested a phrenologist.

"No. Don't tell. I understand . . . everything."

Well, that's a relief, thought Luckacz savagely. That might be useful, to understand everything. Luckacz himself, for example, was quite confused, though he feared the worst. Antonescu had blown up the train. It was obvious he had known there were armaments on board. But who had purchased the cargo? Who had paid for it? What purpose was it supposed to serve?

"Let me remind you that the terminus . . . was in Bucharest."

Luckacz stared down at the row of canisters. These words so accurately reflected his thoughts that he mulled them over for a few seconds before glancing up, startled. Where had this tongue-tied idiot learned such phrases?

"Ammunition, guns, explosives, and of course these." Dr. Beck ticked them off on his fingers.

"They could have been intended for international transfer," suggested Luckacz feebly. "They could have been reloaded at the Gara de Nord."

"I do not . . . think."

Luckacz knew where this was headed. The conclusion was obvious, and the policeman had already arrived at it, though he could scarcely yet admit it to himself. But still he might sabotage the German's train of thought, blow it off its tracks:

"So then perhaps it was intended for these other rebels and agitators, of which there are no lack in my poor country. I mean the supporters of Miranda Popescu, the daughter of Prince Frederick Schenck von Schenck, who betrayed our interests in the old days, as we then conceived of them—this is more than twenty years. But do not be concerned. My men have bottled her in the Mogosoaia woods."

"I do not . . . think. Where is money, influence for these things? To bring from . . . Congo?"

Precisely. Yet the third alternative was painful to consider. Luckacz scratched at his moustache.

"Bah! No reason to guess. Purchasing will make a . . . path." The doctor shrugged, then changed the subject. "And this . . . disease. Psychosomatical, do you . . . think?"

It seemed absurd. The symptoms, after all, were real: fever, erratic heartbeat, delirium, extreme thirst. Seventy-eight adults had been affected, and more than a hundred children. Thankfully, no one had died. "I had thought obviously the results of this African poison. How could there be another cause?"

But Dr. Beck shrugged his massive shoulders. "The dosages are . . . what is this word?"

Behind them came the sounds of the workmen, the thump of sledgehammers, the whistle of the engine, also cries and shouts. Luckacz rubbed the palms of his gloved hands together. Pondering the mystery, searching for the word, the doctor stared down at his boots. His chin, pressed into his breast, now disappeared in folds of flesh.

"Negligible," he grunted finally. "After this rain."

"But of course this radium was planned to be a weapon," protested Luckacz. "Otherwise what was the possible intention?"

From the marshland on the other side of the embankment came the sound of cawing crows. Suddenly again Luckacz felt an irritation that was almost violent; his hands itched. The world seemed airless under the gray, damp sky. He found himself kicking at lumps of mud. His trousers were spattered—was it possible that he also was succumbing to this sickness? Surely he must go away, return to Bucharest where he had other more important responsibilities. This was a matter for the district health commissioner!

The feet of Joachim Beck, by contrast, seemed rooted in the dirt. "A weapon . . . yes. But not to be . . . employed . . . like so."

Luckacz clapped his hands together. "Well, I must make my report to the Baroness Ceausescu," he said. "With any chance we will soon apprehend this woman, Miranda Popescu as she calls herself. I will be able to question her as to her intention."

At the mention of the baroness's name, Dr. Beck glanced up quickly. For the first time Luckacz was aware of his powerful small eyes. "Ceausescu," he said. "You will not mention this . . . to her."

The arrogance of this potato-eating doctor! Again Luckacz felt like pounding him on the head—a reaction which, he had the sense to realize, was not entirely normal. He was not, after all, he reminded himself, a violent or impulsive man. But how could this fellow now presume to give his orders to the police chief of Bucharest? How could he imagine he could tell him not to discuss these matters of importance with the Baroness Nicola Ceausescu? Though her position was not precisely an official one, surely in these dark days of occupation she still represented the unbroken heart of Great Roumania. It was obvious she must be kept informed of these events, if only because they involved the suffering of her citizens.

"You will not . . . mention . . . this . . . to her," repeated the German.

RECENTLY IN BERLIN the Committee for Roumanian affairs had approved a motorcar for Luckacz's official use. As he slogged toward it over a muddy road between two pastures, Luckacz wondered if he should take the time to stop at the telegraph office in Oltenita, perhaps, and send a message on to his personal physician. His wife often accused him of hypochondria. But this was not his imagination, these feelings of anger, this itching in his palms. As he walked, he stripped off his leather gloves, put his hand to his forehead, ran his fingers through his gray hair.

When he reached the main road he had calmed himself. Seated in the back of the luxurious Mercedes, he wondered why he had allowed himself to forfeit his composure. As he opened up his dossier of official papers for the drive, he even allowed himself some generous thoughts about Joachim Beck, who was not the fool he had appeared, and who also had a function to accomplish. Nor had he shown any anxiety about staying in Chiselet. When Luckacz left him he had turned his big back. Hands in his pockets, he had strolled away, returning to the corner of the work site where he was to meet the director of the regional hospital in Slobozia.

So the policeman did not feel any personal vindication in the news that followed him to Bucharest. He did not feel anything but alarm. When the railway crews at Chiselet began their mutiny, Dr. Beck was severely beaten. With several other German nationals, he was among the first patients in the field hospital he had been attempting to set up.

For Luckacz the news only added to the mystery that had already appeared insoluble during the long drive back to the capital over muddy rutted roads. From time to time he fingered his black moustache, glanced at his pocket watch. He had an appointment with the Baroness Ceausescu in the People's Palace.

After sitting in the back of the car awhile, he began to contemplate another mystery, the problem of the baroness's beauty and its effect on him after these five years. Nor could he guess that these two mysteries were related, and had their source in what Aegypta Schenck had called the hidden world.

Luckacz would not, he decided, mention to the baroness the details of his conversation with Joachim Beck. Nor would he convey to her the doctor's suppositions, at least not yet. It was clear, though, what the man suspected: that the baroness herself had purchased the munitions on the Hephaestion, that she herself bore responsibility for this accident.

There was no reason to upset her, not yet. Luckacz would make his own inquiries and decide what to do. In the meantime he lay back in the velvet seats, tried to relax—the road was better beyond Soldanu. He closed his eyes, trying to summon in his mind an image of the baroness's face as she sat poised over her piano, studying the score of her great work, picking out the themes sometimes with difficulty. In the motorcar, Luckacz couldn't hear them. He had no ear for music. Instead he concentrated on the little grimace that distorted her small mouth, revealed her perfect teeth. A frown puckered the skin between her eyebrows, brought lines to the edges of her purple eyes—she was almost forty, after all! Still she was beautiful—her chestnut hair cut at the line of her jaw, her creamlike skin—with a beauty that was not only decorative, but seemed to achieve, at least for Luckacz, a desperate significance.

Even intelligent, rational persons, daydreaming and dreaming, sometimes at moments can achieve a kind of access to the secret world. If in his imagination's eye Luckacz had looked backward through the rear, flat, oval window of the Mercedes, perhaps even he would have caught a glimpse of the disaster that still roiled the sky above Chiselet. He would have seen flashes like lightning burst inside the clouds, which were lit also from beneath by explosions and fires. Near the wreck along the train line there was a raw wound in the earth, a crater almost half a kilometer across. Fires burned in both the marshland and the town among the shattered buildings.

2 In the Mogosoaia Woods

MY DEAR NIECE, this will seem astonishing to you, except for the experiences you have already had in the town in Massachusetts where I protected you. Let me explain how there are places in Roumania and other countries that form an access to this secret world of ghosts, symbols, and animals. One of these places is in Insula Calia where I have written you this letter. One is also in Mogosoaia where you must go and find the key that I have left for you alone. I have hidden it from other prying eyes. This will be for you like opening a door. But you must learn to open it yourself, and wedge it open when it threatens to crash shut. Nor can I help you with this, because I could never find a way to enter through the door as a living woman, and I know about it only in experiments and signs. You come from a mixing of your mother's and your father's blood, the mixing of two traits that are not dominant. It is for this reason that I introduced them in Brasov on Saturn's festival, and I helped her overlook his faults. I hope by God it is enough and I have prepared you sufficiently, though far from my hand. Otherwise the fault is both of ours and God's as well perhaps. . . .

This part of the letter was covered by Miranda's fingers when she awoke, stretched, smiled at something, the tail end of a dream. She opened her eyes and saw de Graz bending over her, his face strange and well-remembered; startled, she raised her hand. But then she brought the smile back again, deliberately this time as de Graz stepped away and stood up straight. He was a menacing figure in the darkness, her father's pistol in his left hand, his right hand covered with a wad of dirty bandages that made it look like a club or a boxing glove. Miranda sat up.

When she slept with her aunt's letter in her hand, dreams came to her that were like memories. It was as if she could absorb them through her skin, as if the fragile paper had been treated in some way.

Because or in spite of her deliberate smile, she felt a little gladness coming back. De Graz had been in her dream. And not just de Graz but Peter Gross, who'd been her friend in the faraway town where she'd gone to school, and who had grown and changed into the hulking figure above her, as she had grown and changed.

"I had a dream," she said. "Do you remember that Halloween party we went to? It must have been in seventh grade. It was at Angela Eusden's house. I was trying to remember the first time I saw you. You know, to recognize. It was by the pool. She must have invited the whole class. I was doing something, and I turned around and you were standing right behind me, dressed as—what were you dressed as?"

De Graz grunted. Stiff as a tree, he stood above her in the pearly dark, his right hand like a club. Maybe he'd been Frankenstein or something, she thought.

Of course in those days he hadn't had an arm at all. His forearm had ended in a stump, a birth defect. That's what she'd thought about on Halloween. She had pitied him as she noticed (now it came back to her) how his costume had given him two arms.

"What were you dressed as?" she repeated, but he wouldn't tell her. Instinctively she'd spoken in English. Nowadays he never talked to her except in French, a language—she was sure—he'd never taken in high school. It was the language of rich people in Roumania.

"Mademoiselle, ce n'est pas la peine . . ."—blah, blah. These days he was all business. These days he always had a scowl on his face, which she attributed partly to the pain in his wounded hand. Not that he complained, or had a right to. He didn't take care of it, didn't allow her or Ludu Rat-tooth to change the bandages. He cursed the Gypsy when she tried. In Massachusetts he had not been so stubborn or so stiff.

Miranda looked around. Where was Ludu now? But with half an ear she was listening to de Graz as he explained again what they were doing here and what they planned to do. In the darkness they would cross the river at Constantin's Ford. It was their only chance, or else a trap.

Soldiers in black uniforms had driven her into this part of the forest, caught her in the river's curve. The Baroness Ceausescu had offered a reward. "I don't understand," she said. "Here's where they've cornered us. How likely is it they don't know about the ford?"

"It is a secret place," muttered the Chevalier de Graz. "Your father showed it to me once when we were hunting."

"What if they're just waiting for us to cross? We'd be in the open. What if they're just waiting for us to show ourselves?"

Left unspoken were more basic questions. What do we do once we're on the other side? "We're just three people," she said. "You need to see a doctor."

He shrugged. Then he nodded, relenting. "I'm surprised you can still read that," he said, meaning the letter in her hand.

"Don't change the subject," said Miranda. She glanced down at the fragile pages, folded them, and slid them carefully into the pocket of her filthy shirt. "Most of this I still don't understand."

She wrapped her shawl closer around her shoulders. It was damp now, and wet where she had lain on it. Beads of moisture were in her hair.

"What if I just give myself up?" she said. "We've gone days like this—no food. She's been chasing me since we first got here. But I still don't know what would happen if she caught me."

"She" was Nicola Ceausescu. With German money and support, she was living in the empress's former palace in Bucharest. "It is your choice," muttered de Graz, his hand raised like a club. "But she would kill you.

"For the sake of your bracelet," he added, and she was aware of it suddenly, the worn gold beads on her wrist, each in the shape of a tiger's head.

"She calls herself the white tyger," said de Graz. "No one believes her. But if she stands on the boards of the Ambassadors Theatre, that bracelet on her hand . . . She lives for that moment."

"There's nothing magic about a bracelet," said Miranda. "What if I send it in the mail?"

De Graz shrugged. "Besides," he said, "you shot a man."

It was true. During the course of another of these endless days, endless escapes, she'd shot a man who'd died.

Miranda fingered the gold beads on her wrist. Chilled, she rubbed her arm. It was odd, and perhaps it was because she was so tired, but she couldn't feel a proper sense of urgency. Kill her—how likely was that? And she had killed a man—how likely did that sound? Since her small glimpse of the hidden world in St. Mary's cave, none of these things and none of this had seemed quite real.

No, it was all real, rocks and stones, reasons and consequences, all of it sufficient for right now. She sat in a nest of old leaves and pine needles under the low, dark clouds. It was her choice, de Graz had said. What did that mean?

Above her he stretched out his bandaged hand, pressed it against the bark of a tall tree. "The Baron Ceausescu killed your father," he said.

This was unfair, and should have made Miranda angry. But she felt suddenly like crying, though she had never known her father, never seen him. What was he besides a name—Prince Frederick Schenck von Schenck? But she sniffed to unclog her nose, and smelled a deep, piney smell. Her fingers, when she rubbed her face, were sticky with a little sap.

"And what if we do cross safely?" she asked. "What then—the three of us?"

"We hide," he said. "There are people who can help us, friends of my mother's in Floreasca. Your father was well loved, as I told you. People hate the Germans, hate Ceausescu, too."

Then he shrugged again, as if irritated to have to think about the future. "Ça ne fait rien. You struggle to the end."

They had been speaking softly. But now they heard a voice

call in the darkness not far away—"Where are you? Miss, what I have seen!"

It was Ludu Rat-tooth. De Graz cursed in Roumanian and raised his gun. Miranda knew he'd chosen this stand of evergreens because the trees grew close together. They gave more shelter than the wide beeches and oaks. But now the Gypsy girl came blundering through, out of breath, excited. "Miss," she said. "Oh, miss!" And then she laughed.

It was a welcome sound. The girl stood with her hands on her hips. Because her spotted face was so familiar, Miranda imagined she could see it clearly in the darkness, even see that she was sweating, flushed. Her coarse brown hair was tied behind her neck and held in place by a silver clasp. Her mouth was open wide. Now, self-conscious even in the dark, she raised her right hand to her lips to hide the sharp bicuspid that had given her her name.

"Be quiet," hissed the Chevalier de Graz. He took a step toward her, menacing with his bandaged hand. He made as if to grab her, pull her down, but she paid no attention. She was too excited. "Miss, I saw it clear as I see you. Oh, I was frightened—the white tyger!"

"Quiet," said de Graz.

But the Gypsy turned her back. She bent down to seize Miranda's hands, drag her to her feet. "I thought I'd never see one," she continued breathlessly. "I thought maybe they'd died out. Or maybe they'd just been a story after all. And it was wrong what I had heard. This was a big animal, as big as you. There was a bird caught in a tree."

"Mademoiselle," de Graz said. "There's no time for this." But Miranda didn't pay attention. Now she was on her feet, following the Gypsy as she crossed over the boggy ground and then into the deeper woods.

"HERE IT IS," said Ludu Rat-tooth. But she wasn't sure. In just fifteen minutes the woods had gotten darker. Had she been this way? Thorns pulled at her long dress.

She had come with Miranda from the coast. She had never been in woods like these and she distrusted them, not just for ordinary reasons. But this was Mother Egypt's place. She had died here in Mogosoaia. And there were ghosts here, ghosts of the dead. Miranda had tried to explain it, quoting from Mother Egypt's letter, which she carried in the pocket of her shirt.

Ludu stood up in the thicket in the dark. A thorn had caught in her necklace, silver and glass beads that Miranda Popescu had bought for her in some little town. Carefully she plucked it loose, then listened. Where was Miss Popescu now? No, there she was—the sound of crashing in the brush behind her. Taller than Ludu, she couldn't come as fast.

The Gypsy turned her head, pulled herself free, stepped into a grove of dark saplings. Heart pounding, out of breath, she was afraid of sudden creatures in the dark. Where were her footprints? Had she come this way? She'd been frightened, yet excited, too—she had not needed to scramble this far through the bushes just to empty her bladder away from the others. Something had drawn her and was drawing her still. "Miss!" she cried out. What was she doing alone in these woods, chasing after a dangerous animal? Oh, but she had seen it! And it had turned its heavy head and looked at her. And there had been a bird above it in the tree. And she had not been frightened, not that she remembered. The animal had stood between two trees. Already the sky was dark, but the white fur along the tyger's flanks had seemed to shine.

Above it in the tree the little iridescent bird had *flap-flap-flapp*ed. And then also it was still. Where was that tree? It had had wide, spadelike leaves.

"Miss!" cried Ludu Rat-tooth. Now she was aware of something new, a smell of burning and also something rotten, a small stink she remembered from Insula Calia in the marsh. It was the smell of conjuring and magic tricks. Suddenly terrified, Ludu pulled out from the waist of her chemise a carborundum strip and a pouch of phaetons, long phosphorus matches.

Now she ignited one. There was no wind, and she held it up. Sparks dripped from it. And in the harsh green light she saw what she had missed, the trail of her own boots. There, just a few meters from her, was the beech tree she had seen, and in the mud the heavy prints of the cat.

The match burned bright. Nearby in a pile of leaf meal at the base of the tree, Ludu saw movement. As if drawn by the light, a tiny, nervous creature showed itself, a mouse or a wood rat, half hidden underneath a tree root. But now it showed its eyes, which gleamed, a little greenish light.

She dropped the match before it burned her fingers. As soon as it was out the darkness covered her, blacker than before. Heart pounding, she fumbled with another match and lit it. There in the tree above her was the bird. Whether it had come back or it had been there all the time, she couldn't say.

It was a brandywine bird, common in Constanta and the flat parts of Roumania, a small bird with an iridescent sheen. It was on a low branch above Ludu's head. It cocked its beak, and Ludu could see something else, something that was also gleaming in the harsh light. Now that she saw it, though, she wondered if it had some other property as well—the stink of conjuring was stronger now, and she could smell it even over the burning phosphorus. She took a few steps to the tree, wondering if the bird would fly away, but it did not. And when she had to drop her match again, she saw that she'd been right. Whatever hung there from that vine or twig had a small purple glow that did not disappear in the darkness, which was otherwise so frightening.

Ludu drew out a third match and lit it. The bird cocked its head. There below it, almost in its feet, hung a berry or a grape. And immediately it occurred to Ludu Rat-tooth that she would pluck it and bring it to Miranda, who seemed so famished and weak, even though Ludu had made her eat up all their meager food over the past day, all their sausage and nuts till there was nothing left. As if it had been whispered in her ear, Ludu knew that she would take this berry or this grape or whatever this was, and she would bring it to Miss Popescu and make her eat it, and refuse any part of it herself, though now she looked at it in the last flare of the match, it looked big enough to share.

She reached up and the light went out. It didn't matter. The glow of the grape or berry guided her hand. It was firm and cool in her fingers as she brought it down, and she thought she would bring it to Miss Popescu, who must be close behind her, must have seen the light from the matches.

But then suddenly she thought she wouldn't, that she herself was hungry and had given up all her food, and Miranda wouldn't begrudge her something she had found in the woods. So in the darkness she brought the fruit to her lips and slipped it into her mouth where it exploded in juice. "Oh, a stone," she thought, which was the last thought she had before she heard a crash behind her in the wood, and then another crash and she fell down.

3 *A Struggle to the End*

MY DEAR, THERE is one other gift I can offer you although I scarcely know its use, a jewel that belonged to a great German alchemist and allowed him, as I understand it from his documents, to pass at will between two worlds. Let me explain another way. This was an ability that he was able to discover and refine, and that he exercised and developed in his mind until it calcified a lobe of his inner brain, a lobe that allows ordinary men and women a capacity for dreams and premonitions. My belief is that this calcification was what killed the alchemist at last, and finally it was dug from his skull in the shape of a great tourmaline. Though more than once when I had money I attempted to purchase this stone from the collector who owned it, still it is true I have not made up my mind as to its dangers. Because this is unclear to me, and because of the constraints of desperation, nevertheless I will attempt to find this tourmaline for you to use or to ignore as you see fit. In the spirit world this stone will take a living form, a piece of fruit. And if you see me as a bird on a branch in Mogosoaia, please . . .

A piece of fruit? Miranda didn't understand this part of her aunt's letter. Even so, as she followed Ludu Rat-tooth into the woods, she found herself remembering these words and the words around them. They had been summoned by what the Gypsy said about the bird in the tree. Miranda found she had a picture in her mind, a small bird with iridescent feathers desperately beating its wings.

"Quiet," whispered de Graz, and they could hear the Gypsy smashing on ahead, snapping the dead sticks under their feet. She even called back to them, called Miranda's name; de Graz seized hold of her forearm and held her. "Idiot fool," he muttered in the common tongue, and Miranda knew what he was talking about. There were soldiers in these woods.

Soon the girl had disappeared ahead of them. They stood in marshy ground amid a stand of dead trees. Above them the sky had lost almost all its light. There was no wind. The air was damp and cool.

But among the dark beech trees there shined a light, the green glare of a phosphorous match. De Graz cursed and pulled Miranda back. They stepped up onto drier land and crouched in a thicket of thorns. "Mademoiselle," whispered de Graz, "je vous en prie . . ." And he was begging her to leave the girl, who was obviously insane; Miranda shook her head. The light of the match dwindled and went out. It was maybe fifty yards away. Then the Gypsy must have struck another match, which flared up, dwindled, and went out.

De Graz held Miranda with his wounded hand. The gun was in his left. Now he seemed to hear something and he stood up. A third match burned itself out. "No more," Miranda murmured, and there was no more. Instead they heard a sound like the popping of a bag. De Graz whispered another curse, and he stepped backward. He reached down to grab Miranda again, this time by the ball of her shoulder, and he tried to draw her up the slope behind them. He tried to draw her away from the sound, but Miranda knew what had happened. She'd heard that noise before. And she didn't have a choice anyway. She twisted away from Pieter de Graz's bandaged hand. She had no choice as she stumbled into the dark woods until she found the place where Ludu Rat-tooth lay.

The girl had fallen onto her back. She was on the bare ground under a tree. And because Miranda's eyes had not been blinded by the burning matches, she could see the Gypsy's eyes were open. Her cheek was against the dirt. Miranda pulled her hair back from her face, and she could feel the girl's wet hair and skin. Her lips were wet with some liquid. Miranda felt an itch or a shiver between her shoulder blades. There was no point thinking about danger, though. It was a horrible thing to be shot or wounded in the mouth, even though the liquid in the girl's hair was sweet, thin, and cold under Miranda's fingers as she combed the coarse hair back. It was not blood. "Get up," she whispered. "Can you get up?"

Where was de Graz? There was some crashing in the trees back where she'd come. Someone cried out. Ludu Rat-tooth tried to speak, and Miranda put her cheek down to the girl's lips, where she could smell the sweet smell of the juice. And was it her imagination, or was there some glow or sheen upon the girl's lips? "Oh, miss," she said.

Maybe if they were still and quiet, the soldiers wouldn't find them in the dark. Maybe if she crouched down like this in the undergrowth, in the thicket of small trees. Miranda found the Gypsy's hands and they were also wet.

"Can you get up?" she whispered. But the girl couldn't answer any questions. She was squeezing Miranda's hands. And her eyes were open. There was a purple sheen on her lips. "Miss," she said, "don't leave. Jesus help me. It's so dark."

"I won't leave you. Can you walk?"

But there was a noise of someone crashing and blundering in the trees, and then the heavy thud of her father's pistol—Miranda recognized the sound. Two gunshots close by, and then a coughing scream. The Chevalier de Graz was there, his bandaged hand around her upper arm. "Je vous en prie."

He lifted her up, dragged her away, but she resisted. Ludu also had grabbed hold of her. Ludu was squeezing her hands. And the girl's shuddering whisper was more powerful than any exhortation, at least at first. Miranda had no choice.

"What are you doing? Leave her! Come!"

There was a light near them, a guttering red flare behind the trees. De Graz crouched over her and pulled at her hands, but she resisted. "This is not the way after all this," he muttered next to her ear. "You have no right to be shot down like a dog."

"Can you walk?" whispered Miranda stubbornly. But already she knew the answer, and she knew why she was asking; the girl's hands were slippery and wet. But it wasn't possible to pull away from her and leave her here alone. Miranda thought she was not strong enough to pull away. The girl's eyes were open and her mouth was open. Miranda could see the sharp edge of her tooth. At that moment, suddenly, she seemed horrible to Miranda, her chapped, spotted skin, big features and uneven teeth, gleaming in the filtered light of the red flare.

"Don't leave me," she whispered. "Don't leave me." De Graz had let go of Miranda and was crouching nearby, his gun held out. Now he turned back, and she could see his disgusted look. She could hear a sobbing sound come out of her, but she closed her mouth, choked it back down. Now she pulled her fingers from the Gypsy's grip, pried herself loose as the girl clutched at her: "Oh, miss!"

Miranda left her. As the red light faltered and subsided, she crawled forward on her hands and knees. At first de Graz was behind her, and then he was in front of her, guiding her across the marshy ground. This was the open swale between the thicket where Ludu lay and higher ground to the south; they staggered up past the evergreens where they had rested and continued up the slope. Though there was dead wood everywhere and scratching undergrowth, de Graz led them quickly, bent almost double in front of her. Miranda thought of how she'd followed Peter Gross through the woods on Christmas Hill when he was younger, uglier, and sweeter, and he wasn't a man yet, and he was missing his right hand. She also had changed.

She felt her body shaking, heaving with dry sobs. At first she'd clenched her mouth shut, breathed through her nose. But soon she was guzzling all the air she could, and then the sounds came out of her, mixing with her ragged breath. De Graz's pace was hard, relentless, punishing as he achieved the ridge and led them among outcroppings of rock beside the river. De Graz was punishing her, but not for the right reasons; Miranda stumbled over a downed tree. The moon had come up somewhere.

De Graz didn't wait. She could scarcely see his gray shirt up ahead, flitting through the saplings like a ghost. Her lungs were blazing and the dry sobs broke from her. Surely he wouldn't leave her as she'd left the Gypsy, alone here in the dark?

She fell and barked her shins. She fell forward on her hands and knees, and when she looked up she could see he'd stopped. A silhouette against the gray-black sky, he stood between two trees, the muzzle of his gun pointing above his head.

Then he walked back toward her and helped her up and put his arms around her. They stood for a while, breathing, snuffling, and listening. The night was warmer now. Miranda's arms and face were wet with sweat.

And they could hear the sound of barking dogs not far away, maybe half a mile. Or else not barking exactly, but the baying of a pack of hounds.

Miranda laid her head against the collar of de Graz's shirt. She closed her eyes and thought of Ludu Rat-tooth lying in the dark.

After a moment, de Graz spoke. "Mademoiselle. Perhaps this would be a time for some of the conjuring your aunt used to speak of. Since I swore my service to your father, I have seen miraculous things. All of them, I think, were ways to help you or protect you. I wonder if you know any of those tricks. . . ."

He had been speaking in French, his voice odd, stilted, harsh. But now he finished with an English phrase, something he might have said in Massachusetts. "Now might be a good time."

It brought tears to her eyes to hear him use those words. She could feel his stiff hands behind her back. One held her father's pistol, and one was thick with bandages. She could feel him flex it once, twice, three times.

"Sure," she said, because she had to say something. In the hidden world she had a tyger's power. Here, not so much.

She laid her cheek against his collarbone. She brought her hand up and laid it on his chest, feeling the swell of his breath, the shudder of his heart. "Abracadabra," she murmured softly.

She had lost her shawl, left it with Ludu Rat-tooth. The afternoon had been damp and chilly, but the night was suddenly warm. And surely the police or the soldiers had found the girl by now. And surely they had a doctor with them who could help her better than Miranda could. She had been conscious, talking, not badly hurt. Surely the dogs hadn't found her.

Pieter de Graz was telling her important things. "From here you go downhill to the river. You'll find it shallow here. Wade in the water upstream. We've led them past the place. When you find the cattails and the three flat rocks, that is the place your father showed me. I think there is some old stonework under the surface that diverts the flow, forces it deep. You will see the eddy turn, and it is shallow and easy all the way across. A strong man can cross if he has to. In the spring the water is too high. Tonight it will be possible for you."

Slowly his breath was coming back to normal, and hers, too. "You still have your money. That's enough. Hide the bracelet. There are towns as soon as you cross out of the preserve. You'll see their lights along the shore. And many small hotels along the river road, but go on into town as far as you can. My mother has a house on Lake Herastrau. There is a fig tree. Seven steps to a door painted red. I will meet you there or send a message. And if not, then you will look for Lieutenant Prochenko. I left him in Chiselet. There are many old soldiers who remember your father. Many others who will fight against the Germans for your sake . . ."

On and on. At some point he had switched back to French. "What about you?" Miranda murmured, and she felt him shrug. The dogs were closer now.

"I'll make a circle back toward Mogosoaia. You'll be safe. I'll leave a message. . . ."

He meant he intended to lead the dogs away. "Take this," he said, and she could feel her father's pistol flat against her back between her shoulder blades.

"You keep it," she whispered against his neck. And she was in his arms, and she could feel the club of his bandaged hand against her back. He bent down and kissed her on the lips. As if the kiss had liberated it, she could smell the bitter smell of his sweat, feel the scratch of his unshaven face, the sharp hair around his mouth.

"Stop," she said after a moment. Her eyes were full of tears.

"Mademoiselle."

"I'll see you again."

"I don't doubt it. In a few days I'll leave a message. Good luck."

And he was gone, striding upright down the hill, breaking twigs and branches now. As she watched, he paused to urinate against a tree. Something for the dogs to smell. Embarrassed, ashamed to leave him, she turned away and ran down the opposite slope toward the water.

Now there was a moon. She pushed through the undergrowth until she stood on the pebbly shore, looking at the lights across the way. The river was wide and quiet here. Dutifully she scuffed away her footprints and went down and stood in the water, a few inches deep around her leather boots, which leaked. She listened to the yapping of the dogs. It came in waves. Sometimes it seemed far away, then close, and then it trailed off.

Dutifully she turned upstream. The water had receded from its banks, leaving a narrow beach. Close at hand, trees and bushes overhung the water, and she kept close beside them as she waded. Sometimes she had to clamber onto the bank again, and sometimes the water rose over the tops of her boots; it didn't matter. She would be drenched soon enough.

Because this was a difficult task—slipping in the mud and clambering over rocks as she fought her way upstream in the dark—she didn't ask herself what she was doing. As was her habit, she concentrated on each tiny thing, one after another in a chain. And she listened to the music of the dogs, and she worried about the obstacle in front of her. Would she recognize the three flat rocks among the cattails, the old stonework? A strong man could cross if he had to. What was that supposed to mean?

But she could feel a constriction in her throat, the tears she was swallowing down. Sometimes she wiped her eyes and nose with her wet hands. People had died to keep her moving forward. Aegypta Schenck had died, Dinu Fishbelly had died. And his daughter lay alone in the dark woods, and Peter also . . . The dogs were louder now. So it was the least she could do to stumble forward step by step. And even if she didn't know where she was going (the river road? Lake Herastrau?), still—first things first. She would find Andromeda, Lieutenant Prochenko now.

In Mogosoaia, in St. Mary's cave, Miranda had found a key

to a hidden world. But in this world also there was a key if she could discover it, something to unlock the mysteries of her unhappy country. It was her duty to search for it, her duty also to preserve and justify the faith of other people—that she'd been somehow chosen by a fate that transcended her own ordinariness. If she kept going, kept striving and fumbling in the dark, then maybe she would find the pressure point, or else a small stone she could struggle to dislodge. Everyone she spoke to claimed the rocks were insecurely piled, and that even a small shift might bring them tumbling: foreign armies, a government of murderers and thugs . . .

With cold, failing fingers she clambered over the wet boulders until she found herself standing in a shallow pool, the water about her shins. Above her loomed a rocky cliff, and all around her there were cattails. She saw three flat stones in a line, and lights across the way. The river swirled in a great eddy. Miranda stood in a detritus of sticks and foam. She had all her money, her purse of gold coins, which Ludu had sewn into the waist of her riding pants. Doubtless now if she escaped, she could find some dry clothes and a bed. Then what? She would lie in it and think, stare at the ceiling.

She climbed onto the nearest of the flat stones, then hopped out to the farthest. She saw no sign of the old dam or bridge or whatever it was, and the water where she stood looked smooth and black and deep. But Peter had led her to this place, and she owed it to Peter to continue on, to try. She owed it to all of them, to Aunt Aegypta, to Great Roumania. "Expedite the inevitable," as Stanley, her adoptive father in Berkshire County, might have said.

The baying of the dogs had died away. But now it surged back close at hand beyond the black rocks that loomed above her. And she heard gunshots, too.

Expedite the inevitable. In an instant, without thinking, she was stumbling back through the pool, through the cattails. She was clambering onto the bank and then along the small path that led upstream and back through the overhanging rocks.

Her boots were full of water. She squelched and slipped through the tall grass. But now she found her way uphill under the trees, and the dogs were barking, and there was some new light beyond the crest of the hill. When she reached the top she could hear voices and see the lights between the tree trunks, a glare below her in an open place. She climbed downhill as quietly and delicately as she could, until she stood under the big oak trees and saw the glare of the lanterns.

For a moment she remembered the scene on the Hoosick riverbank when Captain Raevsky had taken her prisoner. Now men in dark uniforms had pulled the dogs away. Leashed, still they jumped and barked. And in a broken circle of soldiers, Miranda saw Peter on his knees, head to the ground, hands behind his back. An officer was standing over him and had bent down to talk, a tall red-haired man with silver buttons on his jacket as Miranda saw when he stood up, frowning and obviously dissatisfied. He had a whip in his left hand, which he must have used to beat away the dogs. And he had picked up a pistol from the grass, the gold-chased pistol of Prince Frederick Schenck von Schenck. He glanced into the chamber and pulled the hammer back. Then he pressed the octagonal muzzle against the back of Peter's head and would have killed him, murdered him, Miranda thought, if she hadn't spoken, hadn't stepped out from the shelter of the tree, hadn't cried out and then murmured, "I give up."

4 Sasha Prochenko

BUT IN THAT *world each living creature has its analogue. In that world the dead will find each other once again, not in these bodies but transformed. This will happen both for better and for worse, because evil men and women also die. There will be fights and struggles. But just as there are places, accidents, and mental habits that dissolve the boundaries between that world and yours, so also there are points of access between that place and another one, above it and beyond, and one beyond that, until we rise up to the throne of all the gods. And underneath those thrones we will be rarefied and distilled. I say this not because I know it, but because I have faith that it is so. And I offer it to be a comfort, my dear girl, when everything seems dark. For through those holes and dissolved places when they are aligned, there comes a light that filters clear down from the top. It is an analogue to sun and moon and starlight, which is the same in all those places under heaven. . . .*

These words of Aegypta Schenck's, written before her death, had not developed out of any practical experiment or test. Instead they had derived from drawings she had seen in books, as well as a complicated metal astrolabe that had once belonged to Isaac Newton. Now a citizen of the world she had imperfectly described, perhaps she would have wanted to revise this passage in particular.

At noontime on the day Miranda was taken prisoner, while

Radu Luckacz was bumping toward Bucharest in his motorcar, a feverish young man stood on the high street in Chiselet under a bright sun. A soldier like the Chevalier de Graz, he also would have rejected with disgust Aegypta Schenck's model of the universe, her nesting spheres around a source of light. He knew the truth without thinking. He knew it in his irradiated bones: The sun shining above him on this unseasonably cool summer day bore no resemblance to the secret sun. They were not aligned, did not partake of the same essence. In the hidden world, black rags of clouds blew across a bloodred sky.

He was thirsty. The sweat was dripping down his arms in the hot air. In the hidden world his tongue lolled out and he was panting. The pads of his feet were sore. Stiff-legged, he stood on the high street of Chiselet among the burning buildings. Patches of his fur had fallen out.

He limped along the road looking for water and a place to rest. But there was no refuge for him. In the singed fields outside the town the water had dried up. And in the town the intact buildings were full of animals. Nor had the catastrophe—the explosion of the train and the resultant fireball—brought any reaction of kindness or solidarity among the creatures of the town. More than ever they'd divided into struggling factions. The older inhabitants had turned against the new arrivals: industrious and energetic rats that had been multiplying all over central and eastern Europe.

Some of these rats had been cornered in an empty cellar, surrounded by a circle of beasts. In the hidden world, the dog or wolf could hear the sound of squeaks and angry cries. Elsewhere, the young lieutenant on the high street in Chiselet showed no reaction to the news that a crowd of angry townspeople had set upon a detachment of German soldiers.

Intent on his own miseries, the lieutenant staggered on the cobblestones until he reached the road out of town. This was a gravel highway on top of a raised embankment through the marsh. Hungry, thirsty, hands in the pockets of a gray suit that neither fit him nor belonged to him, he stumbled along under the noonday sun, sweating in the cold north breeze.

The leather boots were a size too big. The suit was an expensive one. He had stripped it from the body of the commercial traveler who had been the sole casualty after the wreck of the Hephaestion. Streaked with dirt when he'd found it, now he'd been wearing it for several days. The underwear, full of excrement, he had left with the corpse.

Nevertheless, he made a prepossessing figure. His pale skin was sunburned, chapped, sprinkled with liver-colored freckles, hidden in a layer of hair that was almost white, and so fine and silky that all of his exposed skin seemed to glow. His body was slim and muscular, his face both pleasing and unusual: dark eyebrows under a mass of yellow hair, gray eyes that were flecked with blue and green, dark lips that seemed gray or purple rather than red. He wiped them often with the back of his long hand.

After several kilometers he came across the scene of an accident. The embankment had descended almost to the level of the ground, which was not flooded here. Rich smells of mulch and fertilizer came to him. Green fields of some anonymous crop stretched north to the horizon. The young man had no experience with agriculture. At the limit of his vision ran a line of poplar trees.

These trees described the boundaries of an isolated monastery whose turnip dome rose above a cluster of brick buildings. Sacred to the goddess Demeter, this monastery marked the end of a road that now joined the highway at an angle. Along the same road, hidden in a patch of woodland, stood the cottage of a large estate. An expensive motorcar had driven from its brick gates to the highway and had slid into a ditch.

Within the past few years, African companies had opened branches in Europe, in collaboration with German tool-and-die manufactories. They had produced competing lines of private automobiles, all of which, however, showed traces of Abyssinian design. This model, a Duesenberg Assegai, had a long, distinctive pointed bonnet that was wedged now in a bush.

In a flat, grassy place beside the road, a man and a woman crouched over a second man, who was laid out on his back. Now the woman, dressed in a long traveling coat, stood up straight and waved, or at any rate made a gesture with her gloved hand. The young soldier on the highway crossed down the embankment to the level of the road until he stood beside her.

"It's our driver," she said without preamble. "He was taken ill."

Now Lieutenant Prochenko could see that the man on his back was dressed in some kind of domestic livery, a double-breasted coat with silver buttons, which the other man was loosening. The chauffeur was a man in his sixties, with gray mutton-chop sideburns and rheumy blue eyes. As without stooping the soldier examined him, he recognized some of his own condition. The man's face was sweaty and flushed, and his hands trembled.

"He's had some sort of a stroke or seizure," said the woman—girl, really, as the soldier could see when she took off her shaded glasses. She wore a straw hat with a violet band, and a quantity of transparent veil around her hair and neck.

Now the third man looked up, and the soldier could see he was as young as the girl and just as ineffective; he had been scarcely able to undo the first of the chauffeur's buttons. Elegantly dressed in a dark suit, he looked up helplessly. And so the soldier squatted down and ripped the coat open with his fevered hands, ripped open the gray shirt and neck cloth, exposing the old throat and withered chest; he could see the flutter of a pulse. He could smell the sweat from the old man's body and could see also he was choking. He knew the symptoms of the illness that affected the citizens of Chiselet. White drool had forced its way into the old man's whiskers. So he rolled him onto his side and pulled the vomit from his mouth.

"Here comes Sorin with the horses," said the girl.

A man led a team of Percherons through the gate onto the muddy road, pulling the lead horse by the cheek patch. His wooden-wheeled cart was piled with fat canvas bags. When he saw the accident he left the cart and came running, holding his skullcap to keep it from blowing off. He wore a dirty, short-sleeved undershirt and cotton breeches.

The girl had been speaking French. But she switched to Roumanian when Sorin approached: "He took his hands off the wheel. He just fell over on the seat."

The old man had retched up a little phlegm and now was

breathing easier. As the crisis appeared to have passed, the soldier stood up. He put his hands in his pockets and let the others take over, the carter and his boy, who now loaded the chauffeur into the back of the wagon among the dusty bags. The elegantly dressed young gentleman was with them, and the soldier took the opportunity to study his sister, as he assumed—the resemblance was strong. And the girl, aware she was being watched, did a sort of self-conscious pirouette. She was a lovely creature, with brown hair and brown eyes, pale skin dusted with powder, and plum-colored lipstick. She was younger than the lieutenant, perhaps twenty or nineteen.

Prochenko caught the scent of her perfume. She wore a pearl-gray cravat and a lavender coat past her knees. She was slender, and tall enough to look him in the eyes. For ten seconds she attempted to hold his gaze and then gave up, smiling and blushing as her brother came back from the cart. "C'est ennuyant, mais je te remercie. . . ."

He spoke in the easy, informal way that was just then the fashion among young Roumanians, particularly since the outbreak of the Russian war. Now he put his hands on his hips as he surveyed his car, which appeared unhurt. The carter had already pulled his horses around. "I'll help you," said Prochenko. And not caring about his clothes that were ruined anyway, he stepped into the mud of the ditch. When the young gentleman released the clutch, he seized hold of the grille and muscled the car up its own skid-marks, a display of strength that surprised even himself, although the car was light and small for a four-seater. It gave the soldier an odd pleasure to strain and sweat to his uttermost, abuse his body as the wheels came clear. It was an odd kind of relief from the fever that otherwise was making his hands shake. He understood the nausea and faintness that had struck the old chauffeur. For the first time that day, straining in the mud, he didn't feel it.

"My goodness, you've destroyed your jacket—look at you," said the girl. She and her brother had both helped him by tugging on the car, and she had taken off her gloves. But his hands were bloody as he pulled them from the grille and wiped them in the handkerchief of the Abyssinian commercial traveler.

"I am Valentin Bibescu and this is my sister, Elena," said the young gentleman.

Lieutenant Prochenko smiled, revealing teeth that were very white.

"I also had an accident," he said.

Predicting something like this, he had been wondering over the past days what he would come up with, whether he would invent a name, a history for himself. His thoughts had been tangled up in sickness, and now the moment had come and he was unprepared. The name Bibescu also had confused him, because it was famous in Roumania. And also because he had known a man during the Turkish war, an infantry officer who had been wounded in the trenches at Gurkovo and lost part of his face. In Roumania he had died bankrupt while Prochenko was still in Constanta with Aegypta Schenck—were these two his children? His niece and nephew? And while naturally there was always a split between the infantry and cavalry, still it was not impossible that these children might have heard of him—it was absurd to think of them as children. Surely now he had to find a way to reconcile what he was, a soldier in his middle forties (though in a way this was the least believable of his three options), with what he also was. Doubtless, Pieter de Graz was having the same difficulty.

It occurred to Lieutenant Prochenko suddenly and for the first time, standing in the muddy track in leather boots that were too big, why Frederick Schenck von Schenck had chosen the two of them to protect his daughter and go with her wherever she went. Perhaps it was because in different ways the chevalier and he were not encumbered with other people—dependents, relatives, friends—though de Graz's mother might be still alive. She had a wooden house in Herastrau. But maybe Prince Frederick and certainly Aegypta Schenck had predicted this transition back. "I was in the Hephaestion when it derailed," he said. "I must have hit my head."

No, it was not just because of his loneliness, his and de Graz's. It was also because of other qualities: courage, perhaps, or loyalty—where was Miranda now? Where was she at this moment? And maybe an odd capability that had allowed him to adapt to all these amazing changes: "It is strange to say, but I don't know. But I had a ticket stub to Bucharest. I thought if I could find my way . . ."

Valentin Bibescu stared at him. "You don't know your name?"

"As I say, I must have hit my head. I woke up in the marsh."

"But they sent a special carriage for the passengers of the Hephaestion. Couldn't you find anyone . . . ?"

"I woke up in the marshland, half a kilometer from the derailment. . . ."

With any luck they had not heard of the Abyssinian commercial traveler whose naked body lay beyond the wreck. Or if they had, they would not make the connection; Prochenko heard Elena Bibescu's trilling laugh. "A mystery! How exciting! Was there anything in your pockets?"

He turned toward her, and again her beauty surprised him, her sweet smell, the dusted powder on her cheek. He stared at her a moment until she dropped her eyes. "I found no papers, which was strange because the train had come from Constantinople. We must have passed through customs at Silistra."

The girl clapped her hands. "But you are not a Turk!"

Prochenko smiled, then went on as if self-consciously. "My mind is not entirely effaced. No, it is full of many things, my memory also. And in all these most vital areas, it's as if I almost remember. My name, it's as if it's on the tip of my tongue, as the English say."

He spoke in the French language. The carter's boy was hurrying down the road from the brick gate. He had come to help them with the car, and between him and the lieutenant they got it on the road again. "Now I think your jacket is completely ruined," said Elena, as her brother spoke to the boy about the chauffeur's care, whether they should send for a doctor now or when Valentin returned from Bucharest.

"Have Mihai make inquiries at the German clinic," he continued, while Prochenko wiped the dirt from his fingers.

In the meantime, Elena Bibescu chattered gaily on. "Herr Doctor Beck might refer you to a specialist—no, you must come with us to the city. Valentin, please!"

"It is the least we can do," admitted the young man, smiling.

"I am pleased to go, to tell the truth," he said. "It is unhealthy here."

"Oh, it will be fun," said his sister, clapping her gloved hands. "I swear we will discover the truth by the time we get to Spantov. Were you going to walk to Bucharest along the road? Do you have any money?"

"Some."

"And what else is in your pockets? I swear, you must be ill as well."

Lieutenant Prochenko had been swaying on his feet. Now the girl stripped off her glove and made as if to touch his face. Her fingers hovered a few centimeters from his forehead. "How hot you are! Valentin, please help me. Were you struck on the back of your head?"

Valentin had opened up the doors of the Duesenberg, and now he labored with his sister to slide Prochenko into the soft seats. Though the lieutenant had never felt stronger, still he allowed the two of them to handle him, because in that way he felt his face close to Elena Bibescu's face, and he smelled her body and sensed its coolness even under her long coat. "Valentin is back from Russia with all sorts of new skills," she breathed next to his ear. "To drive a motorcar is nothing. We are going back to Bucharest. Time is short before he must return to his regiment."

Prochenko caught a glimpse of the carter's boy, standing in the road and waving. Then with his face very briefly against the front of Elena's traveling coat, he must have lost consciousness, if only for a few seconds; when he came to himself he was in the rear seat of the Duesenberg and Valentin was in the front, signaling with his hand through the driver's side window as he pulled onto the road. Then he wound up the window as they joined the highway.

The car smelled of leather, oil, and tobacco. The motor made a large popping noise. They jolted along at perhaps thirty kilometers an hour. But Lieutenant Prochenko was comfortable in the plum-colored backseat, which was soft and richly upholstered. Elena had put down the armrest between them, but she was leaning over it, her hat askew.

After a few minutes, as he said nothing and lay back against the seats with his eyes half closed, she undid the veil from around her neck and pulled the hat off entirely. "How hot it is!" she complained, shaking out her brown hair; now he could see it soft around her face. Her brother, by contrast, was wearing a hat, though before he'd been bareheaded. And he gripped the wooden steering wheel with leather driving gloves, at the same time his sister had lost her gloves entirely; was it possible they were twins? In the rearview mirror he stared back at Prochenko with frank, assessing eyes.

"Well, do you remember your given name?" asked Elena beside him. "What do you know about yourself?"

He shrugged. "There is something—Sasha—Alexei, I suppose."

"A Russian name!" protested Elena, and the lieutenant was aware, again, of Valentin Bibescu's scrutinizing eyes. The mirror was mounted on a vertical wooden dashboard. "But you are not a Russian, either. What languages do you speak? French, certainly, and Roumanian without an accent." How did she know this? He must have said something to the carter or the carter's boy.

"So, a Roumanian and also a gentleman, anyone can see that," said Elena. "What is in your pockets?" To his surprise, she fished into his jacket pocket and produced a wristwatch: rectangular, moderately expensive, and with a leather band. "It is from Abyssinia," she announced. "What did I tell you?"

What indeed? Prochenko had a hard time remembering. His thoughts and feelings roamed over a landscape that had no point of similarity with the scenes of rural peace that now surrounded the car on all sides, the pairs of yoked oxen, the wagons piled high, the green and flooded fields. Or else the point of similarity was in the lieutenant's burning, nauseated body.

"I think you must be pulling our legs," said Elena Bibescu. "Again as the English say. Do tell me—it's not kind. I am so gullible."

"What?"

"I don't believe you are—what is it called? Amnesiac? Where is this bump on your head?" And she put her hand up as if to touch him behind the ear, fluttered her fingers a few centimeters from his scalp.

No, but to collect his thoughts, to prevent himself from coming apart, the lieutenant took a kind of refuge in a mental exercise. And so while he spoke to her and tried to make himself charming, and tried to appeal to her in any way she wanted, at the same time he scarcely listened to what he said. But with a savage single-mindedness he tried to clear his consciousness of anything except the physical sensation of sitting next to Elena Bibescu and feeling the proximity of her body. He tried to eliminate all smells from the inside of the compartment that were not her smell. And with an interest that was both clinical and desperate, he examined the delicate curl of her ear, the line of her neck as it disappeared into the collar of her coat, the purple mole above her clavicle, the smell of her hair and the shine of the long curls that hung down near his shoulder.

Because of the noise of the road and the dust and stones that were thrown up by the wheels, the car windows were all closed. And at moments, the bucolic scenes outside appeared too perfect to be true. At moments the lieutenant imagined how they might be painted on the glass, and if he wound down the window crank he might reveal a different reality, and feel in his face the hot, gritty, irradiated wind. Or else if he reached out with his fingernails he might be able to scratch ribbons of paint from the glass, revealing . . . what? "My brother and I are nineteen," said the girl. "I think you must be a few years older. No more than that!"

In time they bumped onto a side road and came to a halt next to a field of grass. Prochenko flung open the door and stood up next to the car. Yes, the air was warmer now, and the sun shone bright in the middle of a cloudless sky. Squinting up, the lieutenant imagined it sucking all the color out of the landscape, a relentless hole of light.

They had stopped for a picnic. Valentin opened the boot and brought out hampers and blankets, which he laid out on the grass. Elena unbuttoned her coat as she sat down. There was cold chicken, potato salad, and champagne in crystal glasses. Smells came to Prochenko as he sank down to his knees. He drank.

"You are in Russia?" he asked Valentin Bibescu.

"In Moldavia. On Thursday morning I must take the train. So we must celebrate while there is time and make new friends. Sasha—it is good not to remember. I myself . . ."

Moodily the young man pulled up strands of grass. "Valentin, please," his sister begged. "There will be enough time for that, and I shall worry every day. But don't let's think about that now. Look, we have cornichons in brine and duck paté, all thanks to my husband. . . ." Suddenly embarrassed, she also let her speech trail away.

"Yes, to Colonel Bocu," said Valentin, lifting up his glass. "Our financial savior, without whom we would be eating dry bread and herring."

"You are married?" asked Prochenko.

Elena blushed, and her brother answered, "Last December. Just in time—the bank would have foreclosed! No, he's a good fellow, though his moustache is a trifle gray," he teased. "And he is inclined to stoutness—no, admit it, dear. 'Any man who walks under a weight of laurels must walk slowly,' said our great aunt at the ceremony!"

But Elena wouldn't look Prochenko in the eye. Her voice was low and sweet. "Today my husband is outside Soroca with the Brancoveanu Artillery. There are worse places and I'm glad. It is true—we all are grateful for his generosity."

"And his pomposity!" exclaimed her brother. "Already he is calling himself Bocu-Bibescu. Need I say it was a match made in heaven? Even that was a godsend. You had no desire to go through life as Madame Beau-cul, no matter how appropriate . . . ."

"Valentin, stop!" said the girl, her cheeks on fire. Then in a moment: "I see you've made your mind up to be disagreeable. Sasha, please! You must not get the wrong impression. My husband is considerate and kind."

She looked into the grass. The humility with which she spoke touched the lieutenant's heart, affected him even through the shield of his illness. Now her coat was unbuttoned, he could see the tight dress underneath, cut low over her chest. In the car she had already stripped away her veil and silk cravat.

Under the tight green fabric Prochenko could see the swell of her small breasts.

Between them they drank two bottles of champagne and two of mineral water. Prochenko got up to urinate and trudged a long way toward a tree in the middle of the field. Hidden from his companions, he pulled down his trousers and squatted behind the wide trunk in the high grass. Afterwards, coming back, he could see angry gestures, hear raised voices which subsided as he approached. But since the accident Prochenko's hearing had been unnaturally acute. "Don't talk to me," said Valentin Bibescu. "It doesn't matter—none of it matters. I'll probably be dead in six months, before my next leave."

Now suddenly in the warm sunshine he got up and began to stow away the remains of the picnic. Prochenko helped him under the hot sun. "I am baking—there is no reason to keep your jacket on," Elena said, and she slipped out of her long lavender coat as if it were some kind of carapace or shell or suit of armor, revealing the light green traveling dress that fell to the middle of her calf.

Since the German occupation, hemlines had been rising in Bucharest. Even since the beginning of the Russian war there'd been a reaction in the dress shops of the capital, under the pretext of anticipated shortages and rationing—Prochenko could see the girl's ankles and legs, encased in silk stockings. There was a ruffled slit in the material that came up almost to her knees. At the same time, her neck was bare.

Slowly, standing in the high green grass, Prochenko unbuttoned his gray jacket and drew it off. She was right, it was ruined, ripped and scuffed, streaked with mud and grease. Underneath he wore a cream-colored shirt without a collar, Turkish-style. The sweat was running down his ribs.

He disposed of his jacket in the boot with the rest of the detritus—empty bottles, smeared dishes. In his present state he was not feeling the wine. But Elena Bibescu was, he thought, as she slid into the car beside him; her brother was eager to be gone. He backed the car onto the track. Then they were on the road again.

They saw no other private cars, but only horse-drawn

carriages and carts. Valentin sped past them, honking his horn. In the backseat, in the stuffy air, Elena subsided onto the padded armrest, and in twenty minutes was asleep with her mouth open and her lips out of shape. Prochenko could see her teeth, hear her breath, smell her perfume, all that. But he looked straight ahead out the windscreen. Sometimes he caught sight of Valentin's eyes in the mirror.

Already he imagined there was some other creature inside the girl who slumped so close to him, as there was inside himself. As he had imagined scratching the paint from the windows, he thought he might reach out his hand and—not scratch her, no. But he would rub the delicate skin around her wrist and around her neck, and it would rub away and show some of the woman underneath, or the kitten or the fawn or the baby bird or whatever it was—would he reach out his hand? It was intolerable to stay inactive in this hot, closed space, with the high, muffled roar of the motor and the wind surrounding him as he plunged forward in exasperated stasis.

What had happened to him? What had happened when the Hephaestion derailed and the baggage car exploded? Surely the accident had changed him, not for the better. Or else—and at this moment his life in Berkshire County, Massachusetts, seemed immeasurably far away. But he thought about the silver canisters that had broken open, and he remembered movies and comic books that had described radioactive accidents in underground laboratories. Spider-man or Batman—a human being merged with an animal, melted or mutated with it. The result was a hero with terrifying strengths and vulnerabilities. But a hero nonetheless. That was important to remember.

In the plush seats of the Duesenberg, Lieutenant Prochenko rubbed his palms together, and then rubbed them on the knees of his trousers. In himself he felt a mixture of two people and an animal, a dog or a wolf whose tongue seemed huge and slimy in his mouth, whose nails seemed sharp as claws, whose heart throbbed unmercifully and whose fever seemed to heat up the entire passenger compartment of the car. A mist or film of condensation—it appeared to him—had crept over the window near his cheek.

In the afternoon they passed through Cernica. And on the

other side of the lake they came gradually into the suburbs south of Vulcan's Gate and the ancient city wall. Here there was more traffic: wagons, carts, and motorized vehicles. At times they crept along or stopped, once for ten minutes to allow a convoy of German army trucks to cross the intersection. Valentin opened his window and lit a cigarette.

Prochenko discovered he was holding the girl's hand. Or at least her palm lay against his palm, and her fingers curled loosely against his. Prochenko now gave all of his attention to the small soft pressure that joined them, and which seemed to offer some chance at respite from the buffeting sensations of his body, some promise of calm. He tried to clear his mind of anything else. Even though he failed, still he could imagine the relief that might come out of success, particularly as he felt her come awake, pull her hand away and then, hesitantly, tentatively replace it. She did not look at him, but like him stared ahead through the front windscreen at the tramway yards beyond the Cernica Temple.

There must have been fifty trucks crossing the road. Valentin cursed softly and then turned back toward him, his arm along the back of the seat. Elena lifted her fingers, and then she also turned her head. "Well," she said. "Do you remember anything?

"This is the Bulevardul Basarabia," she continued after a pause.

"I—I don't know."

"Then we will take you to my husband's house," she said. "Valentin can lend you some clothes. I'll send a note to our doctor, though it has gotten late."

The weather had changed again. A cold wind came from the north, and a cold mist. Suddenly the air seemed saturated, difficult to breathe. The car started up again, and they drove slowly down the boulevard between the long brick walls of industrial buildings or warehouses. Prochenko examined a row of enormous posters, each one announcing a series of performances at the New National Theatre of Roumania. And though the posters did not specify the title or performer, each showed the same image of the same woman. She was alone onstage with her arms raised, the footlights shining off her helmet of chestnut hair.

"That is your head of state," murmured the lieutenant. He had seen photographs in Adrianople.

"See, you do remember!" said Elena Bibescu.

And when the row of posters showed no sign of ending, her brother elaborated. "That is the white tyger, she calls herself. Really, she is just a hired functionary for the Germans, whom she abuses in all her speeches—it is quite amusing, if it weren't a question of one's own country. But I must not say these things too loudly. My brother-in-law is an admirer, needless to explain."

"Oh, Valentin, I don't care what you say. You don't have to . . ." Elena's voice trailed away. Prochenko was conscious suddenly of her knee against his own.

"Well, you will see straightaway the level of absurdity," continued Valentin. "We are coming into the Piata Markasev."

Sure enough, after a few hundred meters the boulevard arrived at a traffic circle in a neighborhood of run-down apartment buildings. In the center of the circle rose a statue of a young man with a pistol in his hand, standing over the corpse of a defeated enemy. " 'Long Live the Patriotic Sacrifice of Kevin Markasev,' " quoted Valentin, reading from the inscription on the pedestal as they drove slowly by. "And there's his portrait," he continued, indicating a bronze profile in bas-relief.

"Tell me the story," said Lieutenant Prochenko.

Valentin glanced at him in the rearview mirror. "Really, my friend, if you don't remember that, now I am frightened for you. Was there anyone who did not learn that song in school? Kevin Markasev the brave, how he shot a German officer right at the start of the occupation, and then was tortured to death rather than reveal the name of his accomplices—really, it is idiotic. The statue was built with German money, naturally."

"What are you saying?" asked Elena. "Are you telling us the story—?"

"—is false, is false, of course it's false," interrupted her brother. "Whoever heard of this person? Where did he go to school? What town did he come from? Obviously if nothing else you will agree that 'Kevin' is an invented name!"

"I don't understand," said Elena. "Why would the Germans—"

"Because they are a federal republic, with laws protecting the right of public discourse, as they call it. And because this officer, supposedly, was abusing a Roumanian prostitute. So they pay for the statue and pat themselves on the back and smile their sanctimonious smiles, and all the time it doesn't matter because they own this country and everything in it—not because they conquered it. The army didn't fight. But we sold it to them, and they paid good money, which we spend on patriotic statues and free performances at the National, which they rebuilt from nothing, let me remind you."

Sasha Prochenko turned his face against the window, cooling his hot cheek against the glass. While the brother argued, and while he pressed his knee against the sister's leg, the lieutenant indulged in his own memories. It was almost as if he had not lied, as if he were in fact a victim of amnesia. It had been twenty-five years since he'd lived in Bucharest. He and some other officers had shared lodgings in Floreasca, which they had given up the year Prince Frederick Schenck von Schenck was murdered, the year Miranda Popescu was born. Afterward he had only come into the city once, during that final mad ride to Mogosoaia when the girl was eight years old. Certainly now as they drove into the city center, he could see much had changed. Much had been torn down and rebuilt. But surely down that road was the Apollo Carrefour, where he had gone to the Chameleon Club. And now they were coming into the Elysian Fields with its double row of sycamores. And here . . . and here . . .

So he was recognizing buildings and establishments he had not seen in a quarter century. And with another part of his mind he was somewhere else. He was in Berkshire County, behind the art museum on Christmas Hill, coming back from the burned-out high school in the middle of the night and seeing Kevin Markasev next to the bonfire, his handsome face under his single eyebrow, his expensive clothes. Even in the crude bronze profile in the piata, the lieutenant had recognized him. And this also was the exercise of an amnesiac, thought Prochenko now. In the cool autumn darkness under the birch trees and among the hummocks of wet grass on Christmas Hill, what kind of person had he been?

One thing was for certain: He was no longer the carefree officer who'd been thrown out of the hotel bar at the Karnac, whose hideous pseudo-Aegyptian façade they were now passing. Nor was he the same man who had made his oath of honor to Prince Frederick Schenck von Schenck and then found seriousness in the prince's castle on the beach, protecting with his wits a little girl and an old woman with the world against them. Nor even the same man who had consented to a desperate adventure he had barely understood, beyond the far side of the universe in Berkshire County. With the dog's part of his mind he pressed his knee against Elena Bibescu's knee, using that pressure as a way of focusing, of concentrating. Outside, in the Champ de Mars, people had gathered for some kind of parade.

"They're starting early," remarked Valentin.

"It's odd," Elena said. "Usually the feast of Athena is a small sort of affair. We came back because Valentin has to catch his train. Something must have happened. Look, there are musicians!"

But then the traffic started again, and they didn't hear the news until they arrived at Colonel Bocu's house in the Strada Italiana. Scarcely had the footman motioned the car in through the gate when Valentin, a cigarette in his mouth, asked for the afternoon newspapers. Obviously the servants had already read them. The type was blurred and the pages had been pulled apart. But, standing on the steps of the colonel's house, Valentin glanced at the headlines and then threw his cigarette into the base of a potted palm. In a quavering voice he read aloud the story: The German government had fallen after a vote of no confidence in the Reichstag. The Teutonic Democrats had abandoned the war coalition over the question of whether to accept a peace proposal from the czar. General von Stoessel and several important ministers were dead under peculiar circumstances. And there were rumors that Felipe Romanov had been released as a gesture of good faith. The czarevich would soon be on a German army train to the frontier, where he would be reunited with his father.

Now suddenly, as if it had been released by the news, Prochenko was aware of the honking of car horns, which had penetrated even this quiet residential street. Valentin refolded the paper and laid it on the curled marble balustrade. Then he burst into tears.

In a moment his sister had followed him through the big doors without a backward glance. Unsure of what to do, Prochenko lingered on the step. Should he wander away out of the gate, try to find Miranda and the Chevalier de Graz? He still had some money in his pocket, thanks to the Abyssinian commercial traveler.

The door was ajar, and the footman stood beside it, a noncommittal expression on his face. Prochenko looked down, and found himself perusing the second article in the newspaper, how the Princess Clara Brancoveanu and Nicola Ceausescu's son, both held as hostages in Germany for many years, were expected that evening at the Gara de Nord, arriving on the train from Buda-Pest. The Baroness Ceausescu would be there to welcome them, together with the German ambassador. So—Miranda's mother, home at last.

There was no sound from within the house. Prochenko wondered if there was any possibility of retrieving his jacket from the Duesenberg's boot. Then he realized he was happy to be rid of it, happy to feel the mist in his hair and the condensation on his skin. It was strange weather, unseasonable for the beginning of summer in Bucharest, and the strange cold breeze was a relief.

But now Elena Bibescu had slipped out the door again and grabbed hold of his sleeve. "Please come," she said, ignoring the footman who was walking down the steps toward the car. And now the girl was pulling him through the high door and up the curving staircase, and through the small rooms of the residential portion of the house. At the same time she was talking to him about her brother, how he'd been part of an advance attack on the Russian lines. The experience had damaged him, apparently, and her husband had been kind enough to pull him from his regiment for a couple of days' leave. "He's not cut out to be a soldier," Elena confided, news which Prochenko didn't take as a surprise.

But he was confused when she kept mentioning the kindness and generosity of her husband. For her visit to the summer house in Chiselet, he had even arranged for a petrol-rationing allowance. Valentin was nowhere to be seen. In an upstairs room with bruise-colored wallpaper and a row of open closets, Elena turned to face him. Now she was tentative, breathless, still more than a little drunk, perhaps, and the lieutenant could smell the liquor on her lips. She came toward him, suddenly abashed, glancing at him for a second and then looking away. "How bright your teeth are!" she said finally. "I must confess you are a little frightening to me."

When he kissed her she made a sighing noise, a musical note that he pressed out of her from time to time, halfway between a hiccup and a song. She kissed him fiercely with her eyes closed, which was just as well, Prochenko thought. Nor did she resist him when he drew up her dress and slipped his hand into her underwear. She did not resist him when he pushed her down onto the daybed, covered with discarded clothes from previous days, he supposed, of choosing her wardrobe. She unbuttoned his shirt and slid it off his arms; the Abyssinian had worn an undershirt, thank God. Prochenko had no desire to expose his chest to her.

Next to her clean, cool, perfumed body he felt rank and filthy, feverish and hot. She ran her hands over his shoulders—"Oh, it is like fur," she said, meaning the delicate white hair that covered him, and which in most light was not even visible. But it ran along his back in two heavier ridges.

Now her mouth was open to him as he kissed her. And though part of him was enjoying this, and grasped at her as if she presented the solution to some kind of mystery, there was another part. He was afraid of what would happen if she ran her hands over his small breasts, or if she found out what could not be hidden forever. Inside his trousers, if she opened them, she would not find a penis. She would find generative organs of the female sex, remnants of the girl he'd been in Berkshire County.

So it was partially with relief that he felt her pull away from him, felt her turn away. She was not ready to take this further than where it was. But she made her little humming gasp. And with her eyes closed she rearranged their bodies so he lay on his back among her discarded dresses. He could smell the fabric and the sweet silk. She lay above him with her fingers on his lips, and when he tried to speak she pressed her fingers against his mouth. Then she lay against his shoulder, making her little sound. Was it possible she intended to fall asleep?

He was uncomfortable against the bunched clothes, his skin burning, his stomach queasy. Behind their gauzy curtains the windows grew darker as the day settled down. His mouth was dry and his eyes itched. From where he lay he could see valuable things on Elena's bureau and vanity—a gold watch, some diamond earrings, even a loose amount of German currency. He wondered if he should take it and find a way of slipping out of this house. Presumably the servants would not question him; they knew where he had been. Or was there some further advantage to be pressed out of Elena and her brother? Could he sleep here? Probably not.

In the dim light he watched Elena Bibescu's pretty face, her pretty mouth pushed out of shape against his undershirt. In his own nose he reeked to heaven. Where was Miranda now? If the war came to an end, if Clara Brancoveanu took up residence in the city, what did it mean?

There was a sound at the door. Suddenly Elena was awake, and with a quick, athletic twist she had vaulted over him onto her feet. In the dim, filtered light of the streetlamp he could see her dress bunched around her waist. Then she was out of the room through a side door, just as Valentin came in from the corridor, a bottle of champagne in one hand, three glasses in the other.

He set them onto the top of Elena's bureau, then fumbled with the gas. "Where is Madame Beau-cul?" he asked in the new, soft light.

Lieutenant Prochenko sat up and put his feet on the floor. "I fell asleep."

"I should think so. I suppose you were waiting for me to try on some clothes."

He pulled open a closet near the bureau. "Elena lets me keep some shirts in here. Please, you might wash. There's a basin right through there."

He indicated the door where Elena had disappeared. Awkward, thirsty, Prochenko followed her into a small cubicle between two rooms, and the door was ajar on the other side. Elena stood motionless next to the toilet, a washcloth in her hands, her dress unbuttoned to her waist. Prochenko went to her and slid his hands along her ribs. Then he was kissing her again, listening to a whispered version of her little gasp. He took the wet washcloth from her fingers and ran it over her neck and face, her shoulders and her breasts, while at the same time Valentin was talking in the other room, discussing the peace proposal in the newspaper.

Elena, smiling, reclaimed the washcloth and wrung it out in a basin of cold water on a lacquered tripod. Then she was touching the lieutenant in the same way, rubbing the rough cloth under his armpits and down his back. Was it possible she guessed the truth? How could it not be possible? But she was smiling in the almost-dark, the only light from the open door, and through it came her brother's excited voice: "There was another story, too—an extraordinary thing. Elena especially will be interested; do you remember a Danish choreographer named Koenigslander, who used to direct the performances at the Dinamo each summer? It's incredible—someone threw acid in his face in his own dressing room in Copenhagen. Vitriol, they say; he's in the hospital. And the police suspect a bastard son he had with a Russian ballerina—isn't that horrible? He's lost an eye."

In the bathroom, Elena barely could contain her giggles. Then she put her lips against Prochenko's ear. "I think there is something else you have forgotten," she said—what did she mean by that? She had pulled up his undershirt, and now she turned him around and pushed him out the door again, hair wet, face wet, arms and shoulders wet.

"Better," said Valentin Bibescu, crinkling his nose. He had poured out the glasses and was drinking from one. And he had taken some shirts from the closet and spread them out on the daybed, silk shirts in startling colors—emerald green, russet brown.

"You should burn that undershirt," he suggested. Prochenko chose a peach-colored shirt with an attached collar and French cuffs. Perhaps he could borrow some expensive cufflinks.

He turned away, stripped off the undershirt. But in the mirror set into the closet door he could see Valentin staring at him as he buttoned his new shirt. "You'll need some trousers as well, and new shoes," he said. "Those ones have gotten mud on the carpet."

Embarrassed, Prochenko glanced toward the bathroom door. Aware now of his lack of underclothes, he could feel the seam of his trousers chafing him. Nor did he think he wanted to undress further under the eyes of this nineteen-year-old—what was he? A homosexual, perhaps. Urning, as they'd been known at the Chameleon Club. No wonder he hadn't been cut out for active service in Moldavia. Shirt buttoned, Prochenko turned toward him, smiling.

"Your teeth are so white," Valentin murmured, as his sister had done.

"I'll rejoin you in a moment," said Prochenko.

Blushing furiously, Valentin took his wineglass and went out into the corridor. Prochenko closed the door behind him and then closed the bathroom door as well. Then he stripped off his pants, boots, socks. He chose underwear from the top drawer of Elena's dresser—soft, without elastic, but it didn't fit. He held it to his face, smelling the expensive fabric, then pulled on trousers from Valentin's closet, found socks and Italian boots—the boy was just his size, or close enough. He found cufflinks in a leather case on Elena's vanity, and filled his pockets with the money that was there, just as Elena knocked and entered through the bathroom. She also had changed her clothes.

Later they shared a collation of cold meats, melon, and cheese. They smoked cigarettes, drank burgundy, and when the first of the fireworks burst above Elysian Fields they put on jackets to go out. There were crowds in the street, all pushing down toward the city center: old people, young people, and even some children who were up late, riding on their fathers' shoulders. In the streets there was an atmosphere that had nothing to do with Athena's feast, and was just as much confused and tentative as celebratory—after all, there was no firm news of anything. But in the course of the past month the German army had reached the gates of Minsk. If the czar made peace, then the soldiers who had marched away so recently could return just as quickly, and that was a good thing, wasn't it? So far the fighting in Moldavia and the Ukraine had been bloody and intense. And Roumanians were fighting also farther north in Lithuania. Still, it felt odd to celebrate a German victory, as it was clear that only a defeat or multiple defeats could drive them from the city of Bucharest, let alone the parts of Bucovina they had practically annexed.

On the other hand, Princess Clara was expected at the Gara de Nord, and that was hopeful, wasn't it? She had been a prisoner since the year of her husband's death at the hands of the previous empress. Having saved her country from the Germans by copying the invasion plans, smuggling them across the border in Miranda Popescu's diaper, she had been held for twenty years in the castle at Ratisbon—she was a hero, wasn't she? Of course the Germans had invaded after all, and the army had surrendered almost without a fight. Now the princess was returning by permission of the German authorities, and the Baroness Ceausescu had gone to meet her. What was to be made of that? Miranda Popescu was still at large. She was in the woods at Mogosoaia, gathering malcontents and shooting at policemen.

Valentin, Elena, and Prochenko moved through the thickening crowds. And when they came into the Champ de Mars they could see the fireworks above their heads. Prochenko found ways of touching the girl, although she often pulled away. Perhaps she was afraid she would see someone she knew. When they got into the area around the university she didn't seem to care as much. The streets were full of students. Once she even kissed him.

Past midnight there were German soldiers on the boulevard, Hanoverian dragoons on horseback, pushing back the crowds. And there were Roumanian policemen in dress uniforms, with their high, old-fashioned helmets, clearing the way for the baroness's carriage. And then there she was in an open coach-and-four, moving slowly down the street.

People cheered. "The white tyger," they cried out. Nicola Ceausescu stood in the open compartment, holding herself upright with her hand around a silver stanchion. Nor did she wave nor smile nor make any other attempt to acknowledge the crowd. But she showed herself before her audience as if she stood upon a stage, illuminated by the streetlights and the fireworks that still exploded fitfully above her, though the main display was long since over. Her eyes seemed glassy, fixed, so much so that the lieutenant asked himself whether it was in fact her body he saw here on exhibit—she wore a tight black dress cut low, and a black leather coat pushed back, hanging from her elbows. But he had heard in the old days that she had used a simulacrum sometimes to impersonate her onstage, during dull bits when there was no dialogue to speak of—a simulacrum animated partially though conjuring and partially through the old country magic of whores, who had other reasons to dissociate from their own bodies and experiences.

Nicola Ceausescu—the lieutenant made a rapid calculation—was thirty-nine years old. How was it possible she still looked as she did, her long legs and narrow hips, her smooth and unblemished face, if not through this or some other alchemy? He had not seen her—again he made his quick subtractions—since she was in her mid-teens, and had appeared to stunned audiences in Klaus Israel's *Cleopatra* at the Ambassadors Theatre. That was before she'd sold herself to the old baron, her greatest conjuring trick.

And it occurred to Prochenko as he watched her on display, staring down the crowd, that they had something in common, the two of them. He also had been young when he'd last seen her, a cadet in his last year at the academy. And here he was still young after all that time, his middle-aged soldier's body mingled (comic-book style) with the body of an adolescent girl in Berkshire County, Massachusetts, not to mention a dog—how old was he in dog years? He suppressed a bark of laughter, and at the same time realized that the baroness's coach had come abreast and she was staring down at him; he dropped his eyes, noticing for the first time the other people in the carriage. Ostensibly, this parade was in their honor.

Prochenko stood bareheaded in the second rank away from the curb, hands in his pockets. Around him men and women shouted, raised their arms. But in between the helmets of the German horsemen he could see them now, a gray-haired lady whose features still held some remnants of something noble and good, though she was terrified now, her face stricken and amazed. Clara Brancoveanu—was there anything of Miranda in her face? She shrank against the pillows and blankets or shied back against the shoulder of the boy, Felix Ceausescu, who did not resemble his mother.

He felt Elena's fingers insinuate themselves into the pocket of his camel-hair coat, searching for his fingers. Would she find the watch that he had stowed in there? The money was in the other pocket, thank God. But Prochenko closed his palm around the diamond earrings, the gold-and-diamond watch, while he plotted his escape; he must say good-bye to this woman and her brother. He would find Miranda . . . and what? What now?

He pulled his hand out of his pocket, transferred Elena's watch and earrings to a more secure location—he had become skilled at these small manipulations from his days as a pick-pocket in Adrianople. Then he replaced his hand and grasped hold of her fingers, squeezing them as the coach passed. And at that moment he became aware of a tall man in front of him in the first row of spectators, dressed in an old coat and a woolen cap.

Always in Adrianople, in the crowds at the marketplace or in front of the old synagogue, Prochenko had learned to keep an eye out not just for policemen, but for anyone whose body language could not easily be understood. The man in front of him stepped nervously from foot to foot, hands in his bulging pockets. And while others had snatched their hats off and were waving them, he had pulled his cap down over his eye-brows, and had half-turned away from the carriage, as if try-ing to hide his face. He had not shaved in several days.

The lieutenant paid particular attention when he pulled a glass jar from his pocket and unscrewed the lid. Since the wreck of the Hephaestion, Prochenko's nose had been as sen-sitive as a dog's, and immediately he was aware of a sharp, in-sinuating odor that brought moisture to his eyes. The carriage was rolling by the curb, its brass-plated wheels just a few me-ters away.

A reflex: He unlocked his fingers from Elena's in his pocket, then reached out and batted down the jar so that it fell among the legs of the crowd. People were shouting and cheering, but the man jumped back. Prochenko saw the oily, viscous liquid spray across the boots of a policeman at the curb. The jar fell to the gutter in a heap of wet refuse that began to smoke.

But the man in the woolen cap turned around with a shocked, startled expression, and Prochenko recognized him. And even if he had not seen his face reproduced in profile in the Piata Markasev that afternoon, the lieutenant would have remembered him from that last night in Berkshire County, when he and Miranda and Peter Gross had come down through the cow pasture on Christmas Hill, and seen this same strange fellow build a bonfire on the slope above the art museum.

Then, caught in a girl's body, Prochenko had admired his dark, single eyebrow, his height, his air of European (as the girl imagined) superiority. Now his face was hollow, haunted, and his hair unkempt, as the lieutenant saw when he snatched the woolen cap off of his head just to make sure. The police could see there was a disturbance in the crowd, even if the man whose boots had been spattered with vitriol had not leapt back, cursing, swatting at the leather where it had started to smoke and foam.

The carriage had continued down the street. But Prochenko was aware of the Baroness Ceausescu looking back from where she stood, studying him with an unreadable expression on her face as he wrestled with Kevin Markasev on the curb.

Ceausescu Triumphant

5 *Prince Frederick's Revolver*

THE EMPRESS VALERIA'S Winter Keep, which Nicola Ceausescu had renamed the Palace of the People, was at that time the largest building in Europe. Constructed on the ruins of a Roman temple, it had evolved over the centuries into a disorganized pile of bricks and stone, a tour of which could illustrate the history of Roumania. There, meticulously restored, were the original Roman colonnades, built on Greek foundations in the earliest days of the city. And there were the innermost black walls of the Gothic castle, and, floating like thunderheads above them, the gold and sapphire domes of the Turkish occupation, built by Dragut Pasha and Kara Selim in faux-Byzantine style.

But it was not until the Brancoveanu restoration that the building had acquired its final perimeter, when the surrounding Turkish gardens were one by one enclosed in rose-colored stone. The largest of these neo-classical façades—Constantin IV's court of Artemis—had been quarried in Petra, dismantled, transported, and then inaccurately reassembled in enormous sandstone blocks. The grand entrance to the entire building was the so-called Nabataean Gate, which had not been used either by the empress or by Nicola Ceausescu until she opened it past midnight to admit the Princess Clara Brancoveanu and Felix Ceausescu, her own son.

That same night, when the baroness finally climbed the stairs to her modest apartments overlooking the Piata Revolutiei, it was almost dawn. But she had left word for Radu Luckacz to disturb her. When he knocked on the half-opened door he knew what he would find. He could hear the sound of her piano in the corridor. And for a while he leaned against the doorpost, listening.

At the Gara de Nord, when the Bavarian Hydra had steamed into the station, the brass band had played some of the baroness's own uncompleted music, triumphant marches from the story of her life, which for several years she'd been composing in an operatic style. Lingering by the door, Luckacz recognized many of the same themes, intimate and melancholy now, transposed into a minor key. And though he didn't claim to be a judge of these things, always he was struck by how poorly she played, at least in a technical sense. In another way the music was sublime, played with a tentative and crude sincerity that was affective beyond measure, particularly when with trembling hands the policeman pushed open the door. There she was in the small room, her face lit with candlelight, a cigarette, ignored, burning in an ashtray like a stick of incense beside her. As always, when he saw her, it was as if she had conjured his heart away, and he could no longer hear any false notes or botched fingering.

She stopped. "Come in," she said in her low voice. "Ah, you startled me!"

As always in her presence, he felt his chest constrict. The air was hard to breathe. To rid himself of the sensation of being buried alive, at once he felt compelled to move and talk. So: tight, constricted gestures with his hat and his gloved hands, harsh, officious speech in his nasal voice.

Pensive and calm, Nicola Ceausescu sat at the stool between the candelabra, gazing at him over the lid of her miniature grand piano. And because his head was still full of her interrupted music, and because she was as still and beautiful as any statue of any goddess in any temple of the city, he felt as if he'd staggered drunk and unwashed into some perfect sanctuary of potential grace. "Ah, ma'am," he continued desperately, "I am privileged to announce to you the culmination of many weeks of investigative toil, which was occurring just as I predicted as I spoke to you last night before the train arrived from

Buda-Pest. My sergeant Vladimir O'Brien, whom I left in command there while I was in Chiselet—a few hours ago he visited me in my office with the news that Pieter de Graz and the Popescu girl have been apprehended—taken alive, according to your orders—and are being held in Mogosoaia. I am unhappy to report five patrolmen were killed, shot in cold blood by that devil with the face still of a boy or a young man, obviously the result of some kind of conjuring or manipulation, as well as the Gypsy girl who was traveling with them and who could not be revived. O'Brien brought me as a token of success, two objects which I know have been of a concern to you, and which you have requested—here."

His voice trailed away. Holding his hat by the brim, he fished into the lower pocket of his coat to remove a cloth-wrapped bundle. This he placed on the closed lid of the piano, and with a flourish that was marred only by the awkwardness of not knowing what to do with the hat in his left hand, he untied the straps to display first a revolver, then a bracelet of gold beads.

A hiss escaped the baroness's lips. Softly she closed the cover on the keyboard and then rose to stand beside him, troubling as she did so the candle flame, the smoke from the burning cigarette.

To Luckacz's surprise, she did not reach for the bracelet, though he knew she coveted it, or had once coveted it: the ancient sign and symbol of the white tyger, which the first Miranda Brancoveanu had worn in the days of the old Turkish wars. Instead she picked up the revolver, a weapon that had once belonged to Frederick Schenck von Schenck. He had inherited it from his father and grandfather—an old-fashioned weapon whose long octagonal barrel was inlaid with precious metals, a device of silver and gold vines or briers that covered the drum and the stock as well. The grip, however, was unornamented, except for two panels of bleached bone from some fallen enemy of the house of Brancoveanu—a macabre weapon, in fact, which had brought nothing but bad luck to Great Roumania.

The baroness's hair shone in the candlelight, a shade that was both red and brown. She stood close to the policeman, too close to make him comfortable, and he could smell the bitter and astringent scent that clung to her. She had changed after the parade and the celebration, and now wore a virginal blue dress with a ruffled neckline that laid bare, nevertheless, the lines of her collar bones. She held the gun up to the ceiling. She peered at the hammer and the firing pin.

"Ma'am, it is unloaded," he said. And he watched a shiver moving up her spine into her neck, a tremor he saw only because he stood so close to her.

"It is never unloaded," she murmured, words that were false and made no sense. Suddenly he imagined this might be the start of some terrible accident; how could that be? Luckacz himself had opened the revolver before he brought it here. He had spun the empty shells into his palm.

"I know you wanted the bracelet, ma'am," he said, his voice harsh and ugly. "I brought the pistol only to show you. . . ."

"Where are they?" she interrupted.

"Ma'am, I have just told you. They are in Mogosoaia at the railway station until—"

"Are they well treated? I ask that they be treated well."

Radu Luckacz shook his head. "A wound is septic on de Graz's hand. He is weak from it, which is lucky for us."

"Please find a doctor to examine him. It is my wish."

"Ma'am, your compassion is well known. But these are dangerous criminals responsible for many deaths, including men from my department who themselves have wives and children. They also are in need of comforting from you."

Her eyes were a violet color. Watching her now, Luckacz saw with astonishment that they were full of tears. "Please," she said.

"Ma'am, I was under the impression that this bracelet . . ."

"Ah."

She replaced the revolver on the piano's lid. She reached for the golden string of beads, then paused. As always, Luckacz studied the imperfection of her hands, her big knuckles, stained fingers, torn nails and cuticles—a peasant's hands, and for that reason touching in the context of such beauty and refinement.

The beads themselves were hollow gold, each in the shape

of a tiger's head. "I wonder if you should give this back to her," murmured the baroness as if to herself. "Yes, I think you should give it back."

"But—"

"It does not belong to me. Nor would it be right to steal it by force. People would laugh."

"But—"

"It is not something you can take or steal," murmured the baroness. "It is something you are, or you are not. If Miranda Popescu herself came to lay it in my hand . . ."

"But ma'am, she shot a man, a policeman in Braila. I assure to you . . ."

Again he let his voice trail away, struck by the moisture in the baroness's eyes—not tears, because they did not fall. But watching her he felt a lump form in his throat—why? For what reason? This was a great day, long anticipated.

"Did you not say," whispered the baroness, "that you took this gun from the Chevalier de Graz?"

"Certainly, and he will be punished for his crimes. But in Braila there were witnesses!"

Now she turned to face him. "Ah," she said, softly and delicately, and he could see her perfect teeth, feel her cool breath, she was so close. "She is just a girl. Who will protect her if I don't? Tonight her mother is my guest, a hero of Roumania. I have opened up a suite of rooms that was long disused. My son—it is obvious my son is much attached to her."

"I see," mumbled Radu Luckacz, which was an exaggeration.

"I thought I could bring her here," continued Nicola Ceausescu. "Perhaps to heal some of this division. I thought of it tonight. Perhaps I could be generous. Perhaps she and my son might enjoy each other's company."

This seemed preposterous to Radu Luckacz. "There is a difference in their ages," he muttered stupidly, and she laughed.

"Not today! Not right away! Please don't make fun of me! I try to think of what is best for Great Roumania."

AND IT WAS true. She had thought about it that evening, when on the station platform she had seen her son for the first time in many years. How grown up he looked, fourteen or so at least! Dressed in an ikat jacket made of purple silk, she had stood in the departure hall under the great clock, surrounded by German officials and Luckacz's men. The crowd, sequestered behind velvet ropes, carried furled umbrellas and raincoats over their arms. The brass band played the music she'd requested, the triumphal march that introduced the third act of her drama, *The White Tyger*. The accompanying text, of course, was still unwritten, and as the baroness watched her son climbing the iron stairs from the train platform, a new idea occurred to her.

Bewildered, shy, dressed in clothes that were too small for him, the boy would not relinquish Clara Brancoveanu's arm. He rubbed his cheek against the shoulder of her threadbare cardigan. The princess stood blinded and wan under the high dome, close to tears, maybe, and overwhelmed. But the boy, Felix—how handsome and how innocent he looked! And as the horns played, for the first time Nicola Ceausescu caught glimpses of how *The White Tyger* might finally end: not in some Ragnarok of fire and death. After all, her shipment of radioactive material had been exploded by Antonescu's partisans, which surely was a sign from the gods.

For the first time she imagined that the ending of this story might not even be with her, Nicola Ceausescu, her apotheosis or else her flaming, doomed destruction. But perhaps there was an ending that might not even involve her, a marriage ceremony that might heal a wound after the potato-eating Germans were defeated, of course. And then the music from the third-act overture would come back reconfigured, intimate and joyous, a wedding march or ode, an epithalamium—that was what it was called. She would look it up.

"You will return this to her," she said now, meaning the bracelet of gold beads, meaning also Miranda Popescu, daughter of Clara Brancoveanu and Frederick Schenck von Schenck. She turned to the policeman and placed her hand upon his shiny cuff, examining, as was her habit, the roots of his dyed moustache. How preposterous he looked, after all! Like an actor on the stage of a musical comedy. Was there a part for him in *The White Tyger*?

Always she took care to stand a little close to him, so she could feel the ticking, sputtering engine of his love for her. That evening already she had given up the tourmaline, forswearing both the jewel itself and the dream it represented. In Professor Corelli's house she had abandoned the chase, preferring to imagine herself standing on her own feet, depending on no one but herself. And so tonight she forswore also the gold bracelet, hoping for a greater and more poignant glory in not picking up what after all did not belong to her. She could be forgiven for indulging herself now, with one hand on Prince Frederick's gun (she would not give that up!) and one on Radu Luckacz's sleeve. She could be forgiven for listening to the labor of his love, the throaty rasp of his breath, the catch in his throat as she squeezed his wrist. It was not for the sake of any jewel or bracelet that he loved her, after all.

"And you will bring her here to reunite her with her mother. I know it works against your sense of justice, my old friend—but we will see." Then, almost as an afterthought: "And you will bring the Chevalier de Graz."

In this she was following the precepts of Hermes Trismegistus to gather all your hostages into your hand, under your roof. That night also, listening to the trumpets under the mosaic dome of the Gara de Nord, she felt a spray of triumph as she realized the princess and the boy—her son, she had to keep reminding herself; how he'd changed!—were symbols of her new power as an alchemist. For they had been the hostages of her enemy, imprisoned by him in his castle at Ratisbon, now freed into her hand. And perhaps because her mind was no longer obsessed with the jewel and the bracelet, she could now appreciate the strength she had. The Palace of the People, which for five years she had lived in like a boarder or a transient, she would set it ablaze with lights. And in various wings and annexes she would gather all these people as her guests. She would throw open the gates to the citizens of Roumania, and would feed upon them not like a tyrant or a jailer, but like a performer on the stage, who holds her audience as if in iron chains, but without them doesn't exist.

She stepped back to allow Radu Luckacz to leave her. But he stood fussing with his hat. "This morning I was at Chiselet," he said in his unpleasant Hungarian voice.

In the afternoon, before her visit to Corelli's house, he had mentioned something about this. Now he knew more—a riot had occurred there after he had left the site of the wreck. He had received a telegram. The work crews had risen against their German overseers. They had disarmed a small detachment of Hanoverian guards, destroyed a clinic, and beaten several medical personnel. The German commander at Giurgiu had responded. Order had been restored.

The baroness shuddered, closed her eyes. Always she felt a small frisson of pleasure at bad news. She had spoken to several German officers that evening. General Schnibbe and Colonel Eulenberg had accompanied her to the Gara de Nord. Why had they not mentioned any of this?

"There is another problem of concern," continued Radu Luckacz. "I spoke this morning to a Herr Doctor Beck about the contraband in the baggage car of the Hephaestion. I suggested that it had its potential terminus in Buda-Pest, Vienna, or even Germany, because I had no knowledge of any group or person here who might require such a cargo. Antonescu himself might come to mind, except it was he who brought the matter to the attention of the German authorities, and of course it was his people in the first place who attacked the train. Then I suggested the supporters of Miranda Popescu, which did not occur to Doctor Beck. But he understood the train was going for Bucharest, nor did he want me to reveal to you our conversation. But—"

Nicola Ceausescu interrupted gently. "Why didn't you tell me this this afternoon?"

The policeman shrugged. He would not meet her eyes. Suddenly he seemed old to her, tired, used up, unable to protect her from the suspicions of the potato-eaters. No wonder Schnibbe and Eulenberg had said nothing.

Radu Luckacz fiddled with his hat, shifted his weight from foot to foot, opened his mouth to answer. But now she was the one to turn away. Placing the revolver to one side, she rewrapped the Brancoveanu bracelet in its cloth package, then laid it in the policeman's hand. "Please, I'm very tired," she said, and smiled. "We will talk about this later."

He brought her hand up to his lips; impatient, she snatched it away. How drab he seemed in his gray raincoat and black suit, how sad his eyes, wrinkled in the corners now, she noticed.

"Go, please—my old friend. I shall expect you tomorrow with the prisoners. Sergeant O'Brien, you must bring him also to accept my thanks."

But the policeman didn't go. He had something more to say. "Ma'am, I ask you for the last time to reconsider this request and instead let justice run its race. De Graz is weak from septicemia. Beyond that he is a dangerous madman, and it is better to remember it. As for the young woman, certainly it cannot be your intention to bring back this parasitic race of kings and queens. . . ."

Nicola Ceausescu laughed. "My friend, you are so serious! Is it so bad to give the people something they can wave at when it marches by? You see how they enjoyed themselves this evening in the Champ de Mars."

"Ma'am, I must insist you do not know. And I insist also these are conjurers and magicians—do not laugh at me! If you could see de Graz's face of a young man, identical to photographs of his promotion in the army when Prince Frederick was alive, more than twenty-five years ago! And the girl, who has been hiding in some magician's secret hole, I mean her aunt Aegypta Schenck the alchemist—"

The baroness raised her hand. "Stop, my friend—I think I had no idea you were so superstitious in these matters. Stop, I will promise to hang their rooms with mirrors and wild onions, smear myself with garlic when I speak to them!"

In fact she was eager to decipher how de Graz had kept himself so young. Radu Luckacz seemed to have diminished just in the past five minutes in her room. His rusty gabardine suit, his porous nose, the rash across his cheeks—he had not shaved. The collar of his shirt was gray and worn. And of course his glossy and absurd moustache—she turned away from him. In the enameled ashtray, her cigarette had long since burnt itself out.

Radu Luckacz excused himself; she did not look at him. Instead she picked up the revolver and hugged it to her chest. She also felt in need of some alchemical rejuvenation, now, after a long night, close to dawn. She also could benefit from studying de Graz's case, listening to his story, though at thirty-nine she was still a beautiful woman, as everyone agreed but her.

From the music room, with its walls of patterned silk, she passed into the bedroom of her private suite. Jean-Baptiste had turned down the blanket, lit the lamp, put out a sandwich and a glass of water, but she did not linger there. Instead she stepped behind a screen and through a hidden door and into a compartment underneath the eaves. What had Luckacz said? A magician's secret hole.

There she had transported all her husband's papers and utensils from the laboratory in Saltpetre Street. Some of the crates and boxes she had not yet unpacked, even after five years. But she knew what she was looking for: her husband's book of experiments and notations, in which she had once read a description of this same revolver. Now she held it against her breasts as if it were the serpent that had stung Cleopatra's life away. Eyes blind in the darkness, she knelt and fumbled at the altar of that deity, after having first deposited the gun onto the offering stand. Then she struck a match, lit the candles, and with a candle in her hand she went in search of the big book.

She found it in a stack beside the lectern. Pressing the candle onto its spike, with her other hand she set the book onto the wooden stand. She pulled back the leather cover and big pages, scanning the lines of the old baron's cramped handwriting, some of it in code she had not been able to decipher.

How had her husband learned about this gun? The artifact itself was famous or at least notorious, handed down in the Brancoveanu family, forged (it was believed) from an ancient core of pitted steel, the shaft of a mace Miranda Brancoveanu had carried at the siege of Turnu Magurele, Kara Selim's fortress on the Danube.

With the mace she had crushed the heads of several champions of the first Turkish war, and with the pistol Frederick

Schenck von Schenck had murdered many others in more recent skirmishes. That history of bloodshed was what made the gun so valuable when, after her brother's death, Aegypta Schenck had disassembled and rebuilt it.

That would have been in the first days before her disgrace, when she was still living at Mamaia Castle with her niece. How had the baron learned about it? They were enemies then, rivals in alchemical power, bent on punishing and destroying each other. Maybe the baron had had spies among the servants, or else more secret sources of information. His wife could only guess at them. No, here it was, as she remembered, the mechanism of the gun drawn carefully on the page in sepia ink.

The air was hot and close. The candle flame burned up without a tremor. The Baroness Ceausescu retrieved the pistol from the altar. She glanced at the icon of the goddess hung suspended in the air above some miscellaneous Aegyptian statuary, property of the late empress, whose house this used to be. She examined it more closely, a painted icon on a wooden board. It was a recent piece of work by a famous painter of religious scenes, whose spirituality, perhaps, had not prevented him from going to the opera. The pose, the modeling, the near-nakedness of the figure had quite obviously been drawn from one of the baroness's performances at the Ambassadors Theatre in the old days, which was why, just as obviously, she had chosen it, although she had not made the connection or understood the reason until now.

Holding the revolver to the candle flame, she opened the clasp, levered down the grip, peered in at the works. There was the alteration Aegypta Schenck had made, the miniature screw that could be set clockwise or counterclockwise to reverse the rotation of the drum. And because no shells were in the chambers, the baroness could see the tiny letters above each hole, as well as the six new points of pressure for the firing pin; the pistol had been scarcely used, it seemed. Maybe de Graz had been ignorant of its new purpose, or had preferred instead to use it as an ordinary gun, storing up its power without expending it.

So much the better. The baroness returned to her husband's

book. Turning the page, smoothing it over, she saw the first of the six powers the gun could conjure into substance—no, that was not the one for her tonight.

From one of her husband's worktables she retrieved a screwdriver and reset the tiny screw. Influenced, perhaps, by the image of the goddess, as well as other forces she scarcely understood, Nicola Ceausescu opened the top of her bodice in the hot, still air, revealing her slip. It was at the moment when she realized how she was betrayed, that Cleopatra revealed her bosom to the asp. As for the baroness, who would be her Marcus Anthony? Who would be her Octavius? Would it be Luckacz, or Eulenberg, or Schnibbe? Certainly now she walked along the dagger's edge, because of her impetuosity and the cargo of the Hephaestion. And if the time was coming when the German government decided to replace her, whom would they choose to live in these high rooms? Princess Clara, perhaps, or her daughter, or else Felix—this would be impossible to bear!—the baroness's only son. So perhaps this was the actual reason she had gathered them under her roof, and generosity had had nothing to do with it.

Now already she realized how foolish and how sentimental she had been—a wedding march! There could be no negotiations with these people. Already she regretted having sent Luckacz away with the bracelet—no, it was better this way. The people of Roumania would lay it in her hand.

Soon it would be time for her to go to bed, and she would take a few bites of Jean-Baptiste's sandwich, and brush her teeth and wash her face and climb among her pillows as the sun rose. But now she turned to the description of the third power, closed the gun and set the drum so that the corresponding chamber was in the barrel. She blew out the candle by the lectern, then turned and faced the altar at the entrance to the room. Like a sharpshooter at the circus she extinguished the flame when she pulled the trigger. The room and everything inside was swallowed up in darkness. But then immediately she saw another figure in the room, illuminated as if by gunfire.

No doubt it would have made sense at that moment of summoning for her to have chosen some powerful and warlike ghost—Sennacherib, for example, the angel of destruction

Aegypta Schenck had used against her. But almost to her own surprise she found that she had chosen from a different category altogether. Her strength as a performer had always been her spontaneity; when she saw the phantasm take momentary shape in her hidden room, she imagined she had caught a glimpse of some new, soft part of herself.

It lingered for a moment before it disappeared into the darkness, the likeness of a naked boy about nine years old, crowned with leaves in his curling hair. Nor was there anything violent about the image except for the feral, savage eyes that the baroness could not see; the boy was turned away from her. Delicate wings spread from his back, the merest tracery. She saw him as if leaning over a rock, staring at a reflection in a forest pool. Then he disappeared.

The spirit creature was named Mintbean. He was a cherub attendant upon Eros, or Cupid, or Dionysus, according to different texts. Even in the darkness after the firing of the gun, the baroness could feel his presence close to her. If she had known the words, she could have summoned him—the words of welcome that were missing from her husband's manuscript.

In the darkness she caught sight of another image, lit this time by a spark of memory. Mintbean, perhaps, had left it as a gift, the memory of the fireworks above her in the Champ de Mars, and she standing in the back of the empress's carriage, and the crowd calling her name. Behind her, as she turned, a scuffle had broken out. A man in a wool cap struggled with a bareheaded man, fashionably dressed in a camel hair coat, and as she watched, he turned to look at her.

His face was lean and wild. He had yellow hair, light eyes under dark eyebrows, eyes that saw her, she thought, saw who she was, or just a glimpse of her before he turned away. Oh, but that was all it took, as she had read about in plays and poems, and everybody knew, perhaps, and everyone had always known, perhaps, but she.

6 *Captives in the People's Palace*

IN THE MIDDLE of the morning two days later, Miranda woke in a small bedroom with cream-colored wallpaper, decorated with a raised pattern of silver fleurs-de-lis. Light filtered through gauze curtains, pulled back to reveal long windows with ornate brass handles. One of these windows—more of a door, really—opened to a stone balcony. Miranda could see a row of squat stone balusters.

She felt the warm breeze on her face and listened to the muted sounds of traffic, filtered also as if through the gauze, or else coming from far away. In Berkshire County where she'd grown up, she'd had a little room on the third floor of her parents' house, and it had overlooked the green, and from it she could hear the sound of cars braking and accelerating for the traffic light. On summer mornings when school was out, she would wake up late and lie on her back against the pillows without moving, as now.

And now especially that vanished time felt close to her, because of her dream. Once Stanley, her adoptive father, had told her it was wrong to imagine dreams had a duration in time, and you could dream the same dream throughout the night. Instead, he told her, they were manufactured instantaneously as you woke up, minted like money or else burned like a CD. He had said money, but she'd imagined a CD, imagined also sliding the new disk into the machine of her memory, while at the same time wondering if Stanley really believed what he was saying. Sometimes it was hard to tell. Sometimes he would experiment with far-fetched theories he had read or heard, reciting them as fact to see how they sounded.

And of course, inevitably, this morning in this room that reminded her of her own childhood room, she had dreamed of Stanley and Rachel and all that. She had thrown off her blankets during the night. Now she lay propped up on pillows under a fragrant, freshly laundered sheet, replaying her memories, which did not have—at least now as she remade them in her mind—any of the distorted, altered quality of dreams. She had been sitting with Rachel and Stanley at the kitchen table, having some kind of argument or discussion about where she might like to go to college, a subject that had always interested Rachel but exhausted Stanley and her. And so as usual they had teamed up to make fun. "I hear there is a marine biology program in Tierra del Fuego," Stanley had said.

And Miranda, giggling: "Isn't there a community college in Novisibirsk?"

And Rachel: "That's just great. Remind me to laugh when you're flipping hamburgers at Burger King."

This mattress was softer than the one at home, too soft for her taste. The bed itself had four posters and a canopy—how long was it since she had slept in a proper bed? Not since the castle at Mamaia—no, there had been a few depressing, fleabag inns around Braila and Macin, where she had woken lumpy with mosquito bites, and Ludu had said . . .

Now suddenly she sat up, remembering Ludu Rat-tooth as she lay on the muddy ground, blood on her face and shirt, sticky under Miranda's fingers. Nor was it possible, once she'd pressed the button, to pause that CD. "Oh, God," she murmured, hugging herself, feeling with surprise her naked shoulders—she was wearing some kind of linen nightgown. How long since she had not slept in her clothes? "Miss, here's your breakfast," Ludu had once said, bringing her a plate of peppered oatmeal, tepid and congealed.

"Are you hungry?" said a soft, low voice. Who was there? The canopy, tied back on the window side, fluttered free on the other side, obscuring a portion of the room. Leaning forward now, pulling the soft material aside, Miranda saw a woman beside the bed, between the bed and a closed door. How long had she been there?

"Oh," Miranda said. Now suddenly she caught a whiff of tobacco smoke. She kicked her legs free from the sheet and put her bare feet on the floor. She knew who this was, where she was. She had heard enough of Captain Raevsky's crazed descriptions. And of course that sadistic pig O'Brien, in the Mogosoaia police station, had told her where she was going.

"Are you . . . hungry?" the woman repeated, her voice low and harsh and toneless. She was dressed in a tight yellow gown that broke above her ankles and displayed her slender waist, her slender arms. She wore no jewelry, and her hair was cut straight at the level of her jaw, a helmet of red and brown. At that moment Miranda saw her as if through the scrim of her anticipation, and because of that she did appear as something mystical and lovely, as Raevsky had described at bleary moments on the Hoosick riverbank.

Miranda even remembered some of the language he'd used. She caught a backward glimpse of some of the images she had supplied when he was talking. But that was then, and this was now, and it was time to forget about all that. The baroness wasn't so much younger than Rachel, after all. And she was just Miranda's height or even a bit shorter, as Miranda saw immediately when she stood up.

"I want to see Peter," she said. "Where are my clothes?"

She had come from Mogosoaia the previous night, and she now wondered if she had been drugged, so incomplete her memory seemed. She had come in some kind of a covered vehicle, a cart or a truck, and had seen the lights of the city as she dozed. Her wrists had been cuffed in front of her. That had been uncomfortable.

Now she rubbed her hands over her wrists—still sore. But her bracelet, which had been taken from her, was in its old place. She fingered it, pulled it out of the raw marks; she had not seen Peter since the night of their arrest. Where was he now? He hadn't been in that cart. He hadn't stumbled out with her into the courtyard of this enormous pile of buildings, that was sure.

But this woman didn't appear to understand what she was

talking about. "Where is the Chevalier de Graz?" Miranda asked again.

Nicola Ceausescu shrugged. And it was true there was something unnatural about her, some weird articulation that made you look at her and try to guess her thoughts. Every small motion seemed significant, as if she were an actor on the stage. Puzzled, she lifted up her hand, spread her fingers by her face. Ah, now she understood! She smiled, swallowed back a laugh that had no appearance of joy or good humor. "There is someone I imagine you would like to see first."

"I don't think so."

"No, I think you do. She is resting, but is eager to see you after twenty-five years."

Suddenly panicked, Miranda glanced around the room. For a moment she recalled another fragment of her dream. She saw Rachel, her adoptive mother, at the kitchen table rubbing her nose, which was her signal that the coffee was too strong again. Stanley had made it and he never got it right.

"Where are my clothes?"

"I had them burned," said the baroness. "You won't need them again. They were unsuitable. I believe a chapter of your life is over," she continued as Miranda saw for the first time, laid out over a complicated wooden dressing frame, some kind of long blue dress or gown. It was ridiculous.

"There was a time," said Nicola Ceausescu, "when I too often dressed like that—in a man's clothes, I mean. Because of the convenience. Oh, for all sorts of reasons. But no longer. My dear, you are a princess of Roumania."

Unrolled over a spar of the dressing stand was a pair of bluish stockings, embroidered with forget-me-nots. On the floor there were some shoes, also blue. "You've got to be kidding," Miranda said. "They'll never fit."

"We measured you when you were asleep."

For reasons that she couldn't analyze, this information brought a lump to Miranda's throat. Self-conscious suddenly, she was aware of the polished floor under her bare feet. Here she was, standing in her underwear and someone else's nightgown, waiting to see her actual birth mother. . . .

"I've put out no jewelry," murmured the baroness. "I didn't

know your taste, though there is a great deal of it here. Pieces that belonged to your own family—you will consult with Princess Clara when you see her. To tell the truth, it is the fashion now to go without, because of me. Once I had a gold ring from my husband, but I don't wear it anymore. I thought I would leave my wrists bare, so that people would notice a gold bracelet when I put it on. Also I imagined a single tourmaline in a platinum setting around my neck, or else having it cut in pieces because it was too big. For the moment I've abandoned those ideas. Please, it's late. I have written out a schedule for you today."

"I won't wear these," said Miranda.

The baroness smiled. "You have no choice."

And as Miranda glared at the dressing frame, she continued, "Would you rather stand a trial for murder like your friend de Graz?"

The sunshine and the soft, warm air came in the window. From where she stood, Miranda could see past the stone balustrade and down into the square. At the mention of Peter's name, Miranda felt like weeping—this ridiculous dress was not the total of her difficulties. There was much, after all, she had to learn.

She slipped the dress off its wooden frame. "Will you give me some privacy?"

The baroness laughed. "Now that's an antique idea! I had expected you to be quite up-to-date. God knows I've had no privacy since I've lived here."

She stood with her arms crossed over her chest. And it was true—she obviously had no intention of budging as Miranda held the dress up and smoothed it over her front. There was no point in delaying once the decision was made, but was it possible this horrible woman was going to watch her the whole time? She walked around the bed to stand in the shelter of its canopy, then, businesslike, slipped off the nightgown so it puddled on the floor.

"Now that is not so bad," murmured the baroness. "You have a pleasant shape."

Clenching her teeth, Miranda stepped into the dress and pulled it up. But of course it fastened with a row of buttons down the back. However she bent her arms, she only got a few.

Beside the bed on this side was a large free-standing mirror in an ornate frame. Abruptly she remembered a series of greeting cards Rachel had used, Weimaraners dressed in human clothes and placed in all kinds of undignified poses. "I look like a dog in a prom dress," she muttered.

The baroness laughed. "Not a dog. Here, let me help you." Then she was behind Miranda, touching her. "Now it is true you have a lovely waist—a benefit, perhaps, of two weeks in the country without food. I suppose I should try hiding from the police in Mogosoaia! What are you, twenty-five, I think? The silk is too tight over your . . . breasts."

She gave a vicious emphasis to the word. Stung with embarrassment, Miranda watched herself in the mirror, the baroness indistinct behind her. "Now the stockings," she said. "You are a virgin, are you not?"

"What?"

They spoke in French. The word the baroness used, "pucelle," was not familiar to Miranda in this context, and it took her a while before she understood. "Oh, don't be a prude! But of course you are public property now, and these things are important. And you have been wearing trousers and sleeping in the woods with a grown man, a dangerous criminal—you understand there's much to overcome. But twenty-five is high time, past time really. I was a mother by your age. You have not met Felix, my son."

While the baroness was speaking, Miranda's emotions had pursued a small, tight circle from embarrassment to anger, then to sadness. Was it true she was twenty-five? How could it be true?

No, it was not true. That was just the time gone by. In the mirror she saw tears in her eyes. "Now, stop," cried the baroness. "I'm sure you will like him. Everybody does, that's what I hear. Of course I myself have scarcely seen him, because of the potato-eating Germans—oh, I know. Sometimes I have wet my pillow with my tears."

She was hateful, Miranda decided. But it was a peculiar kind of hatefulness that seemed deliberate. Now the baroness stepped away beyond the end of the bed and crossed her arms, again, over her chest. Miranda watched her in the mirror. "You must brush your hair, but it's good you've cut it in my style. You will see it is the fashion because of me."

"I'll wear the shoes, but I won't wear the stockings," Miranda said. "Can you take me to Peter now?"

The baroness ignored these last words. She pursed her lips. "Suit yourself. The dress is long enough. We will not experience your legs. Luckily there is no hair upon your ankles, not that I can see. Later we must powder it or else we scrape it off. It's a pity you're so dark."

Then she continued as Miranda stared at herself, tried to make the image in the mirror correspond to something she was familiar with, or liked about herself: "When I took your clothing to be burnt, I found a letter in your pocket from Aegypta Schenck—the policemen had already given a report. My dear, your aunt was some kind of alchemist or conjurer, for which she lost a high position in the household of the former empress. It's not wise for you to read or own such things, but I must ask you: Was there another letter—no, how shall I ask? Sergeant O'Brien also recovered a revolver, I believe it's called, something from your father's family. Let me ask you. Who gave you such a thing?"

"At Mamaia Castle," whispered Miranda impatiently. She watched her lips move in the mirror.

"And was there another letter with it? Perhaps there were some references you didn't understand . . . ."

Maybe that's where it started to go wrong, Miranda thought—the letter from her aunt that she had found with her father's gun and had not read. Later it had been destroyed because of her carelessness. Maybe if she'd followed the directions in that letter, she would never have ended up this image in this glass, her tanned, chapped arms and shoulders.

"So if there is such a thing and you would like to show it to me, perhaps we could puzzle it out. But I tell you it's not wise to get mixed up in this sort of language, these superstitions about ghosts and whatnot, though at one time it was the fashion among wealthy families. This did not protect your aunt, and you see your position is precarious already. So I will keep the letter for you, though there is no place you could keep it now. Alas, there is no reticule or pocket in that frock."

Miranda turned from the mirror so she couldn't see herself. "My face I don't mind it because I'm behind it," she thought, something Stanley had quoted more than once. Words to conjure with. Besides, what did any of this matter now?

And if this was part of being a princess, maybe there was another part. Maybe people would do what she told them, just because of who she was. "Please," she said. "You must take me to the Chevalier de Graz."

She turned to face her persecutor and stare her down, a woman who—Miranda guessed—was beautiful at any moment or in any clothes. Now she smiled, her thin lips cruel and delicate. "I believe you already have a rendezvous."

"No, please. He's here, isn't he?"

"Yes, he's here. You have guessed it. But he also has a . . . schedule."

Miranda closed her eyes, then opened them. "What do you mean?"

"He is a dangerous man. And he has required medical attention. When we took him he was very ill, because of the wound in his hand. Really, he might have died."

Miranda was staring at the expression of the baroness's lips after she said these words. I'm looking at a smirk, she thought. This was what a smirk looked like—she'd never known.

All Nicola Ceausescu's expressions seemed to come with words attached, they were so clear and definite. "He was very careless," she said.

"But—but he's all right now."

She had to believe it. The baroness shrugged. "He would be better if they'd used sufficient morphine in Mogosoaia. But you understand, a prisoner under guard. He was not yet under my protection—would you like to see? Maybe he could spare you several minutes. I thought it would be natural for you to want to see your mother first. More convenient, too, because he is in an older section of the keep. For the sake of our security. He is a dangerous man, I must insist."

She opened the door, then slipped in front of Miranda to lead the way into a long gallery, lit with chandeliers and decorated with portraits of men in blue uniforms. Grumbling about the inconvenience, she nevertheless was smiling as she walked. Miranda could see her face reflected in the mirrors between the paintings, the curl of her thin lips. It was obvious she was only pretending to be glad to do this for her guest. But whatever her expression and whatever she said, Miranda suspected she really was glad to do it, though for reasons that had nothing to do with pleasing her, but probably the reverse.

Even so, Miranda felt she had prevailed. And she wondered if part of what allowed her to prevail was the distance she had kept from her emotions. Of course she was worried about Peter and desperate to see him. Of course she was worried about Clara Brancoveanu and desperate to avoid her. And when one surge of feelings threatened to overcome her, she would force herself open to the other, according to the method Stanley had once taught her. More than that—she had been able to concentrate on her idiotic clothes, the absurd spectacle she must be making right here and right now, as a way of managing the rest of it, which was a chaos of anxiety and dread. What had the baroness said about the morphine?

But as they began to pass by clumps of actual men who seemed to be doing nothing except standing there in the portrait gallery, Miranda let herself imagine the worst, partly to be prepared for it, and partly as a way of reducing her present embarrassment—these men, in coattails or again in uniform, just stared at her as she went by. One old fellow with muttonchop sideburns was actually clapping his gloved hands, as if Miranda were an actress making an entrance. At least the shoes didn't have heels, though they seemed too flimsy to run in. The air was sweltering out here. The small high windows were all closed.

Then they had passed that gantlet, but one of the men had peeled away from the wall to follow them, a narrow-shouldered man dressed in some kind of livery, a short jacket with red piping that took the place of lapels. He had a high bald forehead and a face like the blade of a hatchet. He was thin, almost emaciated, with an Adam's apple that stuck out above a collar that was not clean, as Miranda noticed with surprise; he was walking close behind her and a little to one side. The baroness had hurried on ahead.

They passed through double doors and around a corner, and rejoined her in a square room with a marble floor where they waited by a pair of elevators. "This is Jean-Baptiste," announced the baroness. "He will take you downstairs. Then to Princess Brancoveanu's apartments." Abruptly she stalked away toward another opened door, where a white-haired woman and a number of military officers were waiting. "The German ambassador," murmured Jean-Baptiste.

Miranda glanced at him in surprise. Then the door to the elevator opened, the attendant opened the cage, and the three of them descended in that hot small clanking space. Miranda, staring up at the massed bulk of the building from the courtyard the previous night, had estimated its height at three or four stories, but already they were farther down than that.

The attendant pulled back the door, and then she and Jean-Baptiste were walking through a maze of smaller, brick-faced corridors. Guards carried long rifles and bandoliers of cartridges. A pair of them stood on either side of a narrow door, which one of them unlocked when he saw Jean-Baptiste.

"Thank you," said Miranda, and no one looked at her. She had spoken in French, but now she repeated in Roumanian—"Multumesc"—but still nobody paid attention. Jean-Baptiste opened the door and stood aside to let her in.

He did not follow her, for which she was grateful. At least I'll be alone, she thought. But there was a soldier on the other side as well. He carried a pistol. The room was stinking, filthy, hot, a stone-faced chamber with a single barred window on the bottom of an air shaft. Outside the corridors had been lit with bulbs of gas, but here there was a candle in a wooden stick next to a chamber pot. By its light Miranda could see a ripped mattress stuffed with straw, and Pieter de Graz with his legs shackled together, naked in his underwear, his face puffy and his body dark with bruises, his hand covered with red bandages.

"You may leave us," she said to the soldier, first in French, then in Roumanian. "Please, go," she said, but he did nothing, didn't even look at her, though she was standing right next to him in the open door.

Angry, frustrated, she stepped past him into the room. De Graz turned toward her and he smiled, revealing his familiar teeth, irregular, slightly splayed. He tried to speak—a broken whisper, and she pulled her dress up to squat down beside him. The guard made no movement as she bent down to hear what he was saying: words she recognized, almost the first English words that she had heard in his mouth since she had rediscovered him in Mogosoaia.

"Oh life is a marvelous cycle of song," he quoted.

Among all the disgusting smells in that chamber, at that moment nevertheless she caught a whiff of hope as he continued:

"Of wonderful extemporanea.
And love is a thing that can never go wrong,
And I am the Queen of Roumania!"

SLUT THAT SHE was, she actually embraced him, as the baroness witnessed in the alchemical laboratory that adjoined her bedroom overlooking the Piata Revolutiei. She couldn't hear what the girl said, but in the center of her crystal pyramid she saw her go down on her knees in the filthy straw—now there was a dress quickly ruined, after all.

The baroness was disappointed. Her interview with the German ambassador, short as it was, had been unsatisfactory, anxiety-provoking. She thought perhaps she'd find some comfort here, or else not comfort, exactly. A woman of exquisite sensitivity, Nicola Ceausescu had imagined she'd be able to decipher something in the undissembling language of Miranda's body. She imagined she'd be able to feel some of the girl's pain at discovering her hero and protector beaten, defeated, maimed—the baroness, also, had suffered a great deal when she was young, and even still.

But as she watched Miranda underneath the glass, again she felt disappointed and impatient. She did not feel the surge of empathy that was as necessary to her as coffee mixed with chocolate. In the girl's gestures she thought she could see anger, certainly, and pity, certainly, but also something else that was not sorrow and was not familiar.

The surgery in the Mogosoaia police barracks had not been entirely necessary. Perhaps a competent private doctor would have been able to save his hand. But de Graz was dangerous in many ways, a fugitive and a criminal who could not have expected the best care. The baroness put her hand toward the crystal surface of the pyramid; she almost touched it. The image was occluded as if a mist or a cloud or some ectoplasmic ghost were in de Graz's cell with him. But through this vague shadow the baroness saw Miranda put her cheek against de Graz's bandaged forearm. And it was true, her shoulders shook with sobs. Doubtless she was in tears. But even so, the baroness's view of the girl's face was unsatisfactory, and her view of de Graz's expression was the same.

Momentarily she expected to hear the bell that would summon her to her appointment with Radu Luckacz and Sergeant Vladimir O'Brien. Still she lingered, disturbed also by the mist that seemed to cling to the inner surface of the pyramid. She lingered long enough to watch her steward, Jean-Baptiste, draw the girl away. Then there was nothing but a foggy blackness until she saw some furniture take shape, indistinct also, the interior of Clara Brancoveanu's sitting room, and the baroness had to move around the table to achieve a better view.

After a few minutes the door opened and Jean-Baptiste came in. There was Miranda Popescu on his heels, disheveled, out of breath—the baroness could see that much. Princess Clara, who had stretched out with a book on the settee, now rose to her feet. But again it was impossible to see their gestures and faces with any precision, and of course nothing could be heard except a faint, ionized roar from the lacquered horn of the ansible in the corner. The baroness brought her fingers to her mouth to gnaw on them, and then she lit a cigarette.

THE WOMAN HAD risen from the sofa, a book dangling from one hand. Miranda stared at her, unable to speak. And maybe it was good to have rushed here from some other place, her head and heart full of chaos. Because it had prevented her from imagining and rehearsing what she might say. Here was one more scene or encounter that was both unreal and fraught; she was getting used to them. She remembered the first time she had spoken to her aunt in tara mortilor after she had come up from the dock with all the creatures of the dead—was this as strange as that? Was it more strange?

"Maman," she said. "Mother, there is a man here who has tried to help us, you and me, and has now been punished for it. You remember my father's aide-de-camp?"

No, it wasn't true she hadn't rehearsed, but this line was the extent of it, conceived as the door opened to the princess's chamber. Once it was spoken, Miranda stood with her hands to her hot face, staring at the woman who put down her book and who also appeared flustered and confused.

They were in a small blue room, ornately furnished. The windows were closed; the window shades were down. Princess Clara was a smooth-faced woman, pale and gray-haired. Though it was stifling in the little room, she wore a cardigan whose sleeves she plucked at nervously. She was smaller than Miranda, and would not meet her eyes.

She had flinched as her daughter spoke, glanced toward the mirror, the window, Jean-Baptiste, who still stood against the wall. When he made signs of leaving she gave him a pleading look. When the steward opened the door behind him, he did so gently and with scarcely a noise, a tiptoeing pantomime of solicitude.

Miranda's mother had been held prisoner in Germany for twenty-five years. Probably the world seemed strange to her. Maybe it was frightening and horrible to have a full-grown child burst in on her. So Miranda rubbed her sweating palms on the cloth of her blue dress and swallowed down her own feelings. And the two women continued to stare at each other like unfamiliar animals, Miranda thought, brought suddenly into the same space.

THE SIMILE OCCURRED to Nicola Ceausescu also as she watched them in the glass. To her they were like cats trying to establish dominance—the white tyger, she mused. She couldn't see the bracelet on Miranda's wrist, but at the ironwood table in her secret laboratory she yawned and stretched, blew on her cigarette ash, frowned, and stubbed it into a gilt ashtray, a gift to the former empress from the Sultan of Bhopal.

Sick of spying, the baroness gave her mind momentarily to other things. Laid out on the surface of the table were two more objects, Prince Frederick's revolver and Miranda's letter from her aunt. And the baroness imagined two more that were missing: first, Kepler's Eye, the tourmaline, about which Aegypta Schenck had revealed a new, important piece of information in her letter. Second, the golden bracelet of Miranda Brancoveanu, the symbol of her authority.

These two objects Nicola Ceausescu had given up, abandoned hope of their possession—not without regret or backward glances. The bracelet especially enticed her. Over the years she had adopted the identity of the white tyger as a ceremonial title. The potato-eaters had been only too glad to encourage her, perceiving no doubt a way to defang the legend of the tyger by reducing it into a civil post and confusing the issue of succession. But it had been a long time since the baroness (whose skill as an artist was dependent on unflinching honesty) had been able to persuade herself that the bracelet could belong to her by any kind of right. And how could she convince others if she could not convince herself? She would be the laughingstock of Bucharest if she ever had the impudence to fasten those gold beads around her wrist. Besides, they would only draw attention to her ugly, big-knuckled, tobacco-stained, chewed and bleeding hands.

So the jewel she had abandoned and the bracelet also. As a reward the gods had favored her with this revolver. Perhaps Cleopatra herself had looked down from the slopes of Mount Olympos, and also Medea, and Hera, and Hecate, and Ariadne—oh, the baroness had played many such parts on the boards of the old Ambassadors! And perhaps the goddesses and their attendant muses had been able to appreciate how she had never tried to seize control of any audience with her own self-regarding art. Instead she had always been a humble vessel for some greater force. In this way she had risen above her rivals, Bernhardt in Paris, Caramanlis at the Meroë Festival, Nakamura in Canton—where were they now? Withered, old, and broken, mothers and grandmothers in rich men's houses, while Nicola Ceausescu was still standing on the stage of all the world.

Yes, Cleopatra and Medea had brought her this pistol by a circuitous path. They also had been passionate women who had suffered much and been unfairly judged. And doubtless if she honored them and prayed to them both in her life and in her art, they would bring her also the key to using it, which she still lacked.

Aegypta Schenck, evidently, had discovered that key and cracked the coded language of the spell. Perhaps she had written out the words and Miranda Popescu had lost them through her stupidity and clumsiness. Or else the Princess Aegypta had intended to bring her niece to Mogosoaia while she herself was still alive. The baroness had interrupted that part of the scheme, throttled her to death in front of Mary Magdalena's altar, a crime that still weighed on her and made her start awake at night—it was not her fault! It had not been her fault.

But what one woman could discover, another could as well. Aegypta Schenck had offered her a clue.

Now the baroness spread out the letter she had taken from Miranda's pocket, separated it into its pages. There it was on the last page:

> *. . . Always remember as Magister Newton tells us the events of this world have no probative veracity. But just as incidents occur differently in memory between two witnesses, also they are different at the time of their occurrence. So if we ask if something has an evidentiary value, first we must ask who had observed it and for what reason. For it is not in this world, nor the hidden world, but in the Empyrean World above, that scientific proofs will stand for equal witnesses, or an experiment, or any ordinary incidence. These events in your life that seem extraordinary, to another they have never once occurred. But oh my dear niece . . .*

"COMME VOUS ÊTES grande—how tall you are!" said Clara Brancoveanu. "You take after your father, obviously! You must know it is terrifying to see you like this with your red face. No, let me look at you—I had not dreamed you'd be so tall! Please, there is cold water in the washstand if you'd like to bathe your face, and I have powder also and a hairbrush. . . ."

This wasn't promising. Say what you like, Miranda thought, about the time she'd spent between Christmas Hill and Mogosoaia, it hadn't included a lot of this. After only five minutes, Princess Clara had begun to remind her of some hideous cross between the Baroness Ceausescu and her adoptive mother in Massachusetts—maybe that's just what it was, to be a mother. Maybe that was just part of the deal.

No, there was more: ". . . Madame la Baronne Ceausescu tells me you've led quite such a life in these last months, hiding in the swamps and so on. I can well believe it now I look at you! She tells me you've been traveling with this man de Graz, whom I remember when he was with your father—just a boy, then! Younger than I! Really, on the train from Germany and as I've been sitting here waiting, I have thought it is past time you are married, and if I can achieve that I will die content. Is it true? I fear it would be better not to see this man again. It was not to be your husband that your father selected him. But he was a servant only, a trusted servant. At least your father trusted him though I did not . . ."

This was just the kind of crap Rachel used to say about Peter Gross. Furious, stung, Miranda shook her hair back from her face. She pushed a lock of hair behind her ear. She looked around the ornate, overfurnished parlor, and then worked her way back to the woman standing between the sofa and the low table. She examined her as if she were another object in the room—how old was she? Fiftyish, Miranda supposed. And yet her skin seemed oddly smooth, worn down. And all her gestures seemed old-ladyish—that was what you got, Miranda supposed, after half a life in prison.

Her gray hair was pulled back from her face, fastened at the nape of her neck. Her eyes seemed both nervous and sad. And if immediately she'd started in with criticism and judgments, maybe that was out of nervousness and sadness. And if she worried the sleeves of her cardigan and made odd, plucking motions with her hands, if she persisted in talking like this, maybe it was because she had forgotten how to behave with people, or talk to them, or else she'd never known. She'd been about Miranda's age when she had gone to Ratisbon.

And in Ratisbon, after Miranda's father's death, she had had a baby, and she had given that baby up after one day. What did she have to teach Miranda now? What right did she have even to talk to her? Did she honestly think Miranda was going to listen to her as she continued: ". . . No, no, I don't care what you say—we must be grateful to Madame la Baronne, whose husband was once your father's friend. It is she who used her influence to liberate me from Ratisbon, as well as her son, Felix—have you met him? No? Well, he is very young. No—here he is!"

TO NICOLA CEAUSESCU, watching in the glass, the princess in her movements had now lost any suggestion of a cat. Instead she seemed like a chicken circling the base of a young tree. She was studying her daughter's clothes but not her face, feinting and darting, jerking forward and then pulling back. And now a little chick came hopping behind her out of another room. Nicola Ceausescu put her hand out, eclipsing the image with her hand. Yes, she was feeling discomfort, embarrassment, but no pleasure at this scene. Where was Radu Luckacz, Vladimir O'Brien? They were late.

But then mercifully the bell began to ring.

7 *The Ouijah Board*

RADU LUCKACZ WAITED where he often did, in an antechamber off Constantin's Mezzanine. He sat with his hands on the black knees of his trousers, perched immobile on the front edge of his chair. By contrast, Sergeant Vladimir O'Brien ranged around the room, examining the paintings and the fabric of the curtains. Radu Luckacz watched him.

The sergeant was a tall man, well formed, slender, with a shock of orange hair above an unformed, freckled face. There was always a sheen of moisture on his thick lips, which seemed vaguely misshapen, and he licked them constantly. So—a thug; Luckacz was a student of criminal physiognomy, and he imagined a careful study of the sergeant's cranium would reveal all kinds of suggestive lumps, evidence, maybe, of sexual perversion and violent impulses. His eyes, too close together, compelled attention nevertheless, a glossy brown color that seemed at odds with the rest of his face and which betrayed his mixed ancestry: part Roumanian, part riffraff from the English isles, washed up in Europe after the wreck.

But he moved in an interesting way—self-conscious, athletic, self-controlled. And his dress uniform was beautifully cut; apologetically, Luckacz glanced down at the greasy brim of the black hat in his lap, wondering what a physiognomist or phrenologist might make of him. In particular, he wondered what he might think if he had been able to examine side-by-side two photographic portraits of himself—the kind of tight, focused portraits taken in prisons or madhouses—one showing him today and one five years ago, the first time he had waited for the baroness in this room.

Perhaps the differences would have suggested to him—an impartial observer—the five-year ravages of drunkenness or an addiction to narcotics. Surely then he'd been a different kind of man, with a young daughter and a loving wife—ambitious, maybe, and willing to compromise. What's wrong with that? The world is as it is.

Everything had been so hopeful then, hope plucked from despair after the collapse of the Roumanian armies and the German occupation of the city. When Kevin Markasev was brought to the police station, and Nicola Ceausescu also, and with her Luckacz had lifted a new standard of Roumanian pride, something for his adopted countrymen to catch hold of and believe in after the empress's flight. The white tyger, born out of the invented sacrifice of Kevin Markasev. And that had been a hoax, but not an evil one. The boy had not been mistreated after all, but had lived in luxury in the Strada Spatarul. Doubtless the Germans would have killed him without qualm. Of course Radu Luckacz had also profited.

Five years later here he was, bossed and bullied by German officials, surrounded by men like Vladimir O'Brien, and no closer to what he most desired.

Nicola Ceausescu swept into the room. Luckacz raised his head to look at her, his absinthe, his morphine, and his schnapps. He sprang up from his chair with his hat in his hands, while O'Brien turned from the window. "Oh, I am sorry I am late!" said the baroness, hesitating and then coming toward him so he could smell the faint, astringent odor of her skin. "Oh, my friend! And is this the brave Sergeant O'Brien? The hero of the Mogosoaia woods—not a sergeant for much longer, I am sure!"

O'Brien stepped toward them, took the hand she offered him, bent over it and maybe even touched it with his rubbery, wet lips—Luckacz couldn't stand it: "I must insist it is too dangerous to keep that fellow here. I mean the criminal de Graz. This morning we have come from the funeral of one man, a patrolman with seven years' experience, a widower with three children who are now orphaned. I have come just now from planning a subscription. If this fellow, this devil had not been wounded and without the use of his right hand, I'm sure the death would have been greater. As it was, two mastiffs had to be destroyed. Five men are dead. . . ."

His voice—harsh, nasal, unpleasant—trailed away. "Oh, I don't believe we have a cause to worry," said Nicola Ceausescu. "Sergeant O'Brien has seen to his accommodations here. A devil, as you call him! So, I wanted to see the devil's face! I wanted to see the man who as you say has caused such damage, and try to understand why anyone would take up arms against this government. We can learn things from our enemies! Please put me down for a contribution of one thousand marks for your orphans' subscription."

She spoke to him, but she was looking at Vladimir O'Brien, who had released her hand. What was she thinking? Was she disgusted, as she should be, by this fellow's ugliness, his lips?

"Madam," said Luckacz, "your compassion is well known. On behalf of the victims—no, I must insist this is not the only scoundrel left in Bucharest. Two nights ago in the Champ de Mars there was an attack upon your carriage, an anarchist or else the agent of a foreign government. Thankfully the event was not successful due to the interference of a loyal citizen, or so we thought. A bottle of vitriol was discovered at the precise locality, and a soldier of the Timisoara Rifles was slightly injured when the liquid splashed across his foot."

Officious, irritating even to himself, Luckacz's voice grew softer and then stopped. What was the baroness thinking now? She turned to him, gave him her full attention, cocked her eyebrow. "Sergeant O'Brien, will you wait outside?"

The fellow actually saluted, turned on the heel of his expensive boot, and departed. She didn't look at him. Her eyes didn't leave Luckacz's face, and she was fresh-faced, happy, smiling until the door closed. Then her expression changed, not because she frowned, flared her nostrils, grimaced, or anything like that. In fact she scarcely moved, scarcely breathed. It was the significance of her expression that she altered, as if she spoke the same word in a different context. Like a sensation on his skin, Luckacz could feel her anxiety and wrath.

"How dare you?" she said. "How dare you say these things to me?"

"Ma'am, I must imagine that—"

She cut him off. "It was Kevin Markasev!"

"Ma'am, as I say we have no confirmation on that point. But if—"

"It is Markasev. Don't you read the papers? There was an attack on Koenigslander in the Danish Opera House. In his dressing room. By his own son!"

"Ma'am, I'm afraid I cannot see. . . ."

OF COURSE HE couldn't. He could not pretend to understand her. He stood with his hat in his hands, massaging the worn brim, his mouth almost invisible under the black moustache that every day seemed larger and more luxurious as the rest of him dwindled—of course he couldn't see. Now he was going on about the other man, the yellow-haired stranger in the expensive coat—the beautiful man, and as if sidelong, the baroness caught a sudden glimpse of his clean face and his bright eyes. But then she was pulled back by Luckacz's droning voice—the stranger who at first (the investigating detective thought) had interrupted or frustrated the assault, but then apparently had disappeared with the anarchist or suspected anarchist, and perhaps was even responsible for hiding him from the police who now were searching door to door in the university district where there were many cheap hotels, and where the trail had led. Even at the site of the attack the fellow's struggle to disarm the anarchist (or alleged anarchist) had resulted in a larger disturbance. Several bystanders had lost their footing, and several policemen and soldiers also; it was during this disturbance that the men had disappeared—one in a woolen cap, one (as the baroness had quite possibly observed) in a camel's hair coat. His identity had not been discovered, despite the questioning of several persons at the scene, including the Bibescu brother and sister, one recently married to the celebrated Colonel Bocu, the other on medical leave from the armed forces in Moldavia.

"I understand now why you waited so long to tell me about this. It reflects on the competence of your department."

"Ma'am, the Timisoara Rifles are serving under German officers, as you know. I myself had gone to Mogosoaia to secure the prisoners there. I did not return for several hours after these events. When I brought you General Schenck's revolver, as you recall, I was not aware of the details."

She did not care about his excuses. "But you must take personal charge of this. You must be the one who catches Kevin Markasev. And he must not make any kind of statement, and no one must see his face—do you understand?"

She was close to him, almost close enough to touch him if she'd put out her hand. "My old friend, this is a danger. Already Ambassador Moltke has brought me an official notice of her government's displeasure over this affair of the Hephaestion and the anti-German rioting in Chiselet."

"Ma'am, I was about to tell you . . ."

. . . Nothing, he could tell her nothing, for there was nothing to tell. Now as he was speaking, suddenly the danger she was in was clear to her, although the day was bright and warm. She was aware of the buzzing of a bee on the windowsill. There were fruit trees in the courtyard. Someone had left the window open. Now the bee was in the room.

Now suddenly her troubles swarmed about her, two at least. First and greatest was the notice she'd received from the German Embassy and the Committee for Roumanian Affairs, advising her of an investigation into the wreck of the Hephaestion—an urgent subject now the violence in Chiselet had spread to neighboring villages. But under her own roof, she could not help but be aware, as if from some malignant self-destructive urge, she had gathered together several candidates for her unofficial but still powerful position, any one of whom the potato-eaters might prefer: Clara Brancoveanu or her daughter, or maybe even the baroness's own son.

And it was true what the Germans obviously suspected. It was she who had brought the radium from Abyssinia. Jean-Baptiste had handled the bill of sale. And it was true also that Kevin Markasev was alive, and her dead husband had poisoned him against her, turned him into a weapon he manipulated from the land of the dead. Doubtless also he was responsible for the attack on Koenigslander. And if the potato-eaters or the citizens of Bucharest ever discovered that the cult of Kevin Markasev had been constructed out of lies, then it would be the end of her as well.

"Ma'am, though I appreciate the difficulty, I must assure you that there is no reason to think the boy Markasev was involved in this event, though as you know my department has been searching day and night for him in workhouses and shelters for the indigent, since you released him from the Strada Spatarul. . . ."

How could he dare reproach her in this moment of crisis? She could not explain to him why she was sure the man in the woolen cap was Kevin Markasev, the boy her husband had given her to make up for the son that had been stolen away. Baron Ceausescu had given her a boy, full-formed, half-grown, and he had loved her and helped her and pulled Miranda Popescu out of her aunt's artificial refuge in Massachusetts—what a peculiar name!

No, there was nothing about the hidden world that could be revealed to men like Radu Luckacz. So the solution to this problem would not lie with him. "Please," she said. "When you leave me, send the sergeant in. I have a word for him."

She was rewarded by a crease of pain across the policeman's face—no, not rewarded, for she felt it, too. When he was gone, for several moments she stood alone in the bright room, watching the light shine through the curtains, listening to the buzzing of the bee, feeling sad for the abrupt dismissal of her oldest supporter and confidant. Nor was she encouraged when the sergeant reappeared, a cold-hearted killer, obviously, and one who now felt free to imagine, she was sure, several types of favors and intimacies. The baroness watched the knowledge of them flit across the fellow's hideous, expressive face.

"I'm surprised the Chevalier de Graz was taken alive," she said.

He shrugged. "Miranda Popescu," he began, then stopped. But the baroness knew what he was trying to say. His face was easy to read. If the girl had not surrendered when she did . . .

He stood against the big looking glass. Nicola Ceausescu examined the reflection of his back—his dark blue uniform with silver braid, his tight collar flecked with powder. She couldn't decide whether it was natural or artificial. For her old friend Radu Luckacz's sake, she was glad she'd put him in his place.

Sulky and defiant, he stood with a smirk on his wet lips—oh, he would work to please her now! "I must be at the theater at seven o'clock," she said. "But come to me at six. I have a task for you and I rely on your discretion."

She also had a task and till six o'clock to find out what it was. "Do not ask for me here and do not come into the gate. Do not wear these clothes. Come to the servant's door below the chapel. Ask for Jean-Baptiste. Do not give your name. I will tell him to watch out for you."

But after she had left him and hurried up the stairs to her own private apartments, she felt sickened with remorse. No doubt it was partly or even mostly due to her bad treatment that Kevin Markasev had turned against her—oh, she had used him and abused him! And for the sake of what strange whim had she told a lie to the ghost of her dead husband, that she had betrayed him with Herr Koenigslander when he worked at the National Academy? Now the ballet master, also, was the victim of her clumsiness. The baroness cast her mind back. He had been a handsome man. He'd had a habit of winking at her, trying to brush against her, trying to kiss her hand, which was why, she supposed, he was punished now.

This much was certain: She herself was the source of all her difficulties. But was this true for everybody? Or was it a mark of greatness? Her own choices, after all, had taken her from a dirt-floored shack in the Carpathians and brought her to this high room overlooking the Piata Revolutiei.

She closed the door behind her, leaned against it. She bent over the washstand to cool her face, then continued on past the ornamental screen into her hidden laboratory. She unlocked the little door and ducked inside.

Some of the machinery, left from her husband's time, she'd barely touched. Now in the cramped windowless space she lit the lamp. With the phaeton still smoking in her hand, she examined the dusty surfaces, the jumbled masses of glassware she had had transported from Saltpetre Street—what for? Her husband had almost beggared her with his experiments when he was still alive.

The ansible she used, the crystal pyramid, the adamantine mirror, and a few other devices. And of course she had read his books, his translations of Zosimus and Trismegistus, among others. She had learned from him, she now conceded; how could he have tried to hurt her in this way? And even worse, how could he have been so cruel as to use the boy? In what alembic or beaker had he mixed the stray cells of her flesh and hair, and surely something from himself as well—this must have been after she had closed her bedroom door to him, and after he had ceased to be her husband in the normal way. Nevertheless, this child had been his last, best piece of alchemy, and he had turned it against her now, stolen away its love for her—oil of vitriol! It made her skin crawl to imagine.

Why couldn't he leave her in peace after thirteen years? What chains of jealousy, desire, or circumstance still connected him to her? Or was it his fate, in the mansion of hell he lived in with all other suicides, to pick forever through the garbage and old bones of past mistakes? And he was here now, she could tell. She could smell the garbage and the old bones, too, the stink of death that clung to him after these years.

She had not summoned him. Still, here he was, an evanescent shadow in the crystal pyramid, and the stink of the barnyard—the red pig of Cluj, as he'd been known in his own regiments when he was Prince Frederick's friend. There he roamed and wallowed on the ironwood table under the crystal roof, scraping his tusks on the smooth surface in which, silvered and occluded as it seemed, Nicola Ceausescu caught a glimpse of her own reflected face. And as always, it seemed small-featured and sour to her, a constant reproach, a vision of herself that only she could see clearly in all the world.

And there was a noise, too, the scratching of a rodent somewhere in the chamber—no, it came from under the eaves. There was the wooden card table she had not used in years, and the ouijah board still on it, and the ivory planchette that now was moving softly through accumulated dust, pushing it up into pillows and long trails as it crept from letter to letter. She stood above it with the lamp. DRTY HORE I KLL U FLTHY & DEMON HORE

His spelling had never been the best. Often she had puzzled

over his manuscripts, trying to make out even simple words. But the meaning was plain now as always, and it had the effect of relaxing her and focusing her mind. Her enemies would not rest. All her life she'd been one woman by herself against the world. Sentimentality and the leisure to look backward—these were luxuries she couldn't afford.

But perhaps it would be prudent to do nothing, and send Jean-Baptiste to turn the beast away: Vladimir O'Brien, the temptation outside her door. And she would let Radu Luckacz find the boy, track him down in the university district, arrest him, put him on trial . . . no, it was impossible. Kevin Markasev was five years dead. Only Luckacz and herself knew it was not so. The Baroness Ceausescu had spoken at his funeral, her first public oration and the first step of her journey to this room. However noble her purpose had been, how could she admit now she had lied? It was only her popularity, the crowds inside the theater every night and in the square outside, that kept the Germans from replacing her. Besides, what stories could the boy not tell before a judge?

She put her lamp on the desk and sat on the edge of her leather armchair. She pulled a piece of stationery onto the blotter, dipped her pen into the inkpot. "He must not be recognized," she wrote.

She blew the letters dry and then put her hand over it as if blocking away the words. This was all useless speculation and self-punishment if she was not able to discover where the boy was hiding—the university district. Five years before, chased from her house in Saltpetre Street, she and Markasev had explored those streets together. She had bought him clothes to match his eyes, conceal the effect of his white skin.

Radu Luckacz would find him, she had no doubt. He would cast a net of officers around the district and then draw it closed, moving from house to house. But she had investigative tricks as well. Methodical police work was not among them.

The planchette on the ouijah board was quiet now. The crystal pyramid was empty. Yet still she felt the Baron Ceausescu's lurking, malicious presence, caught a trace of his barnyard stink. She lit a cigarette.

There was much about the crystal pyramid she didn't

understand, and she imagined she employed it to a small percentage of its capacity. There was no mention of it in her husband's notes, but this she had discovered on her own: Even without precise coordinates, any room or street or house that she had actually seen, any place that she had actually visited, she could conjure up a vision of it within the glass, as if through an exercise of memory. And some of these images would be ethereal and ghostly, and some as sharp as diamonds with each detail intact, according to the value of her memory. So now she summoned a small vision of the Strada Inocentei and the alleys branching off from it near the School of Mines. It was an area of cheap rooming houses and student cafés, bookstores, flea markets, butcher shops, and bakeries. Because she'd been happy there, or at least because she remembered being happy, soon the tiny streets behind the Dance Academy took shape, at first with missing blocks and buildings. But because memory is the father of the muses, and because great artists are above all skilled in the mnemonic arts, soon the ghostly, wavering, silver streets acquired edges and colors, as if at the moment of sunrise over the chaotic rooftops—soft and dusty hues at first, but then harder and deeper as morning wore on.

At first the baroness sat with her back to the pyramid, blowing on her cigarette, examining the glow. But then she got up from her leather chair to stand above it like a goddess who had conjured it to life.

In all creative arts there is a moment when an exercise of memory turns into something else, some power that is uncontrolled and separate, and corresponds no longer to anything interior or subjective, but instead to literal truth. So as the baroness stood up with the lamp in her hand, now suddenly she could see the place not as it was five years before when she had lived there with Kevin Markasev, but now. And not just bricks and cobblestones, but people, too, and animals—there was a cart stuck in the gutter with a broken wheel, right there at the corner of Rosetti Mews. The driver, with liquor on his breath, stood with his whip and cursed.

And after an hour of looking, she found him, a stranger in expensive clothes, moving through the crowd. He carried a walking stick, had a newspaper under his arm. He had yellow hair under a slouch hat, and a face that was both wild and delicate. Now she saw his eyes were gray, gray with flecks of blue and green. The baroness reached out her hand, almost touching the smooth surface of the pyramid. And when he finally paused before the steps of a narrow building, she bent her neck to peer inside.

One day soon she would need spectacles. But for now she could still make out the number on the blue enamel plate affixed to the crumbling pilaster. And she had recognized the door even before she saw the number—351 Strada Camatei. Of course Markasev would have found it again. She and he had stayed there briefly in the old days.

8 *A Murder*

LIEUTENANT PROCHENKO STOOD with his hand on the rusty railing. He looked up and down the street, searching for policemen in the lazy summer crowds. In uniform or out of uniform—in the piata he had seen an omnibus disgorge twenty men in identical blue suits. They had gathered to receive directions from a single police officer.

He could not shake the impression he was being watched. As always since he'd returned to Europe with the Chevalier de Graz, he could imagine several reasons for the police to be interested in him. That day, for example, he was just returning from a pawnshop in the Strada Stavropoleos, where he had dispensed with Elena Beau-cul's diamond earrings and her brother's overcoat.

But that was a small matter. If the authorities were searching for Kevin Markasev, he'd have to be careful not to get caught in their net. He had entered the country illegally on the Hephaestion, and had no documents of any kind.

But even that was a small matter. He was capable of living indefinitely by his wits. More was required of him, and of the oath he'd sworn to General Schenck von Schenck. Those words, spoken with his fist clenched to his heart, had sustained him in the strange life he had led.

One of the blue-suited men had come into the bend of the street. Prochenko turned to set his back against the warm wall of number 351. He unfolded his newspaper, hooked his stick over his arm, pulled his hat over his eyes, and settled down to watch the policeman, who appeared to be bargaining for something with a roadside vendor. A cone of roasted nuts, Prochenko saw—he imagined he could smell them even at that distance. The policeman, fat and badly dressed, ate his cashews in the middle of the street.

The newspaper was just a blind, but an appropriate one. There on the front page of the *Roumania Libera*, after the war news but above the speculations on the possibility of a cease-fire, was a story about the general's daughter.

Apparently she had been freed from the manipulations of a retired soldier, a former captain of dragoons who'd been arrested after a murderous rampage. The young woman, named "Popescu" as a sort of honorific title, had been reunited with her mother in the People's Palace. There was no mention of the dead policeman in Braila. But a Gypsy girl had been shot and killed by the ever-watchful metropolitan police. And it was speculated that her father had been the leader of a criminal Gypsy band who had kidnapped Miss Popescu and held her captive for seventeen years, ever since her aunt had left Mamaia Castle. Just this spring they had released her to take part in some criminal scheme against the government and her own family.

"Patty Hearst," the lieutenant murmured to himself. Where had that name come from? A rich girl who'd been kidnapped and trained to rob banks in California . . .

In the warm air of Camatei Street, pungent with the smell of garbage and fried food, Sasha Prochenko remembered something. He heard the English words as clearly as if they had been whispered in his ear: "When you want to trust what you read in the papers, you've got to remember the misspellings and mistakes in any story when it's something you know something about. . . ."

Who had said that? Now he remembered the flat-roofed 1960s house on Syndicate Road where his American mother had tried to teach him about the world.

As he watched the man in the blue suit walk methodically down the road, first to one side and then the other, it occurred to him that his safest and most rational course was to leave

Kevin Markasev where he'd said good-bye to him after lunch, in the fifth floor room they'd shared since the other evening in the Champ de Mars. The lieutenant had all his money, everything he owned and then some, in the pockets of Valentin Bibescu's trousers.

What had he told them at their champagne picnic in the sun, with the Duesenberg parked by the side of the road? What had he told the Bibescu soeur et frère—that he was suffering from amnesia? Then he had meant it as a lie, a way to avoid awkward questions. But it had turned out to be true, and it had required Kevin Markasev to show him. From the moment he had seen the boy's gaunt tortured face and stripped off his woolen cap in the Champ de Mars, he had felt an odd awakening in his body, an ache like blood returning to a sleeping hand or foot.

Nor could he give it up, for somewhere in that new remembered knowledge was the key to his own nature, which since the wreck of the Hephaestion he'd fumbled after without finding it, a drunk on the steps of his own house. Now he pushed his hat back, refolded the *Libera*, took his stick in his right hand, and clambered up between the pilasters of number 351.

It was a building full of students and Turkish immigrants with large families. At every landing of the splintered stairs he paused to listen to the shrieks of children. All the windows and the doors were open, and at the end of every corridor he paused to look out over the courtyard, crisscrossed with laundry lines.

As he climbed up he felt his heart grow light, even as he pondered his next steps. All that time in North Africa and Adrianople with the Chevalier de Graz, they had scarcely spoken of their plans. To cross the frontier and to find Miranda, that seemed difficult enough. And perhaps they had assumed Aegypta Schenck would tell them what to do, Aegypta Schenck who had been dead for years—how stupid they had been! How much time they had wasted! And then everything had blown apart with the Hephaestion, and now here he was alone.

Or not alone. Kevin Markasev was with him, and maybe finding Kevin Markasev had been an act of fate, and maybe he was always meant to play a role in this story. Markasev knew many secrets about the Baroness Ceausescu. Over the past day and a half he had revealed some of them: how she dabbled in sorcery and conjuring, how she had kept him prisoner for five long years. If nothing else, Prochenko thought, the boy's existence was enough to bring Ceausescu down, and maybe he could help Miranda in that way.

He climbed up through the storage boxes on the last flight of stairs. Now he stood in the last corridor, rubbing the point of Valentin Bibescu's boot into a crack in the floor where the fiber mats had worn away. For a moment he thought maybe he should go to the German authorities or else the offices of the *Libera*, or maybe even tell his story to the fat man in the blue suit. That would kick over a wasp's nest, he was sure. No, it was impossible—the boy trusted him. It would be cruel to betray that trust for some advantage he could not even foresee.

All the boy's life the baroness had used him. And there was something about him that had touched the lieutenant's heart. He remembered the assessment of the girl inside of him. "Cute," she'd called him in that town in Massachusetts, in that house on Syndicate Road, meaning partly he seemed older than she was, already shaving. And partly she was talking about his dark, single eyebrow and his menacing, tragic, European sophistication, about which she knew nothing, obviously—it didn't matter.

Now Prochenko paused before the door, its green chipped paint. In the Champ de Mars he had wrestled Markasev away from the curb, pulled him into the crowd. Once away from the street, it had been easy for them to slip away from the police, who seemed confused and doubtful about the nature of the attack—there was no mention of it, for example, in the newspaper. Harder to shake was Elena Beau-cul, who had grabbed hold of his sleeve. He had twisted away from her, not without regret. But Markasev had recognized him instantly, which had made his grip the stronger; he had come without resistance. As the lieutenant pulled him through the crowd, already he was mumbling and muttering about the few weeks he had spent in Berkshire County. And when Prochenko had brought him back to his lodgings—here—even then he could not shut up about the time he had spent in that lost, mythical, artificial world, as if it were the only place his life had had a meaning.

In the pawnshop Prochenko had bought a heavy walking

stick with a silver handle in the shape of a wolf's head. Now he knocked it twice against the door and waited for Markasev to unlock it. He heard the crunch of the stiff bolt and pushed open the door. "We've got to leave," he said before he'd even crossed the threshold. "We can't stay here."

He spoke in English. Naked to the waist, Markasev stood in the slanting light, rubbing his shoulders with one of the stupid cotton rags that passed for towels in this country, so different from the fluffy ones Prochenko had grown up with—no.

"Yuck, gross," he thought, again as if someone had whispered the words into his ear. And then he smiled because he was not in fact disgusted in the core of his girl's heart. There was nothing threatening about the boy as he stood there, tall and famished in the warm light, his skin so pale it was almost green, his long face wet from shaving, his eyes dark-hollowed under his big brow.

"Please . . ." he said in the broken English Prochenko remembered from Massachusetts, the fifty words or so that he had learned in the few weeks he had been there, but which he used with an odd expressiveness. "Please, stay. Don't . . . go . . . again."

Did he recognize the girl he'd known at school there and then later that last night on Christmas Hill, when he had burned Miranda's book, and fought with Peter Gross, and started all this? Did he recognize Andromeda Bailey who lived on Syndicate Road? Yes, because from the moment she had snatched him from the curb he had not spoken except in English words. But he'd said nothing about what he saw in her, what changes he had seen. And what could he have told her? Who was it who now stood in front of him in Valentin Bibescu's clothes?

"I . . . am . . . too . . . much . . . scared."

The night before, he had told Prochenko what he'd been doing in that time and place, how he'd been sent by Nicola Ceausescu to bring Miranda here to Bucharest. And if he'd failed, it was not his fault; he'd done everything the baroness had asked. But he'd been punished nonetheless, punished by the lady of comfort and tears, locked up in a cage and then in a rich house. What had been his crime? And now he was punished even more by these dreams that visited him nightly, or else sometimes when he was sitting by himself or even walking in the street—the old baron's ghost, which he had seen and recognized in his attic dungeon in Saltpetre Street. Or sometimes when he closed his eyes he could see the face of the wild boar, the red pig of Cluj, who had threatened and cajoled him and brought him to that curbside in the Champ de Mars, a bottle of vitriol in his pocket. He had told Prochenko about this as they had lain side by side on the little bed, awake in the middle of the night.

Now he started in again. "I dream of porc rosu—red pig," he said, rubbing the towel under his dark armpits, over his sharp ribs, down into the scraped-out hollow of his stomach. "He tell . . . man come . . . kill."

Great, Prochenko thought. Just great. He put down his hat, stick, and paper on the enamel-topped table and surveyed the room, as if a trace of the red pig might remain. Not under the bed, whose sky-blue coverlet had been pulled tight. The night before, they had lain on top of it in the warm air, dressed in their clothes.

"We should find another place," he said. Maybe even something swankier, he thought. He had been paid in reichmarks for the diamond earrings, and Markasev, also, had no lack of cash. "We should get you something new to wear."

"Too . . . much . . . scared."

"Oh, for Pete's sake," thought Prochenko. It had been a favorite expression of his mother's on Syndicate Road. Because of the appeal in Markasev's dark eyes, the intensity of which attracted and repulsed him, he picked up his stick again and walked into the corridor. Muted cries—squeals of childish laughter, childish wrath—came up through the stairwell from the other floors.

The stairwell formed a long, flat oval on one side of the narrow building. Prochenko looked over the banister and then pulled his head back. His hand tightened on his wolf's-head stick. Even from the corridor he had heard the heavy stamping of a man on the stairs, the stertorous breath of the policeman. His sense of hearing and his sense of smell were sharper, he had noticed, since the train wreck.

On the banister two floors below him, he had seen the fat

pink hand, the cuff of the blue suit. As a soldier, Prochenko had never been ashamed to run, to find a devious way—de Graz, of course, would already have been jumping down the stairs. But the lieutenant pulled back just as the hand paused on the banister, and he imagined the policeman sticking his head into the stairwell and peering upward—fat-faced, and maybe even wiping his forehead with a white or red-spotted handkerchief. In his mind Prochenko looked up with him, the stairs unpromising and choked with wooden boxes and debris, and dark and silent in a way that suggested inactivity, particularly after the noise and smells at the bottom of the building. It was true: Markasev was the only occupant on the top floor, and all the other rooms were full of old furniture and junk. And the concierge maybe was absent and could not be questioned. Prochenko had not seen him or her the day before, and not that morning when he'd gone out.

Soon he heard the clump, clump, clump of the policeman retreating down the stairs. Lighthearted suddenly, Prochenko made a flourish with his cane. Coming back to the green door, closing it behind him, he placed himself in the window alcove and looked down into the street. When Markasev tried to say something, he raised his hand. But when he saw the policeman totter out the door and down the steps, he turned. "Put your shirt on. Let's get something to eat. Is there still that Abyssinian café off the Corsairs'? I'm starving."

"Please . . . is too . . . much . . ."

"But we can't just stay up here. Come on, it'll be my treat. Aren't you hungry?"

He affected an optimism he did not feel. In Massachusetts, Markasev had been a different person, bold and reckless. He had lit the school on fire, for Pete's sake. Now he could not be budged, and with foreboding the lieutenant promised to go out looking for a new room in another part of town, and bring back some beer and sandwiches. Under cover of darkness, they would move.

"Please, don't go."

But he had to go. The little room seemed airless, stark, uncomfortable. In Berkshire County he had had a mountain bike, had ridden all over town. He couldn't stay here with a half-naked Kevin Markasev or whatever, complaining about his dreams. Prochenko's dreams were weird enough.

AT A LITTLE before six o'clock, Jean-Baptiste paused before the baroness's bedroom, dressed in his disheveled livery with the red piping. Because of his long service, and because he had known her in both wealth and poverty, he took liberties without asking. Now he pounded on the door and opened it. He spoke into the half-lit space. "There's a man to see you as you said. A dirty scoundrel, if you want my plain opinion."

Through the half-open door there came a hiss. Then in her lowest, softest, throaty voice: "What is he like?"

"Well, he's dressed in a green jacket and he's sweating. He's a big man, and his clothes are new. Red hair. He's not a gentleman, of course. What do you want with him?"

"A simple errand. Don't come in. I'm dressing for the theater. Is my carriage ready for the National?"

"It's at the Spanish Gate."

"I'll be down. I have something for that fellow."

"If I were you, ma'am, I'd do nothing about that. He's got narrow eyes. I wouldn't send him on any errand of mine."

"Do you think so?" came the low voice behind the door, tinged now with sadness and anxiety. "But would you trust him if you were alone in all the world?"

Jean-Baptiste was accustomed to his mistress's exaggerations. This one might have made him laugh, were it not for the sincere misery in her voice. "Ma'am," he said, "I wouldn't trust him to break an egg. You have other men to help you. I mean Domnul Luckacz first of all."

"And the other?"

Her voice was so close, she must have been standing in the darkness just inside the door. What had she said—that she was dressing for the theater? Surely all her costumes were already at the National. Why wouldn't she open the door?

"Ma'am, you know who the other is. Sometimes you've relied on me. I'm referring to the money in Geneva. And of course those boxes on the Hephaestion . . ."

It was a mistake to mention this. Jean-Baptiste was interrupted by another hiss. It wasn't fair: He'd done his part, which was to negotiate in secret between the Abyssinians and the Central Bank. Radu Luckacz had known nothing about it. Jean-Baptiste had been preparing to receive the boxes when the news arrived that Antonescu had blown up the tracks.

"My friend, I do not blame you. . . ."

Which meant she did. What was in those boxes? he asked himself, not for the first time. Just as important, where was the baroness now? Was she standing barefoot, perhaps, or in just her slip, inside the shadow of the door? Perhaps there was a candle burning on her bedside table, something he couldn't see.

"My friend, some things must be hidden from even you. I mean for your own sake. Take this. Go."

And her naked arm snaked through the gap in the door. Her bitten, stained fingers held an envelope.

"Have my coach ready in four minutes," she said. That was the errand he attended to first. Only later did he make his way back to the servant's door, the baroness's letter in his hand. The sealing paste had softened in the humid air, and the flap of the envelope had come unstuck. In the Corridor of Mirrors he held it to the outside window where the long light streamed in, pressed it against the glass.

Then the envelope was open in his hands. There were two banknotes inside, each for a thousand marks. And then a note he didn't stoop to read, except for several lines and phrases that stood out. "He must not be recognized . . . 351 Camatei"—it was in the university district. "Anything it is in the power of a desperate woman to bestow . . ."

And there was something else inside the envelope. It felt like a large coin, but lighter. A button, he thought, and then it was in his hand, a medallion of pressed tin. There was a time when everyone had had one.

It showed in profile the face of Kevin Markasev the martyr. This was a boy who'd lived in the house on Saltpetre Street years before. After the baron's death, Jean-Baptiste had had his mistress to himself there until the boy came. But the old servant hadn't begrudged him anything, an indigent the baroness had discovered on the streets of Cluj, before she'd had to sell her country house to pay her debts. No, in a way the old man thought the boy had brought them all closer together, an odd family in that cold house, but suitable for three people who had had no families of their own. Most of the time the boy had lived upstairs in the baroness's attic, in a cage that Jean-Baptiste had labored to make comfortable—he'd always felt strange about that. He'd brought him food sometimes he'd made with his own hands.

Then at the time of the German occupation, when the former empress fled the city, Jean-Baptiste had been imprisoned in the old court. There he had thought more about what life must have been like for Kevin Markasev, and had resolved to do better when he was released. He'd resolved to adopt the boy or find a home for him. But he was already dead when the murder case collapsed against Jean-Baptiste.

So—what was this nonsense? He sealed up the envelope again. Then he delivered it to the red-haired man in the green coat standing in the alley. He watched him read the note and lick his lips. What would he make of the phrase, ". . . anything it is in the power of a desperate woman to bestow"?

Jean-Baptiste turned away and climbed the stairs. How sad he felt! How melancholy in the dying afternoon. Once he had been willing to give his life for Nicola Ceausescu.

And yet there was nothing to be ashamed of. He gave his orders to have dinner in his own apartment. There it was already waiting for him in the lower kitchen, cabanos prajit with cartofi, and he asked one of the scullions to pack it into a bundle along with two bottles of beer. Holding a bag of greasy paper, he climbed to the upper floors again.

When he passed Miranda Popescu's door, he could hear her weeping. Sensitive to the sound, he put his ear against the cream-colored door, decorated with a discreet pattern of rosebuds. He reached for the glass knob, but then he hesitated.

That afternoon, following her interview with her mother, Jean-Baptiste had escorted Miss Popescu back to her own room. Then also she had been quite obviously upset, had closed the door without a word, which had irritated Jean-Baptiste. What did she have to complain about?

Now, coming back dispirited to the upper floors, burdened with thoughts of Kevin Markasev, Jean-Baptiste found himself more sympathetic. Surely it was not an unmixed pleasure to discover as a full-grown woman the lost mother you had never had. Surely it was not an unmixed joy to find yourself in this enormous building, separated from your friends. Surely this was a cage for her, just like Kevin Markasev's. Standing at the door, Jean-Baptiste grew philosophical: Surely this is what we all do at the end. Find ourselves a cage and a locked door. If we're lucky we can procure nice furniture, comfortable quilts, good food.

Miranda Popsecu had refused supper. Jean-Baptiste had learned that in the kitchen. Now he rubbed his hand against the door, wondering if he could coax some difference from the sound of grief inside, a lessening, a pause.

The door was locked from the outside, he knew. But he had keys to most rooms in the People's Palace. On this upper floor, in this east wing, the locks were interchangeable; his own key, which he was already clutching, would open this door. He slid the bar into the hole, and twisted it, and listened for the snap of the bolt.

Miss Popescu was on her knees, bent over the bare mattress of the bed. She raised her tear-stained face. Light came from a lamp on a high chest of drawers, a piece of furniture solid enough to be intact. Most of the others—the chairs, a bedside table—had been overturned, though the washbasin on its metal stand had not been smashed. The curtains had been torn down, the pillows thrown around the room.

"Oh," he said. "I'll send a chambermaid."

Miss Popescu, as he'd come in, had gotten to her feet, hands clenched, jaw set, as if expecting some continuation of her struggle with the room. But his words took the spirit out of her. Her shoulders slumped. "Please don't," she said. "I'll clean it up."

This surprised him more than anything she might have said. In the baroness's service he'd become accustomed to displays of temper. He was accustomed to picking up smashed glassware, crockery, and Dresden figurines. "I'll clean it up myself."—Nicola Ceausescu never would have used those words, even if she didn't mean them, and even though she had been born to peasants in a mountain village as all the world knew.

Seeing the armchair on its back, Jean-Baptiste immediately had wondered at the similarities between his new mistress and his old. His mind had leapt ahead. But now he wondered at their differences. Miranda Popescu stood with her back against the dark chest of drawers. The light was in her hair, cut short in the baroness's mode.

Her eyes were dark blue, which she had from her mother—Brancoveanu eyes, common among the rows of portraits downstairs. She was a woman of middle height, broad-shouldered and strong, but with a pretty bosom that was well set off, he thought, by the blue gown she wore—Jean-Baptiste was a judge of such things, though his own clothes were often stained and creased, his jackets perpetually too tight. Her skin was chapped and sunburned, which had never been the style, and yet was no doubt appropriate to the life she had led, sleeping out of doors or in the woods, all day on horseback, all that.

Like everyone in Bucharest, Jean-Baptiste had stood in the crowd to watch Prince Frederick Schenck von Schenck ride up the Calea Victoriei after the Peace of Havsa, his white horse curvetting to the grandstands. The old Baron Ceausescu had been there, too, before his marriage. But all eyes were on the prince; watching his daughter now, Jean-Baptiste saw some of his sharp features and high-born ugliness, but softened through her mother's beauty. She had her father's small, protruding ears.

But what was most remarkable, he thought, was the dissonance between her woman's body and her childlike face—no, not childlike, that wasn't the right phrase. But there was an innocence to her, a vulnerability, and a sincerity to her expression that contradicted the reports of the Gypsy's life she'd led, and formed the greatest single difference with the Baroness Ceausescu, whose ability to mimic all those things was legendary. But Jean-Baptiste had known her a long time in many circumstances. She couldn't fool him anymore, he thought wistfully.

"Please," he said. "They told me you had nothing to eat. I have some sausages here."

This is what he missed above all, the informality of his life with Nicola Ceausescu in Saltpetre Street when she was poor. It was true she never paid him, and he had to rely on his own meager sources of income sometimes to buy food for her as well. The reward was the simple pleasures they had shared, not like here in this enormous building. At first, though, even here they had lived in one small wing. The Germans had allowed only a single candle burning above the Piata Revolutiei, a vigil for Roumanian nationalism.

Now, as in imperial times, the whole façade of the Winter Keep was set ablaze with lights, this time to welcome back the Brancoveanus, allied throughout their history with prominent German families. New majordomos had been hired, answerable not to Jean-Baptiste but directly to the Committee for Roumanian Affairs, which was run out of the German Embassy. They in turn had hired dozens of new servants Jean-Baptiste had never even met, dressed in clean linen and brass-buttoned uniforms.

Tomorrow, he thought, he would walk down to Saltpetre Street and open up the house. He had a suspicion the baroness would soon be needing it.

"Is that a bottle of beer?"

The girl—woman, he corrected himself; why did he persist in seeing her as younger than she was?—spoke Roumanian with a French accent, which he found charming. But there was something else as well, some odd intonation that still lingered from the life she'd led, the prison world her aunt had invented for her, and from which the Baroness Ceausescu had delivered her.

"Two bottles. Would you care for one?"

And so, incredibly, he found himself sitting with her on the Turkey carpet in the wrecked room. He thumbed aside the wire-and-ceramic stoppers and let the bottles froth. After a while he unwrapped the sausages, which she ate with her fingers. They even talked a little bit. Later he couldn't remember. She wouldn't look him in the face at first. But then she turned to him, her eyes wet and blue. "Please, you seem like a nice man. I must see my friend, Peter Gross. We must bring him some food, too. I'm afraid he is . . . no, I'm worried about him. I—I must see him. Will you do this for me?"

Jean-Baptiste was familiar with the name "Peter Gross," an alias the Chevalier de Graz had used in foreign countries, and under which he'd crossed into Roumania. "Miss," he said, his heart aching, "put him out of your mind. Don't give him what he doesn't deserve. This should be a time of celebration."

But she wouldn't let it go. Again and again she found different ways to ask him.

THAT SAME EVENING, at that same moment, the Baroness Ceausescu stood alone behind the footlights. For this performance she had chosen the most intimate of the four spaces in the Roumanian National Theatre, a beautiful small stage, reopened with great fanfare the previous winter. The German government had provided funds for the refurbishment, and German touring companies had played in the main hall. But this stage was off-limits to foreigners, a circular platform and three rows of steeply banked seats. It was a venue designed especially for soloists, either in the classical or folk tradition; that evening the baroness had preempted a Gypsy guitarist for her own performance, which she had transferred at the last minute from one of the larger halls. Much of her audience was disaccommodated, but she had wanted to feel them close around her. Besides, as a matter of public policy, it was preferable if the demand for seats exceeded the supply. Let the guitarist plink his tunes against the main proscenium.

She had chosen a flautist, a violinist, an oboist—always for decisions like this she relied on instinct. She had at her hand's length her entire classical repertoire, as well as her more recent and more personal compositions. Scarcely knowing why and scarcely caring, in her dressing room she had found herself stepping into an old and immodest costume, some crows' feathers, some paste emeralds, some leather straps, some artificial blood. Dressed like this she had achieved one of her greatest triumphs in a part she'd played in many different versions. Medea had been a Roumanian princess, after all, from Colchis or Constanta on the Black Sea.

She'd had herself raised through a trap door. The men and women in their evening clothes seemed close enough to touch, separated from her by a ragged screen of light. Already she was sweating in the hot circle of the lamps, the leather chafing at her breasts and thighs; she started to move.

This was a style of performance she'd invented over the past few years. Now in most of the European capitals she had her imitators, but she was still the source, as even the most scandalized of the German, French, or Russian critics were forced to admit. Before her first retirement she had scarcely once received a negative review. That was different now, but they were fools, all those critics were fools, and she no longer paid attention to their idiotic opinions. The sacks of mail in her secretary's office, the crowds of people who waited for her to show her ankle out of doors, the thousand men and women who waited all day in the piata on the chance of buying tickets—that was enough.

Surely they understood what the critics didn't: that they were witnessing a new and transforming thing. And because it was unfamiliar, whether they liked it or disliked it was not important; what are these words anyway but reflections of ourselves that our tastes and vanity throw back at us? When something is new, that's the only time you can perceive it as if naked on a stage, unhidden by remembered or half-remembered versions, or similarities to other artists or performances.

In another sense, of course, she depended on those scrims of memory. For she was always playing with her audience's familiarity with the traditional repertoire, and even with her past performances. A phrase or block of words, barked or shouted through the veil of her accompaniment, meaningless or dissonant in itself, would nevertheless bring with it an entire scene from a half-remembered opera or libretto. A sequence of movements, furious or languid, but always extemporaneous, unprepared, unrehearsed, would nevertheless bring with it a half-remembered solo from an earlier ballet, even a pas de deux.

So: out of ugliness and chaos, beauty and order, not so much onstage as in the mind.

Extemporaneous, unprepared, unrehearsed. That way, each performance was a discovery not just for the audience but for the artist. Why, for example, that night had she chosen the character of Medea, who had murdered her own children? It was a collection of sounds, movements, and emotions that she hadn't thought about in years. No, but now was the moment when the body of her son was discovered—Kevin Markasev—the name cut through her. Of course. That was it. There was always an explanation.

She paused, frozen and immobile on the stage. She let the musicians go on. Confused, finally, they stumbled to an end. If she just stood here without moving, how long would it take for that man with his boiled shirt and military decorations in the first row to whisper to his companion that he couldn't understand this? How long before he left the theater in disgust; how long before the manager would summon medical assistance? Ah, God, the pain of this terrible night! What was happening right now at 351 Camatei? At least Medea had had the strength to do the work herself!

But because she was an artist and a professional, she gathered herself together. And with a breaking heart she danced a last unaccompanied rondeau to Kevin Markasev, the brave hero of Great Roumania, whom she had saved from death and then delivered to it—yes, that was it. Death had waited for a little while. Death could not be cheated after all.

Streaked with sweat and artificial blood, she looked out and saw tears on the cheeks of the gentleman with military decorations. He would not forget this night. Neither would she.

Then she fell into a lull or trance, which happened every night. Later she would not remember what she'd sung or where she'd moved upon the stage. Often this lasted to the final blackout, but not now. Now she came to herself suddenly, recognizing the man who stood against the wall at the back of the house, half-hidden in shadow, Vladimir O'Brien.

God in heaven, how could she bear it? Should she call the manager, the police? What would she say? There he was, and he was waiting for her at her dressing room when she came off.

Policemen ordinarily kept the backstage corridors free from her admirers and provided her protection when she slipped into her coach. O'Brien must have known someone or else have shown someone his badge of identity. The dresser was in the green room, but O'Brien stood beside her door, and he followed her inside when she pushed by him without a word.

She wore a cloak over her costume. For a moment she stood watching herself in the big looking glass, watching also the man take shape behind her. Always she was drained, vulnerable, receptive after a performance, but she would not let him speak. He had a bouquet of flowers in his hand.

She would not let him say what he had to say. She turned around, her back against the table, and she started in: "So did you see him? Did you give him the money? He must be far away by now!"

Confused, he paused and licked his lips. "He's far away," he said at last. The monster actually smiled. "Here are some flowers from his nightstand."

He was a tall man with a discolored face and red hair slicked back. Or no—close-cropped since she'd first seen him that day. What was wrong with his mouth? His lips were too big, puffed up like a bruise, and he wet them with his tongue as if to soothe them.

"What did he say when you told him he must leave the city?" she asked. "If he sends me his address, I will give him a remittance of two thousand marks a month. What I sent with you was a down payment. There was a yellow-haired man with him. You did not . . . hurt him?"

Disgusted and confused, the fellow shook his head. His mouth slid open. "I took the money as a payment for myself," he said. "As for the rest—what was it? 'All the reward that a desperate woman can bestow?' I'll take that now."

And he actually put his hands on her, opened up her cloak and grabbed the leather strap between her breasts. He threw the flowers at her feet.

She would have struck him or cried out, except for the weakness she felt from her performance. Shivering and sweating, she felt his hand clutch at the strap between her breasts as he pushed her back against the table and the mirror. "Please," she said. "Let go. Please go away."

He smiled and licked his lips. "I don't think you'll be calling for help. Not tonight. I've got your letter in my pocket—look at you! Is this what you offer the entire city? I've seen dancers in a Turkish brothel with more clothes."

He kissed her then and forced his mouth against her mouth. Nor did she cry out. But even in her fragile state, when her skin felt as delicate as eggshell, still she had something to fall back on, some little conjuring. Onstage she disdained to use it, except for small effects at transitional moments, to ease an entrance or provide a misdirection. But here she remembered it with the monster's lips against her lips, and she allowed her tongue to flicker out between his teeth. At the same time she spoke a word she knew, and let a little poison slip out of her mouth, so he fell back, bewildered, rigid, and exhausted. She pushed him over onto the floor, and he slid down. She squatted above him, and he lay with his back bent, his jaw clenched, and for good measure she kissed him again, slipped her tongue into his mouth again. At the same time she was searching in the pockets of his dinner coat for the letter he had mentioned—the few lines of her handwriting. Where was the tin medallion? Searching, she drew out the rumpled envelope, and what was that? A pair of driving gloves, still damp with crusted blood.

She stripped off her cloak, wrapped everything into a bundle. Then she flung open the door, called to the dresser and the stage manager: "He must be drunk!" But the monster was already coming round.

9 *Ghosts*

THERE WAS A bookcase against her bedroom wall, and after Jean-Baptiste had left, Miranda tried to read some pieces of French novels, and later on some poetry.

Near the bookcase stood a writing desk with gilded cabriole legs. Sometime during the day a servant had delivered some personal items that had been found in a barn near Mogosoaia. They included Miranda's diary, which she had brought from Mamaia Castle on the coast—her childhood diary, which ended when she was eight or so. Now past midnight, after she had tried to sleep and failed, she lit the lamp, unlocked the metal clasp with the metal key, stared at the blank pages at the end of the book. There were pens and pencils close at hand; what could she write? Itemized lists occurred to her: one, two, three—lists of mistakes, beginning with the night she had surrendered her aunt's book to that boy Kevin Markasev on Christmas Hill. Like a passive idiot, she had sat cross-legged while he dropped it in the fire—no, that wasn't it. She had thrust it into his hands, practically begged him or demanded that he burn it. No, not passive, but destructive, self-destructive, destructive of a whole world.

She was paying now for her rebelliousness or curiosity or whatever it was, and Peter was paying, too. Still, since then she had saved his life not once but twice, apparently. A third time would pay for all, maybe. Jean-Baptiste had told her, after she begged. They meant to hang the Chevalier de Graz.

Maybe so, but Peter Gross was the man she wanted to save. All other goals now seemed flimsy and far away, impossible to put into words. Instead of plans, she was filled with longings and regrets, which involved her mother, her dead aunt, and the elusive search for justice and some rational or independent government in this strange country. But she would save Peter's life; she would prevail upon the baroness; she would send a message to Madame de Graz in Herastrau, or she would use her own power. In Mogosoaia through the cave she had come into another, hidden world, and she'd been able to transform events because of her own strength. In that shifting, symbolic landscape she had had an instinct about what to do, an instinct that was failing her now.

There, for a moment or a day she'd been the white tyger. Here she was Miranda Popescu, and she had not even been able to protect the life of the girl she'd brought with her from the coast, a single Gypsy girl. In the corner of the blank page in her diary, with her pencil she found herself drawing a small picture of a rat eating a piece of cheese. Often at her desk in her high school in Berkshire County, she had filled pages with her doodling.

And when she tried again to fall asleep, Ludu Rat-tooth came to her, a ghost in the middle of her dream. She had opened the windows to the noise of the distant street, and lay on top of her damp bed in a ridiculously frilly nightgown—part of a whole new wardrobe of princess clothes. In her dream she imagined herself in her room in Massachusetts, the dark armoire looming at the bottom of the bed, full of unworn dresses her adoptive grandparents had sent her from Colorado.

Now the door to the armoire was ajar, and a scratching and a scurrying came from inside it, a little animal among the delicate pink clothes. Then Ludu Rat-tooth was there, coming toward her out of the shadows—"Oh, miss, I'm glad to find you. Let me hold your hands."

Miranda raised herself up on her elbows, and in the dream she wasn't frightened, but concerned. "Come here," she said. "What happened to you?" And she was relieved to see the girl wasn't dead after all, even though she knew she was, must be. But she sat up to embrace the girl when she got close. And though there was no smell to her body or her hair, still Miranda found a comfort in the sight of her rough, spotted face, her crooked nose and sharp teeth. But, "What's the matter with your eyes?" she said or only thought.

Ludu knew what she meant. "I'm blind now," she replied. "You'll be my eyes."

Then the dream was over. Miranda was waking up. And when she was awake in her bedroom in the People's Palace, twisted up in her sweaty sheets, some of the relief still clung to her, along with a new sense of hopelessness and sadness. And when she heard another scurrying in the darkness, she was preserved from fear by an impression of unreality. For a moment she thought she'd fallen asleep again, and this was another dream, or else a continuation of the old one. Because Ludu Rat-tooth was with her once again. In the muted streetlight through the long windows, the light fell on her heavy hips, the shadow of her pubic hair.

Unsure whether she was awake or asleep, Miranda went up on her elbows again. But then with a rising sense of horror she watched the Gypsy stumble toward her over the polished floor; she couldn't move. The girl was close to her now, standing beside the bed, and Miranda could see her breasts all smeared with a black liquid. In the light, Miranda knew, it would be red.

"Oh, miss, I can't see you. I'm so cold," Ludu complained in a well-remembered whisper, which nevertheless had something new in it, a dry, choking gurgle. Stiff with horror, Miranda watched her. But the pity she felt, together with her guilt for the girl's death, mixed into a combination that was a little like courage. And anyway, if she'd learned anything in this bizarre world, it was if you just breathed deep and waited around for a few minutes, everything seemed normal. Fear and horror are not to be sustained, which is why they must be constantly renewed.

So she took one of her sheets and threw it over the girl's shoulders, and that made things better. There was nothing ghostly or ethereal about Ludu Rat-tooth. Her body was as solid as it ever was, which helped. After a few minutes Miranda found herself kneeling on the bed with her arms around the girl, touching her rough hair and her cold face, comforting her as she often had after Insula Calia—a night, after all, no stranger than this one. Miranda found if she held the girl close, concentrating on her nose or cheek or bleared blind eyes, she felt braver than if she looked at her whole face, whole head, whole body, braver than if she'd stepped away, something that was "interesting because counterintuitive," as Stanley, her adoptive father, had often said. How ridiculous to think of him now here in this place!

"Miss, don't laugh," Ludu reproached her. "There's no reason to laugh. I've had a hard time since I saw you in Mogosoaia."

She gulped and gurgled for air, then continued. "Let me tell you, I crawled out on my hands and knees. I thought King Jesus would find me. I crawled down on my own through the dark with no one. I could smell and see the animals but that's all. And the small rocks and then sand. I could smell the salt. It was like Dobruja again, and I was coming down the sand near Mamaia Sat. I thought I'd see my father or my brothers. But at the water's edge the woman told me to go back. I couldn't get onto that boat. I heard the gangplank drawn up. They left me on my knees in the warm water."

Miranda knew what she was talking about, the ferry into tara mortilor. "Why?" she said, combing the girl's hair between her fingers, examining the cold, pimpled skin.

"Miss, don't you know? It's because of the stone in my throat. I found it in the forest, hanging from a branch. It was meant for the white tyger, but I took it. That's what she said, the woman on the shore. I had no right to it, I guess."

"What?"

"The stone, miss. The tourmaline. I got it caught in my throat and it won't come out. Mother Egypt meant it as a gift for you. But I took it. Now I'm punished. Do you see it?"

And Miranda did, a glimmer of a green or purple radiance in Ludu's neck, pulsing below her jaw—a small effect. And when she opened her mouth Miranda could see a stronger glow.

"I was hungry, that's all," said the girl. "Now I can't eat or drink or sleep. My eyes—it is like light and shadow, not all the time. You know there is another world outside of this one."

"I know," Miranda whispered.

"It takes a blind girl to see it. Now I know where you were in Mary's cave."

She meant the shrine in Mogosoaia. "It's a terrible place," she said. "The white tyger lives there and all the animals are afraid of her. They creep in the grass and hope she won't notice—I didn't see her. But I thought she could help me cut the stone out of my throat, tear it out with her strong claws. So I came here."

None of this was what Miranda wanted to hear. Eyes closed, she pressed her lips against the girl's cold forehead. She listened to her try to swallow, try and fail, a strange, glugging noise. "I'll go down to the docks again by the porpoise rock. When the boat comes, I'll climb over the side. When I come into the kingdom, my King Jesus himself will meet my boat. He'll bring me ashore into a white tent. I'll marry him like all the girls. He'll fill me up, and I'll have twins and triplets. My father told me. I didn't believe him then."

Interesting because counterintuitive, Miranda thought. She smiled without joy, imagining for a moment her adoptive father's long, thin face. A king in the dead world—what should Miranda do? Her aunt had written her about the tourmaline, she didn't quite remember what. That crazy brute O'Brien had taken her aunt's letter.

"Can you show me the other world?" she asked.

"Oh, miss, it's all around you. I'm the one who can't see. Where am I now?"

So Miranda described the room to her, and described its position in the People's Palace as best she could: just the pattern on the coverlet at first, and spreading out from there. She looked at things as she described them. Now she studied the blotched bloodstains on the sheets. In the morning, what would she say? That she'd had a nosebleed, or gotten her period during the night?

Thinking her own thoughts, hearing her own voice wavering at first, she took courage as it grew more certain, its descriptions more sure. Then after a time she got off the bed and led the blind girl around the room and out onto the balcony where Miranda could see the courtyard under its pattern of lamps. A cat walked down one of the gravel paths and paused near a park bench.

Beyond, on the open side, Miranda could see deflected moving patterns from the Piata Enescu, between the palace and the Athenée Hotel. "What about the hidden world?" she asked again.

"Oh, miss—close your eyes! I'll show you."

ELSEWHERE IN THE building, overlooking the Piata Revolutiei, Nicola Ceausescu lay restless on her narrow bed. Unerotic by nature, sometimes she was troubled by erotic dreams, as now. Moaning, she threw off her sweaty sheets. Sometimes the god of love would visit in her dreams—not so often, lately, but here he was again. Half-awake, she clutched her pillows, watching him take shape against the windows, a massed silhouette. But where was Mintbean, his assistant? And where were his stag's horns?

Then she recognized him, standing in the gray light: Markasev.

Later she couldn't tolerate it, the uncertainty above all. Before dawn, dressed in a cap and working-man's overalls, she slipped out one of the tradesmen's entrances and made her way circuitously to the Strada Camatei. She did not grimace, change her face, or do anything except tuck up her hair. But she was unrecognizable. The clumsy stride, the stink of cigar smoke, all was perfect.

There were policemen in uniform on the street, and even in the half-light of morning, a crowd had gathered opposite the steps of 351. Traffic was closed off. She was in time to see the body brought down, wrapped in oilcloth, carried on a stretcher. Radu Luckacz was there, and also the stranger, the yellow-haired stranger she had seen twice before, a face in the crowd, an image in her glass.

With some of the citizens she moved across the street to stand next to the steps behind a police barricade. Because she could not bear to watch the wrapped-up body loaded on a cart, she watched the stranger. He moved with an animal grace that was interesting to her, even though his hands were locked behind him. And even though his arms and shirt were bloody, and even though men and women in the crowd were already cursing him and calling him a murderer, his face was calm, enigmatic; the baroness stood near him now and saw his gray eyes flecked with blue—eyes that betrayed, she thought, a concentrated suffering, although his face showed no emotion, nothing but contempt. His clothes, she noticed, were expensive.

In that crowd she felt invisible, but he was watching her. And she could not tell by any change in his face, but she thought he knew her suddenly, recognized her, understood she wasn't as she appeared. Abashed, she pulled at the brim of her cap, looked down at her feet, and then glanced up again. He had turned his back. Radu Luckacz had him by the elbow. They disappeared into the crowd.

Whom had she come to see, him or Kevin Markasev? Ashamed, she looked away and watched Kevin Markasev's body loaded in the horse-drawn cart—so small, he seemed, a small wrapped bundle. Tears in her eyes, she hoped his death had been quick and without pain. God curse those, she thought, who had made this necessary. God curse the monster who had committed this crime. In her hand she grasped a paper bag. Before she could reconsider, she dropped it into the gutter, kicked it with the heel of her work boot into the accumulated refuse. It contained the gloves Vladimir O'Brien had forgotten in her dressing room.

She muttered a prayer to Argos, patron of the ever-watchful metropolitan police. She prayed they might be competent enough to find her gift to them, prayed also (because this was always her sad, dual nature) they would not. As always this was a dangerous game she played.

By the risks she took she could define her life and her success. Shuffling back toward the palace, hands jammed in her pockets, she cast her mind forward to the job of insinuating herself into the stream of tradespeople underneath the Brancoveanu Gate.

She changed in a downstairs cloakroom, for which she kept the only key. Once in her apartment, though, she scarcely had time to undress and take a bath. Jean-Baptiste was knocking on the door with a message that had come from the Committee for Roumanian affairs.

He left it in the music chamber. She read it in her dressing gown. The stationery was crisp, rich, embossed with the arms of the German Republic.

Madame la Baronne,

It is with regret that we receive the answers to our first enquiry, which we undertook following the wreck of the Hephaestion and the outbreak of violence. We should like to provide the opportunity for you to challenge the authenticity of the cargo receipts and bills of lading that we have recovered, both here and in Constantinople.

In the meantime, after consultation with the foreign secretary, it is the request of the committee that you remove yourself into your former residence in Saltpetre Street, until such time as all these facts have been revealed.

Etc., etc., she read—generous annuity, years of service. And then this:

We are pleased to learn of the return to Bucharest of Mlle. Miranda (Brancoveanu) Popescu Schenck von Schenck, and of her reunion with her mother. Because she is the daughter of a Roumanian patriot, whose love for his motherland was only strengthened by his descent from an ancient Prussian family, and who gave his life for the dream of a Roumanian-German federation that would be a political reflection of his own mixed ancestries, it is the opinion of the committee that Mlle. Popescu might provide an appropriate replacement for you in your official duties as the "white tyger," until such time as you have cleared your name. Would you, then, convey our interest to Mlle. Popescu in this matter . . . ?

Despite their power in the world, in some ways, the baroness reflected, these potato-eating Germans were like babies. What did they think? That the white tyger was like some kind of deputy assistant secretary? Or did they think, after all these years of knowing her, that Nicola Ceausescu would slink back to Saltpetre Street like a frightened cat?

Or perhaps, because they were so powerful, they thought

ordinary diplomatic politesse was now beneath them. "What's that news?" Jean-Baptiste called out from the corridor. He had left and come again to stand beside the half-opened door.

She shrugged, although he couldn't see her. After her performance, her unsettled night, and difficult morning, and now this, she felt exhausted and squeezed out. Nor had she even begun, as the potato-eaters might have said, her official duties for the day.

No, maybe she was not the daughter of a famous German family. She had been born in a wooden hut in the Carpathians where pigs lay in the mud. But she would rather die than give up what she'd won from her own courage with the world against her. In the name of all the goddesses who struggle against the gods, she'd rather die. Which was why, she supposed, the goddess had delivered to her Prince Schenck von Schenck's revolver, taken from that girl's unworthy hands.

No, the baroness was far from defenseless. The gun was sufficient power, if she could find a way to use it. What was it Isaac Newton had said? No, Aegypta Schenck had said it, in the letter to her niece: *Always remember as Magister Newton . . .*

"I've opened up the house on Saltpetre Steet," said Jean-Baptiste from the other room. She could hear him fussing around in there. What did he know about this?

But she would not be distracted, and she recovered her thoughts: What did Aegypta Schenck know about Isaac Newton? Magister Newton, as she called him. Only in his alchemical research had he used that title, and those books were hidden, secret, lost.

After the destruction of the English islands, many thousands of refugees had floundered ashore, Isaac Newton as a lecturer in optics at the University of Krakow. Later, the Prussian king had brought him to Berlin, where he had published his *Principia* and many other treatises on natural philosophy. But in time he'd been invited to Roumania, where alchemical research was not yet illegal. There he had commenced the last work of his life, his black book of alchemical inquiry, which was not published. Even the hint of its existence was enough for the German authorities to silence him, censure him for blasphemy, heresy, conjuring, and prestidigitation. He had died of syphilis and mercury poisoning in Potsdam, a drunken, broken man.

The black book was never found. It was thought to have been destroyed. Quotations from it survived, small excerpts in the work of other censured writers. These her husband had collected in his notes, and Nicola Ceausescu had read all of them, she'd thought. But the words Aegypta Schenck had mentioned in her letter, those were new.

Despite his precise diagram, the baron had not predicted any of this. He had not known—the baroness saw now—anything much about it. The phenomenon Aegypta Schenck had captured in her brother's revolver before she died, surely that was only explicable in terms of Newtonian metaphysics. Even the names of the eminences, carefully incised in tiny letters around the bottom of each firing hole, were English: Mintbean, Treacle, Abcess, Rotbottom, Flimsie, and Thorpe.

Magister Newton had been given to puzzles and word games, apparently. These idiotic and demeaning names, did they contain some clue, or else some English joke? Where were the instructions to unlock the mystery? Where was the letter of instructions to the girl, Miranda? She'd lost it, didn't have it, never had read it, obviously. Had it been destroyed?

All this time Jean-Baptiste had been talking to her, and she hadn't been listening. Now he knocked again. "Domnul Luckacz is here."

"Tell him I will meet him downstairs."

Then after a moment she continued: "Arrange breakfast for us, please, although he will have eaten. For me the usual, though of course I am not hungry. My friend, you must allow me to dress!"

That month "the usual" meant poached eggs on black toast, which she had eaten every day since Victory Day, the anniversary of the Peace of Havsa. Often the baroness had cravings that transformed her diet for six weeks at a time or so. She would eat one food to the exclusion of all others until, finally sated, she abandoned it without regret. At official dinners she would spoil and pick at any number of lavish dishes, only to gorge herself in private on tripe and breaded brains, for example—a recent infatuation. Since the murder of Aegypta Schenck she'd eaten a great deal of meat, a penance, she imagined, though it felt more like a compulsion.

Having changed into a light yellow gown, she stood at the top of Baltic Stairs. She watched Radu Luckacz plodding toward her over the marble floor, an explorer trudging over arctic ice. Grim as death—when had the joy gone out of him? His black moustache, his pinched, creased face. His hat seemed heavy in his hands.

Touching the brass banister, she descended to meet him. At the landing she could smell the poached eggs in the Court of the Sarcophagus, where Jean-Baptiste had pulled a glass-topped table against the railing. The baroness felt her stomach rise. All kinds of falsehood and hypocrisy disgusted her, which was the secret of her artistic success. She almost felt like confessing everything that had occurred. Before she could open her mouth, Radu Luckacz started in, looking up at her from the bottom of the stairs.

They were alone, but he spoke softly: "Ma'am, I am the unlucky carrier of unlucky news, which is as usual that I might have trusted your instincts, for you were right. Now, is there somewhere we are able to speak privately, for this will be a blow. Perhaps we can be sitting down."

A blow, and she could feel it on her heart. Sometimes it was difficult to breathe. But always one of her great gifts on the stage was the ability to swallow down her own emotions; with a puzzled expression on her face she reached his level and then led him through the door into a quiet corner near the railing, between two stone cenotaphs of an enormous size, brought from Luxor in the reign of Queen Sophia.

"Please," she said. "I asked Jean-Baptiste to prepare something." She motioned to the table, on which was laid out two plates of eggs, toast, watercress, sardines, and juice from Turkish oranges. Obviously disgusted, as he had every right to be, Luckacz raised his hand. But he sat close beside her on the delicate, wrought-iron chairs.

She saw tears in his eyes, and he looked away. "Tell me," she said. "When Princess Aegypta's house in Bucharest was searched after my husband's death, you said the police discovered an alchemical laboratory that contributed to her disgrace. You did not say: Was there a library?"

In Aegypta Schenck's two cottages near Mogosoaia in the woods, the baroness could not remember having seen a single book except for *The Essential History*, which she had burned before she set the house on fire. And in the other house, of course, she had pulled the soft cord tight around the old woman's neck until she died, an old lady who had never done her any harm! Oh, she was an evil woman, and now she also felt tears on her cheek. Looking down at her plate, she saw the two eyes of her eggs staring up at her.

She listened to the soft, ugly, Hungarian-accented voice of the policeman. "Ma'am, your compassion is well known, and I am not fooled by this attempt to enter into other subjects, because I am afraid this one can't wait. I think you know why I am here."

What did he mean? How could she know? Was her guilt as obvious as that? It crossed her mind for a moment to imagine he was here to arrest her either for one murder or another, and it would be as much as she deserved. But no, he would not have come alone like this, would not be pawing uselessly at the glass tabletop, as if he wanted to take her hand.

"Tell me," she said.

"Ma'am, I must tell you I have brought you two small objects that we found at three fifty-one Strada Camatei in an upstairs room. This was the locality where we'd observed the assassin from two nights ago in the Field of Mars, whose attack was prevented there. I mean the traces of vitriolic acid that were recovered. At the time you suggested a certain identity, which I found unlikely to believe. I would have done better not to doubt you, because of your woman's instinct in these matters. Now I tell you one of these two objects is immaterial, but the other . . ."

He drew an envelope from the inside pocket of his black coat. He drew out a tin medallion, stamped with the head of Kevin Markasev. And then much heavier, a golden locket on a chain.

"I ask you whether it is possible to remember . . ."

Opened between the policeman's dirty thumbs, the locket

showed a photographic portrait, together with a lock of chestnut hair.

"That was a gift to him," she said. "How could I forget?"

Time went by. "I realize this is an event with sensitivity," said Radu Luckacz, finally. "The body is now resting in the city morgue."

"And was he . . . recognized?"

"No, ma'am. There is no use worrying on that subject."

"Why?"

"I do not want to say. Because of the nature of his injuries . . ."

She understood. But always she wanted to go a little further. "I don't understand."

"Ma'am, he was cruelly beaten."

She felt she could not breathe. She remembered the feel of the gloves she had taken from Vladimir O'Brien. The leather was crusted, scored, still wet with blood.

She turned her head to look over the railing at the four painted sarcophaguses in the palm court. "And was anyone arrested?" she asked.

"Ma'am, there was another man staying there. Others in the building were the witnesses to what he said. When he returned after seven o'clock last night, the crime was already made. He could not have accomplished it in the clothes he wore, nor did he have any others. It was this man who brought a doctor. There was no reason to misjudge him, finally. And we discovered other evidence. Another man was seen leaving the place at the hour of the first disturbance. Witnesses have placed it."

She felt the tears drip down her cheeks.

"Ma'am, I promise you that we will catch this murderer. I swear it to you. It is not possible that a man should kill our citizens under our moustaches in the middle of our capital. . . ."

"Thank you, my dear friend. I can depend on you, I know."

And in a moment she continued: "The man living there—what was his name?"

"Andromed, or Andromedes. Turkish or Greek, mixed parentage, he claimed, although he spoke Roumanian without an accent, so my deputy says. I myself am not a judge of this. I come from asking him these questions. He has plenty of money but no papers of identity. He has moved from that place, but we have him under watch."

"Ah," said Nicola Ceausescu. She blotted her cheek with one of the napkins from the table. The soft cotton square was embroidered in one corner with a tiger's head.

"Will you bring this man to me?" she said. "Not today, I couldn't bear it. But I think he must have been the last to see my boy alive."

10 *Cold Soup*

SOME DAYS LATER, Miranda stood in her mother's apartment on the third floor of the People's Palace. "Can we speak in English?" she asked.

"If you would like. I must confess I am not current—how is it?"

"Fluent."

"Ah! But I will struggle on."

After some missteps, she thought, Clara Brancoveanu had made progress in these daily visits, which at first had been awkward and painful. Of course she had said all the wrong things! But what could be expected after so long?

She sat on the chaise longue beneath the window. Her daughter, standing upright in the middle of the room and wearing neither powder, rouge, nor jewelry—except for the Brancoveanu bracelet—was strange to her. No, not entirely, for the girl was like her father, not so much in her face (though there was some of that) as in the language of her gestures. Always there was force behind her, strength. Aegypta knew this language, too. Aegypta also, when you saw her in a frock, looked as though it were the first time she had ever worn one. What was it she had said once? It had seemed scandalous. "You don't need good manners if you're rich enough."

"I want you to tell me what I can and can't do," Miranda went on. "It's like I'm always breaking rules, and I want to know what they are. Can I go outside, for example? I notice you never leave this room."

"Where—in the street?"

"Yes, in the street. Can I take a walk?"

"But where? Where would you go?"

From the impatient, dismissive gesture of her daughter's right hand, the princess knew she'd made another mistake. She tried to concentrate. "I suppose you could take a carriage or a motorcar. But you must advise the steward. And there would be crowds."

Again the angry movement of the hand. Aegypta Schenck von Schenck, the princess's sister-in-law, had had these gestures, as if there was a force of will behind the smallest movement, and always you could tell what she was thinking.

Aegypta had been able to bully her. Aegypta had made so many of the decisions that composed the princess's life, ending with her long imprisonment—she would have taken her baby in her arms and left Ratisbon on that first day. Was that so terrible? Was that such a selfish crime, to have held her only child to her breasts? Later, she'd had to tape them up to keep the milk from flowing. She must have been sedated from the pain of childbirth, to have given Miranda up so easily.

Now it was too late, almost, to reestablish these bonds of nature. But she would try! "That means everyone knows what I am doing in advance," Miranda said. "I want you to advise me. This morning I had a meeting with the German ambassador. She came to meet me here. Ambassador Moltke—does everyone know what she talked to me about?"

"I don't. . . ."

" 'We want you to come out more often, so the people see you. Go to the theater or to social gatherings. . . .' These are her words."

She had her hands on her hips now, and more than ever the princess was reminded of her dead husband, who also was a stranger in most ways—she'd been so young! She'd seen him in Kronstadt a few times when she was a child, picnics and so on. Then for a few weeks, and they had gotten married. Then he was always away, and she would read about him mostly in the newspapers until the Peace of Havsa. He was a hero, naturally. But always she had felt the weight of his authority, when he was standing with his hands on his hips like that.

"I don't know. I think the people love to see a beautiful young woman of your social class. . . ."

These words, which had meant to soothe, now had the opposite effect. "Oh, come off it," Miranda said—what did she mean by this?

Perhaps she did not consider herself beautiful. Which was true in some ways. Her dark hair was cut as if she herself had hacked at it with scissors. Her eyebrows had never been plucked. Her rough, country complexion, as if she'd lived outdoors. Her mouth that was too big. Her solid shoulders, her ears sticking out—all that could be hidden or repaired. It was this language of expressions and gestures that was more difficult. Truly, you could know what this girl was thinking just by looking at her, as if she were a child.

The Baroness Ceausescu, now, there was a woman to be admired, if for no other reason but her taste in clothes. But her face also was expressive, within a subtle range—she barely seemed to move it. The difference was, whatever she appeared to think or feel was just that: an appearance only, though sometimes you felt you had to sit up and applaud, the performance was so cunning. That was what a lady was like, her best protection in a world of men. Aegypta had never learned the skill and she was dead, murdered by some soldier, the baroness had confided, though the mystery had not been solved.

"I'm sure the Baroness Ceausescu's opinion would be more useful than mine. . . ."

Oh, could the girl ever learn to restrain herself from frowning like that, shrugging her big shoulders? "Please," she said, "don't tell me to talk to her. She's a terrible person. Can't you see that?"

Then, after another moment: "I want to know how to behave so I can get what I want. I feel everything is in this kind of code. And what I want is to help Peter, get him out of here. Can you help me with that? I'm standing here dressed like a Barbie doll, while downstairs in this same building he's . . ."

Barbie doll? What was this? But Miranda's anguish was plain to see. "The Baroness Ceausescu has been very kind to us," muttered the princess. "Perhaps she didn't have the advantage of a high birth, but the world is changing. I am sure there is no question of bad treatment for the Chevalier de Graz."

Stubborn, the girl rolled her eyes. And the Princess Brancoveanu had no desire to get into another conversation about Pieter de Graz, his suitability as a friend or even an acquaintance, or the advisability of ever seeing him again. In her mind she returned to the earlier question: How must a woman behave to get what she wanted?

But why would anybody ask her that, of all the women in the world? What information could she possibly offer on that subject? To deflect her thoughts from it, she came back to Nicola Ceausescu, who was after all an authority. "I must tell you the truth. It is entirely inappropriate how she mentions her son for you as a companion. You are right to laugh."

Only it wasn't laughter, but just a coarse expulsion of breath: "Believe me, mother. I can vividly remember my fourteenth birthday party."

What did she mean by that? It didn't matter. "Mother," she had said, a word that was like a drop of water in the center of a thirsty flower—though it did not have the same charm, for example, as the French "maman." Still it was enough to drive any thought out of the princess's head, until the boy himself came in from the next room, Felix Ceausescu, the baroness's son. He also had not been raised by his own mother, which was a bond of longing, doubtless, between the two women. Or it could be a bond of longing between the two children—doubtless also.

THE PRINCESS COULD feel these bonds, though the baroness could not. She stood beside the ironwood table in her laboratory, watching over her crystal pyramid. She saw the boy as he entered Clara Brancoveanu's sitting room, saw his flushed, small face.

Since his arrival in the palace, she had not spoken to him directly, of course. What would she say? No, her task was to watch over him and protect him from his enemies. One enemy in particular: her jealous husband, the old baron, whose wrinkled spotted hands, she imagined, were now stretching out to grasp him from the land of the dead. Now and always she regretted having told the ghost her terrible lie, that the boy was not his child but Koenigslander's.

A terrible lie with terrible consequences, not just for the Danish choreographer. But the Baron Ceausescu had used Markasev to strike against her—not that she cared about that. Her life was always balanced on a tightrope. But now Markasev was dead, grotesquely murdered because of a misunderstanding. And Vladimir O'Brien—after the incident in her dressing room, she'd had him sent back to Mogosoaia in disgrace.

In any great tragedy or comedy, any performance where a woman stands alone upon the stage, the way forward is full of obstacles of her own making. There is no triumph in overcoming anybody but yourself. Here in her secret room, she felt the presence of a brooding, watchful eye above her, an audience of the dead. Couldn't his father see, she thought, how the boy favored him? Couldn't he see himself in Felix Ceausescu's empty eyes, his long, grasping fingers? The baroness could see these things, and they disgusted her.

Now she heard Jean-Baptiste pounding on her bedroom door. Suppressing a smile, she closed the lamps in her laboratory, locked the door. She moved quickly through her sparse, ascetic chamber through the long squares of summer light that slanted from the windows. She was surprised how late it was.

"Here I am," said the voice of Jean-Baptiste. He was waiting outside in the music chamber. "What do you want?"

Always his rudeness was refreshing to her. Perhaps he was the only one who saw her as she truly was, treated her as she deserved. "Thank you," she said, opening the door. "Come in."

He hesitated in the doorway. This was unusual; she rarely invited anybody into her intimate space. The bed was unmade, the windows were locked. The air was humid, and it stank of her, her perfume and the smells of her body, though she was modestly dressed in a long green robe that covered her arms.

"Thank you," she repeated. "My old friend."

And he looked old as he stood there, a spry, emaciated figure with long arms and legs, always dressed—as some sort of ironical statement, she imagined—in an untidy livery that was too small for him. The collar cut into his neck. She watched his Adam's apple swallow and subside, swallow and subside. She admired his high, bald forehead, his sharp, big, narrow nose, his eyes too close together.

"I have heard you have been taking your meals with Miranda Popescu," she said. "I want to thank you for that little gesture of welcome. She must feel she is alone in a strange world."

He grunted, looked around. The baroness watched the flare of his nostrils as he took in the rich smells. Her chamber pot was under the bed. No one had emptied it.

"I would like you to continue doing that," she said. "Eventually, of course, time will have passed. People's memory will blur, and she will be able to take her appropriate place at social gatherings and so on. She will be seen. And by then she will have learned some things about how to dress herself and what to say. How to sit at a proper table. I was even thinking you might want to talk about these things. I remember all the lessons you used to teach me when I first married the baron. How innocent I was! You taught me how to be a hostess."

It was true; he'd been invaluable. What must he be thinking now, standing in this room where she lived like an animal in a cave? Perhaps all his lessons had been for nothing, which fork to use. But the world had changed.

She continued. "I was wondering if I could play a part in welcoming our guest and making her at home. I've given orders to the kitchen to prepare meals for her. Perhaps you could bring them on a tray. Simple, country food, which I think is more appropriate. No doubt she'll crave it later, after a few banquets at the German embassy. There is a cold potato soup that my mother made for me when I was young, cold potato and leeks in chicken broth and cream. My mother made it to comfort me. I would like you to bring it as a gift."

JEAN-BAPTISTE GRUNTED. BUT later he remembered what the baroness had said, when he stood outside Miranda Popescu's door with the cold soup on a polished silver tray. He had stopped by the kitchens as the baroness had requested, and had received there also the greasy packages that contained his own supper; he carried them and the bottles of beer that had become a ritual on the same tray. But the soup was in an elegant porcelain dish, and beside it lay a silver spoon.

"She came down and fixed it with her own hands," the kitchen maid had said. "Not prepared it, but attended to it. Served with her own hands."

Now as he knocked and entered, Jean-Baptiste indulged himself in a cold feeling about this cold soup. But only for a moment; the girl turned and smiled. Woman, he corrected himself, but there was still something girl-like in the way she came to him and took the tray. An impulsiveness, maybe.

"I was hoping you'd come," she said. "What's this?"

She put the tray down on the carpet and sat cross-legged next to it, as if they were on a picnic. With a little bit of difficulty he sat down also. His pants were too tight for this kind of thing.

"Please, don't mind me," she said. "What's this—vichyssoise? My mother used to make it. Stanley said it was invented in the Fifth Avenue Hotel."

Jean-Baptiste found it hard to imagine Clara Brancoveanu making this particular dish. Or Aegypta Schenck—was that whom she meant when she said "mother"? And who was this Stanley? And where was this Fifth Avenue?

He unwrapped his meatballs and tomato sauce. There was enough of it to offer her some when she said, "But it tastes a little strange."

He chided her gently: "You should try to eat a little more. The Baroness Ceausescu . . ."

But he was relieved when Miss Popescu turned her spoon over as she heard the name, turned it over onto her napkin and gave the bowl a little pat, a childlike, definitive, charming gesture. There was still a good deal of soup left in the dish.

"The beer is from Bohemia."

"I don't mind if I do," she said, and smiled.

The beer was unusually gaseous. After a while she gave a little burp. They talked about several things—the floor plan of the palace and the entrances and exits, and where it might be appropriate for her to go. Other state properties and so on; Jean-Baptiste didn't know much about it. As she spoke he was imagining his small room in Saltpetre Street where he had lived with the baroness and been happy. And even here at first, when they'd just opened one small portion of the building. Now there were all kinds of people hired directly from the German embassy. Whole wings were now being used as a hotel for foreign visitors and bureaucrats. Soon there'd be no room for him or the baroness either.

"They have intentions for you," he said.

She shrugged, made a face, wrinkled her nose. What was it about her? At times—no, it was absurd. But at times she reminded him of the baroness herself, not as she was now. But when the baron first brought her to the house, and she was—what—fifteen, sixteen? She'd had some of the same transparency. She'd given the same impression you could know her thoughts by looking at her face. In the baron's wintry house she'd circulated like a current of spring air. When had she learned how to deceive? Or was she deceptive and manipulative even then? Already that year she was a famous actress. She'd been invited to the Venice Festival.

Now Miss Popescu was talking about a subject Jean-Baptiste could have predicted. It was the possibility of visiting Pieter de Graz in his cell. "I inquired about it," he said. "These guards are bored and they need money. Luckacz doesn't pay them much."

Her expression was both hopeful and disappointed. "That sadist stole my money in Mogosoaia."

"Whom do you mean?"

She told him. Then she talked for a bit more, and he interrupted her. "Miss, do you love him?" meaning the Chevalier de Graz.

Like her father's, her ears protruded slightly. Now he watched them turn pink. "No," she said. "He's just my friend."

But like old men everywhere, he thought, he was happy to warm his hands at a little blaze of love. Like Luckacz, too, whose name he'd just mentioned; later he sat waiting for Luckacz in his room. He brought the tray up with him, and while he waited he sat looking at the white soup in the bottom of the dish.

He had an hour. So while he waited he went down to the

kitchen again, where one of the boys had a box of kittens. He brought a kitten up—long-haired, black and white—and put the bowl down for him. The kitten circled the dish and put his tongue out experimentally; he had to climb inside the dish to get at the cream soup. But at the last moment Jean-Baptiste picked him up. Then he sat reading with the kitten on his lap until Radu Luckacz knocked at his door.

The policeman never seemed to go home anymore. Once a week for a year now he had found himself in Jean-Baptiste's apartment, where they would sit and play chess. And in this past month he'd come more frequently—several times a week. It was a habit they'd adopted when Jean-Baptiste was in prison.

Five years later, neither of them was yet proficient at the game. They would swap openings and defenses, and sometimes analyze the board as if both were playing on the same side. Friendless, elderly men, even with each other they had not achieved any obvious intimacy. Sometimes entire matches would pass without a word.

Now, toward nine o'clock, they sat on opposite sides of Jean-Baptiste's table, studying the outcome of a Queen's Gambit. Neither could understand the point of the doubled pawn. "Tell me," said Jean-Baptiste. "I read in the newspaper about a crime, a murder in the university district."

"Three fifty-one Camatei," murmured the policeman.

Jean-Baptiste was aware of the address, which he had read in the *Libera*, and previously on a piece of notepaper in the baroness's handwriting. But it hurt him to hear it said aloud. "I was disgusted to read the details," he said. "I wondered when I'd hear of an arrest."

They sat on stools. Radu Luckacz touched his luxuriant gray hair, touched the end of his black moustache. "There was evidence recovered at the scene," he said. "Also in the street outside."

Playing black, his pieces in a muddle, Jean-Baptiste peered doubtfully at the board. "So you're close," he said. But the policeman didn't respond.

The kitten was asleep on a pillow. Radu Luckacz rubbed his nose. "What is this smell?" he asked.

The porcelain dish was close at hand, perched on a chest of

drawers. "It is soup," said Jean-Baptiste. "The baroness made it."

"For you?"

"For Miss Popescu. But she didn't like it."

Jean-Baptiste made a move almost at random. The policeman pondered it. "The girl doesn't deserve it," he said at last. "She is guilty of murder, conjuring, and prestidigitation. Still, the baroness's compassion . . ."

Drawn to the dish, he got up and bent down over it. "You didn't taste it?"

"It was not for me. Besides, I didn't know what was in it."

Jean-Baptiste spoke carefully as he studied the board. But he could not prevent the policeman leaning over his shoulder and removing one of his pawns.

"You are dozing, my friend. What is in it? I smell chicken and potatoes. So?"

"I didn't know what was in it," Jean-Baptiste said again. And then he changed the subject. "Miss Popescu has given me a complaint. She tells me there's a Sergeant O'Brien who took money from her in Mogosoaia."

Luckacz strolled around the room, hands in the pockets of his drab black coat. "Miss Popescu has nothing to complain about," he said. Then, "Of course thievery and corruption will not be tolerated. This O'Brien is a criminal. You have not seen him here?"

Jean-Baptiste shrugged. One of his rooks was now in jeopardy.

"He broke into the baroness's dressing room," the policeman continued. "You have not seen him here?"

"I WOULDN'T KNOW him," said the steward.

"Then let me delineate him. Tall and with red hair." Then Radu Luckacz continued, describing the red-haired scoundrel with his cleft palate or whatever it was, his wet lips. In an excess of jealousy he described him, watching the steward to see some trace of recognition—yes, there it was. A startled look. Had the creature been invited here, the baroness's guest?

Hands sweating, he sat down. Now, examining the board, he realized suddenly that by taking his opponent's pawn, he'd left his knight uncovered—what stupidity! After all these years! It was because he was distracted, sick, unwell. At night he'd lie awake with a racing heart, his fat wife beside him sunk in sleep.

"It has been difficult," he confided. "You read in the paper, but there is a lot you cannot read. Yes, there is a truce in Moldavia while the cease-fire is discussed, but this fighting could be recommenced at any moment. Now there are these riots in Chiselet and elsewhere the Germans have put down—what will become of this? Now this murder you speak of. I know why you ask, my friend. I know how it is painful that this boy, this Markasev—the baroness is disheartened also. But you knew him, is it not so? Also when he was a guest in the Strada Spatarul?"

Again that startled look. "What do you mean? Kevin Markasev died years ago. It was before I was released. Otherwise I might have—"

"Yes, of course." Hand to his lips, pondering his knight, Luckacz nevertheless glanced sidelong at his latest blunder. Was it possible the steward had not known the boy was still alive? What else didn't he know?

"What do you mean?"

Radu Luckacz put his fist to his mouth.

"Are you telling me the boy at three fifty-one . . . ?"

"Please," said Luckacz, frowning. "I cannot speak about a case that is continuing."

But Jean-Baptiste wouldn't stop staring at him, even as he reached out for the knight. "Pah, what a disaster," murmured the policeman.

The steward did not smile. "You will have better luck another day," he said.

But he was wrong. On the subsequent evening Radu Luckacz performed even worse. This was partly due to the recurrence of his sickness—the fever he had picked up in Chiselet from (he was convinced) the radioactive contaminant. The nausea and headaches had diminished on his return to Bucharest, but now they had come back and they prevented him from sleeping.

And for the next few nights he returned to the palace to be defeated there. This was particularly irritating, as he and

Jean-Baptiste had long established a rough parity in their level of play. Surely his sickness had something to do with his new inability to concentrate. Surely his insomnia had something to do with it.

After a checkmate that had seemed inevitable from the first move, he would find himself wandering the halls of the People's Palace, hoping to catch a glimpse of Nicola Ceausescu after everyone else was asleep. No doubt she also had a secret burden, a sadness that kept her awake. Sometimes he would wait in the corridor outside her apartment, hoping to catch the sound of her pianoforte.

He felt he could not approach her or speak to her until he'd caught the murderer of Kevin Markasev. Yet how could he even attend to his own work, distracted as he was? No, his only comfort were these chess matches and (admit it!) the soup he drank in Jean-Baptiste's room, which had become an odd sort of addiction.

It was always the same. The steward would tell him he had brought the soup back to his own room after the Popescu girl had rejected it—the arrogance of these Brancoveanus and von Schencks! Didn't she realize? The baroness had made this food with her own hands, or else caused it to be made—what condescension!

Evidently Jean-Baptiste was too kindhearted to return it to the kitchen untasted. The baroness had sensitive feelings, it was well known. Radu Luckacz approved of his delicacy in this matter. But why then did he insist repeating the same story over and over, while all the time he was staring at Luckacz with his narrow eyes? Why was he so reluctant to offer him the soup, even when the other option was—as he insisted—throwing it away? Why did he ask him over and over whether he was sure he wanted it? Why did he purse his lips, shake his head, rub his badly shaven chin? And why in God's name did he never have any himself? It seemed a crime to waste it.

11 A Reunion

LIEUTENANT PROCHENKO, WHEN the summons came, had moved away from the fifth-floor room in the Strada Camatei. On the evening of the murder he had gone out to find different lodgings for himself and Kevin Markasev. Now he lived there, down the street and off an alleyway. He was easy to find. As instructed, he had left his new address with the captain of police.

In the hidden world, a radioactive effluent was still poisoning the area around Chiselet, and there were riots there. Feverish and disgusted, Sasha Prochenko spent his days rediscovering the streets of Bucharest, spending the money from Elena Bocu's diamond earrings. At night he lay sleepless in his single room, alternating between plans for the future and visions of the past. He would find Miranda Popescu.

Already he detested the sight of German soldiers in the cafés and piatas, smoking and laughing. He detested the sound of their arrogant voices. He would find Miranda and—what? Most of the newspapers were full of German propaganda. But from the *Roumania Libera* he learned she was a prisoner in the Palace of the People.

Always in the streets or sleepless on his bed he was tormented by images: a seven-year-old Miranda in the castle of her martyred father or else on the beach, looking up at him with eyes full of girlish admiration. Or Miranda in high school in Massachusetts, or playing soccer after school, or riding bikes in the woods, everywhere just trying to have fun. Oh God, it was not so long ago.

These images sometimes were interspersed with more recent ones, things Lieutenant Prochenko was trying to forget, and against which he had raised a wall of memories. But it had many gaps, through which seeped a tide of bloody liquid: He had returned around seven o'clock, and Kevin Markasev was still alive.

Against this memory he had erected others that led to it specifically—other moments when he had seen or spoken to Kevin Markasev, in Berkshire County in the field on Christmas Hill. Or else here in Bucharest during the brief time they had spent together. His single eyebrow and his handsome face: These images Prochenko tended as a kind of memorial, different from the stone monuments that disfigured the city, or the stone mausoleum in Baneasa Cemetery, five years old already, where Kevin Markasev the brave had supposedly been buried. Sometimes as he lay awake Prochenko wondered whether now at that moment the sextons were breaking the lock, slipping the new body inside. Or had they found him a new unmarked grave?

How to progress? And then in the morning, the summons came. It was delivered by a policeman. A printed note. The Baroness Ceausescu would like to speak to him.

Walking to the palace, he was amazed at her boldness. Surely it was the baroness herself who had committed this murder after the incident in the Champ de Mars. Surely she had dispatched one of her assassins, and the police detective—Radu Luckacz—must have been aware of it. What a farce! All the time he'd been questioning Prochenko, the policeman must have known the truth. He must have known the truth or guessed it as with a look of real anxiety he scratched the edges of his Groucho Marx moustache, more boot polish than hair!

In the bright sunshine Prochenko arrived in the Piata Revolutiei. He strolled the length of the palace's eastern façade under the ionic colonnade. He loitered in the crowd in front of the wrought-iron gates; he'd never been inside this building. In Prince Frederick's time this had been the winter residence of the Empress Valeria and the center of her political party.

Enemies of the prince, they had destroyed his reputation and then killed him, scattering his followers to Mogosoaia, Mamaia, and other places.

Valeria had been the tool of Antonescu and the generals. Through her, under emergency powers they had dominated the country. Prince Frederick was a danger to them, a military hero who was nevertheless a liberal, eager to experiment with land reform and parliamentary self-rule.

Most of his ideas he had distilled from German political philosophy. So it was a disgusting irony to see German soldiers at the palace gates. Whatever freedom was enjoyed by ordinary citizens in the German Republic, none of it had crossed the border with the army.

Full of a suppressed fury that seemed to creep under his skin, Prochenko delivered his letter to the German officer in charge. Deliberately insouciant, swinging his wolf's-head stick, left hand in his pocket, he strolled up the steps between the Prussian guardsmen. Waiting, he whistled a folk song from Moldavia before a footman appeared to guide him through the maze of the palace's first floor.

In the big corridors there were crowds of people doing nothing. The footman led him to the bottom of a staircase. Miranda stood above him on the landing, surrounded by a bunch of women with their hair pinned up.

She was wearing a yellow dress that almost touched the floor. She looked like a total goofball. Once in Massachusetts, the high school drama department had tried to do a production of *Tartuffe*.

They looked at each other for a few moments, Prochenko at the bottom of the staircase, Miranda above him on the landing. Knowing her so well, Prochenko saw a kind of defiant embarrassment in her expression, in her eyes. She drew a lock of hair out of her face, perched it behind her ear.

"That is the Princess Popescu von Schenck," murmured the footman at his elbow. "Please, if you come this way . . ."

The lieutenant paid no attention. He forced himself to smile, then pursed his lips to blow a little kiss. What a freakout, he was thinking, an expression he had learned from his mother on Syndicate Road.

In that warm high atrium he felt a chill. And he felt the baroness's presence before he saw her, felt her and smelled her, too—a mixture of bitter herbs and lemon oil and rank sweat. At first a gentle insinuation, in a moment it had all but overcome the other smells, the warm stone, the waxes and the powder. Prochenko recognized her with an animal sensitivity that made the hair stir and rise between his shoulder blades. The note in his pocket had delivered some of the same smell.

But all this time he was looking at Miranda on the stairs. He didn't turn around. After a moment, among the soft echoes of the atrium he heard the baroness's throaty cough, her soft, low voice. "She is a woman of no importance. Blink and she will disappear."

"She is beautiful."

A hiss of indrawn breath. Then a slow exhale that brought with it a tobacco smell. "Domnul—sir. You should not praise one woman to another. It is not polite."

Above him on the stair, Miranda was speaking to someone. But her eyes were on him, and when a lady passed in front of her, she turned her head so they could still keep contact. "Oh, but she is young," he said. "You should not be jealous, a woman of your experience."

He was enjoying this. A cold-hearted animal—he could feel her by his elbow. "I admire her freshness," he went on. "Look, she's had the sun in her cheeks."

"Because she's been sleeping outside like a Gypsy whore," murmured the baroness. "Domnul—sir, I'd like to speak to you."

Now he turned to her, a slender woman standing too close to him. She had changed since he'd last seen her on the boards of the Ambassadors. Because she was so close, he could see the lines around her eyes, the blood vessels at her temples.

Behind her stood a man dressed in a jacket that seemed too small. A fellow like a scarecrow, thin and gangling, with high shoulders and a bulging Adam's apple. He had scarcely shaved. His hair was clipped short on his high forehead, and his narrow eyes were bright. He came forward without a word to take Prochenko's stick and hat, which the lieutenant was holding by the crown.

"Domnul, please come this way," said the baroness. "This is the Peacock Room." She led him away from the staircase into a chamber decorated in a stuffy, old-fashioned, cluttered style. The walls were panels of dark wood, ornately carved.

The steward left with his hat and cane. The footman took his place inside the door. But the baroness drew Prochenko toward the window, where she turned to stare at him, a game she couldn't win.

After a moment she averted her eyes. They were a peculiar violet color, much discussed in the vanity press, as he'd discovered in the past few days. Up close, the hue was quite unpleasant.

"Domnul Andromedes—is that what I should call you? Your papers . . ."

". . . Were destroyed. I was on the Hephaestion. I lost my luggage in the fire, including my passport from the embassy in Constantinople. I would like all that replaced, so I won't be inconvenienced by these questions."

He was enjoying this. The baroness glanced up at him and looked away. Her hair was a peculiar shade, as though she dyed it in henna. She wore a gray velvet dress despite the heat.

"Sir, I asked you here because I wanted to hear from you about that horrifying crime, that boy who was killed, that young man, I suppose. Because you were with him when he died—you shared a room with him. Tell me, did you know his name?"

"We talked about a lot of things."

She glanced up at him with a pleading look, but then quickly dropped her eyes again when he bore down on her, his eyes steady and impassive. "He told you his name?"

"He told me everything."

A flash of defiance: "No one will believe you!" But he ignored her. He just had to wait and she came round again. "It was all lies," she said. "He was a troubled boy. But it is true we were acquainted. I gave him money . . . places to stay . . . charity. Many orphans without homes—there was a house in the Strada Spatarul. The name we called him, it was a joke, of course. A stray resemblance to a national hero."

"It was the truth."

She gave a little laugh. "How could it be the truth?" And

when Prochenko didn't respond, she continued, "I just wanted to know. He was like a son to me, he and those others, those orphans I spoke of. Did he tell you about me? What did he say?"

He stared at her. He guessed she was struggling with two thoughts. She was anxious to know what Markasev had told him. At the same time she was sincere. Prochenko could tell she was sincere.

"A man beat him to death," he said.

Yes, she was sincere. She winced and dropped her head. "He came in when I was in the street," Prochenko said. "He broke all the bones in his face. Kevin didn't say much, I can tell you that. Nothing about you, not at the end."

Were those tears in the baroness's eyes? She made Prochenko angry. "I don't believe you," he murmured at last. "What a hypocrite you are! What a murdering, lying hypocrite."

The footman stood inside the door, shoulders back, chin up. He was too far away to listen. Prochenko leaned forward so he could speak in the baroness's ear. "It wasn't the police, though they were looking for him. He wasn't robbed. He had money in the drawer and so did I. A golden locket on the floor. Whom does that leave? You and your secrets!"

When she turned toward him, their heads were close together. Her lips were near his own, and he could smell the cigarettes and something else, some astringent mouthwash. "Oh, domnul," she murmured. "You have looked inside my heart."

"You are filth," he whispered, enjoying this.

"You are dog shit," he elaborated, translating into French an American phrase that had been popular with the girl, Andromeda. "You are like dog shit on someone's boot that has been tracked in here. Tracked all over these nice floors." And then after a moment, "Your secret is safe with me. Needless to say."

Later he remembered standing close to her, filling his lungs with her smell, and he imagined he could have done anything he liked in front of the high windows of the Peacock Room under the blind gaze of the footman. He could have touched her any way he liked. He could have—and this is what he pictured at the time—reached out and bitten her on the cheek or on the ear or on the lips. He could have bitten her until the blood ran down her dress between her small breasts.

What sort of freak was he? His nausea rose to choke him as he stumbled down the corridor, searching for his hat and stick and some way into the street, into the fresh air of the piata. His fever rose in him. But there was the steward in his tight livery and red lapels, obviously waiting, gesturing at the end of the hall.

When Prochenko approached him, the fellow reached out and took him by the sleeve. "Come with me," he said with peremptory rudeness; Prochenko snatched his hand away. He didn't want to be tormented. "I've come from Miss Popescu," the fellow said.

Suddenly Prochenko remembered her above him on the stairs, remembered also the whole point of coming to this palace of decadence and lies. It hadn't been to see the Baroness Ceausescu!

"This way," said the steward, and he led him through a pair of swinging leather doors into a servant's area that smelled of boiled vegetables. There was a deep, dirty, four-sided stairwell. Down they went.

The vegetable smell got worse, and the humid heat. He is taking me somewhere, and he will turn on me and try to kill me, because I have insulted the disgusting woman they all love, Prochenko thought. And it was true there were soldiers in these brick-faced lower hallways. He is taking me somewhere and he will kill me or imprison me, Prochenko thought. "Let them try," he mumbled, and his fingers itched as he said the words. He felt an itch in his fingers and his palms, something it had never occurred to him could actually happen outside the pages of some overheated book.

"What?" said the steward. And in a moment, "You were saying?"

They stood outside a plain wooden door, much scarred and seamed. "Let them try," Prochenko repeated, and the strange man seemed to understand him. He unlocked the door. There, together on a stinking straw mattress in a stinking cell, holding hands and leaning back together against the stinking, greasy, stone-faced walls, sat Miranda Popescu and Peter Gross.

"Hey," Miranda said.

"Hey," answered Sasha Prochenko.

It disturbed him they were holding hands. His own hands itched and trembled. Had he come all this way for this?

Light came from a kerosene lamp on a wooden box. "Go in," said the steward behind him. And Miranda got to her feet. "It's all right," she said in English. "This is Jean-Baptiste—he's helping us. He got back my money and now we can pay off the guards. It's all right—she can't spy on us. These are our free hours when she leaves for the theater."

All this came out of her tentatively, breathlessly as she approached. She put her arms out, and Prochenko felt the itching in his palms. Tears were in his eyes, which Miranda misinterpreted. She put her arms around his shoulders, patted him awkwardly on the back. What kind of freak am I? Prochenko thought. "Nice tits," he whispered savagely, in English.

Miranda still was wearing the ridiculous yellow dress. Embarrassed, she stepped back. She brought a nervous hand up to her neck. But then she smiled. "Oh, A.—I know it doesn't seem so long. But it's been a long time."

"A." was what Miranda had called him sometimes in Berkshire County, a nickname. She was still talking. "I guess it's been since we were on the river and all that craziness in the snow."

The steward—Jean-Baptiste—had closed the door, leaving the three of them together in that hot, small place. "I don't remember," murmured Prochenko, and it was true. There was just a strange, four-footed dream he'd had before he woke up in the Aegyptian dig, naked with Peter Gross—not that anything had happened between them.

Since then he'd lived suspended between three points, a man, a woman, and a beast. And what had happened at the wreck of the Hephaestion, to burn or anneal those three creatures into one? Was it the result of that radioactive disturbance, those empty canisters? If so, it didn't seem to have affected the Chevalier de Graz or Peter Gross or whoever he was. He made no attempt to get up. He sat back against the wall, his eyes cold and suspicious. His arm was bandaged. He was missing his hand.

"Sit down," said Miranda. "We were talking about what to do. I was telling Peter what had happened—I had another meeting with the German ambassador. You know it's all a kind of diplomatic language. No one says what they really mean. But they're really sick of you-know-who. I guess they'd like to make a change."

Prochenko didn't sit. He stood with his hands in his pockets. "Part of me just wants to go with that," Miranda said. "You know, choose your enemies one at a time. But that's not why I'm here, to open hospitals for the German government."

What was she talking about? Prochenko felt the tears in his eyes. Unbidden, a memory now came to him, something close at hand. He'd come running up the stairs of the house in the Strada Camatei. . . . Now he tried to chase that thought, that picture from his mind. "What are your choices?" he said, his voice a throaty whisper.

"Jean-Baptiste can help us. I suppose we'll have to try and take my mother—she just sits here doing nothing in one room with the curtains drawn. Then she tells me how terrible it was to be a prisoner. You have no idea what a farce it is, this princess thing."

Then Peter spoke. Prochenko saw at once that there was more of de Graz in him than he had first assumed. Surely he had lost some things when he had lost his hand. Lost them and recovered them, but of course not everything was gone. So maybe Peter too felt something of this fever of discomfort. But not like this; his words were reasonable. "You're still thinking about this as some kind of family fight," he said. "You know, kick the Germans out, and the empress, and General Antonescu, and this crazy baroness. You know—defeat all your father's enemies and your aunt's. But things have changed. Most of those people aren't even around anymore. Now Lieutenant Prochenko's here," he said—he knew enough to give him his right name. "He can tell you the same as me. If this was what Aegypta Schenck had wanted, she would have made a different plan."

"What do you mean?" asked Miranda.

"You told me what she said. That dream you had. You said all the bad things in history were just a way of protecting you. Historical projections, but it's not that simple. This was a clever woman. Prochenko knew her as I did. Everything was for two reasons. Maybe all those things—Vietnam, civil rights, Iraq—were like a lesson about what could go wrong. But maybe some of it was an example."

"I'm not sure," Miranda said. She was flushed, and her skin was damp in the heat. As Prochenko watched, she drew back a lock of hair and pressed it behind her ear. But it was too short to stay.

"You can't assume," said Peter, "that's what your aunt wanted, some kind of return to the past—queen of Roumania—wise and kind and powerful. All your enemies crushed. Maybe she was trying to give you a different model. I mean in America."

"You mean like in civics class. The New Hampshire primary."

"Sure, maybe."

They smiled at each other. Prochenko felt sick, ready to throw up on his shoes. It would be a pity, because he'd scarcely yet been able to clean the blood out of the leather. When he'd knelt beside the bed in the Strada Camatei—what were they talking about? Prochenko had come in and they'd been holding hands. This was easy for them, he thought.

And he remembered standing in Queen Sophie's guesthouse in Mogosoaia with the Chevalier de Graz. This was before Miranda was even born. That day he'd given his parole, made his promise. General Schenck von Schenck was standing by the window with a book in his hands. He'd been wearing boots and dress trousers with no jacket. With de Graz beside him, Lieutenant Prochenko had told him he'd protect his wife and unborn daughter—this was half a year, maybe, before Prince Frederick's death. Prochenko had sworn with his hand over his heart, and the prince had interrupted him, concluded matters with a handshake. In every way he was the enemy of false formality. But Prochenko had asked himself, Why me?

That was a question that had changed his life. No doubt de

Graz had never asked himself. It had never occurred to him he wasn't the bravest and the strongest. It had never occurred to him he didn't deserve whatever he wanted.

Now Miranda and Peter Gross were going round again. Their conversation made a small, tight, optimistic turn. Miranda was talking about her mother, and Prochenko remembered how the princess had taken the train without them after Prince Frederick's death—she hadn't liked them or trusted them, her husband's aides-de-camp. She fled across the border to Ratisbon and started all this.

It was Aegypta Schenck who'd brought Miranda back, put her in their care. Years later, when she'd come up with her last, desperate plan, they had not hesitated. They had not known or guessed or been told how much it would cost them. Death was preferable to this magic, triple life, this triangle of lines that divided you from everything you were.

"You want to make it so no one is using you, so you're not beholden to a bunch of assholes," Peter said—good advice, actually. "My father told me that."

Miranda frowned. She was making plans, Prochenko thought, but what plans would make a difference to him or her—Andromeda—or it, the cage of creatures and experiences inside his skin? It was jealousy that let him understand, he thought, and now the sobs burst out of him, softly, silently at first.

"A., what's wrong?"

"You don't need me," he said. "You've got it figured out."

And he was A. at that moment. He could feel the girl inside of him, conjured into existence by the English language. "You're still talking about this as if it is a game or an adventure. A game you can win."

Then he told them about coming up the steps of the house in the Strada Camatei and finding the door open. Kevin Markasev was on the floor next to the broken window. Prochenko had gathered him up, lifted him up, laid him on the bed, wiped the blood from his mouth and eyes so he could see a little bit, talk a little bit before the end. And the only thing he'd talked about was Christmas Hill and sitting by the fire on Christmas Hill.

Prochenko had listened to him as he'd tried to stanch the blood. And in his mind he had climbed down the hill into the town to find the people there.

BUT, "YOU ARE dirt from a dog," he had said not long before. "Filth from a dog, spread on all these floors . . ."

"Oh, domnul, you must not talk to me this way."

But this was not, the baroness decided, because she had any power over him, or because she was giving him a warning. She leaned back against the wall as he stood over her, his face near her face. And it was odd, the phrase he used, because when he opened his mouth she could see his shiny teeth—too many of them, it seemed, for his mouth. And she could smell his warm, carnivorous breath. His skin was dusted with brown freckles. Close as she was, she could see the soft white hair along his jaw. His gray eyes, flecked with silver and sky-blue, never seemed to blink.

She felt she could disappear into those eyes, that they were searching and examining every part of her, and yet at the same time dismissing her as something of no interest. "Your secret is safe with me," he said.

She felt a crushing sense of gratitude. What was the source of this unexpected gift? Bathed in his breath, which suggested to her a luncheon of ground meat, she tried to understand the expression on his face, to understand him and penetrate his heart—this was not usually so difficult for her. This was a skill she had, developed over long years of working as a prostitute when she was small and then later on the stage or in the inmost chambers of power. It was a skill she had—to give an illusion of transparency while holding something back, a guarded central core. It was a skill she had—to discover other people while pretending to show herself.

Now in the empress's Peacock Room, leaning back against the carved panels of the wall, she felt exposed as never before. Perhaps not even in the performance that had made her famous, when she'd stood onstage at the Ambassadors, nearly naked in Klaus Israel's *Cleopatra*, had she felt this sudden vulnerability. At the same time she imagined she could not penetrate this man who stood above her now, could not crack him open, or penetrate beyond his skin, or reveal anything of the mystery she knew was hidden there—a complicated nature, only she could tell, that struggled with itself.

Above all it seemed to her that she could sense an artist's soul, an artist like herself. By an artist she meant one of the small circle of the cursed and blessed, whose gifts made immaterial all moral laws and social conventions. Instead they could be judged only by the pleasure they gave, the beauty they achieved. They could be judged only by the unflinching honesty that was their mark, and which they pursued for its own sake whatever the risks. Dog dirt, he had called her—dog filth, a murderess, here in the People's Palace of Roumania! Oh, he had touched her heart!

As he leaned over her, she had felt the burden of his presence like a weight pressing down on her, a weight that made it difficult to breathe. When he was gone—and later she didn't even quite remember seeing him leave—she felt giddy and intoxicated, floating, as she imagined it, a few centimeters above the ground. In his presence she'd felt vulnerable and sapped of strength, but now alone, moving through the corridors and up the stairs to her own apartment, she was full of power and resolve. "Not now," she murmured, "not now," to the importuning gentlemen who clustered near her antechambers, including the severe and disapproving German diplomats who always seemed to talk to her these days—potato-eating fools!

Once inside the doors of her hot, somber, airless, pungent, comfortable room, she paused. Stripes of shadow fell obliquely from the blinds. Soon she must be dressing for the theater for her evening's performance.

She unbuttoned her gown and stripped it from her shoulders. There was no time to waste and yet she wasted it, standing in her darkened bedroom in just her slip, staring at herself in the upright mirror, examining herself as she imagined Domnul Andromedes had examined her, like an object and not a person, an object with certain flaws.

She pushed her hair back from her forehead.

Now suddenly the image of Miranda Popescu came to her as if floating on the mercury-coated glass. Andromedes had praised the girl, called her beautiful. Before she left from the Spanish Gate, the baroness would reiterate her standing order to the kitchen, though, to prepare her special chicken and potato soup—potato for the girl's German half, needless to say. The drug she'd mixed in it had yet to take effect . . . stubborn girl! She was tougher than she looked. Perhaps a double dose tonight, and her dark hair would come out in clumps. Let her play at the white tyger then!

MIRANDA, IN PETER'S prison cell, stood watching her friend. Oh, A., she thought. Andromeda was in tears and Miranda felt them, felt them inside of her as well. As she listened to Andromeda tell her story, as she imagined her kneeling by the bed where Kevin Markasev lay dying (how strange all of this was! How could he be the same boy they had known so far away, the first one who had spoken about people and places that were now familiar—Mogosoaia, Aegypta Schenck?), she remembered also the dark night in the muddy woods, and Ludu Rat-tooth dying in the dark, alone. These things were like sores that had scarcely healed, rubbed now by abrasive memory.

"Oh, A.," she said, her heart too full to state the obvious, that here they were. After everything, now here they were, and they must look forward to move forward step by step. First things first. And yet . . .

So in the hot, filthy cell she stood watching her friend and envying her. She looked good as a man. Her big eyes and disconcerting teeth, her freckled skin that seemed nevertheless to glow. Her yellow hair. Standing in her tailored suit, her leather boots, she seemed older—but of course they were both older. Only Peter seemed now closer to the boy she remembered, closer than when she'd first seen him again in the Mogosoaia woods. He seemed to have lost some years, cut off with his amputated hand.

Okay, so she was sympathizing and remembering, but feeling a little impatient, too. It was more important to figure out what happened next—to figure out a strategy, say, for Pieter de Graz's trial, which could start any day. Or figure out a strategy for what to do, how to compel Jean-Baptiste to let them go, escape out of this place, and her mother, too, she supposed. Or else make a deal with the Germans for de Graz's life—he hadn't killed any of their men after all, or had he? There had been that incident in the woods before he found her again.

And if they left this place, what would they do? Where would they go? One thing was for certain. She wouldn't wear these clothes again.

But Andromeda couldn't talk about these things and didn't want to talk. Later, when Miranda had sat down on the straw bed again, she paced back and forth inside the room, from the door to the barred window, in tears or close to tears. And when those had dried up finally she didn't want to talk, only glared at them as if angry—wasn't there room for some small kind of celebration here? Or maybe not: Miranda suddenly remembered the odd, triangular tension of that last night of Christmas Hill, the odd tension on the Hoosick riverbank, though there were no words then, no possibility of an explanation.

So finally Andromeda announced she was off to the Moskva bar to have a drink. When she was gone, Miranda almost felt relieved—it shouldn't be like this. Peter didn't notice or else pretended not to notice.

And so she sat down in front of him cross-legged on the dirty straw, flushed and sweating. And together they talked reasonably. They still had an hour or more. Jean-Baptiste waited outside. The guards were gone somewhere. He had persuaded them a change was coming, that the Baroness Ceausescu would soon be living a reduced, private life and that Radu Luckacz, also, would not remain their chief.

Jean-Baptiste had hinted at this and Miranda had understood. Needless to say, it all depended on the Germans and on Ambassador Moltke—a tall, impressive, white-haired woman. Whatever Miranda's long-term plans, she must continue to make herself available to her, to come out gradually into the public eye as she had advised. For her reward she would request the life of Pieter de Graz.

Or was it possible they could claim some kind of mistaken identity, that Peter Gross was not the man who had killed those soldiers in the wood? This they also discussed, sitting cross-legged on the straw pallet—certainly he didn't look the same. Maimed, his right hand lost, he no longer carried de Graz's identifying mark. And he looked smaller, diminished, less threatening, softer, though as Miranda looked at him, it was suddenly unclear to her how to characterize those changes. Already the way he'd been in Mogosoaia, even the way she'd felt about him, had faded a little bit, supplanted by this new reality. What had Berthe Moltke said about her people? "We are heirs to an enlightenment that never penetrated here." The Germans above all would be unable to accept the claims of Luckacz and the others: that this man was the fearsome Chevalier de Graz, famous in the army more than twenty years ago?

Much could be done. In the meantime as they spoke about these things, Miranda sat and watched him in the greasy cell, wondering how she felt—how strange this was! Here they were, alone together and unsupervised almost for the first time—what should they do? Now painfully she was aware of what she was, a girl in a woman's body, and what he was, a man inside a boy. Because he was not the Peter Gross she remembered; she could see that even in the way he moved, a language of his body that seemed powerful and grown up. Or even in the way he didn't move, the way he sat, as now, leaning back with his eyes half closed, as if he was thinking about other things—as she was, obviously, whatever they talked about.

A girl in a woman's body, a man inside a boy. But maybe everyone always felt some version of that. Suddenly Miranda felt exposed and vulnerable, and she wished Andromeda was there again. In the hot room she could feel the gooseflesh on her arms, a tightness in her chest. What would she do if he, you know, tried something? What would she do? In the woods he had kissed her. Then he'd been a man.

Too much thinking, maybe. "C'mere," he said now. And then they kissed for a while and groped each other for a while, but that was as far as things went before Jean-Baptiste knocked at the door. Even that seemed like a lot, though.

RETURNING FROM THE theater, the Baroness Ceausescu caught a glimpse of the girl at the other end of the Corridor of Disenchantment—so named because of the nighttime walks the second empress used to take there in the years following her marriage. Jean-Baptiste was with her—Princess Brancoveanu-Popescu Schenck von Schenck, as the potato-eaters called her. He had a taper in his wrinkled hand. The light shone on her dark hair. She glared at the baroness over twenty meters of parquet floor before she turned away.

Nicola Ceausescu's own footman left her at the door of her apartment. She wouldn't let him inside. She took the taper from him and lit the gas. And when the door was shut and she was alone, she made a leisurely circuit of the room, touching various objects for good luck. She ran her hand down the keys of the pianoforte. With her forefinger, she picked out a tiny theme. Still invigorated from her performance, she paused to pour a glass of Abyssinian whiskey from a decanter. She lifted up the crystal tumbler, a gift to the former empress from a Spanish count. She held it up against the light. More than sensitive, more than alive, she imagined she could see the odor rise until the smell of the liquor saturated the entire room.

She was always like this at these moments. It was as if she trembled on the edge of some revelation, or else some sexual ecstasy. She had changed quickly in her dressing room, departed as her audience was departing. But while they were spreading out over Bucharest to late suppers in expensive restaurants, bottles of champagne, romantic liaisons from which they would rise sated and happy, still she stood here, trembling, close to breaking, like a crystal goblet struck too hard.

But at these moments, also, she could feel her power. At these moments she felt an intuitive command of the conjurer's art. Others—her husband, the Elector of Ratisbon, Aegypta Schenck von Schenck—had been more knowledgeable. They had studied for years, made experiments, learned arcane languages, pondered translations, weighed ambiguities, all that. Where were they now? Dead and buried, because they had not possessed what she possessed.

Now she opened the door to her bedroom where she paused to throw open the windows over the Piata Revolutiei. With the muted sound of traffic, the soft night air came in. With the whiskey in one hand, she filled her lungs with it, receptive at that moment to subtle emanations borne on the night wind—so she imagined.

She took a sip of the burning liquor. Fortified, she changed her clothes, stripping off her clothes, replacing them with a silk robe over her underwear. Then she made her way past the ornamental screen and into the small chamber where the planchette of the ouijah board still moved from letter to letter, sliding over tracks cut through the dust: DEMON DEMON DEMON HORE. With an impatient shove, she sent the planchette skittering across the table onto the floor, until it fetched up in a corner between two pieces of laboratory equipment. It would lurk there, she imagined, like a mouse, motionless until she turned her back.

She lit the candles by the altar, and carried them to the long table and the pyramid. Now its sides were burnished, opaque, solid as adamantine. Soon they would be clear as glass.

Behind her was the battered ansible, painted with scenes of exploding stars. She laid out the charts and tables, then typed in the coordinates on the round, ivory keys. A faint mutter of ionic dust rose from the lacquered horn.

Then she sat back in her leather chair and waited, sniffing at the whiskey in her glass. While the machine sputtered and hummed, she imagined herself as fine-tuned as a wireless receptor, sensitive to tiny particles or waves that came to her through the open window and the open door, filtered through the carved screen. She let her robe fall open, spread her knees, unsnapped her garter belt; the planchette was on the card table again. It must have crawled up one of the legs.

DEMON HORE U KILLD HIM MRDRER U KILLD R SUN—etc., etc. He was so boring, the baron—yes, that was it. He had bored her to distraction when he was alive. Besides, all this was his fault. Him and his vitriolic acid, which conveniently he had failed to mention. How could he reproach her now?

She turned her head. The pyramid on the ironwood table had begun to glow. She almost expected to see some manifestation of the baron inside, perhaps the pig of Cluj itself. Almost expected to see its red eyes glowing in the heart of the pyramid, smell its barnyard stink despite her calculations, the number she had pressed into the machine.

But no—she caught a tiny, hesitant fluttering noise as the glass came clear. She sniffed a smell of Eau de Floride, one of the bottles she had seen on Aegypta Schenck's bedside table five years before in Mogosoaia. An old lady's scent—at the time the baroness had mocked it to herself. God help her! Her hands were still burning from the friction of the rope.

And now came the *tap tap* of the planchette: DEMONIC WHORE. Oh, she was laughing at her. Aegypta Schenck was laughing at her, wherever she was—it served the baroness right. When Nicola Ceausescu died, her spirit would not take this insubstantial and delicate shape, which now stood on one leg in the center of the pyramid and ruffled out its long, iridescent feathers. The baroness had long since given up the idea of ever finding in herself a trace of a tyger or any other noble or even beautiful beast. Perhaps a ripped-up alley cat, something like that. Yet even so she had succeeded in dragging out Aegypta Schenck from the Elysian Fields or the Brass Circle or wherever her soul lingered, happy, perhaps, or else in pain.

She finished the whiskey in her glass, then lit a cigarette, a Turkish sobranie. The smoke made a wayward spiral round the candle flame. "Tell me what I want to know," she murmured.

The planchette paused, was silent. "There were no books in your house in Mogosoaia," the baroness went on. "Or in the house that burned. In Mamaia there was nothing, or in the servant's cottage—I had them searched. Nor in your house in Bucharest, where you had your laboratory. It is an orphanage now, maintained by the German government."

Silence. No longer could she hear the flutter of the bird's feathers. The smell of the cologne also seemed to have dissipated, or else the baroness had gotten used to it. The planchette didn't move.

"Where is the black book?" she said.

After a few minutes, when the cigarette had burned out, she reached over to her desk. She unwrapped the gold-chased revolver of Prince Frederick Schenck von Schenck. "I see what you have done," she said. "This is your inheritance, your legacy. And because of your niece's carelessness, no one will know. These spirits you have made—Magister Newton's spirits. No one will ever know. Surely it was your intention to use them . . ."

She paused. Then, ". . . for the good of Great Roumania," she went on. But while speaking she had snapped open the drum, had seen the word Mintbean incised under its hole. And that word brought a sudden image of Domnul Andromedes, his gray eyes, his predatory beauty.

She was not a strong woman, and the revolver was too heavy for her wrist. It sagged down, and she could feel the ancient steel on her cheek, and then her neck, and then her chest, and then her stomach and her thigh. She rubbed it on the cuff of her silk stocking, slipped it inside. Suddenly flushed and overheated, she felt the cold steel as a relief; she didn't know much about firearms. But this was an object of enormous power, she understood.

Thinking about Andromedes, she leaned back in her chair. Nor did Aegypta Schenck say a word to her. But in time she looked over to the long table with the pyramid at one end. On the table lay a figure she knew wasn't real. There was no reason to be afraid.

It was a skeleton, almost a skeleton. Rags of flesh still hung from it as well as rags of cloth. It was the figure of a woman, the baroness guessed from the long gray hair. A woman of medium height. She had a book clasped in her bony hands.

Nicola Ceausescu leaned forward. She replaced Prince Frederick's pistol on her desk. She picked up a letter opener and then rose unsteadily to her feet. She almost intended to use the brass letter opener to pry the book out of the woman's hands. But this was not real leather, real cloth, real flesh, real bones. When she reached out with her own hand she saw the difference, just before the skeleton dissolved, sighing in a breath of wind.

12 *The Chief of Police Loses His Hair*

IT WAS HIS daughter Katalin who first noticed it one Saturday when she was home from boarding school in Brasov—Kronstadt, as the Germans had renamed it formally. "Father," she had said, and it was true. That morning his comb had been full of hair.

Radu Luckacz didn't think of himself as a vain man. He was past sixty. But both his father and his mother's father had kept their hair—iron gray like his, combed back straight. As for his moustache . . .

This had been an anxious spring, the city during wartime and under occupation—nothing new, except the people were dissatisfied. In Chiselet, Oltenita, and Calarasi, German troops had fired on the crowds. Daily he expected riots and demonstrations in the city.

It was possible whatever fever he'd contracted at the wreck of the Hephaestion, combined with gastric distress that was now chronic, had resulted in this. He slept poorly, and he was exhausted, after all. Because he had pledged his word to Nicola Ceausescu, and because the crime scene had affected him, he devoted many hours every day to the case of Kevin Markasev—he didn't call him that. At the house in the Strada Camatei, the boy had registered under a false name.

When his wife asked him why he expended so much energy on this case, he couldn't tell her. This Markasev was an anarchist, after all, thwarted in the middle of a conspiracy.

But independent of his promise to the baroness, Radu Luckacz found himself affected. There was something in the boy's fate that suggested the fate of his adopted country, caught between larger powers. Five years before, when Luckacz had questioned him after the assassination of Sergeant-Colonel Blum, it had been clear that Markasev had scarcely known what he had done. Morbidly suggestive or else hypnotized, he had struck somebody else's blow.

Now, obviously, something of the same kind had happened again. What possible motivation could he have for an attempt against the baroness's life, a woman who had saved him and protected him and been a second mother to him, in her house in the Strada Spatarul?

So on the second day of the week, for the second time Radu Luckacz took the train to the Mogosoaia station to question Vladimir O'Brien. The first interview had revealed Miranda Popescu's money—gold coins still in a woman's filigree bag—carelessly thrown into a desk drawer. The man had scarcely bothered to deny what he had done. Then he had persisted in imagining that Luckacz wanted a percentage. The fellow had criminal tendencies and no pride, and it gave Luckacz pleasure to take away his rank. What had the baroness said? "Sergeant O'Brien—oh, but not a sergeant for much longer, I feel sure!"

Now, of course, the matter was more serious. On the soft banquette of the first-class compartment, Luckacz felt an ache in his belly. Why had he not taken his own vehicle and a detachment of officers? No, he was afraid of what O'Brien might have to say for himself. He could scarcely admit it, but he was afraid.

He himself had taken charge of the investigation. He himself had traced the gloves found in the Strada Camatei—an expensive pair in an unusually large size, sold only in a few fashionable shops. O'Brien was a dandy, after all. And Luckacz himself could remember having seen those distinctive fawn cuffs as he waited with O'Brien in the People's Palace, the same day of the murder, as it happened—he had promised the baroness he would solve this ghastly crime. She had begged him with tears in her eyes. He would not disappoint her.

But still he had an ache in his stomach. When the doors

opened for Mogosoaia he almost didn't leave the train. But then he wandered off the platform, through the gate, and down the street to the police station. It was dusk.

Entering the small sub-prefecture, he found more evidence of how much he had changed. The officer of the watch didn't even recognize him. As was his custom in the evenings, he was wearing ordinary civilian clothes, his rusty black gabardine suit and his slouch hat.

"O'Brien, he has gone to Mogosoaia to the shrine. He said there was a disturbance."

This was common. Gypsies and superstitious peasants often drank and visited at Mother Egypt's grave or Mary's fountain. They slept out in the woods, waiting for apparitions and seeing them, too—they drank so much.

In Buda-Pest, already under German influence when he was born, there had been less of this nonsense. Always it was unthinking faith—or in this case some sort of folk mythology—that was the enemy. Claiming to lift men up, it dragged them down into the mud. Faith, irrational faith, was a source of misery. Faith in government, or law, or in oneself or one's own feelings—these were the devil's weapons. Doubt, as every policeman knew, came from God's hands.

In the warm evening, Luckacz took the track into the woods. Hundreds, perhaps thousands, of ignorant people made this journey every year. The way was well marked. Gravel had been laid down for the first kilometer or so along the lakeside. Across the water he could see the massed dark bulk of one of the old Brancoveanu palaces, visible intermittently through the trees. He turned into the darker woods. Perhaps he'd meet O'Brien coming back.

But instead after an hour's walk, in the full darkness he saw a circle of pilgrims at one of the registered camping sites. They had lit a fire. He almost thought he would ask them for their permit, but he had other work. Someone was playing a guitar and someone was singing—women's voices, pleasing, actually—and he could smell the roasting vegetables. Nor was there any obvious drunkenness or signs of struggle. As always in these wartime days, he saw mostly women and old men. No, two boys in uniform. Maybe they had been called up.

Luckacz stood among the trees, looking into the clearing. After a few minutes he came forward into the light, and demanded (harshly, officiously) if anyone had heard of any sort of disturbance, which had been reported, so he understood, to the police.

There was silence, then one old man in a wide-brimmed hat spoke up. His eyes were rimmed with red, and he had a Gypsy's silver chain around his neck. Was he drunk? No, Luckacz decided. The Gypsy told him, on the contrary, the police were already here. A single policeman had said the shrine was closed, had kept them away, told them not to pass the last marking stone, which you could see beside the track up ahead.

So: the opposite of a disturbance. What was O'Brien doing here, off-duty, in the dark?

"He had a shovel," volunteered the Gypsy.

"Multumesc."

Useless to speculate. Luckacz continued on until he saw another light up ahead. Ordinarily the lamps were lit at the small house where Mother Egypt had died. It was built into the cliff-face near the entrance to the sanctuary, and the doors were always open. Light came also, ordinarily, from hundreds of small oil or kerosene lamps, or else candle stubs in pear-shaped jars that were for sale in the town. These were set in niches on the grave itself, a mound perhaps a meter high and covered with flowers, books, photographs, rosaries, letters, handwritten lists of supplications, coins, sticks, medallions, crutches, food, bottles of Florida water, as well as many other miscellaneous cult objects. All of it in Luckacz's grim opinion gave the grave a tawdry, ragged look, suitable for an alchemist and conjurer whose meddling in natural philosophy had done a great deal of damage over a period of years. The place stank of incense and superstition, and something else.

A carbide lantern hung from a sapling branch and threw a harsher light than any of the others. It illuminated the back side of the mound, the entrance to the grave itself—a square padlocked gate low to the ground. A man stood there with a shovel in his hands, and from the way he reeled and staggered Luckacz understood he was the drunken one. He was the disturbance. Now he unbuttoned his pants and urinated in a long stream on the threshold of the shrine, a rough hole in the rocks leading back to Mary's pool.

It was Vladimir O'Brien. As Luckacz watched, he buttoned himself up, rubbed his big hands together, took up the shovel again. He hesitated for a moment. Then Luckacz could hear the blade of the shovel grinding on metal. From where he stood among the trees, he could not see the entrance to the grave. Instead he saw the man from the waist up, his face made frightful in the lantern's oblique glare. But Luckacz knew what he was doing. He was breaking the padlock, desecrating the tomb.

Not long before, the first time Luckacz had attempted to arrest Miranda Popescu in these woods, he had cornered her right here, only to be thwarted by some superstitious manifestation. News of it had doubled the number of pilgrims here. Luckacz found it hard to imagine what their response might be to what Vladimir O'Brien was doing. There would be violence, certainly.

Now the man raised the long shaft of the shovel high above his head and smashed it down. Luckacz couldn't see the blade. But he heard the blows on the iron grate and he stepped forward. "O'Brien!" he called out.

The man staggered back, threw down his shovel. He pulled a pistol from inside his shirt—an expensive fabric smeared now with mud.

"Oh, it's you." He slid the gun inside his belt again and laughed. His misshapen mouth was wet with sweat. Luckacz could see his teeth. Some had gold in them.

"You here to help me?"

What was he talking about? Luckacz began to speak, his voice strange and foreign in his mouth: "I must warn you that after less than a week, I now find you indulging in another crime. Before I thought that I might give you the benefit of my doubts, because of your assistance in the apprehension of Miss Popescu. Naturally I did not think that I would find you now disgracing yourself, when I had come to discuss with you another far more serious matter, and had made a special trip by rail."

O'Brien laughed again, a short gruff sound in which

Luckacz nevertheless could detect a trace of desperation. "Stop it—stop your sermon. She's got you by the balls the same as me."

Confused by this vulgarity, Luckacz didn't pause to decipher it. Unarmed, unafraid, he put his hands out. "Please step away. Please come with me."

Ignoring him, O'Brien wiped his forehead. Then he spat ostentatiously on his big palms before he picked up the shovel again. There was another crash as he pounded it down into the grate.

Luckacz could smell the liquor all around him. There was an open jar of raki in the grass. Deliberately he kicked it over as he passed, as he seized hold of the shovel and tried to wrest it away. But O'Brien pushed him in the chest, and he stumbled backward and fell down.

"Enough," O'Brien said. "I'm already a dead man."

Then in a moment, "Did she kiss you, too? God, I can feel the poison on my lips."

From where he lay Luckacz could see the broken padlock and the sagging iron grate. Inside, he supposed, there was the stone sarcophagus—the drunken fool stood over him, the shovel in his hands. He laughed. "Chief," he said, "you're going bald!"

Bugs flickered around the carbide lantern. O'Brien stuck the shovel into the earth. Then he turned, knelt, and pulled open the grate. At full length on his stomach, he tried to wriggle through it into the tomb.

But Luckacz seized hold of his legs, his expensive boots. On his knees he tried to drag him out. "Now I must tell you that I am here to apprehend you for the murder in the Strada Camatei, and I ask you to surrender peaceably. There is no reason to alarm the people in this place. I must command you to return to the bureau in the village. There I will apprise you of the charge, which I have had typewritten and witnessed. I will take your statement. . . ."

His voice drifted up into the night air. Now he was quiet, overcome with sudden nausea, a byproduct, he supposed, of the sickness that had pursued him since Chiselet. A byproduct of the condition that had caused his hair to fall out in bloody clumps, his moustache to turn gray, had caused him, in short, to become an old man suddenly and without warning.

But now there was something else. At first he thought it was the bugs, drawn to his sweat in the hot night air, a swarm of midges, perhaps. He tugged on O'Brien's slippery boots; one of them came away, revealing a sock with holes in it. Luckacz sat back on his heels in the tough grass, the boot in his hand, and he watched an emanation or a manifestation take form above the grave—he should be used to this absurdity! Still there was something about it that weakened him and sapped his will, even when he was looking for the trick.

He had seen Aegypta Schenck before. He had seen her in the old days during various court proceedings and then later after the baron's death. He remembered her big nose, gray hair, coarse features. She looked more like a farmer's mother than a princess. He recognized the big hands that flapped around his head—no, not her hands, of course. But an insubstantial phantasm, a conjuring trick that nevertheless had the power to horrify him. He could almost feel the dead hands on his shoulders and his face.

Her hoarse voice whispered in his ear. "Tell me what you want from me. Tell me what you want." It was like a horror story in a ten-sou broadsheet at the bouquiniste. And yet like the gullible reader of one of those cheap stories, he found himself distracted. His gorge rose.

But this apparition had no effect on Vladimir O'Brien. He was still at his ghoulish work inside the tomb. Luckacz heard the stone lid of the sarcophagus slide and crash. He put his fists over his face. When he took them away again, he found himself lying on his back in the damp grass. O'Brien was standing over him.

He said, "There it was, just as she told me. Caught in her bony hands. Ugh, I stink of death."

Luckacz smelled the liquor and the sweet cologne. Disgusted, he grabbed hold of O'Brien's foot and twisted him down. He expected a fight, but he didn't get it. Drunk, O'Brien sprawled beside him as he got up. And he was rolling back and forth and laughing. "Oh, you want to take it yourself. Be my invited guest. I beg you. I don't want to see her again. That hell-cat—"

Luckacz straightened his jacket, dusted the mud from his sleeves. It was important to take command of this situation, in which he had not yet distinguished himself. "I am asking you again to reaccompany me to the bureau. As I said, I will accept your statement as to the events of—"

This brought more laughter from Vladimir O'Brien. "Chief," he said, "I'll give you my statement now. You can do what you want with it. You know it all already. She paid me two thousand marks. I've never done anything like that before. I tell you it's a black business. A man slaps a baby because it won't be quiet. On and on—we've all heard stories like that. On and on, it never stops. It was like that. One, two, three . . . Oh, I was there for twenty minutes."

Luckacz picked the book up from the grass. There were some cobwebs on the moldy leather binding, and he wiped them with his sleeve. "Two thousand marks for a thing like that," O'Brien said. "You ask me why this doesn't bother me, nothing like this. Nothing ever again."

Luckacz hadn't asked him anything. He left him there. He said nothing to the Gypsies when he passed them in the clearing, even though they stopped their music and the old man called to him. But Luckacz came back through the woods as quickly as he could. He would send others to apprehend O'Brien; why had he wanted to come alone? Was it because he was afraid of something like this?

He wanted to put as much distance as he could between himself and those stinking smells. He scarcely looked at what was in his hands until he was sitting in the night coach to Bucharest. He knew what it was, or else the kind of thing: one of a list of proscribed volumes, published and updated for the Baron Ceausescu's office when he was still alive.

Actually, it was the first book on the list, as he saw when he opened the slimy cover. From the Gara de Nord he took a hackney carriage to the palace, arriving after ten o'clock.

He spoke to a steward and an underfootman and lingered on the stairs, waiting for them to send up word. Then he made the long, slow climb, it seemed to him. The door of the music chamber was open when he arrived, and so he knocked. He waited for the sound of her voice. Under his armpit he carried the book. In his hand he held the document he had received that morning from the Committee for Roumanian Affairs.

Standing by the pianoforte, the baroness was in deshabille. She wore a simple peach-colored robe of Chinese silk. It fell below the knee. Always she had the power to astonish him; how could she receive him, dressed like this?

But she was one of those people who broke all rules because she made them and controlled them. She had silk slippers on her feet. She stood beside the lighted candle, smiling at him. If she saw the book, she gave no sign. But there was also some worry and concern in her expression. "You find me going to bed. But I must always discover time for you—my dear friend," she said, "have you been ill?"

How could he not confide in her? He was feeling old and tired. Now she came forward and reached out her hand. She almost touched his hair.

He heard a hiss, a soft expulsion of breath. "Have you changed your routine?" she asked. "I am concerned for you. Has your diet remained the same?"

He couldn't think, couldn't remember. It seemed to him he scarcely ate. "Come sit down," she said. "Whatever you have to tell me, it can wait."

"Ma'am," he said laboriously. "I am afraid that you are incorrect, and what I have here cannot wait. I confess I am here to tell you of this document that I received, demanding that I find a way to . . . compel you to vacate these apartments and take up your former residence in Saltpetre Street. As it is expressed, this is a test of my competence, and my ability to continue in my present position of responsibility, which also in other circumstances might be expanded. The language is unequivocal. As you see."

The baroness gave her low, throaty laugh, which at that moment seemed as nourishing to him as food, as her own soup. "They do not equivocate, these potato-eaters," she murmured. "Please don't concern yourself. These are just words. We will speak of them another day. Come sit down so I can look at you."

Heartbroken, he put himself down on the settee, while she stood over him with her hands on her hips. "You remember," he said. "Downstairs in this same building I promised you that I would find the murderer of Kevin Markasev or else the person who employed his murderer for two thousand marks. I am here to tell you that I have not broken my promise, and I must ask you to consider this offer from the Committee for Roumanian Affairs, which must be the best choice after all."

"Ah," whispered the baroness. She brought her hand up to her cheek. "Do you turn against me also, my old friend?"

"Ma'am, I must implore to you that I am speaking as a friend."

She let a few moments pass. Then she shrugged her shoulders. "I see you've brought something for me."

The book was beside him on the pillows of the settee. "Yes, I must say it is a painful circumstance. This was a proscribed book. The list was prepared for your dead husband years ago."

Night air came from the open window, carrying with it a smell of petrol and manure. Luckacz could hear the sound of distant music. Several nights a week musicians practiced in the bandstand in the Piata Enescu, amid the soft horns of the carriages and motorcars.

Again he heard the soft hiss of indrawn breath. "Do you know why my husband published such a list?"

"Ma'am, all Bucharest knows, if they remember him. The baron was a man of principle. In this matter he had sworn himself the enemy of conjuring and superstition. It was because he burned these books, destroyed them when he found them."

The baroness laughed, a noiseless sound. "It was because he wanted them for himself. And this book in particular, for his own library. Come, I want to show you something."

Beyond the room Nicola Ceausescu used for entertaining and for musical composition—this room, her public room with its yellow walls, its bookcases of scores—lay her bedroom, Luckacz knew, though he himself had never crossed the threshold. Often he had imagined what it might be like, an intimate, delicate space with paintings of a feminine or romantic nature on the walls. Floral still lifes, he had thought, or genre paintings of ladies and gentlemen. Or else in the French style painted panels over the hidden closets that contained the baroness's wardrobe and a color scheme of ashes of roses, set off perhaps with golden borders. And in the center, a large four-poster bed with a canopy of gauze. He had seen it in his mind a thousand times.

"Come," she said, and he could hardly believe it. She was opening her bedroom door, revealing the dark inside. But not completely dark, because a light shone behind an ornamental screen. "Come, bring the book," she said.

She touched him, led him by the hand. Immediately in the half-dark he could smell a pungent smell, and grasp an impression of disorder. Dresses and ladies' undergarments were piled on the surfaces. He passed a narrow unmade bed in an iron frame, and then was past the screen and in a small, low-ceilinged space without a window. A hidden alcove under the eaves. Candles burned on the altar of a personal shrine.

His heart thudded in his chest. This was a night of so many strange emotions. He was in Nicola Ceausescu's bedroom. He hardly dared think it. Yet he had clasped under his arm the black book of Isaac Newton the conjurer. And in the shadows of the alcove he could see a great deal of dusty, old apparatus; he knew what he was looking at. He had seen an alchemist's laboratory before. He had heard descriptions of the secret chamber of Aegypta Schenck, which the police had discovered in her confiscated mansion here in Bucharest.

"This is where my husband wrote his books and designed his experiments," said Nicola Ceausescu. "No, not here, but in his workshop in Saltpetre Street. I brought his equipment to this room for sentimental reasons, I suppose. I myself have no use for most of it."

A portrait of Cleopatra hung suspended above the shrine, which consisted of candlesticks, jars, bottles, and a few pieces of Aegyptian statuary. There was Prince Frederick's revolver, too, laid out on a small table.

"Please, the book," the baroness continued. And when he handed it over, he found he could only watch dumbstruck and drained of his last capacity for astonishment. She stood in the candlelight, dressed in her silk robe, on whose sleeves now he could see various embroidered motifs. She opened the book, leafed through it. "Ah," she said. "This was what he might have been looking for." And then she quoted in her low sweet voice some words in English from the text: " 'January Seventh. At dawn this morning in our house at Crevedia, I managed to extract from my alembic a quantity of pure white gold weighing the twelfth part of a gram. Present in the room with me were . . . ,' " and then a list of names.

She turned to him, the book open in her hands. "Do you understand now why the Germans hate me and want to be rid of me? Would you be happy to see me ruined and humiliated while that Popescu girl takes my place? Let me remind you of the effort you expended to search for her and bring her to justice. Let me remind you how she shot a man, she herself. You bring me this story from Vladimir O'Brien, hints, perhaps, and accusations—whom do you believe? Me or that criminal, who murdered a young man in the flower of his life—do you know how I have suffered since that night? Do you know the tears I have wept here in this room? Two thousand marks—it was payment for the boy to go away. I had a place of refuge for him in Cluj. Vladimir O'Brien wanted the money for himself."

Through the open window in the adjoining room, Luckacz could hear the faint orchestral music from the bandstand. Now as the baroness approached him, he could smell the bitter odors of her body. Now she was close enough for him to touch if he reached out his arms. Was it possible she wore no undergarments beneath her robe? The intimate clothing he had seen in her bedroom—was it possible that she had stripped it off in order to receive him after the underfootman had announced his presence on the stairs?

With a savage cry he reached to clutch her. Palm toward him, she put out her hand. And the silk was slippery; he found himself sinking, sliding down. Overcome, he fell to his knees, pressing his face into her leg and the peach-colored fabric. She stood above him with the book against her chest, and in time he felt her fingers in his hair. "So," she murmured. "You are still with me now, my dear old friend?"

Then in a little while she raised him up, pushed him back

into a leather armchair. "Let me convince you these phenomena are real, though I am not such an adept as my late husband whom you so admired. And I must tell you—there is a door for everyone, and if you step through you can't go back. Let me show you something. Hand me the revolver now, behind you. There—it is unloaded. Let me show you."

13 *God's Sewing Bee*

THAT SAME EVENING, at a private dinner at the German ambassador's house, Princess Clara and her daughter had sat not in the formal dining room but in a smaller, quieter chamber on the same floor. Contiguous to the embassy and recently refurnished, Ambassador Moltke's residence projected the same modern practicality as she did herself. There were none of the cluttered spaces of the People's Palace, the dark wood and glass-fronted armoires filled with bric-a-brac, the beaded lampshades and Turkey carpets. Instead the floors were polished wood, the furniture blond and severe, taking its beauty—as the ambassador explained—from the richness of the material and the purity of the form, rather than the density of the embellishment.

Instead of figured wallpaper and elaborate curtains, the walls were painted in subtle shades, and the windows let in natural light. In the evening the new electric lamps shone overhead. During supper they had eaten cutlets and steamed vegetables from simple porcelain plates, each one decorated with the seal of the German Republic. Now afterward they sat on hard gray pillows on the wooden chairs, drinking Riesling from unornamented crystal glasses.

The ambassador was dressed in a beautifully tailored suit, a man's formal jacket, a white shirt and black necktie, together with a skirt below her knees. Miranda felt overdressed and uncomfortable in a jeweled necklace and ridiculous dark gown, chosen by her mother—she supposed she had to get used to calling her that. But the word still conjured up for her an image of her adoptive mother in Massachusetts. There, needless to say, she'd avoided the word and even the concept, preferring to call Rachel by her given name.

She took little sips of the sweet wine. Like most people in Bucharest, Ambassador Moltke spoke in French: "Vous comprenez—you understand. There is no reason, I think, why women must be accompanied at a gathering like this, and we have much to discuss. Miss Popescu—you don't mind if I call you that? I feel I can speak frankly to you."

That might be a relief, Miranda thought. There wasn't a lot of frank talk at these places, not in her experience. She smiled in what she thought was an encouraging manner, nodded her head.

The ambassador spoke. "So in this morning's editorial opinion in the *Roumania Libera*, I think we can see an example of Nicola Ceausescu at work—the artist, the white tyger. Have you seen her performances at the National? No? Really, it is worth the wait for tickets. But the same gift that makes her so effective in that sphere makes her a dangerous adversary and an ineffective symbol of German-Roumanian cooperation, especially in times like these. Really, I was expecting with the pension that we offered she'd be happy to return to private life."

"I didn't see the story in the paper," ventured Clara Brancoveanu.

"No? There's a copy on the sideboard. But let me summarize. It is a way of sabotaging your daughter's position by reminding readers of the death of that fellow in Braila—we've talked of this before. You were involved in a struggle for the ordinary rights of the Dobruja Gypsies in the courts. This was for the sake of the family who took you in after your aunt was confined to house arrest under the old regime. And of course your mother was in Ratisbon, for which my government, again, extends a formal apology—we are not all like the Elector of Ratisbon! I believe the father of that Gypsy family was murdered by that same scoundrel Codreanu and his legion of assassins. These are the men you are accused of fighting, is it not so? It was a struggle against criminal injustice. Really, this is something to be celebrated. I am always pleased when women play these parts. We are preparing a story for the evening newspapers tomorrow. . . ."

Miranda decided she wouldn't read it. Conjured by the ambassador's words, images now came to her like importuning ghosts—Dinu Fishbelly with the blood on his lips, the policeman in the garden with his hand held out. They were painful to think about, difficult to think about, but even so the truth was preferable to these lies. Because the lies robbed her, blurred the pictures in her mind. These people in Bucharest, lying was like air to them the higher up you climbed. And it was hard not to breathe it in.

Now suddenly she could almost imagine herself fighting for the Gypsies against Zelea Codreanu and his thugs. She shook her head to clear it. "Aegypta promised me she'd keep you safe," murmured Princess Clara.

Miranda shook her head, took a mouthful of disgusting wine. "And Peter Gross?"

She also, she was thinking, was not perhaps the best symbol for German-Roumanian cooperation, in times like these or any times. Ambassador Moltke clicked her tongue, touched the front of her white shirt. "Well, that is more complicated. I must tell you I have spoken to my government. They are concerned this might be perceived as an internal matter. The Chevalier de Graz—they are suggesting we let justice take its course."

"This is not justice," said Miranda. "This is a mistake. Peter Gross is not the Chevalier de Graz. How could he be? It's just their names are similar."

Ambassador Moltke's hair was prematurely white. Her face was changeable—florid and sharp sometimes, or else pale and kind. The surface of her skin was covered with fine wrinkles, more noticeable whenever she smiled, as now. She looked not at Miranda, but at Clara Brancoveanu. "That is a concern," she said. "Peter Gross—tell me his history. Where is he from? Why is he in prison for a crime he did not commit?"

Miranda said nothing, only brought her hand to her forehead. "You will notice," the ambassador continued, "that the story in the paper will contain no mention of the Chevalier de Graz."

Then she relented. "It is true the Baroness Ceausescu is exerting pressure to bring this to a rapid trial. But we also have pressure we can bring. I think it might be possible to make a bargain for the sake of both our countries. Have you considered the attention you give him might itself be the source of the danger he is in? And if you gave him less attention then the danger might disappear? Really, the Baroness Ceausescu uses him to affect you. She knows you are under our protection."

"This is what I've told her," said Clara Brancoveanu. "But you know, a mother's advice . . ."

The word "mother" brought a small quick image of Rachel's dark hair and intense face. She also hadn't liked Peter much. Miranda shook her head.

How exhausting she found this kind of talk. Exhausting and dispiriting, because she wasn't good at it. There was a way forward, she knew, a combination of words and lies that would get her what she wanted.

She wondered, was it true? Was Peter in danger because of her? If she relinquished him then would the baroness lose interest, give up what Jean-Baptiste claimed was her stated goal, a private trial and a public execution in the Piata Revolutiei? Or was Miranda his only hope?

She sat on the gray cushion in the yellow wooden chair. The ambassador's expression seemed to her astonishingly bland. Was it possible this woman and her mother—her actual mother, as she had to constantly remind herself—had her best interests at heart? And was it possible also that she had selfish motives, that she held onto Peter with a kind of desperation, because he knew her, remembered her, knew all about her, knew what she was?

But what did that matter anymore? She wasn't sure if it mattered. Was it possible for her to imagine living here like this, dressed in these clothes and living in these rooms, trying to learn the language of telling lies until she was old like these women? No, she couldn't imagine it.

No, Peter was right if he meant what she thought he meant: Her purpose, the purpose her aunt had given her and she had chosen for herself, wasn't in these false negotiations, these little increments. Her strength was in the hidden world, where enormous changes could be made.

Now she was aware the ambassador was speaking. "I am glad you're listening to me. I heard perhaps that you were blind to reason, but I see it is not so. I have discussed this subject with your mother. Both of us agree that Nicola Ceausescu's first proposal was inappropriate and indecent, because of the difference in your ages. In any case, she withdrew it yesterday. After next week of course there will be no advantage to such an alliance, because the woman herself will be in retirement, or perhaps on an extended tour of foreign countries with her son."

What was she talking about? Her face seemed to have no expression. "With your mother's permission I am able to extend half a dozen preliminary offers. Let us say this is a gesture of acquaintance. No reason must be given—these affairs are not subject to reason, after all. As I know, it is a matter of an eyebrow or a chin, the smell of some cologne. At least in my country, the time is past when a mother can compel her daughter in these situations. Any of them might be suitable, so much we are agreed. Because of the liberal traditions of your family, these are modern, forward-thinking young men. Also I admit, because of your age and the exotic circumstances of your life so far—these men are of a type to find that interesting and appealing, perhaps more so than their other choices. Naturally there should be no secrets between husbands and wives. But discretion also is a virtue, we can all agree."

Now a man had come into the room from behind Miranda's chair, a dark-haired man in a dark suit. Horrified, she imagined for a moment these two women had arranged a kind of demonstration, a sequence of forward-thinking young men who would walk a figure-eight around the room as if on a model's runway. But no—he brought an envelope to Ambassador Moltke, who opened it, shrugged, smiled, nodded.

Shoes squeaking on the polished floor, the sevant or attaché now brought Miranda the contents of the envelope, a half-dozen large posed photographs, portraits from a studio in Berlin. Some were sepia, with a granular, soft texture. Some were black-and-white.

And as she gazed at the faces of the forward-thinking men, Miranda felt tears come. But then she made them stop. She read the biographical information printed on the back of each photograph: dates of military service or of graduation from the university. Some of the young men had long, complicated names. All of them were German, which came as no surprise.

She examined the face of a handsome stranger, heir to the Graf von something-or-other. At least he had a nice smile. What was he thinking when this photograph was taken? Did he know what it was for? Was he at that moment gazing at a photographic portrait of herself? And if so, what weakness or secrets—jail, maybe, or drug addiction—made her acceptable to him? An acceptable compromise: She wondered how her own biographical summary might read. It was obvious why there were only liberals and free-thinkers in this bunch. No kings or dukes or princes either, she noticed. But there were several bankers and the sons of some prominent industrialists.

"I haven't any money," she murmured. Suddenly she was convinced it was not true.

Ambassador Moltke had not stopped smiling. "We have something to say about that. A number of properties were confiscated from private citizens under the old regime. This includes a house in Bucharest, site of the Tears of Freya orphanage. Then there is the castle at Mamaia beach, the island in the marsh near Braila, and almost thirty thousand hectares around Mogosoaia, including the preserve. In documents we discovered your father's elder sister willed all this to you in the case of a political change. Some of it was held in trust after your father died, and some of it was hers. Your father's sister had no heirs but you."

Miranda turned to look at her mother, whose expression also was unreadable. Then she spoke. "Aegypta never married. There was no need. It's a sad story. There was a man, of course, an older man. A widower, I think, or else divorced. He was killed in a hunting accident."

"Everyone has a misfortune," murmured the ambassador. Then after a moment: "So. Shall I write to Ferdinand? I know his family well."

"Who?"

She nodded toward the picture in Miranda's lap, the liberal, progressive, gold-digging young man with the nice smile. Startled, Miranda shook her head. He looked a little like Peter, she decided. Again she felt tears come but made them stop.

But the sadness returned later. Back in her own room after dark, she opened the long windows to the balcony and stood looking out. She didn't light the lamps, but stood in darkness. Again she reminded herself of where the battle must be fought.

Then she took her clothes off and got dressed for bed. She lay down in the dark. "Come to me," she said, and in a little while she was dreaming.

At first her aunt was in the room, she knew. But she couldn't see her. She had no peripheral vision, and when she moved her head her aunt was gone. But she could imagine how she looked, queen of the dead, maybe, with a crown or coronet on her bony brows. "Don't believe what they tell you about me," said a bony voice.

Miranda didn't want to hear about that. Bones aside, she had no desire to talk to Aegypta Schenck, who occupied so many different holes inside her mind, and about whom her feelings were so mixed—no. She was aware she was dreaming, and she was aware she had some kind of incomplete control. After a while the dark room was empty.

Then there was a mouse in the armoire again, and Ludu Rat-tooth came out from behind the curtains to stand by the bed. Maybe it was because of Miranda's new lucidity, her new sense of power over events, but she wasn't so threatening this time. Nor was she in need of comfort, but almost the reverse. Yes, the Gypsy girl was naked, but the details weren't as expressive or as clear. Yes, she was wounded, but the blood no longer flowed. Lying on her back, propped up on her elbows, Miranda could see the girl's throat shining with a green and purple light, glowing from the tourmaline inside. This time it didn't choke her or cause her pain. She stood beside the bed, a tentative smile on her face, although her lips were shut. That had also been her habit when she was alive.

"Are you ready?" she said in the Roumanian language, and Miranda caught a glimpse of the corner of her tooth.

Dressed in her underwear and nightgown, Miranda slid out of bed. The girl followed her with blind eyes. They moved around Miranda's face without taking purchase anywhere.

"The door is locked from the outside," Miranda said. "They lock it unless they know where I'm going."

Another small, closed smile. "Take me to the balcony."

Miranda led her through the French windows. They stood looking over the stone balustrade with the warm wind in their faces. "Be my eyes," the Gypsy said. "Tell me what you see."

So Miranda described the interior courtyard with the formal garden and the small statue in the middle of the hedges and gravel paths. She saw it all clearly under the big moon, though from above she had not yet been able to determine what the statue was. Some days she saw a man playing a violin. Other days he was a hunter with a crossbow, depending on her mood.

Surrounded on three sides, the courtyard debouched onto the street, visible beyond a sharp, tall, wrought-iron fence. Then there were streetlamps, and a soldier's guard box near the gate, and carriages, and muted noise from the Piata Enescu. Above them the stars shone, small and weak around the moon, of course, where also there were milky clouds.

Smaller than she, holding her by the upper arm, the girl moved around behind her back, then reached up with both hands to cover her eyes. Miranda thought she could feel the pressure of her face against her shoulder blade. "Close your eyes," said Ludu Rat-tooth.

"We're in the open air," she whispered, and Miranda could feel her lips move against her shoulder. "Let me tell you," she said, and then haltingly, inexpertly, she began to describe a different landscape. Miranda saw a wavering line against the black background: "It's the high rocks. And we can see a long way. . . ."

Each word lightened the darkness, brought a new detail. In time Miranda could see something. In time she could see it all from where they stood on a rock escarpment over the Roumanian plain. The moon shone on the fat, coiled river many miles to the south. Beneath them there were stands of trees, some alive. But some stood stark and dead with the water at their knees. And there were flat streams of grassland to the horizon, where the ground rose into the Carpathians, a glittering, sharp range of snowfields and granite walls that seemed to rise up forever against the sky.

All that was pure and cold and lifeless, but below them Miranda could smell the humid marshland and the plain. In the tall grass below her everywhere she looked she could see creatures crawling around, insects and reptiles and animals. The ground was thick with them. Birds chattered in the trees. But she stood with Ludu the Gypsy in the high rocks.

"I suppose we should go," she said.

"Miss, they're waiting."

This was the part of the dream she felt she could control. She climbed onto Ludu's naked back, which was covered with moles and discolored patches of bumpy skin. She twisted her hands into Ludu's coarse, wild hair, and then the girl fell out of their stone perch with her arms and legs spread out. At first she dropped straight toward the ground but then she flattened out over the trees with Miranda on her back, gripping her hips between her knees.

In her lifetime of powerful dreaming, Miranda had never dreamed of flying before now. And when the first sickening drop was over and she felt the girl rise under her, then the experience was all she imagined it might be, the sudden swoops and falls, the rushing wind. Not knowing what it was, from high up she could see the burning storm that lingered over Chiselet. Then they turned over the river and then rose north and east over the marsh. There was the sea on her right hand. And the delta below her, full and stuffed and struggling with life, and they crossed into Moldavia. There also she could see the line of the tempest, the lightning flashing through the mist, the thunder like distant guns.

But this she recognized from other people's talk: the section of the line where the Roumanian sixth army held the fords of the Bug River south of Kiev, and the bloody Fedorivka Salient. Now she could see the line itself under the storm, a blasted piece of ground and a wide, shallow trench of slithering white snakes or fish or tangled worms, or so it seemed as they flew low through the sudden rain. Thunder and lightning and they fled from it, turning west and north into the mountains, riding the updrafts higher and higher until they reached an elemental landscape of snow and shattered rock and ridge after ridge of barren peaks. Miranda saw no life or movement, and the air was cold.

That spring she had come from Dobruja on the coast, riding her black gelding over some of the same country. The first two days she had been aching and sore—not just her thighs but her whole body, until she got used to all those hours in the saddle. Now she found some of that soreness had returned as, finally, Ludu Rat-tooth paused above a horizontal shelf of gleaming rock, then settled down. Unsteadily Miranda climbed from her back and almost fell.

The air was sharp in her lungs, and there was gooseflesh on her bare legs and arms. They stood on the shores of a pool of ice. Above them rose the higher peaks.

"This is Borgo Pass," murmured the Gypsy.

Miranda shivered. "Why are we here?"

For an answer, Ludu pointed up the slope. There, silhouetted against the lighter moon-filled sky was a new ridge—spires of rock, Miranda had supposed. But now she saw some of the stonework was artificial, some of the rock towers were inhabited. Light shone from high, narrow windows. Smoke rose from a chimney.

"Castle Dracula," said Ludu Rat-tooth. "The dragon's lair."

This was far-fetched even for a dream. Miranda had watched her share of vampire movies, read her share of graphic novels. She thought she had disposed of all that nosferatu crap with Zelea Codreanu's corpse. But here it was again or else some other version of it, recycled out of some deep place inside herself or maybe not so deep.

Now as she looked up she saw details she hadn't noticed, solid steps leading up through a tumbled slope of scree. A collapsed wall of masonry, a line of headless statues. A rock half-finished in the shape of a dragon's head. Everywhere was ruin and neglect.

"Miss, I'll wait for you. Tell me what you see."

No—ruin, certainly, but not neglect. The place looked better than it had in years, Miranda thought for no reason at all.

She didn't know anything about it. But the light was cheery in the windows and in the open door, and the rubble had been cleared into heaps on both sides of the path. Someone was standing above her on the stair, and Miranda wondered with mixed feelings if she were going to see the ghost or woman she had last seen at Insula Calia or in tara mortilor, and before that in the Mogosoaia train station and a dozen dreams—Aegypta Schenck. No, this was a younger woman standing barefoot on the square rocks, a woman in a ragged dress and shawl. But she was pretty and plump and yellow-haired, and not much older than Miranda, however old that was tonight—fifteen or twenty or twenty-five, or else some mixture of the three. The moon cast long soft shadows underfoot.

"Come on up, now, there's your girl," said the blond-haired woman in English. She spoke loudly, confidently, quickly, but in a strange accent. And all her words and phrases seemed a little distorted. "Come, is that your person there? Call her to be warm behind the fire. There is food. But there's not a stitch on her. Is she a real Gypsy? She will catch death."

Miranda looked back. Ludu stood naked by the ice. The jewel was shining in her throat. But she didn't move, didn't come closer even when the woman yelled and beckoned. "King Jesus keeps her warm, I must suppose," she said. Then, "Hey!" She stripped off her shawl and held it up, then wrapped it in a ball and threw it down the steps.

"Now give me a look at you," she said. "You will meet the others in some moments, so."

Miranda continued up the steps. She kept the odd composure she was used to in these dreams. But she knew that she'd wake up and her memory would be incomplete, no matter how much she tried now to capture every detail—the feeling of the cold stone underfoot, her own stiff awkwardness as she was pulled into an embrace—"Ah, at last!" Plump and soft and smelling of dirt, the woman had two yellow braids.

As always, Miranda felt herself a witness here as much as a participant. She reassured herself that even if she saw terrible things, they would mean nothing. Symbols, maybe, symptoms of anxiety, or a reaction to other people's pain and trouble. She herself was safe in bed, wasn't she?

"I am Zuzana Knauss," murmured the woman. Now she drew Miranda up into a stone courtyard. Battered gargoyles clung to the wall above her, and there were bats flying around.

The door was big and thick and studded with iron nails. It was made of many layers of splintered wood, as Miranda saw when she got close; it hung ajar. Firelight spread from the opening across the stones, and in it stood another woman—gray-haired, older, yet giving an impression still of beauty and elegance. "My name is Inez de Rougemont," she said. "Please come in."

Her English was careful and correct, and her voice was soft. She didn't touch Miranda as Zuzana Knauss had done, but stood aside to let them enter a room that seemed not to coincide with the broken walls of the stone fortress. Miranda was expecting a cavernous drafty hall, but instead the room was small and comfortable. Nor were there any doors or corridors that led to other places in the building. But it was as if suddenly they had stepped into a single-roomed cottage with overstuffed embroidered pillows and old but serviceable furniture and painted plaster walls. Light and heat came from a fire on a raised hearth.

And there were several other women standing or sitting around the room, knitting, or mending clothes, or pouring out tea on the brick hearth, or toasting scones. "Please come," said Inez de Rougemont, and then she was introducing all of them. Even as she heard them, Miranda could feel their names slipping away, replaced instead by a general impression of spectacles and smiling faces—this was something Miranda remembered from her adoptive mother's dinner parties in Massachusetts, this tendency to forget important information even as it was offered her. Often when she was a child she would ask for directions or instructions, then stop listening the moment they were given.

But she understood the women came from different countries: France, Bohemia, Sweden, Russia, Bengal, and the Turkish Empire. One tiny old lady in a silk jacket was from Japan. All spoke English with differing amounts of fluency. The Indian lady, dressed in a pink and purple sari and a lot of gold jewelry, said, "Please sit down here beside me. You are taking tea? It is from Assam! But I must inquire, one lump or two?"

She spoke in a melodic sing-song. "What am I doing here?" Miranda asked. In her mind she was comparing this place with the strange cold restaurant in tara mortilor where all the food was papier-maché and all the cups were empty. But here the tea was real and fragrant, though intolerably sweet.

"Oh yes, I thought you must be wanting to know." The Indian woman laughed. Mrs. Chatterjee, her name was. She had a dot in the middle of her forehead, and the part of her black hair was lined with red.

Inez de Rougemont sat at a worktable, where she was piecing a quilt out of a basket full of scraps. She had put on steel-rimmed spectacles that glittered in the firelight. "You must understand how we are curious," she said. "It was a grand experiment, and we desire to know how it turned out."

"Excuse me?" Miranda asked. In her dream she was on her best behavior, perched on the edge of an upholstered chair, her teacup in her lap.

"Well, I supposed we might look at you and judge for ourselves," continued Inez de Rougemont, smiling in a way that seemed both skeptical and encouraging. "Aegypta had such unusual theories. We would argue for hours, but none of us were convinced. No, sometimes I could see, but it helps to have an illustration. You must have guessed—we told her to make a model to try out. Darwin, Copernicus, Einstein, Marx—you see I know these names. I read the manuscript as it was first prepared. Most of us heard some of her lectures here in this place in the old days. That what you might call truth would follow from a theory. For her the idea always came first, facts afterward."

Already Miranda felt hot and flushed. Mrs. Chatterjee sat by her right hand on a low bench, and there was a plate of cookies.

Maybe outside in the icy rocks, Miranda could imagine she had climbed up to a place of pure ideas. But not in here. "What do you mean?" she asked.

De Rougemont's spectacles glinted in the firelight. Now

Miranda could see she wore a lot of makeup. "Well, it is obvious. She wondered how the world could be improved if she improved the theory—these were her ideas, or partly hers. It is all in Newton, really, and the other English scientists."

"I thought it was for me," Miranda said.

Mrs. Chatterjee gave a trilling laugh. "Now you see that is the solipsism of childhood," she said. "Now you are older, and you must admit that all of this was slightly too elaborate for what you say. All these invented countries and so on. Invented continents, invented histories."

De Rougemont nodded. "These were failed experiments. Models for evolution, heliocentric . . . what is it? Fairy stories. A world where dreams mean nothing. Where the dead are dead. Where dreams are not the portal to another world, no matter what this fellow says, this Sigmund Freud and others. Where stars are only balls of flaming gas and planets are dead rocks, and so we are only responsible to our own selves—do you think she would invent all this for you?"

The solipsism of childhood. "Probably not," Miranda muttered, and around her the women smiled and nodded. Some of them seemed to want to speak, but Inez de Rougemont wouldn't stop: "It was an afterthought, I tell you. Protecting you, it was an afterthought to her experiment. I'm talking about during the catastrophe, when she was arrested the first time. Then she did need to protect you from the empress, and she had the model close to hand."

"Catastrophe?" Miranda asked.

"I mean when the Baron Ceausescu was deputy prime minister. When he drafted the first anti-conjuring laws. At first it was a joke, though there were circus magicians who were imprisoned. But then Aegypta Schenck was arrested in her house. Later she was questioned in the Palais de Justice before a judge. I myself . . ."

Mrs. Chatterjee laughed again. "Yes, dear . . ."

"I myself had to remove myself into a quiet life. I myself had to make a pretense of disease and death. I myself must find a place to hide—it is not amusing!"

Her painted cheeks shone. Miranda sat between the two of them, de Rougemont at her table, and Chatterjee on her bench with one leg tucked up under her. Her feet were bare, the soles colored red. She wore golden toe rings.

The rest of the women had begun their own circle of conversation. But when de Rougemont raised her voice, they quieted down: "It is not humorous to live in a secret place with only some friends you have informed. To read my own obituary, it was disgusting. I had none of these cancers in my family."

Miranda heard clucks and sighs of sympathy. But Mrs. Chatterjee was irrepressible. "Yes, you see we are all suffering for our art. It is not dancing only we give up, or visits to the theater."

Zuzana Knauss was sprawled out on the carpet, lying back against some pillows. Her hands were folded on her belly, and Miranda saw how dirty they were. Her nails were chipped and lined with dirt. "Ach, shut up," she said. "This is not what we agreed on talking. Not the questions we must ask. Tell me—" she said.

But Miranda interrupted. "Why was it a failure?"

"What, child?"

"She said that the whole world was a failure."

"Ach, that's too big, too hard. She also saw the difficulty in overmaking . . . what is the word?"

"Overdetermining," suggested Mrs. Chatterjee.

"Yah, sure. Social or political building. Engineering. Your aunt described the danger. What could she do? It was one great engineering project. One from many. Now we see in Europe also there are many politicians who think like this."

"One must not seem immodest," murmured Mrs. Chatterjee. "But our dear Aegypta's experiment could only fail, because you see she always was attempting to maintain her own authority. There was no place in it . . . for us."

She had golden earrings in the shape of little parasols. Also a quantity of facial hair; lilting and musical, her voice drifted away. Miranda turned her head, and then she found herself studying the black lines under Zuzana Knauss's fingernails, studying also her ripped and dirty smock.

Suddenly tired, she had almost stopped listening. Idly, without much concentration, she wondered what would happen if she dozed off in her seat in this comfortable warm room. Would she penetrate down deeper into something else? Or would she wake up in her bed in her third-floor room in the People's Palace? Or would she wake inside the failed experiment and stumble downstairs to eat some breakfast before the school bus came? No, but it was summer vacation. She'd missed almost the whole year.

Now she realized the room was quiet. And when she looked up she saw everyone was looking at her. Some of them seemed curious and some beseeching. But she felt a kind of urgency that did not dissipate, and so she cast her mind backward to grasp hold of the last slippery words before they disappeared. "There was no place in it . . . for us."

"What do you mean?"

The silence continued for a moment. Then Zuzana spoke. "So, it is for contemplation and for guidance when we come together. Some from many countries, though many other places have no voice. That is obvious. But we sit and make these horse-swapping bargains. Now you see the world is on the blade of war. One step, then we fall. But now you see Olga Karpov takes the Russian part."

Here she nodded toward a black-haired woman in the corner, an ugly woman with a sharp, emaciated face. She had enormous, hungry, haunted eyes and lips that were oddly scarred. She did not smile.

"Now that snake of Ratisbon is dead, so I must take the German part," continued Zuzana Knauss. "It is my blood. And there are others who help—Inez, of course. Now the cannons have stopped firing and all wait. All are quiet, while in this room we are making the political alchemy. Shit into something—well, it is not gold. Not yet. But General von Stoessel is dead and the czarevich will also die. This war was his father's gift to him to make him happy. So, a bargain."

God's sewing bee, Miranda thought. Every other Thursday evening her adoptive mother in Massachusetts had gotten together with some friends. It was something Miranda and Andromeda had never failed to mock. Now in this room there wasn't any sewing or knitting or quilting that was actually going on. They had paused over their work. Everyone was staring at her.

"Of course she knows about Stoessel and Ratisbon," said Olga Karpov. Listening, Miranda had an immediate sense of something mean and sour and cold.

"Yes, of course," repeated Inez de Rougemont. "She has been part of this. But does she recognize me from this river in the snow where I stood with my plate of waffles? Belgian, I believe. I was there to guide her for Aegypta's sake—she made me promise. This Ratisbon, he could move pictures only. He could not carry in his mind a living creature over the sea, just in one blink. Mental picture—I gave him a mental picture of myself while he sat dreaming in his chair."

Miranda had no idea what to make of this. For several minutes she had wanted to ask a question. Now seemed like a good time. "And will my aunt . . . come here?"

Nobody spoke until Mrs. Chatterjee said, "My poor child—she is dead."

"And the dead never . . . come here?"

"No, child."

"But she knows all this," interrupted Olga Karpov in her cold, insinuating voice. "Because of what she did, because of this we have these problems."

Others protested, but Karpov kept on speaking. "Of course she knows! You let a bird out a cage, it flies away. It is no mystery."

Now Miranda knew what they were talking about. In a previous dream like this, a lucid dream, she had taken the boat across the water to the land of the dead, to tara mortilor. She had followed her aunt's instructions. And if finally she could not do what she'd been told to do, still she'd managed to free a little bird—her aunt's soul or spirit, as she'd thought. Not till this moment had she imagined she'd done wrong.

"But you see she does not know," said a new voice. A girl or woman not much older than Miranda sat in a rocking chair. Her name was Jeanne Petite, and she was wearing a skirt much shorter than anything Miranda had seen in Bucharest. She crossed one knee over the other and then clasped her hands together over her stockinged shin. Her fingernails were painted pink.

"But it is by chance she comes like this, par hazard," she

said. "Permit me, it is not a place like this. Death, le mort, we call it many names. In my country as you know it is Les Champs Elysées, like the Parisian boulevard. Perhaps for some of us it will be a street like this, with shopping also! Disons que, let us say it is a dream, different every time. It is part of us! We make it for ourself. And so sometimes you see it is a boat, so many creatures! I think you know about this. Sometimes it is a palace like Versailles where King Jesus reigns, or else some other fellows also—" Here she nodded toward Mrs. Chatterjee. "But it is not always like this. . . ."

The others smiled and shook their heads as Jeanne Petite went on to explain how there were some who could not enter tara mortilor until some new conditions could be met. "Because they have destroyed themselves!" The Baron Ceausescu, apparently, still roamed the hidden world, as well as the Elector of Ratisbon, who had held Miranda's mother prisoner.

Others had crossed over and then had managed to return. Aegypta Schenck was one of these, as shown by her appearance in Insula Calia and some other places.

"For this, my dear, you must assume responsibility," continued Mrs. Chatterjee, holding up a cookie. She had ivory bangles on her wrist that clicked together as they fell toward her elbow. Her dark arms were thin as sticks. "This is why we are coming here, you see. And we are assuming that there can be a great suffering in death, because these people have become more mad or crazy after all, if they were not mad first or fantastical—your aunt, I knew her. We all knew her. It is thinking too much about the interest of her own family—well, we can forgive these things. Now it is worse, and she has caused a terrible weapon to come into the hands of a terrible person, who might employ it to undo all of the benefits that we are making here, especially Olga and Zuzana with the compromise they are developing—now do you understand?"

"I . . . I think so," said Miranda, and she almost told the truth.

Inez de Rougemont made a gesture with her hand. "It is the gun," she said. "Set one way it stores up death with every firing. Death and death's power in a type of reservoir, I think, in the bone handle. Set another and the creatures feed on it as they come out, one after another. I did not think it was possible what she accomplished."

One wire hook at a time, she stripped the spectacles off her ears. Her gray hair was pulled back tight. Unsoftened now by the lenses, her face was thin and painted and intense. De Rougemont stared at her, and Miranda couldn't meet her eyes. Once again, obviously, she'd made a terrible mistake.

She had known her father's pistol was important. Gregor Splaa had told her about it before he died. Her aunt had hidden it for her to find and left her clues as well as some detailed instructions. At least that was probably what they were. Who knows? Miranda had lost them without reading them through a perverse carelessness, she told herself now.

She felt tears on her cheek. She imagined she must ask these women what to do. But when she spoke, it was to ask another question, which took shape slowly out of her chaotic thoughts. "I don't know what I want to say."

She faltered and went on. "Evolution, Copernicus, the big bang. These were the things I learned. Fairy tales. But they were what I had, even if I didn't understand them or even pay attention. They were the explanations. So now what?"

She looked around the room. No one spoke.

"I mean," she said, "what takes their place? Failed experiments. But what are the explanations that are true?"

Again nothing. The heat in the room now seemed oppressive. No one had fed or tended the fire, yet still it flared up in the hearth. Miranda saw the reflection on the ceiling, which seemed lower now, a burden that pressed down.

"My dear," said Mrs. Chatterjee at last. "We were hoping that you could be able to tell us. Do you see?"

Miranda bowed her head, but not so quickly that she didn't see the woman indicate, with a sidelong glance of her almond, black, kohl-lined eyes, the bracelet on Miranda's wrist.

"You are the white tyger," she continued humbly.

Jeanne Petite had lit a cigarette. She blew the end off it and then examined the smoke as it spiraled upward. "You see we are always searching for truth in the secret world," she said. "Le monde secret. We think there is the key, or many keys, I suppose. When we learn there is someone who can travel to this place, we think she can tell us many things. The nature of the planets or the gods. If the aether is a liquid or a gas. If the sun moves in the sky—we argue about these things. People argue, and they publish books that say one thing or else another. But the truth, perhaps, it is like a fruit hanging from a tree in a dark forest. People tell a story how a god was tricked and captured by these Germans in their scientific explorations, locked up in a tower. And either you must think this is a great event, and all these new discoveries and experiments and alchemical conjuring, it is all possible from this, the modern world, or else you must think also that it is the source of all our difficulties—already this was several hundred years ago. But in the secret world I think that time is not the same. . . ."

"I thought this was the secret world," Miranda cried. "Where we are now!"

Some of the women smiled. Zuzana laughed aloud. Inez de Rougemont shrugged her shoulders. "Oh, this mountain has many names. There is nothing secret here, but you can see the place we spoke of from the crest. Down in the dark, where the creatures live. You came up from there, flying. We saw you."

Miranda started to protest. But she was interrupted by the pleasant voice of Jeanne Petite. "Please, enough of this. I want to verify that she will understand what we are asking—I think she is not such a clever one. But this adversary is quite clever, I think, and she is capable of desperate acts to save herself, as we have seen from the burning fire over Chiselet. I want to know that she will understand what she will do, that is to take this weapon and destroy it, perhaps, or hide it or bring it to us here. She must owe us this. She has been careless in the past."

"I understand," Miranda said. She could not look at Jeanne Petite. So she watched Olga Karpov, dressed in a wool cardigan and a fur collar, regardless of the heat. Then she turned her head, and found herself looking into the face of a woman who had not yet spoken in that group, the Turkish woman who had sat the whole time without moving in an upholstered armchair. Or she had not moved her body, but her hands were busy, knitting or crocheting an unusually ugly afghan. Now they paused. Looking at her flat, stolid, pock-marked features,

Miranda thought she felt a gust of something nevertheless, a breath of some hostility or some anticipated triumph.

Troubled, Miranda tried to stare her down. "I'll do my best," she murmured.

Mrs. Chatterjee's jewelry made a jingle as she moved. "My dear, we are not asking more than that. After all, this is a question of your family's property. This is a weapon that was handed down—"

"Not for this purpose," interrupted Olga Karpov, her chin sunk in her ratty white fur collar. And then there was a light bickering as Miranda's thoughts moved elsewhere, back to the question she had asked before.

The Turkish woman's head was round, her neck was fat. She dropped her eyes back to her lap again, and Miranda could hear the click of her knitting needles as she resumed.

What is the mountain with names in many languages? Miranda thought. Peter had told her about the cave or hole he had found in time and space, that had brought him from the snowy woods into an archeological dig in the middle of the Egyptian desert—the Aegyptian desert, she corrected herself. He'd told her some ideas about how time was different in different places, how it moved slower or else faster at the edges, where it was like the waterfall that poured off the circumference of the flat earth. That was his comparison. She didn't know what she thought of it—half the world seemed abandoned, dark. West of the Hudson, east of Japan, people said there was nothing. What did that mean? Literally nothing? Or no place you could go?

In Massachusetts in Miranda's house, no one had really believed in God. They'd gone to church sometimes when her adoptive grandparents showed up from Colorado. But even they seemed to be Christians more for political reasons, to be part of something here and now.

Or there and then. But was there a God here? Mountains that rose up to heaven? Circles of ether—aether, she corrected herself impatiently. Planets that were alive like watchful eyes. Time like a bowl or an inverted bowl—which way? And if there was a God here, an actual God, maybe that explained why all the churches seemed so feeble, and no one believed in anything.

The Turkish lady had ringlets of oily red hair. Her chest was huge. Click, click, click, came the sound of her needles.

Later, when she was safe in bed and Ludu Rat-tooth was gone, Miranda sat up wondering. Later still she went onto the balcony and looked up into the sky.

14 *A Defeat on the Bug*

THE NEXT MORNING, Sasha Prochenko sat at the bar of the Hotel Moskva.

For most of the past week he had done nothing except walk the streets of Bucharest and play at whist or Boston in the upstairs rooms of the Flamingo Club, which he had joined under an assumed name—the rules were not so strict anymore. Any riffraff could come up and play.

In the afternoons he sat at the long bar reading newspapers. Especially he followed the society gossip in the *Evenimentul Zilei*, which represented German interests in the capital.

Twice during the week he had brought private letters, sent to his rooming house in Floreasca. He had opened them and smoothed them out on the varnished mahogany, as now. This third letter was like the others: "Dear A., I can't come to see you. I'm like a prisoner. If they turn you away, just ask for Jean-Baptiste. Please help me."

The handwriting hadn't changed. Always Miranda had written in a careful, precise cursive, like an elementary school teacher. Always Prochenko had found the sight of it a little bit irritating; the paper was expensive and embossed. He smoothed it out next to his brandy glass, then folded back the flimsy pages of the newspaper again. He was interested in several different articles, already a day old. Already he had glanced at them, episodes in a coherent narrative. Or else several different narratives, depending on the order he looked at them. His fingers were smeared with ink.

This was the order he now chose: First, the chief of the metropolitan police had been replaced in light of the continuing emergencies—the riots in the south and now a religious disturbance close to the capital in Mogosoaia (a policeman had been attacked by Gypsies in the vicinity of St. Mary's Fountain). Inspector Luckacz's replacement had a German name, and was a member of the German-speaking minority in Bucovina. He had not yet arrived in the capital to take up his post, and it was to be wondered if criminals or subversives would take advantage of an opportunity.

Second, representatives of the German Republic were to present the State Medallion of Achievement to Mme. Nicola Ceausescu in a public ceremony. Traditionally considered the final capstone of an illustrious artistic career, the medallion brought with it a public pension, which matched the people's gratitude for contributions to the allied cause. In anticipation, Mme. Ceausescu had already refurnished her mansion in Saltpetre Street.

Third, Princess Popescu von Schenck was expected to reopen the new Targoviste Bridge, after the original had been damaged in an anarchist's attack the previous year.

Fourth, Felipe Romanov, the czarevich of all Russia, had died suddenly of a heart attack only a day after his release from German custody, as his train arrived at Vitebsky Station in Petersburg. No one knew how this might affect the balance of ongoing negotiations. The czarevich, of course, had been a leading advocate for war.

Fifth, a man named Peter Gross had been found guilty of kidnapping and murder, and was scheduled to face a police firing squad at Jilava Prison in one week's time.

Since Chiselet, Lieutenant Prochenko had been nursing a low fever. Now he rubbed his forehead with a linen napkin from the bar. This was the first time he'd seen Peter mentioned in the paper, even—as now—in a fragment of a larger column of criminal news.

As at many other moments since the crash of the Hephaestion, Prochenko tried to decipher his own feelings. Jilava

Prison—that was where Prince Frederick met his end, shot down, supposedly, while trying to escape.

Now, clueless as to what he thought, the lieutenant brought his attention down to the messages of his own body: fever, trembling, giddiness, nausea. Anger, that was it, and now his eyes were watering. He wiped them on the napkin—this was an insult to Prince Frederick, and the Ninth Hussars, and the honor of the Roumanian army. The Chevalier de Graz, after all, was a hero of the Turkish wars, decorated with the Order of Hercules. It was contemptible to sneak him to his death, and under an assumed name.

Images of Pieter de Graz now came to him—at Nova Zagora returning from Turkish lines, his face marked with blood, oil, dirt, and a demented joy. At Sophie's guesthouse with the prince. And then many discrete images from Mamaia Castle on the beach, where they had lived with Aegypta Schenck when Miranda was a little girl—all that seemed distant and confused, hard to remember, hard to put into a story. What had they been doing all those years? Babysitting, fending off occasional attacks, pursuing intrigues with women from the villages. Closer to hand were pictures from Berkshire County: Peter Gross cutting his lawn on White Oak Road, running the power mower with his left hand. Or that moment on Christmas Hill when everything had changed. Kevin Markasev had been there, too.

So the world was full of violence, currents as strong as wind and water. These wars, these political upheavals, and people on their little boats alone, spinning in the flood. Markasev had already gone down. Peter Gross was foundering. No, by God, the lieutenant would not sink like that. By the untouched breasts of Artemis the Great. Something could be done.

Face flushed and hot, eyes watering, Prochenko took a gulp of brandy. In the long mirror above the bar he was able to survey the diners in the restaurant behind him, an area of small round tables and white tablecloths where fashionable couples were eating lunch. Someone was watching him—no, he looked up and there was no one. But when he turned his stool he saw, beyond a wrought-iron balustrade not ten meters away, Elena

Bibescu sitting with a man. Fiftyish, powerfully built, with a gray moustache and close-cropped hair, he was stylishly dressed in a military uniform that nevertheless displayed no insignia or identifying marks. Prochenko had no doubt he was observing the notorious Colonel Bocu, who had saved an ancient family from bankruptcy for reasons that were plain to see.

Light came through the high windows and played with the massed crystal, silver, and empty dishes; they must have just arrived. Waiters stood around. Prochenko watched Elena's beautiful face in profile. She was aware of him, he knew.

Supported on his elbows, Prochenko leaned back against the bar. Idly, to distract himself, he watched the colonel's face as he watched his wife. Palms on the tablecloth, sitting forward in his chair, he had evidently asked her a question. Prochenko examined his intelligent, expressive face, which nevertheless in that light seemed to demonstrate a kind of coarseness and sensuality—why did Prochenko think so? Was it because of what he knew about him, the rumors and gossip he had already heard at the Flamingo Club? Or could you really tell these things by looking?

He watched Elena Bibescu's beautiful ears, just tinged with red. Her brown hair was gathered up on top of her head, held in place with a tortoiseshell comb. Because it was a warm day, her dress was light—a lavender and purple floral print, with ruffles around the neck and sleeves. She wore jewelry. With a start Prochenko remembered her diamond earrings, now in a pawnshop off the Strada Stavropoleos if they hadn't been sold.

Well, so maybe it was time to pay his tab and leave. Prochenko sat up on his stool, and at the same time Elena turned to look at him.

Men—he had always had a hard time understanding them or reading their faces. Women—that was different. There was no anger in her gaze, or else not much. Instead he saw a kind of wordless appeal, which he would have been churlish to ignore.

Besides, there was something in her face that spoke to him, the simple surfaces that made her cheekbones, jaw, nose, neck, forehead. She was like a sketch made of a few thin lines, and easier to read than something full of subtle contour or complicated colors—Miranda, for example. What was Miranda to him now? A combination of stories that couldn't fit together, and in each of which Prochenko played a different role—oh, he had been lonely these past days.

He let Elena's gaze fall over him. If she had been alone he would have smiled, would have made a gesture with his hand. But now the husband had turned his head, was looking toward the bar with a brutal malevolence that seemed intended to repulse just such a handsome young man as he appeared to be; he yawned, scratched his jaw, left his money next to his glass.

Then he sauntered toward the cloakroom out of sight in a small maze of corridors beyond the lobby of the hotel. He waited in an alcove that contained some kind of bell pull. He had a long time to wait, but it was worth it just for the expression on her face. She had expected him, she had not expected him. She was angry, she was not angry. It didn't matter; he pulled her into a small secret place behind the coat racks, and she was in his arms, and he was kissing her, and she was making the same small exclamations of surprise that he remembered from the half hour in her room. Oh, he remembered this all right, the sweetness now intensified because he'd seen her husband, and recognized in him the kind of man who must be punished for his money, his power, his arrogance, his success, punished in all the intimate ways. How dare he have a wife this young, this sweet?

At the same time Prochenko imagined he had missed this girl, and all the painful disassociations of the past few days would have been easier if he'd been with her like this, if only for stolen moments. He needed comforting, and she could have comforted him; he pushed his mouth against her mouth, rewarded by her little gasp. He wanted to mark her in a way that he only could see, a way that would be hidden from her husband. At the same time he had lost himself in all her smells, and was clawing at her bosom until she said, "Enough," and pushed him away.

"I lost you in the crowd," she said. "The police came between us and I lost you. I was afraid I'd never see you again—have you remembered your name? Or was that just a lie or something like that? I must go back to Colonel Bocu—where are you staying?"

He gave her the name of the place. "Sasha Andromedes," he gasped. Then she put her hand on his mouth—she was the one who had marked him. He could taste the blood on his lips. "You must not think this is not difficult for me," she said. Then in a moment, breathlessly: "The colonel is returning to his regiment." Then she was gone, and again he remembered the diamond earrings and the stolen money—gifts from her husband, he told himself. So she must not have cared about them.

He pulled himself together, straightened the lapels of his linen jacket. Emerging from the alcove, he examined himself in one of the high mirrors. Bellboys moved back and forth behind him in their brass-buttoned uniforms and pillbox hats. Any one of them could have seen and recognized Elena Bibescu. Yes, she had bitten him or something. There was blood on his upper lip. He licked it away.

After retrieving his gloves, stick, and hat from the consignment desk, he walked straight across the lobby with his left hand in his pocket, not even glancing at the entrance to the restaurant and bar, from which now issued the sounds of a piano. He pushed out through the revolving door into the bright sun. He had several kilometers to walk before he reached the area around Lake Herastrau—he knew the house he was looking for. He had had it pointed out to him from across the street.

Whistling a tune from *Kiss Me, Kate*, a favorite of Andromeda's mother in the house on Syndicate Road, he strolled along the sidewalk until he reached the alley between two rows of houses—a shortcut if you could manage to avoid the drainage ditch. But he'd scarcely gone a dozen meters when a man called out from behind him. Silhouetted in the alley's mouth, the sun behind him, he looked harmless enough. But when he came close, Prochenko saw he wore the same kind of unmarked uniform the colonel had worn in the hotel restaurant—cream-colored broadcloth buttoned to his chin. His neck was thick, his skin was flushed, and you could say he was as thick and ugly as a fireplug, and no manners either. Maybe he understood that dogs or wolves like Prochenko had pissed on him his entire life and he was sick of it, especially because he knew or half suspected it was about to start again. A bully, in fact, though he showed signs of anxiety and nervousness the way immediately he started asking for papers and identification, all of which Prochenko still had not a sniff.

"Who's asking me?" Prochenko asked, because you had to be high-handed with these fellows.

"Oh, so that's it. Don't you know there's a war on?" the man said. "We'll soon put you right. We've got fairies like you in the Branco Artillery," he said, naming Elena's husband's regiment. Immediately Prochenko understood what this was all about.

"Your colonel's a piss-pot," said Lieutenant Prochenko, to hasten things along. He wanted to get this over before other men like this one joined them in the alley behind all the overflowing garbage cans from the hotel. He shouldn't have come this way. It stank.

"You tell him I said so," he continued, looking back toward the alley's mouth. Then he turned and struck the fellow with the heel of his hand below the nose. Then he hit him with the wolf's-head stick, imagining how satisfying it might have been to tear apart the bully who'd attacked Kevin Markasev, a bully like this one. What did Bocu think? That he was going to have beaten up or arrested any man his wife even glanced at casually in a crowded hotel?

"'Oh, kiss me, Kate,'" he murmured. "'And twice and thrice . . . '" He'd never really been able to carry a tune.

The man had stumbled on the filthy cobblestones and fallen over. Prochenko stood above him, massaging his gloved fingers. Whatever happened, he was glad of this, because already he'd been in Bucharest long enough to see how the power in the city had devolved into the hands of bully-boys like this, members of private militias who were connected on one side to criminal or quasi-criminal enterprises. And on the other side they were protected by corrupt colonels or corrupt bureaucrats, all flourishing under the German occupation—though to be fair, Antonescu and Ceausescu and Valeria Dragonesti had been just as bad. A general, a baron, and an empress—no, you had to go back to Frederick Schenck von Schenck to remember any kind of hope, Prince Frederick whom they'd put against the wall at Jilava, doubtless the same courtyard where they planned to shoot the Chevalier de Graz—his friend.

Where was Miranda now? Prochenko thought. Was she still wondering what deals she could make with the German ambassador?

He put his expensive boot—purchased with Elena's money—against the fat cheek of the bully-boy, and saw for the first time how young he was. The tail of his jacket had pulled up, revealing a pistol in a holster. "You are a complete and total fascist piece of shit," Prochenko said in English.

But maybe he had managed to make some signal after all, because Prochenko could see men gathering at the mouth of the alley. He could see their shadows flickering in the light. He bent down to remove the pistol from its holster. It was a fine, light, modern weapon, spring-loaded, Prochenko thought, African or German made. Then he turned and ran up the alley; he knew this area of Floreasca well. It hadn't changed in twenty-five years, the twisting, dark, cobblestone streets, remnants of the Wallachian medieval town.

But then he was among the shacks and shantytowns and on the wooden bridge across the cesspool of the canal. On the other side was parkland, the hippodrome, Dinamo Stadium. He reached Lake Herastrau in the middle of the afternoon. In a block of wooden houses backed onto the shallow, reedy water, he mounted seven steps to a door once painted red.

This was the residence of Magda de Graz, much reduced in circumstances. At one time hers had been an inspiring story. Daughter of a Ploiesti shopkeeper, she had won, in blind competition, a government scholarship to the national university, where there were seven women in her class. Active in republican causes, she had met and married the young Count de Graz—not because of her looks, as had been endlessly reported in the press. Small, big-featured, she had eventually learned to ride and had taken up fox hunting, according to the German style. But she had always kept her interest in politics, and her husband had been one of the earliest supporters of Prince Frederick Schenck von Schenck. In the coup d'état that brought Valeria Dragonesti to the throne, the count had been arrested by Antonescu's thugs, despite the heroism of his son in the war against the Turks. And when Ceausescu's perjured testimony had brought down Frederick Schenck himself, most of his political supporters were shot outside of Brabova and buried in mass graves, supposedly for treason. This was at the time, of course, when General Antonescu had repulsed the first incursions of the German army at Kaposvar.

De Graz's property had all been confiscated except for this one house, where his widow still lived. She rented out the upper floor and gave music lessons in the parlor. Standing on the weathered porch, looking up into the branches of the old fig tree, Sasha Prochenko listened to the sound of a viola deep within the house, playing endlessly a sequence of a few bars.

Birds chattered in the tree, making an uneasy and equally repetitive counterpoint. Prochenko stood waiting for the lesson's end, and he looked up and down the rutted dirt road, studying the peeling façades, the porches with their wooden gutters and old gingerbread fretwork. There was a fountain of Demeter at the end of the cul-de-sac, but the bowl was dry and the water no longer flowered or even dripped from her stone, eroded breasts.

Flies buzzed. Nothing moved in the warm afternoon. Prochenko, as he often did, now surrendered himself to his preternaturally acute sense of smell. Closing his eyes, he turned his face from side to side, allowing small odors to come to him, some singly and some together—the hot wood, the paint, the dust, the mud, the grass, the rot, the bat shit, the yellow reeds, and the dozen stenches of the lake. Behind him the window was ajar, and a number of old-lady smells came seeping through the dusty curtains: furniture wax, and Madeira, and scented water, and farts. Prochenko opened his mouth, stretched out his tongue.

When the door finally opened, he felt he already knew this woman, whom he had met once years before, after all. The student, a young man, carried his instrument case under his arm. Madame de Graz was with him, whispering to him, a little woman with white hair, her back bent with osteoporosis. Prochenko stood motionless in the shadows, hidden by the tree that grew so close to the house that part of the porch had begun to shape itself around it, the thin balustrade slowly buckling. Dressed in rusty black, the old woman stood in the open door, watching her student stroll down the brick path and down the street—no, she didn't watch him. Like Prochenko she sniffed the air, moved her head this way and that, and the lieutenant saw that she was blind or nearly blind, her eyes milky with cataracts. But she had some peripheral vision, and when he moved she turned to him and did not look at him directly.

Prochenko could see nothing of her son in her. "Ma'am," he said, "you might not remember me. My name is Sasha Prochenko and—"

"Lieutenant," she interrupted. The way she said the word seemed as complicated as a poem to him, a poem or a song that was full of sadness and hope, patience and fear. "Sir, I am pleased to see you."

He came close to her, stood in the light, and she tilted her head so she could look at him out of the corner of her left eye. "Will you not come in?" she said. "It is a warm day. I believe there is some lemonade."

Prochenko had already removed his hat and gloves. Now he put his stick into the old-fashioned ceramic umbrella stand beside the door. Madame de Graz stood aside to let him enter the house. In the parlor next to the piano, he stood among pieces of furniture that had been meant for a larger space. The old lady asked him to sit, and he chose a leather armchair. Immediately she was gone through an inner doorway, probably searching for some refreshment.

The room was cool and dark. Above the fireplace there was a painting of Prince Frederick Schenck von Schenck, dressed in civilian clothes. It had the unmistakable look of a posed portrait, rather than something painted from a photograph, or else some idealized scene. The prince, never a handsome man with his protruding ears and weak chin, nevertheless in his eyes and his expression managed to project an impression of wisdom and strength. Watching him, Prochenko felt a terrible surge of sadness and regret—what had happened to his country after the death of this man? Even more poignant, against the mantel, furled yet still recognizable, stood one of the faded old banners of the prince's party, the tricolored flag of the Republic, throttled in its infancy by Valeria Dragonesti, Antonescu, Ceausescu, and the others. Once it had flown over half the roofs in Bucharest.

Pieter de Graz's Star of Hercules lay in a glass case on the sideboard, along with several other decorations. And there were photographic portraits of horses and even dogs, and the old count in riding clothes, and several other men and women—de Graz had had brothers and sisters, Prochenko remembered now.

All the photographs were edged in black crepe. Or all but one, a larger picture of the Chevalier de Graz in his captain's uniform with the high, embroidered collar. Pieter de Graz, Peter Gross—now the old lady had returned, carrying a silver tray with a glass pitcher. Ice had made it sweat.

He rose to take it from her hands. "I suppose it is very hot today," she said. "Ordinarily I open the windows off the back veranda, and there is a breeze through the house into this room. But we've had so little rain, except for that storm two nights ago. Even so there was lightning, but in the morning the ground was scarcely damp. I'm afraid the weather will affect the fruit season, with the prices so very dear. Please, there is a compote."

He placed the tray on a low inlaid table that, like many of the objects here, seemed too precious for this humble house. He let her talk. She stood in front of him, cataloguing the weather, wringing her hands. Unlike any other part of her they were smooth, unwrinkled, untouched by age or, he supposed, arthritis—why had he come? She spoke of the rain, the prices, the crops with a politeness that veiled but did not mask the greediness with which she stood and waited for information, any information after all these years alone. And what could he tell her? He had no good news to bring. Now more than anything he felt he must prevent her from having to decorate, at long last, the central photograph on the sideboard with its band of crepe. Did she have it prepared already, perhaps a roll of it with scissors, too, somewhere in some drawer?

He cleared his throat and she fell silent, licked her lips. "Please sit down," he said. Immediately she perched on the edge of the horsehair settee, her head bowed as if awaiting some punishment or blow.

"Ma'am," he said. Then: "Ma'am, I hope your health is good—"

And she interrupted. "Oh, sir," she said, "for God's sake, please." Immediately she was in tears, sobs that shook her little body as they emerged, tears that drenched her cheeks. "Forgive me," she said. "Please forgive me. I'm so sorry—please, just tell me, for God's love."

She had a handkerchief in the bosom of her black dress and now she used it to wipe her eyes. Lieutenant Prochenko studied his dusty boots. On his trouser leg there was a greasy stain, which he must have acquired in the alley behind the Hotel Moskva; "I'm in Roumania after years abroad. We crossed the border after Dragonesti moved against the prince's sister. It was our duty to protect his daughter where she'd be safe from her enemies. . . ."

"Forgive me, please—I know all that," sobbed Madame de Graz. "I received letters weekly from Constanta from my son. Then nothing after that. Not a postal card. Now Mademoiselle Popescu is in Bucharest—you read it in the newspapers. And some story about Gypsies that no one believes. And here you are. . . ."

Lieutenant Prochenko sat down again. "Yes. Well, let me tell you that the Chevalier de Graz is in good health. I have seen him in the last few days."

He'd thought this would calm her, but he was wrong. Instead she collapsed onto the carpet on her knees. The tears came out of her as if she were vomiting them up; she clutched at her white hair. For a moment, panic-struck, he studied the row of buttons down her spine, each one corresponding to a section of vertebrae that he could see all too plainly. He wondered how she managed such small buttons every evening and morning. Then he was with her on the floor, helping her up—"Oh, domnul, please!" And to his intense embarrassment she kissed his hands, held them against her cheeks. "But my God, your hands are burning," she said. "Please, you have come a long way just to comfort an old woman. You say my son is well—what about you?"

ABSENT FROM PROCHENKO'S copy of the *Evenimentul Zilei* was any mention of the anti-German protests that now gathered every afternoon in the Piata Revolutiei and the surrounding streets. These had begun modestly and furtively after the first disturbances at Chiselet, but had intensified especially after the attack on the Mogosoaia Gypsies. Radu Luckacz had done nothing to discourage them, and in the *Roumania Libera* there was speculation that the new chief of police would be more rigid in his attitude.

Late in the afternoon, as Lieutenant Prochenko and Madame de Graz searched for a taxi stand in the streets of Floreasca, a company of mounted Bavarian dragoons entered the piata and attempted to disperse the crowd. In this they were partially successful. But the core of the demonstration refused to budge. Under pacifist and anti-German banners, the representatives of the trade unions and artists' guilds maintained their position in the center of the piata, around the cannons brought back from the siege of Prague. At three o'clock their spirits were lifted by the appearance of the Baroness Ceausescu, who climbed onto the monument to address the crowd, exhorting them with the memory of Kevin Markasev. She was alone, without any kind of bodyguard or entourage, but by the pure force of her character she appeared to push the Germans back, especially the horses, which seemed frightened and difficult to control. Enthusiastic and relieved, the crowd shouted her name and waved small flags, each one cheaply printed with a white, furry face.

Miranda watched this from a third floor balcony. After the baroness left for the theater, she saw the soldiers return, a battalion of infantry this time. So she was in a position to witness the so-called martyr's massacre, when with fixed bayonets the soldiers put the crowd to flight. These were the troops of Sergeant-Colonel Carlos Maschmann; superbly trained, pelted with vegetables and stones, they never fired a shot.

Nevertheless, a half dozen men and women died in the stampede, and several children were injured.

Though she saw from a distance huddled knots of confusion, Miranda didn't hear about the casualties until the next day. Several times she left the balcony. But always she returned. She felt more fury than sadness, and she made three decisions as she watched. The first was to reject all further contact with Ambassador Moltke and her representatives. The second was to screw up her courage to demand from Nicola Ceausescu the return of her father's gun. The third was to find Peter and escape this place. Already her time in the woods, and before that her journey from the coast through the Roumanian plains, and before that her adventures on the Hoosick riverbank, all of it seemed like a forgotten paradise. She couldn't even think of anything before that, in Berkshire Country or else trips with her family to Florida, or Colorado, or Westchester, or Maine.

So when darkness came, the soldiers lit carbide lamps. The cobblestones were covered with discarded clothing and pieces of paper and the small flags. Miranda kicked at the ornate iron balusters as if they were the bars of an iron cage, and then she went in through the French windows into the third-floor portrait gallery, where the chandeliers were lit. There at the end was Miranda Brancoveanu dressed in armor with her mace in her hand, standing in triumph over the prostrate Turkish captains. She had been very beautiful, apparently.

She reached her suite of rooms and there was Jean-Baptiste waiting outside with two other people, and one of them was Andromeda, dressed as before in a man's expensive suit, and looking every inch a handsome young lieutenant—Sasha Prochenko, she supposed. Miranda went toward her with her hands held out, then found herself looking into the face of an old woman. Shoulders hunched, she peered up at Miranda through milky and occluded eyes.

"This is Peter's mother," said Andromeda.

Jean-Baptiste, unshaven, stood with his hand against Miranda's door. Despite his slovenly, ill-fitting clothes, there was something gracious and punctilious about the way he held himself. Glancing at him as if for clues, Miranda saw a submissive look that was in contrast to his usual rudeness and informality. "I'm very pleased to meet you," she said, holding out her hand.

And she was surprised by the force in the old woman's fingers. Madame de Graz tilted her head to one side and the other, as if searching for an angle that would make Miranda's face come clear. "Mademoiselle, I am so pleased. My husband and I were great admirers of your father. . . ."

But if there was a formality in Jean-Baptiste that was at odds with his wild appearance, then there was the reverse in Magda de Graz, and soon the wildness came out of her, an explosion of tears. "Mademoiselle," she gasped when she could speak. "Please, for your father's sake—please, for the love of God, please save my son."

And Miranda, who at quick intervals during the day had felt some of this same passion, now pulled the old woman into an embrace, so that her white hair was against her shoulder. She could feel a resistance. She could feel the old woman's body against hers, and it was rigid and unyielding. But Peter's mother gripped her hand so hard it hurt.

They stood there for an odd, long, awkward moment. Glancing up, Miranda saw the steward's expression change. Then she heard a noise behind her, several people in the long corridor—murmurs, laughter, and heavy steps. When she turned, there was Nicola Ceausescu back from her performance, and with her an enormous man in military uniform. His bald head shone in the light. And on her other side there was a woman whom Miranda recognized with shocked surprise—sour, emaciated, dressed in a fur coat despite the heat: Olga Karpov from her dream.

The baroness wore a long red coat unbuttoned down the front. She came to a stop in the middle of the hall. And then a hiss came out of her, which was in its own way as unexpected and disconcerting as Mme. de Graz's explosion of sobs. "Domnul—sir," she said, and Miranda could see that she was looking at Andromeda. "I understand you have ignored my requests. I understand you prefer other company."

And then to Jean-Baptiste: "Go to your room. I will send for you. I don't know how it is you could deceive me like this."

"Ma'am," the steward said. "It is to protect you from others. . . ."

The baroness laughed. "I see we're all friends here," she interrupted. "You know General Antonescu, I am sure. But who is . . . ?"

Miranda had released Magda de Graz. What was Antonescu doing here? Weren't they enemies, he and the baroness?

She watched a contortion of disgust pass over the old woman's face. But she was still in tears, and now she stepped forward unsteadily. "Ma'am," she said, "I am the mother of the Chevalier de Graz. Please, I am here to beg you for his life."

"Go," said Nicola Ceausescu to Jean-Baptiste. "Escort Madame Karpov to the elevators and the Spanish Gate. General," she continued, turning to Antonescu, "I will wait for your dispatches." She held out her gloved hand for him to kiss.

And when Jean-Baptiste had led Olga Karpov down the corridor, and Antonescu had turned back the way they'd come—not before giving her, Miranda thought, an insolent, assessing smile—Nicola Ceausescu stood alone in the middle of the hall. Then she also came forward and took Peter's mother by the hand. "Madame," she said, "I beg you to be patient. All is not lost. These potato-eating Germans—we are doing all we can."

Her voice was full of sadness and concern. Liar, Miranda thought, but she said nothing. It was Andromeda who said it. "Liar," she whispered, but she smiled.

Then it seemed to Miranda that she saw a complicated mix of emotions pass over the baroness's beautiful, exquisitely expressive face—fury, amusement, and then a sort of furtive pleasure. Momentarily she closed her eyes.

"I assure you," she continued, "we are doing all we can. And do not give up hope. Hope is our most important commodity in times like these. . . ."

"Liar," murmured Andromeda, and again Miranda followed the baroness's expression.

"Alas," she said, "it is so difficult to keep hold of oneself, living in this public way. Always under public scrutiny. Domnul Andromedes, you must not judge me. You will see that it is difficult what I attempt to do."

Then she detached her gloved fingers one by one from Madame de Graz's grasping hands. "Your son will die in one week's time," she said. "I don't care about it one way or the other. You must console yourself. It is his duty as a soldier. I myself do not expect to die of old age."

Then she turned back to Andromeda. "Is that better?" she asked. "Do you admire me now?"

"You are such dog shit," Andromeda murmured in English. It had been one of her favorite phrases, and Miranda was surprised to hear it. There was little else she recognized of her old friend.

It occurred to Miranda suddenly that maybe they could kill this woman, Andromeda and she. And what would happen then? It was a wisp of a thought rather than a plan. But some version of it animated Magda de Graz, who now reached out with both her hands to seize hold of the baroness's shirt. And before she had time to react, Miranda heard her question answered. In this palace if you thought you were alone it was an illusion. Two men in livery came running down the hall.

"No, it's all right," gasped Nicola Ceausescu. "Take Madame de Graz and return her to her carriage—you must not use any of the doors to the piata where the potato-eaters are camped. All of them are closed; ah, you have no carriage? Domnul Andromedes—always the gentleman! Doubtless he will escort you home."

She was enjoying this, Miranda saw. Her shirt was ripped open at the throat. "Madame de Graz," she said, "your honesty has touched my heart. Tomorrow I will ask for an interview with the new chief of police—you understand I am a citizen like you. Especially after today—these are dark days for our country. If Domnul Andromedes will call for me at two o'clock? I could have an answer then."

"Unbelievable and total dog shit," murmured Andromeda as she led Mme. de Graz away toward the elevators, and the baroness smiled.

One of the footmen stayed and pressed himself into the wall a discreet distance down the corridor. As far as could be seen, Miranda and the baroness were alone. "What do you have?" she asked when all was still. "You are not beautiful, not intelligent, and you have no art or culture or style. You are not touched by the muses or the gods. But de Graz and this other—are you a whore for them? Is that the explanation after all? But they are not jealous. Why is that?"

Furious, Miranda put her hand up to her neck. "They are my friends," she said.

The baroness laughed. "I see you have a lot to teach me, mademoiselle. I myself have no friends. Jean-Baptiste, have you also stolen him away?"

She stood with her hands in the pockets of her long red coat. She wore boots and tight pants, and her yellow shirt was torn around the throat. Her chestnut-colored hair seemed to glow in the muted light. Miranda caught a little of her body's bitter smell, mixed also with cigarettes.

In her mind's theater, though, Miranda was not watching the baroness, who stood alone under the lights as if onstage. Or else she also saw something else: Colonel Maschmann's soldiers, moving with fixed bayonets over the stones of the Piata Revolutiei. And then at other moments she saw Mme. de Graz tilting her head from side to side, the tears running from her milky eyes.

Miranda had imagined for much of the past week that she and the baroness were fighting to manipulate the only power in Roumania, which was the German army. And it was a struggle Miranda knew she could win if she wanted—already she'd been of two minds about that. This evening, though, watching the soldiers from the balcony, Miranda had begun to understand something. Later, seeing General Antonescu and Olga Karpov in the hallways of the People's Palace, another puzzle piece had been added in. Now she knew instinctively that German power in Roumania was at an end, and in the larger struggle the baroness's position was unbeatable. In the piata the crowds had chanted her name, waved their little flags.

So this entire conversation was a form of gloating, of amusement. By confessing weakness, the baroness was confessing strength. There was no reason, for example, to have Miranda arrested or confined to her room, though it was easy to predict that that might come.

So the fight was lost before it had even really started. But there was another place to resist, which was the hidden world. "Tell me," she said. "In Mogosoaia that policeman stole my bracelet, my money, and my father's gun. Later Domnul Luckacz returned the bracelet and the money, as you see."

Already on the morning after her dream, Miranda had asked Jean-Baptiste to find the gun for her, search the baroness's room for her if necessary, during the evening performance. And Jean-Baptiste had raised his eyebrow without saying a word. So Miranda had imagined she might try, except in this building there was always someone with her or near her. Now, maybe, with the Baroness Ceausescu standing triumphant in the middle of the corridor, something could be done.

Hands in the pockets of her red coat, she smiled. "The bracelet—I couldn't take it from you. Soon the citizens of Bucharest will fasten it around my wrist. Already they know what you are—a potato-eating spy. So you may wear it a little longer. It has been in your family a long time. But the pistol, would you like to see it now? It has not been fired. You must have guessed tonight would be the night."

She turned to lead Miranda the way she'd come. She didn't look back, but spoke over her shoulder, because she knew Miranda would follow. "You know it has come to me just now. Why would this man Andromedes have brought the mother of the Chevalier de Graz to see me? What connection could there have been—I see it now. De Graz was your father's servant, and he went with you to that place—what was it called? Massachusetts. Such a peculiar name. He was in the newspapers. But there was another one whose face I never saw. A lieutenant. So I think I know who that is, and why he comes. It is not for love, which is a relief."

She was talking about Andromeda. ". . . This man who insults me so freely. Sometimes in my life I have been cursed and despised. Other times they lick the dog shit from my shoes—that is his phrase, is it not? If I'm bored from that, so who can blame me? He is a handsome man, don't you think so? Now I could have my servants follow him. But that will not be necessary. You will live to see him come to me."

They had left the portrait gallery and passed down several other shorter corridors. Now they stood at the door of the baroness's suite of rooms overlooking the Piata Revolutiei. It was ajar. "Enter, enter," said Nicola Ceausescu. Pushing open the door, she led Miranda into her music room and stopped.

An ornamental fixture stood out from the wall. A glass bulb hung from it. The baroness fumbled at the screw with her right hand. The gaslight flickered up, revealing beyond the draped piano, at the entrance to the inner room, the shadow of a man.

A hiss from the baroness. Then she spoke over her shoulder to Miranda. "I'm glad you've come. I promise you there is no danger—who is it? Domnul Luckacz, is it you?"

The shadow didn't move. The baroness let her coat slip from her shoulders onto the floor. Then she stepped over to the empty grate and seized a poker from the hearth. "Sir, show yourself," she said. "Have you come to steal from me? I have nothing here."

Jean-Baptiste stood in the doorway to the baroness's bedroom. Miranda could see him now. "Ma'am," he said, "there is no reason to be frightened. I have brought some linen."

It was true. He carried a pile of sheets and towels in his hands. But his tone was too formal to be sincere, Miranda thought, and the baroness again let out a hiss of expelled breath.

"Oh, my friend," she said. She had the poker in her hand. She looked back at Miranda. Then she smiled. Her lips were elegant and small.

"So you have come to rob me after all, while I stood talking like a fool. This is the plan for both of you, I see."

"No ma'am, I brought the pillowcases." The steward's voice was soft. But he was nervous. Miranda could see the anxiety in his high, narrow shoulders, his thin face. What did he have to hide?

"Forgive me," he said now. "I came to speak with you. But I did not expect . . ." Hands full, he gestured toward Miranda with his chin.

"Here I am," said the baroness. "Speak to me."

He looked down at the floor. "Forgive me," he murmured with uncharacteristic humbleness. "I know it is not my place to come here late at night."

Miranda clapped her hands together noiselessly, a gesture

her adoptive father had sometimes used to show embarrassment. "Well, I guess I'll be moseying on out of here," she almost said. There was no chance, she thought, of retrieving the gun now. More important was to escape from this place, this prison. But what about Peter? What about her mother—Clara Brancoveanu?

The baroness anticipated her. "Please stay. You could not think that you might trick me and then go to bed." Then to the steward, "Speak to me."

The miserable man bowed his head. Sweat stood out on his high forehead. "Ma'am," he said—"Downstairs. I saw Madame de Graz in the lower gallery."

"And?"

"And she was in tears."

The baroness let the point of the poker sink down. "I don't believe you," she said. Then she stepped across the room to the piano. With her left hand she pushed away the long embroidered cloth that covered its closed lid, revealing a box. She opened it awkwardly with her wrong hand, and drew out something wrapped in leather.

Miranda knew what it was. She could tell by the shape and the weight, the way the baroness's slender wrist sagged down. "Is this what you were looking for?" she asked. "She wanted it, the whore. Did she ask you to steal it for her?"

"No," said Jean-Baptiste, which was a lie, of course.

It must have shown on his face. "Come here," said the baroness.

She laid the poker on the piano lid and unwrapped the gun, and switched it to her right hand. Then she held it up with both hands clasped together. It didn't seem to Miranda that she knew how to hold it safely, and perhaps the steward thought so, too. His eyes were big. Nevertheless, he placed the cube of folded pillowcases onto the piano stool, gave the top of it a little pat, and moved closer to the light.

The baroness came to meet him with the gun in her hands. She reached out with the muzzle of it and touched his unshaven cheek and chin. With the inlaid steel she caressed his neck and the front of his stained shirt, a gesture that seemed intimate and dangerous at the same time; Miranda longed to be elsewhere. What would happen if she left? No, she couldn't leave now, even though she could not believe the baroness would actually shoot this man, not with that expression of longing and remorse on her face. But maybe he thought so, because he cleared his throat and began to speak. "Ma'am, I didn't have any plan like that, I swear. You've known me a long time."

"Yes," murmured Nicola Ceausescu. "And I did not believe you'd feed my soup to Radu Luckacz. I thought he was a friend of yours! I see you didn't even taste a drop. Didn't you trust me?"

Miranda thought he would take the gun from the baroness's hands, bat it away. But he scarcely moved. "Ma'am," he said, "I shouldn't have come. These people—Madame de Graz—they didn't know you, but I know you."

The sweat stood out in drops on his high forehead. "For years I've seen you every day. Believe me when I tell you this is changing you, all this. Kevin Markasev—how could you have done that? We lived—the three of us—in Saltpetre Street. In those days you complained to me about the Germans, how they took your son from you. Stole him away. And now he lives in the floor below this, and you don't visit him. Yes, you spy on him, that's all. But I remember when you first came to the baron's house, so humble yet so proud."

Miranda brought her hands together. "Gosh, look at the time," she almost said, although as long as the gun was in the baroness's hands, she couldn't leave.

Nicola Ceausescu tapped the steward on his breastbone with the muzzle of the long revolver. "You must not chastise me," she said at last. "What are you saying—I'm a monster? Yes, I've felt you pull away."

She glanced at Miranda, and then looked back. "Don't think I haven't noticed and it hasn't hurt me. Don't think it doesn't hurt me to be judged by someone I trusted, and for choices I've made not for myself. Don't you think it would make me happy to leave this prison, let go of these responsibilities? Live with you and Felix in Saltpetre Street, devote myself to art?"

Will you look at that? I've got to fly, Miranda thought.

But at the same time she felt as always a perverse admiration for the baroness's skill. These were obvious lies, the words she'd spoken. No one in the room believed them. Nor was she helped in any way by the language she had used, which was stilted and insincere. It was as if a mediocre playwright had written a mediocre part for a superb actress. "It hurts me so terribly," she said. "As for the revolver, it is not loaded."

Miranda had scarcely breathed since the baroness had pulled the gun out of the box. Now she gulped at the air, took physical pleasure in her sense of relief. Jean-Baptiste managed a smile. But his eyes were still big, and there was still a sheen on his high forehead and his narrow, bladelike nose; he opened his mouth to speak. But the baroness continued, and the playwright had gotten a little better this time, and the words themselves were disconcerting—"Not in the conventional way. Mademoiselle Popescu doesn't know. The time has come for her to learn. Always we must learn new things. Mademoiselle—please—there is a book inside the box. Magister Newton, Isaac Newton—you have heard of him? Read me where the marker is."

She still held the gun in her clasped hands, the muzzle pressed against the steward's shirt. Her fingers were against the trigger. If she'd meant to murder him, surely she would not look like that, her face expressing remorse and triumph, pity and contempt and a dozen other things, the gaslight in her chestnut hair.

Miranda walked behind her to the piano. The box underneath the embroidered shawl was wide and flat, ornately carved. There was a book in the bottom of it, not like the book she had lost, *The Essential History*. But it was bigger and older and it smelled of mold, and the black leather binding was turning into dust.

The pages were still strong, and seemed to be made of a kind of cloth, as Miranda saw when she opened the book. "Read where the marker is," the baroness said again.

Jean-Baptiste gave her a pleading look, and Miranda paused. "Please, mademoiselle. You have no choice," said Nicola Ceausescu.

The marker was a wide, flat ribbon close to the end. "Can

you see in the light?" asked the baroness. "There are matches by the candle."

Both of her index fingers were locked around the trigger of the gun. She didn't look back at Miranda, but stared instead at Jean-Baptiste. "Read it," she said. "Where it starts at 'Mint-bean.' "

Miranda lit the four candles in the candelabrum on the right side of the keyboard. More things were visible now, and she could see, for example, the sheaves of handwritten music on the stand. And in the book she saw the place the baroness meant. Two-thirds of the way down the big page there was a rubric in red ink.

The black book also was handwritten. Except for the rubrics in the right-hand margins, the letters were heavy and brown. Miranda glanced up at Jean-Baptiste again, but in the new light she couldn't see him quite so well; he was out of the flickering circle. And the gun wasn't loaded. The baroness had said so. It couldn't be loaded. This was just a joke to scare them both, a stupid, cruel joke.

This much was true: She had no choice. The text was in English, which surprised her. But some of the letters were unfamiliar and hard to read. Opposite the rubric was a double line, written in a different, spidery hand. Hesitantly, she spoke the words:

Flee to me remote elf.
Egad a base life defiles a bad age.

So that doesn't make much sense, she thought, relieved. But there was obviously a puzzle, and she was good at puzzles. She started to think about the words, which must hold some kind of clue. There was a crash, and on the other side of the piano Jean-Baptiste staggered back. The baroness had fired the gun.

Miranda, who was used to the sound it made in the open air, was confused to hear it so much softer in the enclosed space. This confusion was the first of a quick sequence of emotions and thoughts: Had the steward's body acted as a kind of silencer? She felt a cold, stunned interest in part of her mind as, horrified, she scrambled around the piano's bulge to support Jean-Baptiste as he collapsed—but he was still alive! And unwounded. Had he fainted from the shock? Or had the baroness put up the gun at the last instant before firing, in which case the sound would have been louder, wouldn't it? There was no stink of gunpowder, no ringing in Miranda's ears.

He had fallen back against a padded armchair and she helped him into it. And he seemed unhurt, his white shirtfront stained only with soup or whatever it was; she heard the chattering of his teeth. When she touched him on his chest, he flinched. So there must be a bruise there; had the baroness used some kind of fake cartridge or a blank? She still stood with the gun held out straight, and as Miranda watched, the barrel seemed to glow. And there was smoke from the muzzle—no, more solid, difficult to see in the uncertain light.

But it was there, a little creature perched on the barrel of Prince Frederick's revolver. "Mintbean," whispered the baroness.

It was human in shape, naked, pallid, male. It moved and swelled a little bit. Miranda saw it had a pair of wings that now unfolded like a butterfly's. And maybe they were wet, and maybe drying in the heat from the gun barrel, for they shifted, moved, almost transparent, almost invisible in the uncertain light. Just a flicker of iridescence above the creature's head.

Breathless, Nicola Ceausescu moved five steps sideways to the window. Keeping the gun immobile in her right hand, with her left she reached behind her to push open the window and the screen. "Go," she whispered in English. "You know what I want."

The creature shifted its big wings. Then it drifted into the air as lightly as a bubble. From the chair Miranda watched it, her arms around the thin shoulders of the old man. He lay back against the pillows with his eyes closed.

No, Miranda thought. No, really, I can't stay, thanks all the same.

The creature drifted up, caught and buffeted by a soft current of air from the open window. "I thought it was appropriate. The white tyger of Roumania could speak the spell," the baroness said.

Her cheeks were painted with a soft glow. Closer to the delicate, drifting fairy, she seemed entranced. But almost before it disappeared, sucked out the window in the soft, rising breeze, she turned away as if unsatisfied, back into the room. "There is another one," she said, "on the next page. 'Abcess.' Read it."

"No," Miranda said.

She pushed the steward's lank hair from his forehead, slimy with sweat. But he was opening his eyes. His lashes fluttered, and he stared up at the ceiling as the baroness stood over them. "No?"

"No," Miranda repeated, more firmly. "The gun is mine."

And she couldn't but punish herself now for having lost her aunt's letter, which doubtless would have made sense out of all this. And she couldn't but punish herself for not keeping the gun safe, and not retrieving it when it was lost, and not grabbing hold of it now—it was an evil tool in the wrong hands, that was sure. No, she would grab hold of it and take it away, as Inez de Rougemont and Mrs. Chatterjee and all the other witches had required in her dream. No, she would—but at that moment Jean-Baptiste came suddenly alive and seized her by the elbow. "She'll kill you," he murmured.

The baroness laughed. "Oh, I will," she said. "Nothing can take this away from me." As she half-turned to retrieve the book, her feet made a little tripping stutter almost like a dance step. Instead of crossing in front of Miranda, she moved the other way around the piano. When she stood in front of the dark entrance to her bedroom, she bent down over the keyboard. And with the index finger of her left hand she picked out hesitantly a little tune, which Miranda in time would come to recognize. In the third act of *The White Tyger* it would build to a crescendo, the whole orchestra sawing and blowing and pounding away: Nicola Ceausescu triumphant as she accepted the burden of her destiny.

Then she reached out for the book and turned it around so she could read it under the candelabrum. "On a clover if alive erupts a vast pure evil a fire volcano," she said. Pointing the gun at them, she fired, and Miranda felt the hot blast of air. She saw fire spit from the muzzle. Holding up the pistol in her right hand, the baroness blew out the candles one by one.

Now everything was lit by the soft glow of the gas, or almost everything. Traces of light still lingered by the baroness's upraised hand. It was a hot red glow, different from before, and the creature that materialized on the long barrel was different also. It crawled out of the muzzle and squatted above it, an ugly, toadlike creature.

Isaac Newton: Inventor of the palindrome, Miranda thought for a split moment.

"Do your worst," murmured the baroness. And the toad leapt immediately for the open window, suspended on the air by a repulsive flap of skin that stretched between its arms and its knees. It glided down to the windowsill and leapt away.

Miranda felt a terrible relief to see it go, a sense of terrible foreboding. Later the relief dissipated but the foreboding did not.

When the creature leapt into the air above the Piata Revolutiei it did not disappear. Already the next morning it was lurking in the corner of the council chamber in Petersburg, where the czar's foreign minister delivered an ultimatum to the German ambassador, together with a public accusation. The czarevich had been poisoned, murdered, destroyed by cruel treatment while he was in German hands, his majesty was sure.

And the next day it was gliding in the wet clouds above staff headquarters on the River Bug, as General Antonescu rejoined his old comrades from the sixth army. Enormous and impressive on his white horse in the rain, he was greeted as a hero by the assembled officers, and by the soldiers also when he toured the forward trenches under his command.

And it hopped in the slippery, fetid mud of the Fedorivka Salient a week later as the Russians began their new offensive. All along that section of the front there was discomfort and disorder, but no bloodshed. And there was hot weather and constant rain, which threatened to wash away the pontoon bridges of the Russian engineers. But there was no artillery barrage, no death in the barbed wire. The air stunk of petrol and exhaust as the new armored vehicles crossed over. The soldiers marched in their raincoats with their weapons on their backs, while the divisions of the Sixth Roumanian Army Group withdrew to their established positions farther west.

15 *Throat Surgery*

THESE WERE ALL scenes from *The White Tyger*, the baroness's opera or song cycle, plotted but not written down. Also plotted was the climactic moment when the German authority in Bucharest, stung with treachery and astonished by the Russians' quick advance through the Ukraine, sent Colonel Maschmann to arrest the baroness in the People's Palace. Their way was blocked by fifty thousand citizens, who sang patriotic songs and pelted the Germans with rocks and bottles until they were forced to withdraw.

At five o'clock, Nicola Ceausescu stood on the balcony to acknowledge the crowd. In the opera, by then the bracelet of the white tyger was already locked to her wrist. The aria she sang there, performed as if upon the great stage of the world, marked the beginning of her third and final act.

But on the night when, gun in hand, she picked out these same musical themes for Miranda and Jean-Baptiste, that hour of victory was still two weeks away. Now suddenly there was a noise in the corridor. Servants, alerted by the muffled sound of gunfire, had come to the baroness's room. Despite the lateness of the hour they pounded on the door.

"Come in," said the Baroness Ceausescu. "You see I've found these two together. Take them away—no, wait. Take her to her room. Lock the door and post a guard. I will secure an order from the Committee for Roumanian Affairs. As for the man, leave him—no, take him away. Take him to the Gara de

Nord. Put him on a train to Cluj. If you set foot in Bucharest again, you are a dead man."

These last words she spoke to Jean-Baptiste, who had risen from the armchair. "Please, ma'am," he said. But then some rudeness and familiarity crept into his voice. "Don't turn me out. It's been too long. Too many tricks I've played for you."

Was that a threat? Miranda thought. He stood shaking and twitching with his hands held out. "Pay his ticket," said the baroness. "I'll give you the money. Nothing else but just his clothes. He came to rob me for his wages after all I've done—I've got no money here. You tell that to all the others. Here I live in my little room, for your sake and for Great Roumania. Take whatever you want. I've got nothing of my own."

"Ma'am," said the underfootman. "On whose authority? Ambassador Moltke says . . ."

"On my authority," murmured the baroness. "Go find Radu Luckacz. Wake him out of bed. Tell him to bring some men with him. I'll show you. Are you Roumanians?"

She stood by the window with the gun in her hand. Miranda could see how she was agitated and upset, and when the old man started to weep, a complementary tear ran down her perfect cheek. "Oh, Jean-Baptiste, what have you done to me? What have you made me do? No—I can't stand it. You see I will not cheat you. I will make you rich. Then you won't look at me like that."

Beside the window stood an ornate looking glass atop a narrow cabinet. "You were in my bedroom," she said. "You didn't find anything there. There's nothing to find. People give me precious jewels and I put them in these drawers—these are things from the Empress Valeria's time. Here, take this," she said, reaching into one long compartment and taking out a strand of diamonds and then another and another. With tears in her eyes she came to the old man and looped delicate gold chains and diamonds and rubies around his neck—"Oh, my friend," she said, embracing him, the gun clasped in her hand. "If you come to Bucharest again, I'll put you up against the wall at Jilava, I swear to God. But this will be enough, won't it? For your little house?"

"Ma'am," said the underfootman. "This is the property of—"

"No," whispered the baroness. She stepped away from Jean-Baptiste and wiped her eyes. "They are mine. Those emeralds were given to me by the Sultan of Byzantium when we opened the new railway line. Put them under your shirt," she said to the old man.

No one had moved to escort Miranda to her room. "She's got no authority to do these things," she said. "In the morning if—"

"Silence." The baroness's whisper was more effective than a shout. Even Miranda strained to hear her. "You have stolen this man from me, stolen his heart. You will not rob him of what I owe him after all these years."

And because of the power of her character, and because also—Miranda surmised—the underfootman and the others had witnessed or heard about the speech she'd made that afternoon in the piata, they took Jean-Baptiste by his thin elbows and led him out into the corridor. He'd stopped crying. There was a cold, desolate expression on his face. Miranda also—two men made a gesture to touch her. But with a flick of her fingers she waved them away, and then preceded them out the door and down the hall toward her own rooms. She didn't turn around, didn't look back. She walked through the portrait gallery as if the men did not exist. And when she reached her chambers she turned the lock herself, and heard them settle down beside the door.

But that night Ludu Rat-tooth came to her. For hours she had lain in her nightdress, waiting in the dark. And there was a creaking in the armoire, and the Gypsy girl was in the shadows, naked, blind. She stepped into the filtered light from the French windows, and Miranda could see her heavy breasts and hips, and the faint glow in her throat where the tourmaline was caught. "Come," she said, and the girl came to stand beside the bed. There were red shadows all around her eyes and stains on her cheeks, as if she'd been weeping blood.

"King Jesus says he'll wait for me," she murmured. "Please let me go to him."

Miranda didn't know what to say. She stood barefoot on the polished wood, her hand over the nightgown's frilly top.

"Take me down," she said. There was no reason, she thought, to go and confess failure to the witches in Borgo Pass. Unless it was to tell them Olga Karpov was a traitor, so Miranda guessed.

"Please, miss, I'm choking." Every time she opened her mouth, Miranda could see the gleam of light between her teeth.

So everybody has a problem, she thought grimly, deliberately. "I'll help you," she said. "I want to find Pieter de Graz."

When she first came to the People's Palace, they had locked her in. As the baroness's power had waned and hers had grown, then she was free to go where she wanted inside the building. Now the guards were at the door again. How much time did she have left?

Peter was gone from his old cell, she knew. Jean-Baptiste had told her. He couldn't tell where he'd been taken. There was no point in pretending someone else was going to help in this world or in any other—no. Ludu would help. "Please, every hour it's worse," she said. "Please, miss, I climbed up to the bridge but it was too light for my weight. King Jesus stood in the middle of the span. I couldn't catch his hand. He had clothes like a Gypsy bridegroom with the knife at his belt. Crossed sashes underneath his waistcoat and a feather in his hat. There's an island where the Gypsies live, he said. He'd built a house for me. He had a room for me upstairs, he said, where I'd lie on my back with my legs in the air."

How romantic. "I thought you took a boat."

"It's different every time." This was what the witches had said, too.

They stood on the balcony and looked down over the courtyard in the steamy summer night. There was traffic in the street beyond the iron gates, horses and lanterns ghostlike in the mist. "What do you mean?"

"Oh, miss, it hurts to talk. Different for everyone—you make it different."

Hurting or not, she continued talking as Miranda looked down into the formal garden and the statue of the violinist or the hunter. The bulbs of the lampposts seemed luminous in the fog, bigger than they really were. "There's the dead world, the secret world, the mountain where God lives, locked in his tower. Maybe more. Here, of course—Bucharest, Great Roumania. They're like different parts of the same country. Sometimes they are spread apart like stars. Sometimes they're inside each other—you can't control it. It's like a dream that way. But you meet the people you know, go to your own places."

Miranda's hair was wet and stringy around her face. Her nightgown was damp. "Like a dream," she murmured. She had been asleep when Ludu Rat-tooth came, asleep and waiting. "Take me down."

"Close your eyes."

And when Miranda opened them, again they stood upon the high escarpment with the mountains in front of them across the plain, and the fat river twisting like a snake. Below them spread the marshland and the dark trees. "That's where we'll go," Miranda said.

"Miss, that's a new place. You've not been there before."

"So you say."

"There's no flying," said Ludu Rat-tooth. "Not from here."

"Why not?"

The girl shrugged. "They'd shoot us from the trees."

Her cheeks were streaked, her dark eyes ringed with dirt or crusted blood. Her hair was knotted, wet. On her knees she searched among the slippery rocks until she found the end of a thick vine that seemed to grow out of the roots of a broken tree. It was as big around as Miranda's forearm, and it hung down over the sharp cliff.

Once before, Miranda had asked Jean-Baptiste for a rope, thinking she might tie it to the stone balusters late at night and let herself down into the courtyard. From there she would find her way through the wrought-iron gate and out into the Piata Enescu. Surely that would be easier than breaking down the door, evading all the footmen and the guards.

He had laughed at her, yet with a sympathetic expression on his narrow face. Everything she suggested seemed to amuse him and make him sad after a few beers. But this was what she'd had in mind. It wasn't impossible. The vine was braided out of three strands growing underneath the rotten, saturated stump. Ludu the Gypsy had already disappeared into the dark. She slid down and pulled the vine taut. And there was some purplish green glow down there. The mist seemed to gather as they descended down a rocky chute, seemed to cling to them and fill the air around them, so after only a few minutes of dirty scrambling she could no longer see the river or the sky. Nor did she look for them, but instead she was searching for ways over the steep, mossy rocks that did not seem entirely real under her grasping fingers and bare feet. Or it was as if she hung suspended on that vine halfway between the world and a dream. No matter how low she climbed, still she hung suspended, even when with aching feet and hands she reached the bottom of the cliff. As she sank to her shins in the wet mud, as she felt the hot breath of the swamp on her skin, still she was looking for the trick. Looking for it and not finding it in her sensations, which seemed genuine enough.

But there was a kind of distance from herself that she remembered from dreams, and in particular the lucid dreaming that brought with it an illusion of control. Maybe that illusion was, she thought, what protected her now as she stumbled into the swamp in her bare feet—the reassurance that in some way all of this was an extension of herself, her own fears and desires.

She trod on something sharp. All the time she was following a little glow, and it led her to drier land. Ludu Rat-tooth was on her hands and knees in front of her. Miranda could see her broad backside.

"There it is," she breathed.

In the half-light Miranda could see a pile of sand or dirt that rose out of the stringy grass. Squatting in her wet nightgown, now she saw what it was: an enormous ant hill that rose in cliffs and towers almost to the level of her knees.

"Find the queen," whispered Ludu.

Everything was quiet. There was not an insect stirring. But Miranda knew if she touched the smallest of the outlying fortifications with a stick or with her toe, the entire structure would erupt into disgusting life. These creatures would bite and sting. Where was the queen?

"Try," whispered the Gypsy.

Somewhere in the deepest recesses of the building, fat and repulsive, lived . . . no. But in a third-floor apartment overlooking the Piata Revolutiei—that was where she might be found. So Miranda did take a pointed stick, and after a little dithering she plunged it into the side of the hill. And she was right, and in a moment all the air around them was full of swarming bugs. Squatting back, Ludu Rat-tooth had a cloud of them around her head, while an army of the soldier ants broke out of the earth. Miranda put her arms around the girl's shoulders and tugged her down into the swamp.

But when Miranda poked her sharp stick into the hill, the world started to change, not all at once. As she brought the Gypsy girl into the water, she saw the light change around them. Before, there had been a copper glow that seemed to gather out of the swamp itself. On the cliff face and on the balcony it had been dark night. But when they'd sunk into the mist, there had been more light down there, and a different light, too.

Now that was extinguished. The only illumination to reach the surface of the swamp came from above the clouds, a rolling front of heat lightning that broke and built up pressure every few seconds. As if under a slow, irregular strobe, Miranda caught glimpses of new dangers in the hot ionic mist, new creatures in the water and among the broken trees. There was a snake in the water; she didn't have to see it to know. But she imagined a cold, flat head would break onto the surface through the duckweed. She didn't have to look behind her. The girl's skin was slippery with sweat, but Miranda pulled her through a channel of deeper water around their knees, away from the anthill and toward what seemed to be an island. The ground scarcely broke over the surface of the swamp. But there were cattails, living trees.

And something else: a man in the dead grass. He came out from behind a green tree trunk, and the light rolled across his face. Miranda recognized him, his yellow hair and formal clothes. She remembered his name. She'd last seen him on the Hoosick riverbank in the snow.

It was Dr. Theodore, the worse for wear. His pleated trousers and white shirt were ripped and stained. He stood above her on the shore with a gun in his hand, a small silver derringer. At first she thought he was waving to her or gesticulating, his face twisted with rage. But then she heard a pop and felt the impact in the Gypsy's body. She heard the whisper in her ear, "Oh, miss . . ."

But Miranda was saved now by the darkness as the lightning shuddered out. Holding her from behind, she dragged Ludu Rat-tooth's slippery, naked body through the water. Dr. Theodore was raging and crashing through the reeds, and Miranda sank into the water with one hand over Ludu's throat.

She let the heavy body down into the mud. One hand was on the Gypsy's neck, but even so she couldn't block the small glow of the tourmaline. There was a snake in the swamp and other enemies on the dry ground. Small blobby creatures had affixed themselves between her fingers, leeches or slugs, and Miranda understood that she was holding a corpse, supporting its head above the surface, feeling its cheek and hair against her cheek, listening to its voice as it whispered, "Miss, please . . ."

Above her came a rumbling of thunder. "Let me go," said Ludu Rat-tooth. Her mouth had lolled open to reveal her sharp incisor and a greenish radiance. Dr. Theodore raged and shouted twenty yards away. Miranda felt a change come over her, a sensation she remembered from Insula Calia and St. Mary's Fountain. The tourmaline bulged in the girl's throat, shined in her cold skin, and in its glow Miranda could see her hand, the cruel claw. But in another way she was still the same, squatting wet and hot and dirty in the shallow water, one arm around the Gypsy's waist. Even so she felt the transformation, and in the darkness she could glimpse the hooked blade of her claw. "Please, miss . . . I'm choking . . . Jesus, please . . ."

Then there was just a little pressure, and the pale skin parted, and the stone was in her hand. Slippery and cold, it throbbed under her fingers as she squeezed it, as if it weren't a jewel at all but rather an organ of the girl's body, something that had held her between life and death. Now she subsided into the water, while at the same time her last breath rose from her mouth. Without further impediment it rose into the air, a sudden radiance. And there was a scratching along Miranda's arm and a little plop in the water. It meant, she supposed, that a wet mouse or a wet rat would soon be creeping up the bank onto the land, where it would find the boat or the bridge or whatever artificial means now led to the island where the Gypsies lived.

The thunder broke above Miranda's head. Someone was pounding on the door of her room. It took a long time to wake her, but then she was awake, standing in her nightgown in the dark. "Qui est là?" she asked. Who is there?

It was Jean-Baptiste. Miranda put on a robe and lit the lamps. She opened the door to let him in. A half dozen men stood outside in the corridor.

Jean-Baptiste had taken off his jacket. He had not changed his shirt, which showed a greasy burn over his breastbone. Miranda stepped aside, and he strode immediately to the windows. "I thought you would have gone," Miranda said.

He shrugged, a tremor of his high, thin shoulders. "You must not judge her. She feels too much. But she is . . . changeable." Then in a moment: "She will change her mind."

He turned to face her, and Miranda saw a mark on his white cheek, a smear of red where the baroness had struck him, she guessed, or else hurt him with one of her diamond necklaces. "Where would I go?" he said. "She will not abandon an old man. You're the one in danger."

He had gone to the armoire and pulled it open, revealing all Miranda's ridiculous gowns and dresses. "She will have changed her mind," he said, "but not tonight. Antonescu has left the city, but she has sent for Colonel Bocu and his men. She will take hold of the palace and dare the Germans to do their worst. There are people camped in the piata because of the murders there this afternoon. More every hour. You can't see them from here."

Standing by the half-opened door, Miranda peered into the corridor at the footmen and understewards, one of whom was picking his nose. "These men . . ."

"Work for the Committee for Roumanian Affairs. It's the German government that pays the salaries in this place. Maybe the baroness will dismiss them all, certainly if she gets the crowd behind her. But until then I've hired them to bring you to the German embassy where you'll be safe."

Miranda stepped back. "I don't think—"

"You don't have a choice," the old man interrupted. "She'll play a game with you, hold you out to show how these Germans have polluted us, the pure Roumanian blood. It is time for a new change, a woman of the people, she'll say, and she'll be serious—she hates you. Remember what happened to your father. When Bocu gets here or his adjutant . . . Where are the clothes I brought?"

"But the Germans . . ."

"Miss, you have no choice! Where are your clothes?"

He meant the traveling clothes she'd begged from him, trousers and boots. "I won't ask shelter from our enemies," she said. "What about my mother and Pieter de Graz? Can you get a message to Andromedes?"

"Miss, there's no time. Captain Sawicki says the orders are already sent. He says most of the guards deserted since Maschmann's troops were withdrawn. When she fired that gun at me it was the signal, but the plans were already made."

Once in social studies class, Miranda's teacher, Mr. Oats, had described the passions of the crowd when they stormed the gates of the Bastille. Just for a moment, Miranda had caught a glimpse of a mental picture—men in long pants and red woolen hats—that returned to her now. The corridor where the understeward picked his nose was dark and quiet. But she could imagine it full of noise and light. "Wait for me," she said.

When the door was closed behind him, she said to herself, "But I won't go to the embassy. And I won't go without the others." She spoke aloud to reassure herself as she fumbled in a chest of drawers for the precious trousers—she had hidden them inside a nest of unworn lingerie in case the room was searched. Time was important, she knew. But after she pulled them on and fastened her belt, after she chose her shirt and socks, she stepped through the French windows onto the balcony and looked down.

In the open air, in the damp summer night, it was as if she'd crossed another kind of threshold. Here she had the tourmaline clasped in her hand. She studied it for a moment, a jewel the size of a plum, and she was not enough of an authority to tell if it had been cut or faceted, or if its shape was natural. It gleamed a little in the dark, a color hard to describe.

And then—did she blink? Or was it an effort of the mind?—she was in the swamp again, and Ludu's body had subsided under water. Dr. Theodore was gone. Miranda had pulled herself up onto dry ground and she yawned and stretched there, kneading the earth in front of her, ripping at the logs and stones with her cruel hands. She was confident of her strength, confident also that her enemies were powerful—not one by one, but in a mass. But she was the white tyger of Roumania, and she had not yet been tested in this place.

Above and far away, she opened the door again and crossed the threshold. "Where is Peter?" she said.

"Miss, there's no time. Our carriage is at the Mycenaean Gate. I'll take you to the embassy—I spoke to Madame de Graz. Just for tonight, I promise you. In the morning this will all look different, and the baroness . . . She is not a monster—I say it again. She will change her mind. Only she is excitable like any person of genius, or any woman touched by God . . ."

The lamps flickered in their sconces. The old man stood rubbing his hands, a pleading expression on his narrow face. His skin was pale, his lips oddly dark, as if he'd put on lipstick—he was trying to convince himself, Miranda thought. And he'd have to go on talking all night, to her and to himself, because the Baroness Ceausescu really was a heartless murderer, as doubtless he was just beginning to understand. So even though he spoke of urgency, and even though the other men glanced nervously up and down the corridor, still he did nothing but talk until Miranda interrupted him. "I know the Mycenaean Gate," she said. "I'll meet you there."

Then she hurried down the corridor the opposite way from the direction he now indicated, ignoring his cry of exasperation—he meant to take the Promenade and then the Summer Stairs, she guessed. It was the closest way. But she turned the corner and then found the servants' staircase he'd once showed her, a square shaft leading down. And down below there was a noise of footsteps and muted shouts; she only descended four turns of the stair before she let herself back into the main building, the second story with its residential apartments. This was King Rudolph's Gallery, which was dingy, dark, unused. The furniture was covered with gray canvas sheets.

But the lights burned brighter up ahead. And there was noise that way, too. She pushed herself against the wall and watched a dozen or so men run past the entrance of the gallery, where it debouched into the corridor. They were looking for the main stairs to the floor above, she guessed. There was no time to lose. Once in the bright corridor she turned away from them and hurried back toward the east wing, the Court of Venus where Clara Brancoveanu stayed—her mother—whatever. The wainscot was gilded here, the plaster painted with rose-colored domestic scenes.

And the door was open, the lock broken. Her mother was not here. The room was dark. Without bothering to light the lamp, Miranda stepped across the carpet to the inner door and wrenched it open—dark there, too. But she heard something, a whimpering.

She waited in the doorway. No reason to frighten the boy, if she wanted him to tell her what had happened. She stood with her hand on the doorknob, silhouetted, she imagined, in the light from the corridor until the boy emerged, Felix Ceausescu. He was small for his age, maybe fourteen years old—smaller than she was. He was dressed in yellow pajamas and his face was streaked with tears. But even so he had some spunk in him. His hands were knotted into fists. "Mother," he said, "is that you?"

Whom did he mean? Not the Baroness Ceausescu. But her own mother, Miranda guessed. "No."

All this was half of her experience. In the other half, she stood up to her shins in the black water while the thunder groaned and the heat lightning flickered above her. And on the shore there was a chicken peering out from underneath some hanging leaves. Miranda kept herself from moving because she wanted to lure it out—an awkward, tiny, yellow bird that now turned away from her so he could fix her with one round little eye.

Before, in Insula Calia and in Mogosoaia, she had experienced the hidden world while inert or absent in this one, sleeping or else sleepwalking. Now, with the tourmaline clenched in her hand, she sensed both places simultaneously, lived in them simultaneously, breathed the divided air. It occurred to her to wonder what Johannes Kepler might have done to keep his equilibrium, calm the greasy, knotted feeling in his stomach, quiet the ringing in his ears. In each world she felt clumsy and half present. But now already she was used to it a little bit, she no longer imagined she was watching herself move, hearing her own voice out of a tape recorder—you could get used to anything. And it didn't take long. That was the lesson she had learned and would pass down to her own daughter if she had one, the way Stanley, her adoptive father, had taught her to keep moving step by step.

But in the hidden world, also, she was divided. No, not divided, that wasn't it. But she had a double nature. Sometimes as the lightning flickered she saw herself standing in the water, her hair lank and wet, her body slick with perspiration, the stone grasped in her hand. At moments she was also something else, a white beast with long, heavy claws. And the strength she felt in her body stayed with her in the People's Palace, where she stood silhouetted in the door. "Come out," she said. "I won't hurt you."

Maybe the boy could sense the white tyger somewhere, because he looked doubtful and afraid. The chicken clucked under the bush. But then it came out, impelled by a need greater than caution. "Mother—where is she?" he said.

"Tell me."

"They were here."

And as he came into the light, Miranda could see he'd been hurt. The sleeve of his pajamas was ripped. The scratch on his cheek still bled. So—not long, and she couldn't stay here long. Whoever had come once would probably come again, once they found Miranda's room empty.

"They said they'd take her to the prison—it's not fair," the boy continued. "She's an old lady, locked up half her life. How could they do this to her? They said for her own protection. What harm had she done?"

Miranda had already turned away. Peter was next—she was wondering if she could find Peter. Listening for any sound in the corridor, she crossed the dark room again. But now the boy was at her heels.

She paused. Felix Ceausescu was a fragile, funny-looking kid, without any of his mother's beauty. Apprehension was mixed in him with a kind of fierceness; in the hidden world the chicken beat his wings, stretched his neck, shook out his feathers. He didn't care about the white tyger. He came strutting and clucking by the water's edge.

"Come with me," she said.

THE MYCENAEAN GATE, leading out into the Piata Enescu, was one of the Palace's most peculiar architectural characteristics, built during the reign of the fifth Constantin, when the Brancoveanu dynasty was already old and tired. Architects had disassembled part of Menelaus's fortress on the Peloponnese and reassembled it into a kind of theater, with hemicircles of banked steps overlooking the ancient stones. A line of ancient columns, blackened with soot, separated the open space from the piata. The steps were divided by the famous lion gate, which led into the palace storerooms. Deliveries to the kitchens were made there. And from the holding cells, occasional prisoners were transferred to Jilava.

Now on this same night, before dawn, Radu Luckacz stood on a balcony set into the outside wall of the east wing, overlooking the amphitheater. Beyond the old columns, unjoined at the top, people were still camped in the piata as a demonstration of support, a protest against the German occupation. In the hot night the open space was marked with torches and small fires.

Out of the darkness beside him, the voice came low, throaty, soft. "Once I spoke to Ambassador Moltke about a grant of money to restore it. Scrub off all the grime, it wouldn't take much. From the German archeological commission—now I suppose I'll have to find another patron! I want it, you see, for *The White Tyger*. A thousand people could fit on the steps. Five thousand more in the piata. I'd build a raised stage. Knock down those pillars. She wouldn't hear of it. A purist."

The baroness laughed. Her hand on the stone balustrade was near his own. A cigarette glowed between her fingers. Even in the hot, damp air, Luckacz could distinguish the heat from it.

He said nothing, but his body was alive to the magic of the night. The baroness had summoned him here to this balcony for reasons that could not help but seem like a pretext. She wanted him to be the one who stood beside her while the world changed, and the crowd in the piata was proof of that. Also the police escort drawn up under the disputed columns, waiting to transport Popescu and de Graz to Jilava Prison as they both deserved; he had recommended this for many days. Now, he thought, the baroness was showing him how she'd submitted to his will.

Hope against hope—surely no one could say he was guilty of impatience. But a balcony—surely it was possible to read something into this, a location that had suggested innocent illicit love affairs ever since that English refugee—what was his name—had included it in his play about the children in Verona. Perhaps the baroness herself did not yet understand the subtlety of her own mind. Since the night when he had brought her the black book and pledged himself to her, he had been waiting for this moment.

He could feel the heat from her cigarette next to his hand. That night she had taken the book and chased him out into the hall, half-dressed as she was, because she was nervous and because she was afraid of what the servants might say—oh, he had been on fire since then. Acquaintances who had known him for years could scarcely recognize him these days. He could not recognize himself. Bald, clean-shaven, the last shreds of hair shaved away, he was dressed in a gray suit, a color and a cloth that was the fashion now. Before he'd been dismissed from his employment by the Committee for Roumanian Affairs, he had always worn civilian clothes—a black, dreary color, it seemed to him now.

Since the night when he had brought the book to Nicola Ceausescu, he had lived in a peculiar state of ecstasy. How astonishing it was to let go of everything that was making him unhappy! How liberating it was to let his mind follow in the path his heart had dug, to convince himself finally that what he loved could not be wrong. No, his scruples had been another word for guilt. Now even in the movement of his body he felt fresh as a twenty-five-year-old.

Why had he held himself back? Surely there was a joy in surrender after so many years. "There, you see," said the baroness. "They're bringing her out now. No, it's the mother. I misspoke."

Under the lamppost in the center of the Mycenaean hemicircle, a modern truck had been brought up. Cavernous, its rear doors hung open. And there were some horse-drawn carriages, too, with all their old-fashioned chains and bits and traces. There was Jean-Baptiste, the steward, Luckacz's friend. He had taken off his jacket with the red piping. He paced back and forth over the cobblestones, under the lamp.

But that wasn't where the baroness indicated as she brought her cigarette to her mouth. A dozen men came up the slot between the stone quarter-circles and passed through the lion gate. They brought with them a woman who didn't struggle, and Luckacz recognized the Princess Clara Brancoveanu. They brought her toward the truck. Two policemen in uniform stood beside an enormous rubber wheel.

"It would be better if they never reached where they were going," mused the baroness. "You said it yourself—they are dangerous. We are too civilized sometimes. Look at the people sleeping like animals in the piata, copulating, eating like beasts. They will want revenge for the damage done. That would be cleaner, wouldn't it? More democratic, surely. Look, there is the Chevalier de Graz."

Another knot of men came through the gate and down the steps. Luckacz saw de Graz with his curly brown hair. His left hand was chained to his belt. His maimed right arm was strapped across his chest.

The policemen brought him to the truck. Then they stopped to argue with the other men.

The baroness laughed again. "I think they're saying it's not proper for the two to ride together. What prudes—they'll be dead in a week. Let me ask you, what harm could they do? I tell you she looks old enough to be his mother. There's some conjuring there. No, I'm teasing you. Where is the daughter? That's the source of intrigue, so I've heard.

"Mother and daughter," she continued. "It would be better if the people washed them from the world. Tonight, perhaps—they're not worth two bullets at Jilava."

Luckacz breathed deep. "What's the charge against her?" He meant the old princess. The daughter, he knew, was responsible for various crimes.

"Treason."

This was astonishing, exciting—a bouleversement, in the French language. That Clara Brancoveanu, who had saved Roumania from foreign domination and then paid for it personally with twenty-five years in a German prison—that such a woman should be taken to the Jilava on such a charge—the world was upside down. His world also as he stood here, his hand near the baroness's hand. "My friend," she said, "don't think I am cruel to her. Tonight is an important night. New generations in a free country will look back at us, standing on this balcony. Friends have become enemies, enemies our friends." And then she told him how Ion Antonescu had left the city and was riding east to take up the command on the Bug river. "The czar is not my rival," she said. "These women and the Germans have been manipulating us. Certainly it is better to have peace."

Certainly it was. What did she mean? "I need men who aren't afraid of a shared dream. We are witness to a great event," she said, and it was true. Standing there, leaning on his hands, he imagined himself part of the audience of a private theatrical performance—an audience of two. Something the baroness had said had put it in his mind, how she would build a scaffold overlooking the piata for a presentation of her great work. In the meantime he looked down on the disused Mycenaean amphitheater as if onto a stage, half a circle of worn stones, lit from five lampposts—five circles of light that did not overlap. And if he couldn't hear much of the dialogue, with great clarity from his position he could judge the movement of the characters: the Chevalier de Graz with his mouth open, straining at his bonds. And the old steward—Jean-Baptiste now hiding in the shadows with his men—why was he here, standing with his hand on the door of his old hackney cab? Policemen arguing next to the open truck. Two separate groups of soldiers and irregulars. The gray-haired princess with the empty circle around her. Was it true her life was worth nothing after all this time?

But Miranda Popescu had not made her entrance. No, there she was. She had not come in through the lion gate. But she had found the door at the top of the amphitheater, not thirty meters from where Luckacz stood. She was dressed in trousers and leather boots, and she was helping someone down the big stone steps, each one waist-high. It was the baroness's son, barefoot and in pajamas.

From beside him in the dark Luckacz could hear a stifled hiss. Together, he and Nicola Ceausescu watched them negotiate the long stones. With his attention diverted, Luckacz didn't see the moment when the drama shifted down below, changed from a static circle around the arguing policemen. Now there was sudden movement, and de Graz was free. He had gotten his left hand free, and one of the policemen was down, and he had the man's service pistol in his left hand—Luckacz knew how awkward and unnatural that would be. But no, the fellow was a perfect devil, ambidextrous, obviously. Luckacz heard the smash of the gun and saw the second policeman stagger back, fall down. De Graz was biting and pulling at the laces that held his right arm to his body, and when four men tried to seize him he slipped between them—a wrestler's trick, Luckacz supposed. Then the fellow darted back to let two men sprawl into one another.

Certainly it was peculiar watching from above, as if standing in the expensive box seats. Had all this urgent motion been rehearsed and choreographed for the stage? With one part of his mind he could not but admire de Graz's cunning and ferocity—he had grabbed one of the men from behind with his maimed arm and was dragging him along not to the shelter of the piata but back into the amphitheater, where Miranda Popescu and the boy came down to join him. But with another part Luckacz was analyzing the incompetence of these men, because it was eighteen to one, after all, even though most of them were untrained irregulars, armed only with sticks. And with a third part he realized with disgust that his romantic dream was over suddenly, at least for this particular night.

"By God, he is the devil," he murmured as de Graz threw down the man and stepped into the circle of the central lamppost and met Miranda there; they clung and kissed.

"Yes."

The baroness's voice was calm, as if she, too, had achieved a sort of separation. "The devil's stink—can you smell? There's conjuring here. This isn't what you see," and she was right. There was some kind of mephitic odor that was tickling his nostrils, a swamplike smell of vegetable decay, borne to him on the hot wet air. "I thought she was a marker in her aunt's dead hand or else a pawn. Maybe she was—not now. This is not de Graz's fight."

Then she turned toward him and her face was near his own. "I need men I can depend on," she said.

For a moment he didn't know what she was talking about. In the amphitheater some of the militiamen had run away, scattered beyond the pillars into the dark square. Luckacz wondered if a detachment of German guards had been attracted by the sound of gunfire. Perhaps that's why the men had fled, though several still lay where they had fallen, wounded or stunned. It could not be that this one man had beaten all of them, even if some kind of sorcery or conjuring or trickery was involved—what had the baroness said? De Graz stood with the Popescu girl like the hero and heroine of some sentimental opera. But they were killers, both of them, monsters of an arrogant, decadent class.

"They must be caught," murmured Nicola Ceausescu. "Don't let them get away."

Was that even a possibility? Surely German soldiers would soon appear to restore order. But what was he doing now, that fool Jean-Baptiste? He had stepped into the light, motioning to his broken-down horse and two-wheeled hansom. Some other man had already stepped onto the box.

"They must not get away," the baroness repeated, fumbling with something in her cloak. Now suddenly her voice was hard with urgency, and she leaned forward with her left hand on the balustrade while she struggled with something.

He didn't want to see what it was. He understood her and his mind leapt ahead. She meant there was a part for him in this drama, if he hoped to claim his prize. One more thing—there was always one more thing for him to do. As he left her, as he climbed in through the French doors, he could imagine the last words of his former self, harsh, nasal, awkward: "Ma'am, I am desolated to remind you that I do not have the correct authority under the circumstances, and no official position whatsoever. The Committee for Roumanian Affairs has seen it appropriate to . . ."

Unspoken, they filled his ears as he made his way downstairs through the dark corridors toward the gate.

THE BARONESS WAS correct. Incompetence or cowardice could not have by themselves explained de Graz's victory over the militiamen and thugs in the stone amphitheater. But in the hidden world the white tyger protected him. She had climbed out of the water in the flickering darkness. And in a circle of dead stumps she had found a shallow indentation or a dell. The chicken ran behind her, clucking softly, its indignation conquering its fear.

There was another animal in the bottom of the dell, an animal she'd searched for and was glad to see. It was hampered or wounded, a small brown ape with a hurt paw. And she knew or suspected or felt the presence of another anomaly, a living insect in the primate's heart or brain, that served the same purpose as the living tourmaline inside Johannes Kepler. Or else not the same purpose but a similar one—analogous, as her adoptive father might have said. Or else not the same at all, maybe, but she had faith. Inside the wounded man was the boy she had once known, a beetle with a scarlet carapace, the prettiest insect in the world, at least to her after long last.

She saw him in the bottom of the stone amphitheater near the open truck. In the hidden world he was beset by a different kind of enemy, a dozen or more wild pigs that were the tyger's natural food. Panicked, they could already smell her. She didn't even have to open her mouth for them to lose themselves in fear. And the ape, emboldened, moved away from the rocks where he'd been cornered. With a few slaps of his paw he knocked one over and scratched open its belly. They were squealing now.

Then in the circle there was another creature that now showed itself, a mother hen. Behind the tyger, the young chicken screamed and staggered down the slope. Wings raised, it beat the air. Miranda was glad and touched to see its energy and courage as it scrambled down the last stone blocks, a boy in ripped pajamas. "Mother, please," he cried.

And he was scolding the militiamen who hung around the old woman underneath the lamppost—not so old, maybe. And even if she'd suffered a long time, still she was capable of acts of kindness, as she showed now in the simple way she reached out her arms. And there was Pieter de Graz, of course, the Chevalier de Graz, a gun in his left hand. Miranda went to meet him in the light.

THEY HAD BEEN careless because they did not think him capable without his hand. They thought he was weak and broken after beating him every day and pissing in his water. They didn't know he was used to this, and had learned to store his strength in the Eski Seray in Adrianopole. Before that in his Berkshire County high school he had understood what it was to be underestimated, a sweet joy when he was younger and now a source of strength.

For days they had kept him in a dark hole below ground level, with greasy brick walls. They had taunted him with news of his condemnation. His wound had scarcely scabbed over, and they had not changed his bandages. But he kept himself clean now. He studied the endless moments even in the dark, searching for his opportunity. He was wiser than the Chevalier de Graz, less impetuous.

Now he stood under the lamppost while Miranda pressed her face into his filthy, stinking shirt. These men turned out to be stupid fools, once he had a pistol in his hand. He pulled Miranda out of the light, while at the same time he could see the steward who'd been kind to him during the first part of his confinement. Kind to him, and he had forced others to be kind. Now he gestured toward a horse-drawn carriage. "It's all right," Miranda said. "We'll go with Jean-Baptiste."

Even in this chaos, he noticed something odd about the way she spoke. Even with his wounded arm around her waist, he noticed an odd distance, a stiffness in her body. Part of her was gone from him, he thought, which made him look around the amphitheater in a wide circle, past the steward, past the middle-aged woman who was soothing the crying boy, past the men who were massing to attack, past the wounded men on the stones, past even the bald man in the gray clothes who was running through the seats above the lion gate—did he recognize him?

But this was not the only movement. High above there was a balcony that jutted from the wall. It was lit from below and to the side. A woman stood there, and when she leaned over the balustrade she cast a wild, gesticulating, enormous shadow on the stucco wall. She had an old-fashioned revolver in her hands, something left over from the Turkish wars—no, he recognized it, too. He almost felt the weight of it, especially when he saw the long shadow of the barrel droop and flutter. The woman was too weak to fire it. Her wrists were too weak to hold it straight. Now she opened it and fussed over the drum—she wouldn't hit anything, he thought, except by luck. It would have been a hard shot even for him. He pulled Miranda down out of the light and did not change the angle of the pistol in his left hand, which searched among the militiamen for the first one with the courage to step forward. The bald man—certainly he had seen his face before!—was shouting in Roumanian. And there was a crash from Prince Frederick's big revolver, and a scream from up above, and the long black shadow of the barrel jumped against the stucco wall and disappeared. She'd lost it, dropped it, missed them by a mile. There were other things to worry about now.

IN THE HIDDEN world, as graceful as a debutante, Miranda stepped into the center of the dell. The wet ground sucked at her boots. The pigs had squealed and run away. But Miranda felt the presence of one more, a big lurking brute of a red boar, above her somewhere indistinct in the dark undergrowth. The mother hen clucked over its chick. Small dangers had been thwarted. Big dangers remained. Unexpected dangers—just as Miranda turned her head, she saw a cat on a stump above the crooning birds. One-eyed, bitten, baggy knees, it was a cat she recognized.

And on the bare stones of the Mycenaean Gate she heard a scream of horror as she pulled away from Peter de Graz. Clara Brancoveanu was on her knees, and the boy—Felix Ceausescu—had been hurt. He lay with his legs twisted and the blood leaking around him, staining his yellow silk pajamas.

"Come," said Jean-Baptiste.

"Mother, come."

But she didn't come. She knelt crooning and crying over the wounded boy. She wouldn't even look at Miranda or say anything to her. But instead she plucked at the sleeves of her old cardigan. Nor was she able, Miranda saw, to offer any solace or comfort or assistance, or anything but her own suffering, her gift to the world.

"Mother—please come," but it was useless. The hen had lost her chick.

That was the image Miranda took with her. After a few minutes, in the cab, she might have wanted to ride forever through the streets of Bucharest, gripping Peter's strong left hand. In the hidden world she was alone, and she took a few steps backward from the bottom of that dell where the mother hen poked at the little yellow body. Other creatures were now appearing from the shadows, but Miranda left them behind. She climbed up onto the high pinnacle of rocks, where she now found herself still dressed in her nightgown, the jewel gleaming in her hand. That place, that rocky overlook, she would recognize it as a fulcrum or a transition point, however it appeared to her; she laid the tourmaline in a mossy crevice at her feet. Once it had left her fingers she could no longer see the ice mountains at the horizon or the steaming wetlands below her, the heavy curve of the river. Her single reality was the dark, cramped, jolting interior of the hansom cab as it raced around the carrefour and up the Strada Stirbei Voda.

She lay back against the ripped leather banquette. She might have wanted to ride north and west forever, away from the gate where they had left her mother and the boy. But after five minutes they turned the corner, and the horse pulled up beside the entrance to Cismigiu Park.

She found she had her eyes closed, and like an animal she was trying to decipher all the smells—the grime and grease inside the cab, the horse and its urine. She felt the springs release as two men clambered from the box. "Come," said Peter. The door opened from the outside.

And she opened her eyes, and Peter handed her down the tiny metal steps. Jean-Baptiste was there. Miranda would have said something, only he started in at once. "Mademoiselle, you must hurry now. Take the path down to the boathouse. The Chevalier will show you. Madame de Graz is there, and the other gentleman."

It was cool and quiet here so close to dawn. They had stopped under a row of enormous trees. Two other private carriages were also at the curb, and the high-hatted coachmen were smoking cigarettes and talking. "What about you?" Miranda asked.

Jean-Baptiste grimaced. "I'll go back. My services—"

"You can't go back. Did you see? She shot her own son from the balcony."

Again he winced. "It was confusion. No one can say—"

"But I saw her. Everyone saw her."

The steward shrugged his narrow shoulders. "You cannot know this. And you must hurry now. There is no time to discuss such things. You cannot know. Did you hear her crying?"

Agitated, he rubbed his pale cheek. Then he blundered on. "You know more than anyone that pistol could not be fired. This was an accident. Your mother will stay there till the doctor comes. Doctor Hartnagel—the boy will recover, you will see. The baroness is brokenhearted now. Who could comfort her if I could not?"

Peter was tugging at Miranda's arm. But astonished by the old man's stubbornness, she would not go. "Mademoiselle," he continued, "I cannot expect you to understand. I say again this is not the safest choice for you. The German embassy is not so far, as I suggested. All of you, I think. It would be better to take refuge there."

"No. We are Roumanians."

There would come a time, Miranda decided, when words like these wouldn't sound so implausible in own ears when she said them. But Jean-Baptiste seemed to buy the concept. He nodded, grimaced, turned his head until she could see the outline of his big blade of a nose in the light from the lamp-post across the street. "You're the one who needs a refuge," she said.

"She will not hurt me. You will see. I will ride to the station and then return. You must be gone by then."

With his foot on the metal step, he whistled to the driver. Peter motioned with his bandaged arm. Jean-Baptiste held the cab door open as the driver cracked his whip. "Mademoiselle, we will meet again in happier times!"

Miranda didn't think so. Frustrated, she turned her back even before the cab had pulled away. Peter hurried her down the path, which divided a sculptured slope of grass. There was a smell of something sweet.

She felt tears on her cheeks, but she was angry at herself. "She wouldn't leave him," she said, meaning Clara Brancoveanu. "And now he won't leave her," she said, meaning Jean-Baptiste. "They'll go to prison for it, maybe worse. It doesn't matter. Not to them.

"But I left her in the mud," she continued, meaning Ludu Rat-tooth. "I left her to die in the mud. I left her twice. I'm not like them. What does that make me? What kind of friends do I deserve?"

Peter cleared his throat. "Mademoiselle—"

"Don't call me that! Please don't call me that. It was horrible tonight, just horrible. You don't even know everything that's happened."

She turned to him and put her hands on his arms. But he was stiff, uncomfortable, and he stepped away from her. "Je vous en prie," he said, and then continued on in French. "It is my mother."

Ahead of them there was some sort of lake or pond. Away from the streetlights, the dark could scarcely be penetrated, even though above them the sky was purple now. But there was a lantern on a raised dais, and Miranda could see some sort of brickwork, and beyond it the glimmer of the water.

Another lamp was lit. A voice came out of the darkness. "Pieter, is that you?"

And with a shock Miranda decided that her problems—what she'd done, what she'd failed to do, what she must do now—were not the only ones. What was Peter thinking now? Because of course his mother had died of cancer in the Berkshire Medical Center not so long ago.

Just a quick glimpse, and then back to herself: Regardless, either of Peter's mothers was likely to be more alive to him than the strange, distant, defeated yet indomitable woman that Miranda had abandoned just a few minutes before. Doubtless at this moment she was in awful danger. If only Miranda had been able to convince her to leave. But if she had come, what then? Could Miranda have protected her? So, another failure altogether, like her failure to retrieve her father's gun. What part of tonight's disasters had been caused by the two spirits she had glimpsed in the baroness's antechamber, hovering above the long, octagonal barrel of Prince Frederick's revolver?

Peter had left her in the meantime, had hurried past her to the gazebo by the shore. The light was burning brighter, and Miranda could see the high, small, cylindrical colonnade, the roof like a witch's cap. There were other people among the pillars, but in the center of the dais Peter bent down to embrace the old woman, Madame de Graz. Miranda trudged up the steps feeling a rueful, self-critical resentment.

She was not alone. Inside the circle, she saw Andromeda leaning against one of the thin, fluted pillars. She was stylishly dressed in a black suit and a white shirt, and her arms were crossed over her chest. As Miranda hesitated at the edge of the light, she turned to her and rolled her eyes.

Then she came to stand beside her. With her back to Peter and his mother and her hands in her pockets, she stood looking out into the dark. As always, Miranda decided, there was something intimidating about her. "Hey," she said.

"Hey."

"Sort of a happy ending," said Andromeda.

Miranda wondered. Sure, the old lady was laughing and crying, which was something she had read about but never seen before. Madame de Graz's eyes shone milky in the lantern's light, and she looked up at her son with an adoring expression, touching his face with her wrinkled hand. If Peter was conflicted, if he was remembering his other mother who had died, he didn't show it. But he smiled as the old lady held the stump of his wounded arm, pressed it against her cheek and chest.

Andromeda giggled. "Please, enough already. Do you remember my dad?"

"Sure."

"Once he came to visit from California. He brought me an autographed copy of a book called *Even Cowgirls Get the Blues*. This was a long time ago."

They spoke in English. "Oh, A.," Miranda said.

But then she didn't know how to continue. "I've missed you," she said, which wasn't what she meant.

Andromeda half turned. She raised one eyebrow, a characteristic gesture. Miranda could remember her practicing it in the bathroom.

"Meanwhile, it's time to go," Andromeda said. She wore patent-leather boots. Now she walked over to the steps. But Peter hadn't moved, hadn't even acknowledged their presence.

"Aren't we going to wait?" Miranda asked. Then, panicked: "Isn't Peter coming?"

"That's what I'm gathering. This is Mrs. de Graz's plan. She made the arrangement with that guy in the bad clothes. You know, from the palace."

"Jean-Baptiste?"

"Yeah. That guy."

Peter and his mother were talking. All smiles were gone, all tears dried up. He was nodding as he looked toward Miranda, and his expression now looked almost angry. No, colder than that. Resolved.

What had changed, all in a moment? Now he came toward her. "Mademoiselle."

And he continued in French: "Already you've stayed here too long. You have enemies, we both have enemies. My mother has arranged a place for you, if you go with Prochenko now. I myself—"

"What are you talking about?" Miranda said. She reached out for his hand and pulled him toward her against one of the pillars. He flinched.

But she didn't know what to say to him, so he continued. "They will be looking for me and my mother, too. Since what happened to that boy—"

"But you didn't have anything to do with that!"

"So what difference does that make? Do you think she'll take responsibility?" he said, again with something like anger in his face. "This is an opportunity for her."

He meant the Baroness Ceausescu. "I made my oath to your father to protect you. Sometimes you make me forget that," he said and paused.

Then he went on: "But then other times I understand it—that boy was fourteen years old. He had no business there. What is clear is that I will attract more trouble to you, at least now."

Mme. de Graz had lingered out of earshot at the far edge of the little colonnade. Andromeda had stalked down the steps into the dark. Miranda and Peter were alone, as alone as they were going to be. "Sure," she said in English. "We'll split up for a few days. Then you'll come find me."

She'd grabbed hold of his hand. But now she realized he was pulling away from her, so she let it go. "You don't understand," he said. "If I go or stay, it won't be what you think. Worrying about me, thinking about me and how we should behave—you don't have time for that. I don't have time for it—you want something, but you don't know what it is."

"I do know," she said, which was a lie.

He held up his maimed arm, held it toward her. "What I know is what you want makes me forget myself. You want me to be some kind of boy, like that boy Felix Ceausescu or some other boy. You want that because it keeps you sure of what you are—not even what you are, but what you were. Listen to me: I am the Chevalier de Graz, and not someone from your past. I was your father's aide-de-camp—I gave my word. And that wasn't to make you happy, but to keep you safe. And bring you safe to your own country, where you could make a place in it—is that what you've been thinking about? Or is it about me, my plans? Or not even about me, but about Peter Gross."

But at that moment, with the stump of his hand held out, he was the most like Peter Gross to her, the least like Pieter de Graz since she had rediscovered him in Mogosoaia. "This is our future," he said. He gestured into the darkness with his maimed hand. "You have something you must do and so do I. Together, we are back in the dead past."

Miranda felt that like a slap. "You're right," she said, although he wasn't right at all.

Mme. de Graz stared at her with eyes that were fierce, worried, blind. Now she bent down to fumble with the lantern, turn the wheel to reduce the flame, which glimmered down. Cheeks hot, Miranda stepped back to the brick edge of the gazebo. As if they had been held back by the light, the sounds and odors of the park now came to her, the dawn birds quarrelling. There in the wet mist. Something splashing in the little lake.

Andromeda whistled from the darkness, her fingers in her mouth. Often in Miranda's yard she'd stood under the trees and whistled like that, a signal for Miranda to come out and play. A wolf's whistle, she had called it.

Peter had to struggle against her because he did have feelings, Miranda decided. Not because he didn't. So to hell with him; Miranda turned around. Then she ran down the brick steps into the dark. She found Andromeda where the bushes closed over a curving path. It led toward the south entrance of the park, and as they followed it, Andromeda let their shoulders touch.

Miranda cleared her throat. "Where are we going now?" she asked in a voice that sounded weak and quavering, even or especially to herself.

Her friend stalked beside her. The patent-leather boots made no noise on the rough slabs. "I think you know her. She said something about it."

Which sounded encouraging. But it turned out to be not true, or not very true. In a few minutes they reached the

Boulevard Magureanu and the roundabout. Two vehicles were drawn up away from the lamppost, a small fiacre and a larger, covered, four-wheeled carriage with a team of horses and a coachman on the roof. Beside it, a gray-haired woman ranged back and forth, and when she turned her head Miranda recognized Inez de Rougemont.

A Cancer of Decadence

16 *Mintbean*

IN THE MIDDLE of the month of Thermidor, the last regiments of Hanovarian Dragoons withdrew from Bucharest for positions farther north in Transylvania.

In his rented room near the university, Sasha Prochenko lay awake. Beside him, tired out from lovemaking, Elena Bibescu lay asleep, the pillow damp under her lips. Her husband was never home, although his men were everywhere. For many afternoons she had risked disaster by coming here.

The first hour of the first day she had surrendered to him utterly and completely, though she'd not taken off her clothes. It had become their habit never to undress, and she'd followed his lead in this. Now she lay in her green shift, her underpants around her knees. His trousers were unbuttoned, his shirt pulled up. Otherwise he was fully clothed; he had not taken off his boots.

And while he thought about the Chevalier and Mme. de Graz, and wondered how they had escaped the net Bocu had laid for them, Prochenko also asked himself whether he would ever reveal to Elena what she must already know. He didn't want to confuse her. When he was with her, after all, he was a man, a lieutenant of the Ninth Hussars, long used to women and their moods.

But she knew also—and it was part of what she had first seen in him—that he was more than that, a creature, as she sometimes told him, out of myths and stories. She felt it in the soft white hair that grew over his legs, the unnatural fever of his body. Still he was damaged from the accident at Chiselet.

Nor did she question him about his past. She accepted the story of his amnesia, even after she had stopped believing it. Maybe this was a strategy to absolve her of guilt; though she often spoke of her own childhood, her anxiety about her brother, she never mentioned her husband. Perhaps that was because he was important these days, his acts and motivations covered in the newspaper.

Her brown hair was undone, tangled around her face. Prochenko lay with his hands behind his head, staring at the ceiling, satisfied but still hungry. Was he meant to live like this forever, equidistant between three natures—or rather, never equidistant, but ranging back and forth over a triple line, a triangle? For in the time he had spent with Miranda after the events in Cismigiu Park, another nature had won out. They had been girls again, for comfort's sake. They had gossiped in English far into the night. Now, thinking in another language, he could hardly conceive of it.

That first day, leaving the city gates at dawn, they had traveled until dark along the Pitesti road. In the carriage they had scarcely spoken, only pausing to change horses and go to the bathroom until they reached the terminus of the cog railway. It was not till after midnight that they reached their destination, a little village in the Vulcan Mountains.

Another black carriage waited for them at the station. It brought them to a hill above the town, a lonely house at the top of a high meadow. It was no mansion, but a simple farmhouse with a wide green roof and black, wooden sides.

This was the house of Inez de Rougemont, who had not come with them from the city. Nor was she waiting for them at the station or the house, though she must have telegrammed ahead. A farmhand dressed in canvas trousers took them to their room on the second floor under the eaves. He had a candle in his big hand, and when he laid the brass stick on the bedside table, the flame stopped flickering. It swelled and lengthened, revealing yellow plaster walls and some religious icons. Also a plate of cold salad: beets, peas, and strips of beef. Also two glasses and two jugs, one of water, one of stale beer.

If Miranda hadn't said much in the carriage or the train, it wasn't because she didn't have much to say. Prochenko could see this. Her face had always been transparent to him, since she was a child at Mamaia Castle on the beach. She sat against the bolster and the wooden double-bedstead, picking at the knee of her trousers while Prochenko opened the heavy windows. He swung the shutters out into the night. There was a moon above the wooded ridge. The air was fresh and cool.

But Miranda took no notice. She sat on the bed gnawing her lips, rubbing her face. She was worried about Clara Brancoveanu and de Graz.

"Madame de Graz is an awesome woman," he said, trying to break in onto her thoughts. "At first I thought she was, I don't know, helpless. The viola lessons, the lodgers in the house. It all seemed a little pathetic. But she's the center of a political movement that's been dormant all these years. Underground. This woman—our hostess is a part of it. And your father, years ago."

When he spoke in English especially he could feel the girl coming out, her cadences and inflections and vocabulary struggling to be heard. And he was exaggerating out of a sense of irony; Andromeda Bailey had not sounded exactly like this. "She was going to take him south across the river, while you and I came north and west. I told her to go for it."

Miranda rubbed her nose. She sat cross-legged on the lumpy bed. She pulled her hair back from her face. How old she looked! Mournful and peevish—older, almost, than he.

"Why?"

Prochenko shrugged. "I'm sick of him. Don't forget, I was with him for a long time. It's not so good, the three of us. We don't need him."

Miranda looked up. "You said that before. You remember when we were going over Christmas Hill to get my backpack from the school."

She didn't smile, and Prochenko realized with surprise he could not in fact guess what she was thinking. Realized also she looked good sitting there, her dark hair, dark blue eyes. It troubled him obscurely.

She looked so tired, but even her tiredness suited her. "Do

you think they'll bring us some fresh clothes?" he asked, changing the subject. He was still wearing what he'd worn to the Moskva bar, when he'd seen Elena Bibescu with her husband. His linen, especially, was disgusting.

"Sure, let's talk about clothes," Miranda said, and smiled. "Oh, A., what are we going to do?"

Standing with his back to the open window, Prochenko considered her. "Have some beer," he suggested.

And she almost laughed, which had been his intention. "I would," she said. "Only I'm not sure about the facilities."

He shrugged. "There's probably an outhouse. And a chamber pot under the bed."

Miranda touched her nose. "I hope there's two of them. I don't want to share."

And that's how it began, because they had a lot to talk about. They had not talked in a long time. Back home (home?), in Miranda's bedroom in Miranda's house, they had used to sit up late listening to music and talking about stupid stuff. In Bucharest, lying on his back next to Elena Bibescu, staring at the ceiling with his hands folded behind his head, Prochenko went over the conversation in his mind, as if he were pulling free one single strand out of a tangled skein, a cord that might lead him forward toward—what? A sense of his own purpose, something he had not had since Chiselet.

In the farmhouse they sat cross-legged on the straw-filled mattress, drinking tepid beer. And Miranda told him what had happened since she had come to Roumania and even before that, since the night on Christmas Hill. And for Prochenko, who had always tried to look neither forward nor back, and whose memory even in the short term had never been good, and whose sense of his own self now waned and fluctuated constantly like other people's moods, it was as if she had thrown him a rope while he was drowning. Drowning and not known it—in the farmhouse and again on his bed in Bucharest he seized hold of this timeline of events, adding to it the chaotic scenes of his own experience, one after another. Once someone had told him that the difference between animals and people was just their memories. Animals didn't have any memories, or a sense of a past that makes the future real.

So, step by step from Christmas Hill, and he had things to add as well, memories of his time in Turkey and North Africa with de Graz—though Miranda knew more than he did about even this, because she'd spoken to de Graz when they were both locked up together in the People's Palace. "I'll tell you this," she said. "One thing I know for sure. Whatever plan my aunt had for me, if it included running some kind of government, or even being some kind of figurehead—I know now I'm not interested. That was where this always broke down. I couldn't picture myself—what? Living in some palace on some golden throne? Telling people what to do? And now I've seen it from the inside. It's the Baroness Ceausescu's thing. Not mine.

"And yet," she continued, "I want to do something. This place is such a mess."

Prochenko took a mouthful of beer. "Your father and your aunt had different plans for you. De Graz and I—our promise was to keep you safe, that's all."

Miranda frowned. "That's what he said, but that's not enough. Aren't you my friend? Haven't you always been my friend?"

Her eyes were pleading, sad. She pushed back a lock of her hair, hooked it behind her protruding ear—a prim gesture that he recognized from long ago. It touched him now. "Of course," he said, and then, halting and unsure, he told her a little bit about himself. "You may think I am Andromeda, but I'm not."

Then he went on to describe all that had happened since Chiselet and the accident. And feelings were never something he'd been good at describing, either as a man or a girl or—God help him—a dog, and so he screwed it up. He didn't manage to say what he meant. But even so she looked at him gratefully, especially when he used his comic book analogy. She interrupted: "Well, that's what it's like for all of us. Peter, me. We're like mutants. My question is, how much of that is just the same as everybody else?"

Hmm, a poser, as they'd used to say, Miranda and she. "I feel so guilty about everything," Miranda went on. "That boy was hurt, killed maybe, for no reason—was that my fault? And my mother—is she even my mother? What does that mean? What's happening to her now?"

"Don't blame yourself for what Nicola Ceausescu does," Prochenko said, the only advice he could muster under the circumstances. "She is one cold bitch."

Now, in Bucharest, in his rented room, lying beside Elena Bibescu as she slept, he translated this comment first into French, then Roumanian, then to English again. It wasn't right. Prochenko knew about dogs, and the baroness was more a cat than a bitch. A cat in heat, and yet she was still cold.

Now Prochenko—the amnesiac Domnul Andromedes—became aware of a noise, the sound of something scratching on the window.

He got up, buttoned his trousers. There was a scratching on the dirty glass. And something, he thought later, must have drawn him to it, away from the beautiful girl asleep in his bed. Some instinct for perverse dissatisfaction. Maybe that was what had attracted the creature across Bucharest from the People's Palace, this creature he saw now, as he stood in his boots next to the window. In the farmhouse in the Vulcan mountains he had stood with his hand on the shutter, feeling the clean wind. He had seen the moonlight on the fields of grass. But in this place he looked into a stinking airshaft, and the glass was streaked with grime.

At first he thought it was a butterfly or an enormous moth. Its wings were as big as his hands. Looking again, he saw it was a boy, a tiny naked boy. And so he opened the window sash as high as it would go, just a few centimeters, just enough for the creature to crawl through. And when, impetuous, he put his hand out, the creature seized hold of his thumb. Without any preamble it bit him. Half amused, half horrified, he shouted, because his thumb hurt, stung as if by a bee. He shook it back and forth next to his face—"What is it?" cried Elena, sitting up in bed, her shirt pulled up over her breasts. And in the confusion, when Prochenko turned back to the sill, the creature had already drifted toward the ceiling.

17 *The Baroness Receives a Visitor*

THE GERMANS WITHDREW from Bucharest as a temporary measure, part of an effort to protect the Transylvanian oil fields from the Russian advance, which had not paused or faltered since the crossing of the Bug. But they had left so quickly and with so little warning, it was as if they had disappeared from the streets of the city overnight. No one in Roumania, or at least no one writing in the pages of the *Roumania Libera*, doubted they would soon be driven back across the border into Hungary.

When the Baroness Ceausescu returned from the conference in Galati on the Moldavian frontier, the crowd was lined up thee or four deep along the Calea Victoriei. She brought with her a treaty of neutrality signed by the czar himself. In a number of related editorials, the newspapers claimed he must have been seduced or bewitched by her tragic beauty. Nothing else could explain the terms of the agreement, considering the weakness of the Roumanian position. No territory was ceded, no rights curtailed, no restitution paid. The baroness in her carriage neither waved nor smiled, though she'd drawn her black veil away from her face, to reveal her neck and chestnut-colored hair.

But the humor of the city was kept somber by an official act of mourning and the state funeral of Felix Ceausescu, the baroness's only child. But in certain neighborhoods all that—the black flags, the suggested curfew—was like a lid on a boiling pot, and there were fireworks and public demonstrations.

In other places these official displays of grief seemed more appropriate. The political transition was defined by public suffering as much as private celebration. When, during the summer festival, black-robed priests carried the centuries-old sarcophagus of Miranda Brancoveanu across the city, their procession was augmented by many hundreds of collaborators, shuffling with their hands behind their backs. By tradition the parade took place at midnight, five kilometers from the Temple of the Sacred Body to the Temple of the Sacred Mind, and in other years it had been sparsely attended. But now the streets were full of people watching in silence as the rich men staggered by, the editors of the *Evenimentul Zilei*, the heads of all the various bureaucracies, the senators and puppet deputies, who had been meeting all these years in Satu Mare under German auspices.

And if anyone grumbled that until a month before, Nicola Ceausescu had benefited from the occupation more than anyone, he did so privately. Her supporters, identified now by enamel collar buttons in the shape of a tyger's head, made pamphlets of her anti-German speeches. It was impossible to criticize a woman who had suffered so much for her country—the death of her only son, shot down by a dangerous assassin who was still at large, though the police were searching house to house.

The assassin had escaped from police custody and fled south toward the Turkish frontier, abetted by a hidden network of counterrevolutionaries and collaborators. In all towns, villages, and cities now controlled either by the army or Colonel Bocu's militiamen, these accusations—complicity with the Germans or involvement in the murder of Felix Ceausescu—were sufficient to transform the nation. Bankers and factory owners were arrested or dismissed.

All this proceeded rapidly. Naïve observers, caught up in an optimistic frenzy, might have supposed they were participating in a spontaneous revolution, made possible by the defeat of the German army. But these were plans of many years, rooted in darkness, now brought violently into fruition by a new nexus of power, a marriage of convenience between Nicola Ceausescu and Colonel Victor Bocu, who despised each other. Radu Luckacz was the link between them, the former chief of the metropolitan police.

And the center of this tempest of activity was the People's Palace, the apartments of Nicola Ceausescu overlooking the Piata Revolutiei. In these hot summer afternoons after her return from Galati, the baroness hardly stirred from her inner bedchamber except to give some speech or issue some pronouncement. She was in mourning for her son, whose death was now conflated in her mind with the death of Kevin Markasev. If her sorrow was profound, her anger had no limit, and was directed inward to herself as well as outward to the world, according to her unhappy custom. This much was true no matter how she squirmed: She had hired a murderer to beat Kevin Markasev to death in his rented room. And from the balcony overlooking the Mycenaean Gate she had fired the fatal shot with Prince Frederick's revolver, before it had kicked out of her hands. Unconvinced by the efficiency of the police, unconvinced that Radu Luckacz could help her, she had reloaded and reset the antique gun, switching the mechanism to its ordinary use.

But everything had been by accident! She had no skill or even competence to shoot a man at such a distance, let alone a child. No, the bullet must have come from the Chevalier de Graz, whose prowess in these matters was notorious. Or at least he had invented the moral circumstances for the crime. And Miranda Popescu had dragged the boy downstairs when he was safe in bed. It was not possible for a mother to stand by and watch her son abducted. Already she had done that once, when Theodore von Geiss had stolen him away to Ratisbon.

De Graz, Popescu, and one other who had been with Markasev in his upstairs room the day he'd died—oh, how that idiotic monster Vladimir O'Brien had tricked her, made a fool of her, deliberately misunderstood her when she'd given him two thousand marks to buy the boy a train ticket anywhere he wanted—out of the country, preferably—with more money to come. She had never cared about money. All she had ever cared about was the safety of these boys who had abandoned her. Who had been so eager to escape her.

All she had ever cared about were her two boys. Ah, God—no doubt that man Andromedes or Prochenko had played a part in what had happened. And Popescu, and de Graz. No doubt the three of them had conspired together in these murders, resolved to destroy her at the moment of her greatest triumph, turn her life into a desert of bitterness and regret. No doubt, finally, they did not act alone in this, but as emissaries from a land of darkness, where Aegypta Schenck von Schenck sat nursing real and imagined slights.

Aegypta Schenck, and the old baron also, the red pig of Cluj. She had smelled him from the balcony—the ghost of her dead husband. Doubtless he had guided her hand, guided the bullet that had killed their son.

Because of the lie she'd told him; in the middle of the afternoon Nicola Ceausescu lay motionless in bed, en deshabille. Of these five enemies the one she thought about the most had harmed her least of all. Unless you could count, as she did, casual insults in a voice of studied disdain. What right had he or any man to call her these things—dog excrement, whore? Oh, he had seen into her heart of hearts. Always she had hated dogs.

But she would have her revenge. Mintbean would find him. Abscess had worked quickly, but Mintbean was more sure. The baroness had released love and death into the world, and they had visited her first of all. Perhaps she could have predicted that. Now already she had paid the price of this last piece of conjuring. The benefit was yet to come.

So she was not surprised when Sasha Prochenko called on her. She was gratified and frightened, but not surprised. Except for Jean-Baptiste, all the previous stewards and footmen had been arrested or had disappeared. The reception rooms on the first floor swarmed with militiamen, and everything was in chaos there. Clara Brancoveanu had been taken to a new apartment in the palace's east wing. Sometimes she sent plaintive messages that begged permission to reopen her husband's summer residence on Mamaia beach—where was the money for such things? It was a mystery to the baroness how meals were produced for her every morning and evening—the sardines and herring and eels packed in brine that she ate now obsessively. It was a mystery how her chamber pot was emptied, how her clothes were cleared away and brought back clean and fresh.

And if these things were magic, Jean-Baptiste was the conjuror, for he produced them out of his hands. She had forgiven him everything; who was she to deny forgiveness? With relief she saw that he had settled in immediately to his informal way of talking. He and Luckacz were her only friends among all these swaggering new people, bullies under the command of Colonel Beau-cul. It was Jean-Baptiste who brought her the news that Domnul Andromedes had arrived. He was waiting for her in the amber gallery.

"You might as well put some clothes on," said the steward from outside her room. "No, the blue is better. And remember about Domnul Luckacz, who is coming later."

Flustered, she turned again to her closet, pulled the clothes down from their padded hangers, though her hands were shaking. What was she, a child? To calm herself, she put her hands on her hips and stared at herself in the long mirror set into the door of the armoire. There she was. Everything was in place, and as good as it ever was. She herself had never understood what the commotion was about.

Now, reinforced, she chose her wardrobe carefully, like a soldier going into battle. Despite the heat she selected many layers of armor—garters and silk stockings, a petticoat, even a corset that laced up the front. And after much consideration she selected—let him wait, the bastard—a virginal light blue with a cream-colored lace trim around her neck and sleeves.

It had not been her custom for many years to wear jewelry or paint her face. But now in a fit of nervousness she sat down at her table with her dress unbuttoned to her waist, and drew out her box of colors and powders. Later she wrapped a strand of platinum and marcasite around her neck, an intricate pattern of interlocking flowers. But she wore nothing on her wrists.

"I'll see if he's still here," commented Jean-Baptiste from beyond the threshold, where he stood with his eyes turned away. "I believe he had an appointment in the new year."

She laughed; she was ready. She hooked and buttoned herself up. Unaccustomed to the constraint, she could feel her heart throbbing as if it were outside of her body, caught between her breasts for all the world to see. What was she afraid of? She was an important woman, after all.

Preceding Jean-Baptiste down the lapis staircase, she sometimes had to pause to remind herself, build herself up, make a list of her accomplishments: an artist famous throughout Europe. And now the white tyger of Roumania, as everybody called her—a title she had not been born to or inherited. These aristocratic dispensations, all that was in the past. You were what you made yourself, a savior, a liberator, a queen.

But it all disappeared when Jean-Baptiste left her at the entrance to the amber gallery—the czar had not even requested that to be dismantled or returned, though it had been the jewel of the Winter Palace in Petersburg in the old days. The walls, ceiling, even the tiles were cut from polished sheets of amber. Anything else got lost in the strange patterns. No, there he was, standing by the window.

She had prepared herself, but he had not. He looked drunk or ill. Mintbean had found him and punished him, she reminded herself—punished him for his disdain. And though there was justice in that and even an amount of pleasure, still she could not but pity him as he stood slack-jawed and slovenly, unshaved, his hair lank and crusted around his beautiful face. As she approached, she was surprised by how hairy he was. She had not supposed she'd be attracted to hairy men.

Nor had she supposed that personal attraction, a new experience for her, would feel like this. How could she not have cherished the qualities that made her strong? Once in a review of a performance in Paris she had read about her terrifying solitude ("solitude effrayante") even on a crowded stage.

Sometimes she'd tried to imagine what it might be like to be like other people, to have had a conventional childhood or to possess an ordinary array of characteristics and desires. But she'd not imagined they would cause her suffering, as now. Love and affection, she'd supposed them to be comforts. The heels of her shoes scraped the surface of the amber tiles, liberating a peculiar waxy smell—really, she should have chosen something else to wear. She felt a mixture of unpleasant sensations: pity, guilt, triumph, and disgust. Was this what Jason had engendered in Medea, her greatest role? Yes, she supposed it was. How interesting to feel it or something like it after all these years, as well as something physical she couldn't identify, a nervousness, an anxiety, a humid itchy feeling on her most private skin, though of course she was overdressed for the heat of the day, even in the coolest chamber in the palace.

Oh, he was in pain, and her woman's heart went out to him. No doubt he felt some version of what she was feeling. She could see the sweat on his forehead and his cheeks. "Qu'est-ce que vous avez foutu?" he said—what have you done?

His linen clothes were misbuttoned, his cuffs and sleeves streaked with dirt. His shirt was open at the neck. His thin, pale, long, dark lips were open, revealing teeth that seemed too big and too numerous, and he licked them constantly with his thick tongue. As she approached she could smell the sweat on him. Why was it that she longed to take him in her arms? Was it because she wanted to comfort him, as she imagined she might have comforted Markasev and Felix when they had evil dreams or fevers in the night? No, something else.

"You grotesque whore, what have you done to me?" He staggered toward her with his arm stretched out as if he meant to strike her. His voice was harsh and indistinct, as if his mouth was the wrong shape for the words.

He slipped and fell forward, and she opened her arms. But his long, sharp fingernails clutched at the front of her dress, breaking the platinum chain and tearing the lace material—she didn't care. She felt his nails on her skin. He dug under the top of her corset and pulled her onto the floor, where she embraced him in a spasm of misplaced surrender—he was the weak one, after all. He was the one who needed comfort and healing. His skin was burning wet. "Bitch," he whispered next to her ear, and then continued in a mixture of Roumanian, English, French—"What have you done? What was in those crates on the Hephaestion? God, you have poisoned me."

The Hephaestion? He didn't know the half of it. Maybe he did; she looked up and there was Mintbean drifting against the ceiling, his transparent wings buffeted by drafts and currents only he could feel.

A SHORT WHILE later Radu Luckacz stood at the doorway to the baroness's apartment on the upper floor, waiting to come in. He had an appointment. He listened for the sound of the piano, or else a whispered murmur when he drummed his fingertips against the door, which was ajar.

But he heard nothing. Lately, in mourning, the baroness had taken to her bed. Was it possible she was asleep? He cleared his throat—"Madam!"—but he heard nothing.

He touched the tortoiseshell buttons of his gray suit, then rubbed distractedly at his bald scalp. He was concerned for the baroness's safety, needless to say. His heart ached for her.

On the night when Felix Ceausescu had been murdered, Radu Luckacz had been the one to bring the terrible news, though in fact she had seen everything from the balcony overlooking the Mycenaean Gate. But she had come in through the long window and stood with her back against the glass, Prince Frederick Schenck von Schenck's revolver at her feet—too late she had snatched it up and dropped it. And her eyes were staring as she uttered little moans. She knelt to retrieve the gun when he started to speak, hid her face in her hands, and for long moments he debated what to do. Should he attempt to comfort her? Lift her up? Take her in his arms? Twenty minutes earlier he had contemplated the same actions in a different context—all that was ruined now, unthinkable. The mood was irrevocably broken. Soon he had left her to go see if he could find a trace of the criminals who had absconded.

Ah, how bitter to imagine what she might have surrendered to him there in the darkness before dawn, or else later in her room, this room! He remembered the clues she'd given him, her cigarette next to his hand. Since then of course he'd had no opportunity, found no appropriate moment to show or demonstrate his feelings. Indeed he felt guilty even to imagine the possibility now, when the baroness was so vulnerable, so prostrate with grief. Instead he had dedicated himself to chasing after Miranda Popescu and the Chevalier de Graz. The girl's trail had come to an end in Cismigiu Park, though he and Bocu had made progress with the mother and her son.

But when he thought about it later and tried to recall the clues and language of her body, the revolver troubled him. Why had she brought a firearm to a romantic assignation? Ah

God, sometimes he suspected he had sold his soul to the devil and had not even been paid the pittance it was worth, not yet.

It was the same revolver he could see through the partially open door, displayed on the lid of the piano. He felt a sudden, terrible despair—was it possible the baroness had hurt herself, punished herself for what had happened? Surely she was expecting him. Perhaps she lay undressed, sedated; he knocked against the door and pushed it open. No one.

But the gun was there, the long, old-fashioned revolver with the octagonal barrel and the plain bone handle. He seized it up, broke it open. There was one spent shell. The other bullets, made of a curious atypical metal, spilled across the polished wood.

Was it silver? Harder than lead, in any case. He tested a bullet with his thumbnail, then dropped it. And with the empty gun in his hand he crossed behind the piano to the threshold of the inner room and cleared his throat again. "Ma'am!"

Still nothing, and he crossed the threshold. There was the virginal iron bedstead where she slept, the sheets in wild disorder, the pillows on the floor. Disgusted with himself, he bent to pick up one of the pillows and buried his face in it, sucked in the smells, a potent, dizzying stew.

"Excuse me."

It was Jean-Baptiste. He stood in the doorway. Radu Luckacz dropped the pillow and turned toward him, the empty gun held out.

Since the night on the balcony he had not known what to say to his friend, if that's what he was, what he had been—fellow sufferer, perhaps. Of course he'd questioned him about the hired coach he had taken to Cismigiu. De Graz had threatened him, pressed a gun against his forehead, he had claimed. It was a lie, wasn't it a lie?

What was the fellow doing there in the first place, at the Mycenaean Gate? Even now, was he holding something back? But the baroness had forgiven him, had brushed away the subject when Luckacz mentioned it. "He would never hurt me," she had murmured brokenhearted, in tears. "Don't take him away from me." So there was nothing further to be said or done.

"Under the circumstances I was apprehensive that she might be ill," he said, his voice in his own ears always striving to a new level of ugliness. Then why was he carrying the gun? He returned to the antechamber and laid it where it had been on the piano. "We had an appointment," he went on, observing for the first time the vanity table with its pots and brushes, the clothes laid out. Was this for him?

"I told her."

"It is important that she must be reapprised of . . ."

Luckacz's voice drifted away. The air was thick and hard to breathe. "Open a window," he said shortly. "My God—"

"She is in the amber room," said Jean-Baptiste.

SHE WAS IN the amber room. Her nostrils were full of the tawny dust. Open and vulnerable, she sprawled across the floor. But this strange man, Andromedes, was not a danger to her. He was too sick for that. She was aware of some slight disappointment.

"Please," she murmured in his ear. "You must tell me where she is. I mean Miranda Popescu. The woman who has killed my son."

Lolling on her back with his head against her ribs, she could feel the heat from his body under her hands. Above them Mintbean bumped along the ceiling, his little face impossible to read. "Tell me," she repeated. "Where is she? For the sake of my dead son."

This phrase brought back a memory not of Felix but of Kevin Markasev, whom this man had known. But that was not the connection. For she remembered Markasev as he had been, tied up for her and waiting in his room in the Strada Spatarul—but there'd been nothing filthy about that, nothing obscene. Nothing to make her body feel alive. But here, no, she must do this to get the information she needed. That was all.

De Graz, she'd have him executed out of hand. But Miranda Popescu, she would punish her, because of her involvement with this crime. And there was no more ambiguity about the baroness's feelings. She would strip the golden bracelet from the girl's wrist, and the crowd would roar for her. She would stand up on the cannons in the Piata Victoriei and the crowd would roar for the white tyger. Nor would they remember the half-German girl, tainted as she was by her father's potato-eating name.

All this was in the baroness's mind as she bent over Andromedes on the amber floor, her dress open at the neck, her corset unlaced. The man had penetrated her defenses, that was sure. She had given something, and she wanted something in return: the golden bracelet. Colonel Bocu was establishing his power in Bucharest and the tara Romaneasa. She needed power of her own. Her skill, obviously, was not in public administration.

She was thinking these things as she pried Andromedes's mouth open and kissed him on the lips—she couldn't help herself. For an instant she remembered the repulsive Vladimir O'Brien and his cold, thick, slippery mouth; Andromedes was not like that. His lips were blistered, dry. Under dark eyebrows his astonishing eyes, blue speckled with darker blue and gray, stared maliciously and sightlessly into her eyes. His pale skin glowed or seemed to glow under a layer of hair so fine it was transparent.

This was a magic, dangerous moment. The door was unsecured. Anyone could walk in on them at any time. Bending over him, pushing his hair back from his forehead, holding his chin in her other hand, the baroness uttered words in the language of Hermes Trismegistus, mispronounced, inappropriate. It was a text she had found in her husband's papers, and with the sheer power of her intention she made something out of nothing, pried open his mouth so she could see his numerous sharp teeth. "Dog excrement," she exulted. "Is that what it is?"

And she was rewarded by a stream of foul words in the English language: "You are such a whore," etc. "Get off of me, you piece of shit. . . ."

And at the same time Mintbean descended as if summoned by these words. He drifted down into the thicker air. The motion was more like swimming than like flying as he kicked down. Andromedes's collar was laid back, and there were many bites or claw marks there between his neck and his shoulder blades.

But at the moment when the little creature somersaulted down out of the ceiling once more, it occurred to Nicola Ceausescu to wonder why she wasn't like everybody else. Why did these situations always fall apart, transform into ugliness and violence despite her best intentions? She had not come here for this. She had dressed herself, painted her face, and for a moment she allowed herself to imagine a different type of encounter with Sasha Andromedes—a table in some secluded restaurant perhaps in Venice or Vienna or someplace far from here. Low, murmuring music. Perhaps some of the new dance steps that had not yet come to Great Roumania—was that too much to ask? Instead she grunted over him like a pig, scratched at him like a cat while he cursed at her. And it was not for her sake he had come, but because of a disease and a compulsion that now forced open his lips, made him choke out a single word: "Stanesti-Jui."

It was the name of a village in the Vulcan Mountains. A convent was there, sacred to Demeter. The baroness flapped her hand, and the air forced Mintbean away. There was no reason to torture this man anymore. Not a single moment more. She wouldn't allow it.

She rolled him over to his back, where he lay delirious and exhausted. She searched in the pocket of his trousers for a handkerchief and used it to clean his face. And then she leaned down to kiss him again, kiss him again and again, run her hands under his shirt.

RADU LUCKACZ STOOD in the open doorway.

As the baroness became aware of his presence, she sat up, put her hand over her chest. Her shoes had come off. Barefoot, she rose quickly and gracefully, but then she didn't turn away. She stood with her two hands spread over her naked chest. Luckacz watched a blush suffuse her milky skin, moving from her neck across her cheeks and to her ears.

Never had she seemed more desirable. Her copper-colored hair shone and gleamed, lent luster from the amber walls. Her bare arms and shoulders were perfect to him, and her expression also, a chaotic mix of feelings that included fierceness, shyness, and confusion. Often he had imagined her lying back on her own bed beneath him, just that expression on her face.

She turned away from him to lace and button herself up. And he could hear his grating and officious voice, coming as if from far away. "Madam, I apologize to have disturbed you. I believe we had an appointment for an interview, and it is already past the hour."

He was enraged. If she had even hinted the fellow had assaulted her . . . But she said nothing about that, only: "Domnul Andromedes is ill."

That looked true enough. So she had been trying to cure him or comfort him. No, Luckacz thought, recreating the mix of passions in her face. Did she take him for a fool?

Still she was turned away, facing the amber wall. "You will send a doctor," she said. "And you will take some men on the night train to Rimnicu. This is important. The Popescu girl is hiding in Stanesti-Jui."

Moaning softly, Andromedes rolled onto his side. This was the man who had been with Kevin Markasev when he died, which made all of this still more indecent. No, she had been pressing him for information. Perhaps that had required some species of false seduction. Ah, God, thought Luckacz. But did she take him for a consummated fool? Go find a doctor, take a train from the Gara de Nord—but why? So she could finish what she started here on the floor like an animal. Oh, this was a bereaved mother with a broken heart!

"Madam," he said. "Let me assure you I had no wish to disturb you. And I am gratified if you have discovered a piece of information or a clue, which might well be significant. As you know we are presently undertaking many concurrent lines of questioning. This fellow especially I was eager to interview—"

An abrupt, dismissive gesture with the back of her hand. She would not even look at him. "It is already done. Please send Doctor Hartnagel and Jean-Baptiste."

"Madam, I believe Herr Doctor Hartnagel is already on these premises. I observed his coach inside the gate not half an hour ago. As for your steward . . ."

If she noticed the wounded fury in his tone, she gave no

sign. Perhaps she was too mortified with shame to look at him, or else she didn't care. "My friend," she said, pulling at the laces on her dress, "this village in the mountains—this is a chance for you. I have spoken with Colonel Bocu about returning you to your old post in the police force. It will be possible for me to persuade him, though he has other candidates from his political party. But I think it would be useful for you to prove your worth. As you know, he is hunting down all the old families."

So that was it! He had to prove his worth. He must be useful to her, and she to him. But these mechanisms of the heart, this was not how they were intended to operate!

She was still fussing with her dress, and as he made his bow she didn't turn around. The man Andromedes had lapsed into something like unconsciousness at her feet. Even so, and even if the doctor failed to revive him, he was the lucky one, Luckacz thought.

He staggered from the room. In tears, for a moment he leaned his cheek against the wall. He'd left the amber gallery, could no longer see inside the door. What was happening there now?

For several minutes he stood listening. He took his handkerchief from his pocket, wiped his face.

Herr Doctor Hartnagel was a neighbor in the Floreasca. Luckacz's wife was his patient, but he was often in the palace now, looking after Clara Brancoveanu. Since the death of Felix Ceausescu she had suffered from neurasthenia and sleeplessness.

Slowly now, the door shut. The baroness had closed it from the inside. Luckacz turned away. There was nothing more for him to see or hear.

De Graz had murdered the boy, but Miranda Popescu was quite obviously his accomplice in this and every other crime. Perhaps that was the source of the old princess's condition, Luckacz considered grimly as he climbed downstairs. He looked forward to the day when these hereditary titles were condemned by law. The Germans had recently considered such a step, but it had failed by a single vote in the Reichstag.

And now this German doctor who had chosen to stay in Bucharest—Jean-Baptiste must already have searched him out, and he met the fellow on the stairs. Dressed in a top hat, carrying a black leather bag, he was hurrying toward the amber gallery.

Despite their acquaintance and their wives' friendship, he would have passed Luckacz almost without a word. But the policeman stopped him on the landing and took pleasure in stopping him, when every moment perhaps counted. Luckacz couldn't help himself. Nor could he avoid imagining Andromedes's prostrate form, spread out along the amber tiles.

"Herr Doctor Hartnagel, you are the one I am most anxious to see. I must inquire as to the results of your investigation into this sad event, as when I spoke to you most lately it was previous to the autopsy, and I have not yet received your report."

"Please, Herr Inspector. The baroness—"

"—is also interested in this tragedy, because it is a matter of her only son. Allow me to insist. Did you find anything peculiar in your observation? Did you for example retrieve the bullet itself, which was lodged, as I recall you explaining it, in or near the young boy's heart?"

"Yes, I did—"

"And did you find something unusual?"

"Not at all. Now, if you please—"

Luckacz had taken the fellow by the arm. Though he was large and prepossessing, like all of these potato-eaters, Luckacz still managed to block his way, because he stood on a higher step. But now the doctor brushed past him, fingering the brim of his top hat. At the landing he turned. "I mean no disrespect. My secretary is just now typing the report. You will have it tomorrow morning, earlier if you prefer. Now I must—"

His voice was pleasing, his Roumanian flawless, better than Luckacz's own. Obscurely disappointed, the policeman turned downstairs, then paused to listen to the patter of the doctor's boots.

He stood in the middle of the Baltic Stairs. Of course he would gather a detail of men, take the night train to Rimnicu, do whatever was necessary to apprehend these criminals. But in the meantime he rested for a moment with his hand on the marble banister.

How could he go on like this? No, it was intolerable. He would have several hours before the train. Perhaps he would go home to wait.

18 *An Act of Mercy*

LATER THAT NIGHT, the Baroness Ceausescu sat at the piano in her upstairs apartment, picking out a tune. Now the dinner hour was past, and she'd been working since the middle of the afternoon on the conclusion of her opera, *The White Tyger*. Now she was inspired to finish it, and she could almost see the end. For several weeks she'd been unsure, dissatisfied by the marches and crescendos of the first part of the last act, all the stirring music that accompanied her political success. But now all that had given way to intimate and seductive melodies. It was to be expected. Much had changed. Her son was dead.

The dividing point was the music of that fateful night, initiated by a song that was both toneless and sublime: "What Have We Done?" Though full of anger and wildness, the composition nevertheless contained a theme of self-recrimination, all the more poignant for having been concealed in the cascades of notes. Later, upon reflection, this theme returned, doubled and changed. As is true with all true artists, it was the tone of this new music that revealed to the baroness what she was feeling—not the reverse. A vital spirit such as hers could not persist in misery. Nor was it inappropriate for this new sequence, which was to determine in different forms the entire conclusion of the piece, to grow out of the old—a mother's love. All love was related. And the pathos that attended the last restatement of the Felix leitmotif—still it was possible to find some hope in it, some vision for the future, after all!

A mother's love, that was the key to it. All her life the baroness had been conscious of an instinct to protect. And if circumstances had conspired to rob her of the satisfaction, still the instinct had flourished underneath the surface. Now for the first time she could let it manifest itself. The potato-eaters were gone! No longer did she have to prostitute herself for them while secretly she nursed and fed the flame, the soul of Great Roumania. Now truly she could be a mother to her country, expending on all its citizens the tenderness she had owed to her son—this was an opportunity. And in it she could see the subtle workings of the gods—this was a theme, too—who take that they might give.

She coaxed out an A minor triad, then the progression, and then the new little tune, as fresh and tentative as a spring flower. Who could have thought her heart could so renew itself, after all her suffering? For most of a week she had scarcely slept, wondering if she would hear on her stairs or in her corridor the footsteps of the metropolitan police or Bocu's thugs, hear their knock on her door.

She played it louder, recombined it, her new theme of love. She was no great virtuoso, but even in the mistakes she trusted anyone who heard her could perceive her honesty, the sincerity of her feeling. Finally (and this was the message she was always trying to communicate), nothing was necessary except that, no diplomatic skill or knowledge of statecraft. Even the details of motherhood were unimportant, the day-to-day pleasures that had been stolen from her. And yet always she could hear the hidden melody of regret—Aegypta Schenck, Kevin Markasev, Felix Ceausescu—moving like a snake through the forest of notes. Even when she took her hands from the keys and closed the keyboard. Or even when, as now, she played as loudly as her small strength would permit.

And it was not just for her own benefit that she played like this, eyes wet, lips trembling. But she imagined she could be heard in the room beside her, which had long stayed empty but was now full. Full of darkness, for the blinds were always closed, the windows covered. The door was locked. She had the key.

How hot and airless it must be inside that room! Now

suddenly she stopped her playing, let her small-featured face sink almost to the level of her hands.

Almost, if it weren't for the man who lay listening through the wall (surely the music was a comfort to him!), she could imagine abandoning this room, this piano, and all her plans and intrigues, leaving it all behind! She could imagine listening to the voice of her own suffering. She had choices. She could go or stay. Right now she could turn and go out through the doors, and call for Jean-Baptiste. He would bring her a valise already packed, which would contain an assortment of passports and papers in different names.

Many times during the past years in moments of despair she'd talked to him about this plan. At first it had been a joke, a way of reassuring herself. But now every step of it was in place; there were passes and letters of safe conduct, scrupulously updated. Nor was there a single way to go, but instead a skein of paths that had proliferated: post horses at various hotels, railway tickets on the local and express trains south, east, west, and even north, for diversion's sake.

What person would she be? Could she still manage the young guardsman, in whose clothes she once walked the streets of Bucharest? No, a woman, she would be a woman, and Jean-Baptiste would accompany her, and she would be his servant for a change—a twenty-year-old peasant girl, not too pretty or too clever; could she still do it? Not for long anymore. Once across the border in Trieste she wouldn't have to hide, and there was money there, enough to bring them in comfort to Geneva and a little house by the lake, and seven million reichmarks in the bank, taken from the discretionary fund of the Committee for Roumanian Affairs. She could live quietly, and perhaps later make a European tour. Jean-Baptiste had handled the details, though she had signed the papers, held the passbook. Several times they had discussed it in the past week alone, a fantasy made real.

No, she had work to do. And the world still owed her pleasure, after all. She pushed herself up. Half-dressed, she strode the width of the small chamber and pulled open the door into the hall.

Jean-Baptiste had put her pickled eels on a tray, perched on a low table beside the door. Was it an hour ago? Two? And he had also placed another tray on the threshold of the adjoining room, some sausages and grilled chops. A plate of meat. All cold now and the grease had congealed; the baroness sniffed the air, repulsed but hungry, too. And she drew the chain with its key from between her breasts, fitted it into the lock, opened the door softly, tentatively. "Domnul Andromedes, are you there?"

Jean-Baptiste had cleared out this room, brought the sick man here, her always faithful Jean-Baptiste. Now she stood in the open doorway, peering into the hot, dark, secret room that might also have been empty for all the noise she heard. No, there was something.

At the limit of her hearing she could sense her lover's soft harsh breath. He wasn't feeling any better. Nor was she able to help him, though her heart bled for him. She wasn't skilled in any of the healing arts. That was a part of alchemy the baron had not studied. Nor had she.

As she stood there in the open door, eyes wet, heart pounding, she was aware of something else. She was frightened—an unnatural sensation, and one she scarcely understood. Maybe she mistook it for another emotion just as foreign, but which shared some of the same signs. Oh, the human heart is such a mystery, especially in the moments that leave us vulnerable and uncovered in the dark of night.

Again she heard the steady, even breath. "Domnul," she said—"Sir, are you there?"

She left the food behind her on the threshold. Cold, piled on its plate, the meat gave off an odor. She imagined Andromedes—lying on the bed? Curled up on the floor?—turn his face into the smell. She took a step into the room and then her feet refused to budge.

How she longed to kneel beside him, push the hair from his hot brow! How she longed to hear something from his lips, a whispered word or phrase that might be different from the insults that had masked, up till now, something more tender, hadn't they? He had come to her, after all. He had come to search her out. Mintbean had seen to that.

So they were alike, she and he, a hard exterior, a tender

heart. "Please, speak to me," she said. But he was too shy. And perhaps he was intimidated by the shell the others saw, the beauty they described in their poems and reviews and newspaper articles. She had never been able to see it. And he also, she could tell, had not been taken in. Oh, he had seen through her on the first day.

Often, though, she had used her body to manipulate others. She admitted it. How could she convince him it was different now, that she had changed? Tonight she had played on the piano, sung her songs—he must have heard her through the walls. Was it enough? What we have is what we are.

She shrugged her loose robe from her shoulders, then shyly spread her arms apart. Could he see her in the darkness? Did she have an odor he could smell?

But his breathing didn't change. After a few minutes she tied up her robe again and left the room. She paused for a moment in the corridor. She did not feel humiliated but fulfilled, a hot flush on her body. If he rejected her now, surely it was no more than she deserved. But she could change; the music had said so. How could she sweeten herself, prepare herself, rededicate herself after all this time?

She reached to shut the door, and then he spoke. Only the faintest murmur from inside the room: "Let me go."

She had not noticed he had a foreign accent or a speech impediment. Almost she couldn't understand him. She stood on the threshold looking back into the dark. "Domnul, it is not safe for you. The streets aren't safe right now. Magda de Graz has been arrested, and I know you were a friend of hers—no, not a friend. I could not vouch for that if I were questioned. But you know her."

It was true she had an instinct to protect. Inside her heart she felt a glow of something like self-satisfaction.

Again the odd, queer, malformed voice: "What is this insect that bites me? Let us go."

Was Mintbean still in there, bobbing near the ceiling in the dark? Was that the "us" he meant?

Frightened, she closed the door and locked it. She turned into the gas-lit corridor and leaned her back against the door. She waited for her heartbeat to subside, but it did not. And in a moment, her anxiety had been replaced by a kind of eagerness; she returned to her dressing room with a sense of purpose. A half hour later, in evening clothes, she found herself prowling the palace's east wing, which was now the headquarters for the Brancoveanu artillery. Colonel Bocu-Bibescu had his offices there, both military and political.

There also were the chambers of the new secret police, a body of men still uncommissioned and disorganized. Matters of jurisdiction and professional conduct were still unresolved. Even so, they had taken over a row of small suites and receiving rooms on the second floor. It was past midnight when Nicola Ceausescu pushed in through the double doors.

There was no secretary at the desk. No one challenged her as she walked the hall. But men with shaved heads and wire spectacles moved back and forth between the rooms, dressed in the shapeless uniforms of Bocu's militia.

This was the center of the investigation into the assassination of Felix Ceausescu, the young baron, as his name was now configured in the press. It was the center of the effort to track down the conspirators, who included—it had turned out—several journalists, trade unionists, and social figures, friends of Frederick Schenck von Schenck in the old days. The baroness knew what she was looking for. Jean-Baptiste had told her. Magda de Graz had been arrested in Tutrakan. Under escort she'd returned to Bucharest the previous day.

And the Princess Clara Brancoveanu was already here—a preposterous miscarriage of justice, the baroness admitted to herself. Bocu was quite obviously a monster; this could not be condoned. Her son had loved the princess, who had conforted him the night he died. When she'd stood up, the front of her dress had been wet with blood.

A man came from the room in front of her, a notebook in his hands. These thugs, these hypocrites, what did they know about a mother's love? Whatever crimes Mme. de Graz might have committed, surely they were for the sake of her only surviving child? The baroness, also, had committed crimes.

And now the man came toward her. Nicola Ceausescu could see how young he was—not twenty-five, she guessed.

Under her heart she felt a stab of pity and remorse. Felix would never grow into a man.

At moments in the past few days, whatever else she was doing she found herself watching the same small surreal drama, performed over and over on her imagination's stage. She smelled the cordite, felt the bruises on her hands. Under the lights, the little figure staggered and went down—God, no.

"Ma'am, you cannot be here," said the officer, his eyes strange and wide. With her new sensitivity to fear, the baroness decided he stank of it; he hadn't shaved. His face was mottled, pale.

"You must tell me," she said. "Magda de Graz—is she . . . well?"

The man stared at her. "Ma'am, what do you mean?"

"I mean she is an old lady. She must be treated with respect. In her situation I would welcome any chance to die for my son, protect him with my death—the last gift any woman may offer to her child. Clara Brancoveanu, too. Please, they must not be mistreated."

Another man now appeared at one of the right-hand doors. The officer gestured to him, rolled his eyes. Perhaps he didn't understand her, and she partly didn't understand herself. The words she'd spoken—"I would welcome any chance to die for my son," etc.—were a quotation from *The White Tyger*, one of the final recitatives. Excerpting it here was not entirely to the point.

The second man was older, dressed in the same uniform without markings. Where had Bocu found these people? Had they worked in the old Siguranta, the secret police from the empress's time? If so, they looked as if they'd spent the intervening years out of the sunlight, underground. They had the same blotched complexion sprinkled with red spots, though the older one had picked up an additional rash as well. His left cheek was lumpy and discolored, as was that side of his neck. He also seemed frightened, as he stood rubbing his hands together. "Ma'am," he said, "that is a point of view. I must assure you it is not a question of mistreatment. We are entirely within our protocols. It is true, though, what you say about these old ladies. They are recalcitrant. Prisoner G. has been unwilling to be cooperative, and she is more than seventy years of age."

Not frightened, but terrified, the baroness decided. Both of them looked ready to wet themselves with fear. The younger one looked at the older one, and the older one looked anywhere except at her—the floor, the ceiling, past her down the hall. "Bring them to me," she said. "Magda de Graz and Clara Brancoveanu."

"Ma'am, that is not possible. My superior could not allow it. If you would make a request for an interview . . ."

"Where is your superior?"

"Ma'am, he is home in bed. It's past midnight. . . ."

So they had homes, these people. Not burrows, caves, or wormholes, but actual houses—the baroness couldn't imagine it. Actual beds! "I can only assume you choose to disoblige me because you have something to conceal. As you know, I am a simple woman, with no patience for your protocols, as you describe them. . . ."

"Ma'am, it's not true! I swear to you they are well treated, both of them!"

What was she doing here? the baroness asked herself. It was true she couldn't sleep. If she wasn't here, she'd be moving back and forth between her music room and bedchamber, or else lying on her narrow bed alone with her regrets. Or she'd be sitting on the threshold of the adjoining chamber, her ear pressed against the door. Or she'd be at her piano, lost in the thicket of notes, pursuing and pursued—"Let us go," Sasha Andromedes had told her. Would he be satisfied with this, her gift to him?

Oh, but there was more. Always she'd delighted in taking risks. Always she had followed her instincts. If she wasn't careful now, Colonel Bocu would carry off the prize. Because of his militia and his presence in the capital, he'd been well placed to take advantage of the potato-eaters' sudden departure. This was how he'd paid her, when she'd invited him to restore order. Already he had taken over this whole section of the People's Palace, while she kept to her own apartment—she, the white tyger of Roumania, who would not stand idle while foreign tyranny was superseded by another type, no less destructive for being native-grown. How dare these fellows use the tragic, accidental death of her only son to tighten their grip on power, or (as she'd expressed it in another recitative) on the throat of the defenseless, naked body of Great Roumania!

And if this was not a meaningful or prudent place to confront Bocu and the others, since when had she ever valued prudence, or meaning either? Every artist knew the truth, that meaning was a trap and a manipulation. Everything of importance, by which she meant the symbolic and emotional pattern of events, hid under the surface. In that hidden landscape she was powerful, though in the surface world she was an ordinary, fallible, and defenseless woman, as everybody knew.

Despite their terror, she saw she could get nothing from these men, these grave-robbers and ghouls, who themselves seemed to have only just recently issued from their crypts. Forever they'd defer and defer, hands trembling, knees knocking in their shapeless trousers. And so she used some of her woman's charm, one of her husband's spells that she had altered to suit herself in the Strada Spatarul, when she'd had Kevin Markasev to play with and work against his will—oh, God, these names, these ghosts, how they tormented her! That, too, had been an accident.

She wore a shawl over her shoulders and her gown. But she reached out with her arms uncovered, and with her ink-stained hands she touched the grave-robbers on their pasty foreheads and their eyes, one after another, the older man first. They shrank against the painted wallpaper. These had been elegant apartments once, now disfigured by dirty wooden desks and iron beds. Oh, she would preserve Roumania from this, the history of her long-suffering country.

These men had the spirits of blind worms, or maggots, or snakes that lie in darkness. She touched their mouths and pushed them back against the wall. Always you thought progress might be made, or that the next success would be the last success required. But there was no end to these people, a tide of derelict humanity, and she was like a boat tossed on its surface until she sank. And perhaps it was the effort of conjuring, but now suddenly she felt exhausted with the struggle.

Ugly, worthless men like this, one day they would vanquish her.

This was not the only time she'd had such a feeling. Colonel Bocu's men inspired it these days.

"I am interested in all these prisoners," she murmured.

The older policeman shook his head, a slow heavy wagging that cost him a great deal. Impatient, with her hand outstretched, the baroness dug into him.

Once again she imagined letting go, leaving all this, turning her back, staggering out through the double doors, calling for Jean-Baptiste and her small valise, abandoning this life. There were two kinds of escape, two that she'd imagined and considered. One was from the final act of Florio Lucian's *Medea*, a version of which she was scheduled to perform at the old Ambassadors the following night. Drawn by dragons, a magical chariot appears, which pulls the queen away from the carnage and the havoc on the stage—where? To Geneva, perhaps, a little house on the lake.

But there was also Klaus Israel's *Cleopatra*, her first critical and popular success, and the performance that had started all this. Always in a moment she could find herself there behind the smoking footlights, a young girl from the country and the streets of Bucharest, standing naked and exposed before the world, the little live snake clasped in her hands, flickering its tongue against her breast. And in the front row the old General Ceausescu, not yet a baron, not yet deputy prime minister. As she stared at his bleached, skull-like face, he leaned to whisper something to his companion, Prince Frederick Schenck von Schenck, hero of Havsa and all that.

Still in her future were Marcus Antony and Actium, or else already in her past. But the snake was always there, bumping its nose against her nipple; she could always feel it. Always, always, always it was possible to escape that way. Afterwards, perhaps, there'd be another journey and a solution to at least one of several mysteries, a partial solution, maybe. Conjurers and alchemists grew into crones and skeletons just scratching around the edges of these things. But there was a quicker way.

She had learned many things in the past five years, studying her husband's books in the People's Palace, perfecting or at least improving various techniques. Even a year before, she could not have coerced these men like this, with all their will opposed to her. The older man had slumped down the floor. He had slid down with his back against the wallpaper and rose-colored wainscoting without even leaving a trail or a stain. He sat on the floor with his legs splayed, his eyes big and unseeing while the younger one pleaded and begged. "Please ma'am, they're all asleep. It's us that keeps them safe and the floors clean. They don't suffer while we're here, you'll see. Even in the daytime it's just questions, I swear. Whatever you heard, it's not true. We would never hurt a woman—"

Then he was quiet, his tongue straining from his open mouth. "It's like rotten wood," the baroness reflected, now examining his voided face. "You just push and push, and it gives way under your hand. There's no source for it, no place where you find the source."

Still she pushed, and the man fell. And the baroness walked down the hall, opening the doors. They were not locked, which surprised her. From the doorways she could see the ugly new furniture and the gilded interiors full of shadows.

UPON REFLECTION, RADU Luckacz had not gone to Rimnicu on the night train. He had not gone to police headquarters to recruit an escort, as the baroness had demanded. Instead, he had chosen to disobey her. No, it had not felt like a choice.

Instead, cut off from his work or his usual pursuits, he had sat drinking chocolate in a late-night café near the station. He had read a foreign newspaper. Several times he had blotted his lips with his pocket handkerchief. Later still, fists in his pockets, he had walked the streets of the old city.

Not long before, he might have visited the steward, Jean-Baptiste, in his room. He might have asked him for a game of chess, a bowl of soup. Or he would have haunted the corridors of the People's Palace. Those doors were closed to him now, he thought. And so, exhausted after a circuit of small streets that had seemed both methodical and aimless, he found his way back to his own house in the Floreasca.

It was on a street of modest houses. Early, before dawn, he

unlocked the door and stood in the hall, listening to the sleeping house.

Until recently, his salary had been paid by the German government on the fifteenth of every month, with regular increases. His wife had always made do, despite some grumblings. It was because she was proud of his reputation for honesty, his steadfast rejection of any opportunity to enrich himself. This included all transactions outside his official duties, even ones that weren't illegal. He had always been precise about this.

Nor did he have cause to regret it now, among his other regrets as he stood in his comfortable hall, decorated with small watercolors of the Hungarian countryside, inherited from his wife's family. His prospects were uncertain now, of course, but he had money put by.

Now he revisited and summarized the musings that had accompanied his walk: It was likely, or at least possible, that Colonel Bocu would require a man of his integrity and experience to run or at least manage the police department. No doubt the actual chief would be a political functionary. That was to be expected. But he might need an assistant or a deputy assistant who knew what was what.

Light came through the colored glass panes in the stairwell, shined on the dark varnished woodwork, which did not show the dirt. Luckacz stood on the coiled rug and removed his overcoat, his hat. He listened to Viorica, the housekeeper, stirring in the kitchen, and then a door opened up above. "Radu, is that you?"

Ibolya was on the stairs, a big woman with a big middle and coarse gray hair that was braided down her back. Wisps of it protruded from her nightcap. She had not dressed for the day.

She stood on the landing above him, her fat hand on the post.

For years now he had carried a secret that had separated them, driven him from the house. He'd been so accustomed to the burden, even now he wondered if he could set it down. But at moments even in these past five years—at dinner, say, or with his daughter in the room—he had been able to see her clearly, laughing at some joke, her teeth still good in her head, her black eyes shining.

"I've come back," he said.

"I've been so frightened. There was gunfire last night on the Promenade. You could hear it from the roof. Broken windows in the shops."

"I believe Colonel Bocu is in the city," he said. "With his regiment. He understands the need for public safety."

He disliked himself for saying this, though every word was true. Still, what a relief to speak in his native language with his wife, the only time he couldn't hear his own voice braying like an ass.

She came down a few steps. "I must tell you. You are to call on him this morning at his house in the Strada Italiana. The soldier came last night."

This was a coincidence, an opportunity. He had not hoped things would move so quickly. And yet he felt suddenly downcast. "What time?" he said. But in a moment he changed course. "Tell me what's wrong."

It was because he knew her well, knew she was holding something from him. She wasn't like the Baroness Ceausescu! She couldn't lead him like a donkey by the nose. "Radu, it's been very bad. People knocking on the door. That nice Doctor Hartnagel sent his family away last week, you know Frau Hartnagel and the little boy. He thinks they're safe in Debrecen, where the Germans still have soldiers. But the police came to question him after the young baron's death—as if he had anything to do with that! He tried to save the boy, he told me. Everything's the opposite now; I'm so frightened. Anyway, last night he came again after supper. Someone had broken into his house. Broken the windows—he said he'd seen you. He had a message for you, some report you wanted, and when he came to the door I—"

Again the coincidence, and if Radu Luckacz been a superstitious man, he might have imagined the workings of some providence or fate hurrying him along, smoothing his path. "Where is he?" he asked.

Already he had promised himself he must search Hartnagel

out, talk to him again, though he had not looked forward to the interview. And now here was the man on his doorstep.

He felt a combination of hope and fear. Ibolya came down the last few steps until she stood in front of him. "He's upstairs. I kept him upstairs in the spare room. He thought you might help him because of the special circumstances. Last night they were going door-to-door, looking for German citizens—"

How long had it been since he'd embraced his wife? He felt like embracing her now. Was it only because the doctor might give him some new information about Nicola Ceausescu? Surely not, or not entirely. "Come," he said. "I smell some coffee."

But even as they sat and chatted in the kitchen, waiting for their daughter to come down, he found himself rehearsing the phrases he might use in a foreign language once again, to discover the two separate facts he needed to know. Both of them Herr Doctor Hartnagel was in a position to reveal to him. This was not providence, but luck, perhaps.

Later, in an upstairs room, he took the doctor by the hand. A large man, he was deflated now. The previous afternoon, when Luckacz had seen him on the palace stairs, he might have passed without speaking. Now he grasped both Luckacz's hands in his. "Your wife has told me you will try to help me. Sir, I cannot express . . ."

Luckacz let him go on. He hoped he had some help to give, some influence in the proper quarters. But he wouldn't show any doubt about that. There would be no point.

After today, it was impossible to guess what might happen. Who could predict the future, even just a single day? Nevertheless it was important for honest and uncorrupted men to show themselves, and to walk forward in the pretense that the world is a simple place, simpler than we know it to be. Men like Dr. Hartnagel would be the beneficiaries. "Tell me," said Radu Luckacz. "My wife mentioned a report you had for me."

"Yes, I was going over my notes. You asked me a question that seemed peculiar to me, and so I went back to assure myself. You remember you questioned me about the bullet itself, which was your phrase. Do you remember asking me?"

His face was big and florid. His thinning hair was combed

into long, separate lines across his scalp. He seemed eager, even desperate to please. These potato-eaters, Luckacz mused, a random thought. "Yes?" he said aloud.

"Well, you were right. I had assumed it was a matter of an ordinary lead bullet, because of the morphology and because I had been shown an example of the service weapon issued to members of the metropolitan police force—of German manufacture, as you are aware. I was not concerned. But after the boy's death and after your question, I went back and discovered that this bullet is of a different metal entirely, lighter and with a larger mass. . . ."

This was the first of the facts that Radu Luckacz needed. Perhaps, he thought, a stronger man would have found it the more important of the two. But he pressed on. "I take it you have prepared a document for me. . . ."

". . . Yes, yes! Signed and witnessed by my assistant . . ."

"That is all correct," Luckacz said. "Now I want you to remember when I left you, because you were on your way to an examination of a person who exists under the name of Sasha Andromedes. . . ."

"Well, yes. Of course."

"And you found this person with the Baroness Nicola Ceausescu?"

"Well, yes. It was her steward who stayed with me after she left."

"And?"

"And?"

"And so what . . . did you observe?" said Luckacz. The sound of his voice came to him, harsh, awkward, foreign, insincere.

The doctor had blue eyes. Staring up at them, Luckacz imagined the fellow had regained some of his superior air: "Well, it's a peculiar case. A high fever, of course. So, aspirin for that. Still, a peculiar individual. Very . . . hirsute, is the word. I believe a Roentgen ray, an x-ray as we call them, would reveal some abnormalities. A properly established scientific laboratory such as the one at Humboldt University—well, I believe these tests would reveal more. There was a report of exposure to the incident in Chiselet."

"So, but he is stable? Out of danger?"

"He?"

Hartnagel seemed puzzled. Was he a fool after all? "I mean the man Andromedes. This is the fellow we are discussing."

The doctor did not blink, did not answer right away. "Without a diagnosis or access to a proper laboratory, I could be of no assistance," he said finally. "But the person you mention, she is not a man."

"Ah," Luckacz murmured. He felt as though he had been stabbed with a needle or a leather-maker's awl in a private place. And yet, how peculiar the mind is! He had known this all along, all this night and day, though it had taken the doctor to tell him. But the afternoon before in the amber gallery, he had passed right next to Sasha Andromedes as he lay on the amber tiles, hoping, perhaps, to give him a little kick with the point of his boot when the baroness wasn't looking. And the fellow had turned over onto his back. His shirt was unbuttoned, his undershirt pulled up where the baroness had caressed him, loosened his clothes for him to breathe. As the doctor had mentioned, his naked flesh was covered with a kind of hair.

"Ah, God," murmured Luckacz.

"I must insist this is a peculiar case," continued the doctor. "When you speak to the authorities on my behalf, you might mention I am prepared to make a new investigation of this phenomenon in Chiselet, provided I am allowed to remain in Bucharest or in Roumania. If there are other examples like this unfortunate woman, it might be the basis of a scientific article."

Luckacz doubted if Colonel Bocu was interested in such a thing. He decided he wouldn't mention it when he saw him, wouldn't mention the doctor at all unless he had to. In the first instance he must try to regain some of his previous responsibilities, if he wanted to help men like Hartnagel or even his own family.

So now he sent him away, paced the floor of his study as he prepared himself for his interview. To be summoned to the Strada Italiana was unusual, and Luckacz had no reason not to be optimistic under the circumstances. But he must be nervous, he decided, as he joined his wife and daughter at the luncheon table. All the gentleness he'd felt that morning had now dissipated, and he found himself irritable as he found his wife and Katalin laughing at some foolish joke. Ibolya had been forty when Katalin was born, and the girl was a younger version of her mother.

Who could predict what might happen? And because Luckacz bore the weight of many responsibilities, it was normal for him to be disagreeable. To laugh at these inanities, to be calm and pleasant and sentimental, that was too much to ask. "Oh, papa, don't be so grouchy!"—what did these women know about the world? He had protected them from it, so they could laugh at his expense.

But he wished he could be sure of the source of his bad temper as he left the house and walked along the street. Someone had decorated the brick wall with an obscene drawing and the words "Beau Cul"—was that anything for Katalin to see not fifty meters from her house? No, there was more to it, other reasons for the sorrow and jealousy that threatened to destroy him. But the political situation was intolerable. In the foreign papers there had been a speculation that the Turks might break the Peace of Havsa.

When he reached the house in the Strada Italiana, he was made to wait, first at the guard's kiosk at the bottom of the street and then inside the gate. The sky was threatening, the air wet. Luckacz had not brought his umbrella, and he protested to the guard, whose face he almost recognized. But Colonel Bocu was not yet at home.

Eventually, though, because his name was on the register, and because he had once been, after all, chief of the metropolitan police, the soldiers let him climb the steps into the house. Then another man in the same anonymous uniform led him to the "library" as it was called, though there were no books in it. But there was an armchair and a desk and a long table with newspapers and periodicals in several languages. Luckacz glanced at the headlines. They advertised the German defeat, the Russian counterattack, the diplomatic triumph in Galati. The Turkish ambassador had been withdrawn. There was no speculation as to why, although Luckacz had heard rumors that alarmed him. There was talk in the city of a secret pact between the Germans and the Turks. Once he had regained his old employment, Luckacz would be in a position to verify this gossip, separate the rumors from the truth.

Then he heard a movement behind him at the door, and he turned. On the way from his house, he had asked himself whether he should first tell Bocu what he had rehearsed, or else wait for whatever news the colonel had for him. The words he'd memorized and gone over now seemed caught in his throat, and he longed to spit them out, disgorge them right away. But it would be more intelligent to wait—there was no need. He had no choice. It was not Bocu, after all.

A woman entered, closed the door behind her, turned. Not yet twenty, he guessed, scarcely older than Katalin, and very pretty with her dark eyes, brown hair. Surely this was Elena Bibescu, the colonel's young wife; how sad she looked! Her eyes were smudged with dark cosmetic powder, rimmed with tears. But her hair was brushed, her hands clean, he noticed at once. She wore a summer dress, one of the gray shades of pink.

All her gestures were furtive and hesitant. She glanced behind her, then stepped into the room. "Oh, monsieur," she said. "You are a policeman, an inspector. Isn't it so?"

He shrugged.

"I want to ask something privately. I have no choice but to assume you are a gentleman. Do you understand me?"

And his face must have confessed he didn't, because she persevered. "I mean you must give me your word. It isn't possible for me to make a confidential inquiry. That's all—no, I've said too much."

"Madame—"

She pressed her hands together. "A woman in my position, there are always people watching, you understand. But you're an honest man, my brother said, the only one in Bucharest to never take a bribe. He's dead now, dead in this stupid war in the Ukraine—what could I expect? He was not a soldier. I knew the minute Antonescu let the Russians through the front; this wasn't the end of all the fighting. Valentin explained it. Blown up by a bomb. The letter came on Thursday."

"Ma'am, I'm sorry—"

"This is not what I want to tell you! I don't need your pity! I want you to promise not to betray me. No, I don't care. We have only a moment. But I have a friend who has disappeared. I must give his name to the police."

"Ma'am—"

"And I know where he is! Sasha Andromedes is his name—he is not well. Otherwise this woman would not have this hold on him. I remember you used to prosecute these women, conjurers and magicians not so long ago. Every month this was in the papers, jail terms and fines. Now you've stopped. Is it because this witch is living in the palace now? Sasha Andromedes was a friend of my poor brother. He is very sick."

"Then you must search in the hospitals."

She studied him. How painful—the sureness of the young. Sometimes his daughter looked at him like this.

But what was the point of appealing to his honesty if she was going to lie to him? A friend of her brother's—was that why she was in tears? Was that why she was afraid to question her own husband? Sasha Andromedes—God curse him. What did he represent? The inadequacy of men.

But Luckacz would not be cruel, not to Colonel Bocu's wife. He could not promise her, but it was true: The baroness would be punished for this last piece of conjuring. Elena Bocu-Bibescu would be revenged on her rival. And he would be the instrument of her revenge—that was a way to think about it. Perhaps there was some comfort there for him. "I do not mean to make a joke," he said. "You understand that in the present circumstances these things are difficult. But I will make an inquiry, as you say, a confidential inquiry as you prefer. . . ."

Behind them there were footsteps and the doorknob jiggled. Quick as a weasel, Madame Bocu slipped forward and embraced him, put her cheek against his cheek. Then she was out the door on the opposite side, just as the door behind him opened and the colonel strode into the room.

For a moment he glanced around and his eyes narrowed, as if he smelled something. Then he came forward with his hand out, a broad-chested man with a powerful grip, younger than Luckacz as so many people were. People of importance. People of influence. He had colorless eyes, cropped hair, a gray moustache. He wore the symbol of his party, an eagle's foot with the talons outstretched, on an enameled button pinned to his lapel, where Luckacz had formerly worn his own pin of the white tyger. And he started in at once. "I value punctuality and I am sorry to be late. My excuse is this Ceausescu woman, who once more has found a way to embarrass me. You will appreciate this, as it is a matter of public order. Four criminals under arraignment, all disappeared from the People's Keep. Two men poisoned or some such, one with a wife and child. I tell you if you get your old job back, it will be your first priority to dispose of this—difficult, of course. The two men are useless as witnesses, I can assure you."

So Luckacz didn't have to choose whether to wait or give his speech. Circumstances came together. "Colonel Bocu-Bibescu," he ennunciated carefully. "I have come to offer you some information."

But he could not help but picture the face of the pretty young woman who had stood here praising his discretion not five minutes before. "Sir," he said, and then he went on in his ugly voice, describing first his investigation into the death of the boy at 351 Camatei—the saturated gloves, the partial interview with Vladimir O'Brien. Then he described the scientific evidence as it pertained to his examination of the bullets in the long revolver, Prince Frederick's gun.

As he was speaking, Colonel Bocu moved around the room. Then he drew out the leather armchair and sat down behind the desk. He took a cigar from a wooden box, sniffed it, crinkled it beside his ear. Then he snipped the end and lit it while he put his boots up on the empty leather surface of the desk, staring at Luckacz as he spoke.

Luckacz watched the toes of his own muddy shoes. He watched the pattern on the carpet spread away from them. So he was taken by surprise when he heard the colonel chuckle and then burst out laughing, while gouts of pungent smoke drifted above his head. He brought his fist up to his mouth to cough, and then sat forward with his eyes wet from mirth. Luckacz stopped talking, reached a kind of end, while at the same time he was astonished by this man—how long had it been since he'd heard anyone laugh like this? Doubtless the colonel now saw his way clear and straight ahead of him. But that wasn't the cause of his laughter; it couldn't be.

"Do you remember," he gasped, "how we used to go see her at the old Ambassadors? And now here she is more than twenty years later and she's still showing her same backside. She's got a performance tonight; she's still got us by the short hairs! Kevin Markasev, you say—Kevin Markasev the bold! Admit it is a kind of genius, all these years."

And he laughed with his face red, his mouth open wide enough to swallow the whole city. Watching him, astonished, even Radu Luckacz was forced to smile.

19 *A Final Act*

LATER THAT AFTERNOON, he arrived at the People's Palace with an escort of soldiers from the Brancoveanu Artillery. He climbed the stairs to the baroness's apartment overlooking the Piata Revolutiei.

She was at her mirror, looking at her face in preparation for the evening performance at the Ambassadors. Lately she had had to ponder the occasional line or crease, and today a knotted blood vessel that seemed to have risen quite suddenly to the surface over her right temple. These small blemishes, of course, were immaterial. They could be hidden with a little powder, and in any case they were invisible onstage.

She knew it was he. Jean-Baptiste had a rude way of knocking, a sudden pounding on the jamb with the heel of his hand. But Radu Luckacz was more tentative, the way he scratched at the panel with his nails.

"Come in," she said, and he came in.

But if his knocking was the same, she had to admit he had changed in other ways. Sitting at her mirror, smiling at him with the long brush in her hand, she thought about the day he'd first come to her house in Saltpetre Street. Not so long. Five years or so ago. And he'd been quite well dressed and quite distinguished, with his gray hair combed straight back, his glossy moustache. After that he had lost weight, of course, and taken to wearing the same black suit of clothes. Now he had shaved, and he was bald as an egg. She was responsible for that. And in place of his ordinary felt hat, now he was wearing this new fashion in official circles, this brimless gray soldier's cap that was constructed like an envelope. And of course this gray uniform of Colonel Bocu's, with its tin button—a bird's foot. She had not seem him wear it before.

She had always excelled at reading people's faces. He almost didn't need to speak. "So," she said. "My old friend."

All day long it had been threatening to rain. The heat and dampness were oppressive. Nicola Ceausescu sat back in her chair. A small book of poetry was lying open on the table, just a dozen pages tied together. She picked it up and fanned herself, a few slow strokes. Even his nasal, officious speech, when it came all in a rush, would be endearing, she decided.

IT DID NOT seem that way to him. "Madam, I have just come directly from the offices of the *Roumania Libera*, where I was able to receive a preliminary copy of tomorrow's newspaper. At the beginning of the week as you must know, the editors will publish an artistic commentary and their theatrical reviews. Because of your long service to the Roumanian people, they have allowed me to show you this."

The article took up most of the front page. It was in the form of a general editorial under a bold-faced headline: THE CANCER OF DECADENCE. And then in smaller type: In Defense of Our Traditions.

The ink was so new, it came off on his hands as he passed her the folded sheet. He watched her spread it out on her small table, watched her grope for her wire spectacles and hook them behind her ears. For the first time he imagined her beauty might have a kind of frailty and one day it might disappear—a thought that made it hard for him to breathe. He watched the lines form and re-form on her forehead as she tried to puzzle out the words. Perhaps she'd assumed, because of what he'd said about her service to Roumania, that she would see the usual list of bewildered encomiums—the *Libera* had always been the more radical of the two daily papers. The baroness had often boasted of her contempt for all her critics, whether they praised her or blamed her. But Luckacz could see she was reading avidly.

How painful it was for him to watch her, because he knew what she was seeing, had seen it himself—indeed, had seen it written. By her various exclamations and expressions he imagined where she might be in the text. He pitied her and at the same time admired her calmness as she sighed, unhooked her spectacles, and turned to face him.

"What garbage," she said.

But he knew her well enough to know she was affected. How could she not be? "Garbage," she repeated. "They must hate everything they haven't seen a thousand times before."

And then she went through the process of putting on her spectacles again so she could quote to him: " '. . . When she retired at the apex of her fame, it was from the purest of motives and in order to pursue another nobler vocation, that of wife to a distinguished hero and of mother to his son. In this she showed herself to be an artist of a pure Roumanian kind. For it she justly earned the plaudits of her countrymen, who saw in this choice a culmination of her entire career, during which she had shown herself over the course of many performances to personify in every changing character the spirit and genius of her race, a true daughter of Great Roumania—' This is not even grammatical! 'Now, since her ill-advised return to the stage, we have seen creep into her performances the effect of many years of German occupation, by which we mean theatrical ideas that flout our traditions for the sake of flouting them, and for the sake of a so-called modernity that was always more appropriate in Berlin. Most unfortunate has been the way she has chosen to reprise her greatest triumphs, betraying our memories and her own gifts. Chief among these is the travesty of her performance of Medea, at the Ambassadors through the end of next week. . . .' Etcetera, etcetera—can you believe it?"

She was angry. "How can they even say such things to me? All that work when I was young, every line of it was translated from some foreign language. Every note of it was foreign. Now finally there is something that is authentic here in Bucharest—the Germans hate it, too! But for these idiots, what do they want except folk tales and folk music—Gypsy girls with fat knees dancing in embroidered dresses, and copies of copies of something terrible!"

She did not mention, Luckacz noticed, a single word of one thick paragraph. An actress at thirty-nine could scarcely hope to re-create the roles she had made famous at sixteen, particularly not in the same costumes—this was what the editors maintained. To Luckacz these lines seemed particularly cruel, particularly untrue. Never had the baroness appeared so beautiful to him, as she ran her fingers through her copper-colored hair, and stripped the glasses from her nose for one last time. She looked—tired, he supposed.

"Well, it doesn't matter. The carriage will come for me in half an hour. Will you come see an old woman perform tonight? You remember when I first met you, it was because of some misplaced tickets."

Yes, he supposed it was. "Madam," he persevered. "Colonel Bocu-Bibescu is fond of Gypsy dancing."

Nicola Ceausecu laughed. "You don't surprise me." Then after a moment her expression changed. "Tell me what you mean."

He told her how the colonel had withdrawn the lease for the Ambassadors Theatre, on the strength of this article and others still to come. He would close it down for renovations. The new National Theatre and Dinamo Stadium, both symbols of Germanic excess, would also be closed during this period of crisis.

She looked at him. He blinked, admiring the late-afternoon sunlight on her perfect skin, perfect teeth. "I don't understand," she said.

Then he told her about the militiamen who waited for her at the Malachite Stairs, and who would escort her to her house in Saltpetre Street and keep her under watch until these charges of murder and conjuring could be investigated.

Despite his anger, despite his disgust and contempt for her behavior, he felt his heart was breaking as he looked at her. One of her big, thick-knuckled hands was laid out on the newspaper. With the other, she touched her hair and neck and collarbone as he spoke to her in his harsh, foreign voice.

He noticed there was no ashtray beside her, and he had not seen her with a cigarette after that fatal night when he stood with her on the balcony above the Mycenean Gate. And the smell of tobacco smoke seemed to have dissipated from the room. Was it possible she'd managed to abandon this dirty habit? He'd always deplored it, thought it was unsuitable for women. She had washed her hands, he noticed. The nails were unlined, unstained with nicotine. So was she capable of change? Was it possible that she could transform herself in the right circumstances?

She rose. She turned, stood with her back to him at the threshold of her bedchamber, where she kept her alchemical machines, he knew. "And this is for the sake of an editorial letter that has not yet appeared. Radu," she said, the first time she had used his given name. "You are a brave man to tell me these things."

But she didn't reproach him, even though he had betrayed her. Even though she must have guessed he had betrayed her. Instead she faltered and went on: "Aren't you—doesn't it occur to you—to be afraid of me?"

Then she turned. She stood by the piano in her summer dress. As was her habit, she wore no jewelry or any other adornment. But he imagined, as he saw her lips move, that she was muttering some kind of spell, because she did seem to change a little bit. And perhaps it was a trick of the light where she stood now in shadow. But she did seem ominous to him, and sinister, and beautiful beyond words. Perhaps she'd released something into the air that made it hard for him to breathe. Even now, he asked himself, what would happen if he forced himself to go to her and take her in his arms?

"These are superstitions, ma'am," he croaked.

She relaxed and smiled. "I suppose you're right."

Her next expression was so melancholy and regretful, he had to speak. "Ma'am, it might not be too late. If I could take you to the colonel and if you could promise to release a statement of support for his people, his candidates in the elections he has planned—something of that nature . . ."

She laughed. "Beau-cul," she said—beautiful bottom. "Perhaps on the election cards there could be a symbol to express his name."

So that was that. But she went on: "There is one thing. This article, as you call it, though it is nothing but slander, as you know. It will appear in tomorrow's edition of the *Libera*?"

"A special edition," murmured Radu Luckacz.

"A special edition. And because of it, Colonel Bocu will close the Ambassadors for renovations?"

"Yes. I will speak to the manager tonight."

"He will be disappointed. Every night they have pulled me back onto the stage with their bravos, sometimes more than twenty times."

"Ma'am, I'm sorry."

She raised her hand, showing her unbitten nails. "That does not interest me. But you must tell me—what about tonight? People will be arriving at the theater in half an hour. The soldiers could take me and bring me back, or to Saltpetre Street. You yourself could accompany me. You will understand that these are lies," she said, indicating the paper on the table. "All of them are lies, except the things you know that are the truth."

She was talking about the death of Kevin Markasev, Luckacz guessed. "Please. My art has been my comfort," she said. "Now that Felix is gone."

It was impossible, what she suggested. He'd always avoided seeing her on stage, because he understood nothing about modern art. No, that wasn't it. But he did not wish to share her in a crowd of men.

Never had she seemed more beautiful to him. Was it possible, after tonight, that he would never again stand beside her like this, intimate in the same room? And in the newspaper he had read a description of one of her costumes. It occurred to him that he would like very much to see her wearing such a thing.

"Please," she said. "Perhaps I've gone on too long—it's true. Perhaps it is time for me to retire. Perhaps you will tell me, my old friend. You'll be the judge. I promise you have nothing to fear from a poor woman with the world against her. But you must not rob me of my last performance, my finale."

No, he could not. And he would not rob himself of the pleasure of her company. Coming up the stairs to her apartment, he had imagined terrible reproaches from her lips. But even without that, everything would change after tonight, and perhaps it had all changed already. He could tell from her and how she treated him. But perhaps that was what the theater was—a pretense of reality, of authenticity. The Baroness Ceausescu was famous throughout Europe for her skill.

And Luckacz also might have hidden talents. Bocu be damned!

But they would have an escort of soldiers. And more policemen would surround the theater. Nothing would go wrong. This is what he would say to Bocu: He was protecting him from moving too fast in advance of public opinion, as it was interpreted in the pages of the newspaper.

He would let Nicola Ceausescu play Medea one more time. And he would sit and watch her or else wait for her backstage. He imagined all this in the corridor outside her chamber, while she composed herself and made her preparations. As he spoke to one of his men and sent him off, Luckacz asked himself for a moment if she might try to trick him or make a fool of him. He checked his watch and hesitated by the door. When all the soldiers were dispatched, he wondered if he should bring them back to fetch her out. He put his hand on the knob to see if she had locked the door, but then it opened inward and she swept past him without a word. She wore her long red coat, and her expression when she looked at him was sad and gentle and contemptuous.

He deserved nothing more. All that day he had nursed his sense of outrage and humiliation, preparing for the moment when she would be gone from him, dead to him, and here it was. He followed her downstairs. And he supposed her attitude, regardless of anything that had passed between them, was natural for an artist putting on a role—she couldn't talk to him, couldn't acknowledge his presence if she wanted to, even if she felt she had to justify herself to him one final time before the end. No, she was the prisoner of her art, and she would treat him like a spy and a thief and a traitor whatever she felt, not that he deserved anything different. Perhaps he was the one who should beg for her forgiveness.

How could she have forced him to do what he had done?

Was it possible he could explain himself? No, the time was past. As he followed her, he could tell she had assumed a personality that was not herself, that would reject all explanation as weak and craven. For tonight, for one last time she was the ancient queen of Colchis, imperious and passionate—not that he knew much about the character of Medea, other than what everybody knew. She had had a palace near Constanta, and she had murdered her own sons in the old days.

"Ma'am," he said, "please . . . ," but she wouldn't answer him. Perhaps after the performance, when she could drop this artifice . . . What nonsense was he thinking? Tonight she would not sleep in the People's Palace. She would not come back to these rooms. No, she was making her good-byes as she walked the corridors to the Spanish Gate, nodding at servants or soldiers or Bocu's officers, or else ignoring them. Tonight she'd spend in house arrest in Saltpetre Street. Was it possible Luckacz would never be alone with her again? That from now on he would have to share her with all the other men who loved her and hated her, all the men who bowed or stood out of her way in these lower rooms?

He stopped and let her go. He watched the back of her red coat move through the crowd in the empress's reception hall; there were soldiers at the opposite doors to wait for her. Several men came up to him and he refined his orders, wondering what Bocu would make of this. Was he disobeying his instructions? He no longer knew. There was some imprecision, some room for independent choices, and the main thing was accomplished. He had caught the white tyger in a trap.

He followed her carriage to the theater. Soldiers on horseback rode in front of her, clearing the way. Soldiers rode behind her with their sabers drawn, while the crowd stood on the pavement; Luckacz arrived close to the hour. He had given himself time to speak to the manager and procure a ticket at the last minute, one of a pair that had been reserved for Colonel Bocu and his wife. The reservations had been cancelled suddenly that afternoon.

Luckacz was relieved. Elena Bibescu would not have enjoyed herself, he felt sure. In his carriage he'd been nervous he wouldn't find a seat, particularly when he saw the people massed between the columns of the porch. He was also nervous he might not be properly dressed—it didn't matter. There were plenty of men like him in Bocu's gray uniform, and plenty of others in Antonescu's black and green. There would be a fight between the two of them, that much was sure.

His fauteuil was in the middle of the third row. The Ambassadors was a brick building in the center of the old city, built in a maze of cobblestone alleys. Bocu was right: The building was in need of restoration, Luckacz thought as he sat watching the people take their seats under the gas chandelier, as he listened to the loud, flat talk. The white paint was faded in the hall, streaked with soot. There was no magic here, no conjuring. The footlights smoked and flickered in a semicircle under the proscenium. Then the room was dark, and everyone was quiet, and Nicola Ceausescu was onstage.

He had noticed in the program a synopsis of the play, which mentioned a number of supporting characters and musicians. So he was surprised to see the baroness standing by herself, dressed not in some approximation of antique royal splendor—he had expected, he supposed, a gold headdress, and necklaces, and earrings, such as he'd once seen in the museum in Constanta when he had first come to Roumania. Instead she wore an ordinary peasant's costume from the mountains, a colorless ragged dress below her knees. And when she opened her mouth, he found he could recognize the tune. There was a flute playing somewhere behind the painted scene.

But he knew nothing of Florio Lucian's music! No, this was part of a melody he had heard the baroness go over late at night while he waited outside her room in the People's Palace. With a dawning sense of confusion and horror and fascination, Luckacz realized he was listening to the overture from *The White Tyger*, which the baroness had been preparing all these years.

Later this work would be performed in all the capitals of Europe and in all the great opera houses. There would be a full orchestra and a stage full of actors, dancers, singers. But at its premiere in Bucharest, it was presented for the most part as an unaccompanied cycle of songs. And when Nicola Ceausescu started to sing, her voice was low, toneless, weak, cracked, and faltering—it didn't matter. Radu Luckacz found himself sitting forward like the others, straining to catch and understand each note, each word.

This was the story of the baroness's life, how she'd been born in a hut with a sod roof, all that. Everyone knew this story. The details didn't matter. But the crowd sat bewildered, hypnotized, and astonished. It was as if they watched a magician or a conjurer produce a series of predictable effects—a rabbit in a hat, perhaps, or a pigeon, or a bouquet, or an endless stream of colored handkerchiefs—yet with an intensity and conviction that suggested an entire world of magic, genuine and menacing and beautiful beyond belief. If the magician's coat is threadbare, it doesn't matter. Even if you see and understand the trick, it doesn't matter.

At each break in the story or else each new song, Nicola Ceausescu would change her clothes. She wouldn't leave the stage. Luckacz saw there were many costumes scattered on the floor in little clumps around her feet, and she would strip them off or draw them on with scarcely a gap in the music. But the footlights would dim and flicker without human agency, it seemed. For a moment, always, she'd be standing unclothed, naked on the boards, making no attempt to hide or display herself. And at these moments she was never more than almost seen, almost unseen, her small breasts and narrow hips, the shadow between her legs. Prostitute, beggar, pickpocket, actress, bride, baroness, mother, widow, bankrupt, conjurer, murderess—all the familiar and hidden stations of her life's journey. Luckacz found himself traveling with her along that road, as if her theme or subject was his own failure and triumph, his own moments of nakedness. Sometimes she danced.

"Ah, God," he murmured as she told the story of the last years, how she'd tricked and fooled her way into the People's Palace. Luckacz was exhausted, wrung out, yet still she didn't lose or let flicker the unbearable concentration of her art. In the crowded theater, Luckacz sat as if alone while she performed on his own private, bare, inner stage. But at the same time he was aware of the combined power of the crowd, especially as she built to the events of the past months, her persecution of Miranda Popescu, her intimate betrayal of Kevin

Markasev. Everyone could guess how the story might come to an end here in this building on this night. Everyone could leap ahead to one of several ends, no doubt for himself or herself as well. Without a single conscious thought, Luckacz came to understand the error he had made, sitting here in Bocu's seat, allowing this to happen. There would be no possibility of his old job, or any municipal employment of any kind. He would be lucky to escape prison. All of this was a public outrage. Tonight he would go home and try to explain things to his wife, and see if he could find some shelter there under the wreck of all his hopes.

He noticed there was no song about Andromedes. But after the murder of her younger son, Nicola Ceausescu made a resting place. What was to come? Here she was. Bocu and Luckacz had tracked her down. From the evening gown she'd worn on the balcony above the Mycenaean Gate, she stripped to nothing once again. And then again the conjurer's trick—she had a snake in her hands, a little, writhing, hooded snake that slithered up her arm and rose above her shoulder. She had a knife in her other hand, a cruel, curved blade, and as every man in the house rose from his seat, she drew it across her naked breasts, puncturing them, and what came out was like blood.

TIRED AND FLUSHED, and sensitive to every small current of emotion, the baroness sat in the secret alchemical laboratory beyond her bedroom in the People's Palace. She had arrived to the end, and she felt some of the peculiar sense of dissatisfaction that came to her after every performance, dissatisfaction and an urge to laugh. What would she do now for an encore? Perhaps she could let the simulacrum burst into flames. That would close the theater, make its renovation necessary.

Or else she would take her knife and plunge it into Radu Luckacz's face while she stood above him naked, poised on the arms of his fauteuil. He had betrayed her—no. Perhaps it was all for the best. Perhaps he was her old friend after all.

Jean-Baptiste pounded on the outside door. "There's no time." And so she let the simulacrum lie, shifting and deflating beyond the circle of lights. She looked around her room without regret. She'd never come here again. She had some belongings wrapped in an old cloth, but now she pulled the bundle open on her lap. It was too heavy. On a whim she discarded the revolver and the black book, laid them out on the lighted altar of Cleopatra—she hoped she had not given any offense. She hoped the end of her performance had contained nothing the goddess might find insulting or presumptuous, because she had rejected Cleopatra after all.

She had chosen Medea and the chariot of dragons. And she'd take with her just a change of clothes, and the manuscript of her musical score. Now she had some new ideas for it, and she imagined an entire new act, which she might work on in Trieste or in the little house in Geneva by the lake.

"It's past time," yelled Jean-Baptiste. Then he left her to attend to the horses, the first stage to Beograd and Sarajevo. She would meet him in the east wing by the cleaning closet and the servants' stair.

She was dressed as a chambermaid in a rough skirt and apron, her chestnut hair tied up and covered with a cotton cap. But she was sure of her abilities, sure that no one would see her or recognize her on the way, even if she strode through Rudolph's Gallery in her most formal clothes, or else stark naked. Again she laughed, a soft explosion of breath.

She stood up, swung her bundle to her shoulder. She walked past the screen into her bedroom, laying her hand for a moment on the iron frame of the unmade bed—oh, she had many regrets. Though at that moment she wasn't thinking about Aegypta Schenck or Kevin Markasev or little Felix. All that was in the past, expiated on the stage of the Ambassadors, where she'd had her first triumph years before. Now a new act was beginning, and she was only thirty-nine. There was much good to be accomplished, she was sure, among the people of Italy or Switzerland. There was much comfort she could distribute as a patron or a model or a symbol for the poor.

She passed the threshold of her music chamber, where she had spent so many happy hours. Then she was in the corridor—no, it was here, the source of her regret, behind the locked door of the adjoining room. There were doctors in Switzerland, competent specialists, she knew. She'd left instructions for Jean-Baptiste. She'd specified a private railway compartment to follow after her; she would meet the train at the frontier. She'd known Jean-Baptiste for many years. He was her oldest friend. But what if he also betrayed her at long last? She knew his opinion of Sasha Andromedes.

She must go. But at the final moment she slipped the key from around her neck and unlocked the door to the dark room, just to say good-bye, or au revoir, or even à bientôt.

Just a minute, only for a minute, then. She locked the door from the inside.

A quarter of an hour later, the exasperated Jean-Baptiste climbed up the stairs from the Spanish Gate, where the black carriage waited. In the corridor he was in time to hear a scream, a single crystalline note that shattered suddenly. He recognized it from the final page of Lucian's opera, when the dragon appears onstage, the beast that pulls Medea's airborne chariot. Muttering and cursing, he pounded on the door; he'd never had a taste for this music. He couldn't believe the baroness would waste her opportunity to escape. This was her plan, after all.

But when he rattled the handle, she didn't respond. He spoke her name, then hurried back to the top of the stairs to listen for Bocu's men. Full of doubts and frustration, he pulled out his skeleton key. Did he have the boldness to unlock the door?

There was a conversation drifting up from down below, and he climbed down to the landing to listen. At the second turning of the stair, he heard a crash from up above.

But he was not in time to see the beast slink down the corridor the other way. He stared in horror at the lower panel of the door, the lacquered wood scratched to pieces. He did not see on the stairs or in the corridor the coarse gray beast, larger and fiercer now than she had ever been in Massachusetts, or on Christmas Hill, or on the Hoosick River in the snow. Larger and fiercer than she'd been in Chiselet.

She hid inside the doorway of the Diamond Ballroom as the servants and the soldiers passed, running for the elevators and the upper floors. Then she made for the servants' quarters, her nails slipping on the marble tiles. Oh, she was clever and secret—Andromeda was used to this. She climbed down through the Mycenaean Portal and out into the piata, which was empty now.

The colonel had imposed a curfew. Past midnight the beast went slinking through the streets to wait outside his house in the Strada Italiana. She leapt onto the roof of a low shed, pulled herself onto a sloping pile of bricks, and reached the garden wall behind the house. When Elena Bibescu went walking among the flowers just at dawn, she knelt in the dirt under the trees to push her hands through the stiff fur. At first she thought the beast was hurt, because there was so much blood.

Turn the page for a preview of

Paul Park

Coming in April 2008

A TOR HARDCOVER

ISBN-13: 978-0-7653-1668-4 ISBN-10: 0-7653-1668-4

HE SQUATTED DOWN and slid his hook into Adira's neck just above his breastbone. Delicately, with the point of his prosthesis, he unbuttoned the front of Adira's tunic. "I felt this before. I wonder what it is."

In the afternoon, Peter's company would return to the front line, and there were rumors of a push. He had no time to waste here, but he was curious about the envelope over Adira's heart—was it the same as his? A memento, a talisman, a good-luck charm? Peter didn't think so. With his left hand he unfolded it, opened it up. Underneath, tucked into Adira's undershirt was a wad of reichmarks. This was what the man had meant when he had talked about paying him.

The paper on the inside of the envelope was sky-blue with threads of silk. There were pages of hieroglyphs drawn in gold. Andromeda might have been able to read them, Peter thought.

So: an African carrying messages from Africa. Under the bare trees in the dead, long grass, the world was calm. Corporal Adira, if that was really his name, was sniveling because of his broken leg. But even that was a hopeless little noise.

There were birds in the branches above Peter's head. And in the dawn light, on the hill south of the town he could see the battery come to life, the men pulling the howitzers out of their pens. It was quiet in that wood behind the line, the day-long hush before the evening thunder.

"Tell me what this says," he said.

"I—I don't know. It is from Abyssinia."

"I can see that. You don't know what it says?" Peter removed the wad of currency. "Where are you taking this?"

"To Brasov, sir. Dispatches. The money is for my sister and my mother. Not for myself—I swear it."

Peter wrinkled up his nose. "And you're from Abyssinia?"

"Yes. No. My father—"

"And you think this will help?"

"Yes. Yes I do. Yes, sir. Something must be done."

"I wonder."

Around them the day was gathering. The men on the hill were unwrapping the long muzzles of the 75-millimeter cannons.

Peter Gross looked up. "Twenty-five years ago, we marched through this country carrying rifled muskets with percussion caps. Now we have machine guns and grenades—from Africa, but they supply both sides. It's for the money, don't you think?"

"I don't know."

"That's what I think. It's too much money to resist."

They spoke in murmurs behind the ruined wall. The trees above them were full of little birds that suddenly took flight, turning all at once. Now a single long shaft of sunlight broke through the clouds.

Deep in the east, the light came slipping toward them over the broken fields and the remains of last year's harvest. "I'm going back," said Captain Gross. "I'll turn this over to my colonel. He'll send someone to pick you up."

"Please, sir, no. For the love of God. It's—it's about Chiselet. The accident at Chiselet. This is an investigation by the government in Addis Ababa—that's all. I swear to God."

Peter turned the papers over, examined the backs of them. "What do you know about Chiselet?"

"Nothing, sir—I'm just a messenger."

Peter laughed. "And not a good one. You're not the right man for this."

He dropped the wad of money in the dirt. The little man, still weeping, lying on his side, clutched at it feebly. "No, sir."

Peter got to his feet. He brushed off the knees of his trousers, stood for a moment squinting into the wide sun, sniffing at the air. From here, looking north toward the great river, you almost wouldn't know there was a war.

He turned and walked away through the orchard toward the communication trench. He would inform the military police after he'd returned to Theta Company. In the meantime he was being followed.

He recognized the scent first of all, an animal and human mixture. In cheap hotels across North Africa and the Levant, he'd gotten used to it. Now he sniffed it with an odd sense of nostalgia. Rank and appealing, heavy and light, there had been a time when it had disgusted him. Those also had been difficult days.

But difficult or not, now they seemed touched with gold, with the warm morning light that caressed every prewar memory, everything that had happened before the Turks had crossed the line. He turned and lifted up his nose, waiting for her to take shape somewhere in the dead weeds—dog, woman, or man. Standing over the idiotic spy, her name had occurred to him. Was that when he had first caught the scent? Maybe not, because he thought about her often, her and Miranda Popescu. Every hour, maybe more.

"Where are you?" he whispered.

"Behind you." Her harsh, queer voice. Maybe she crouched on the other side of the stone wall. But he heard her clearly. "Don't turn around," she said.

They spoke in English. "What do you want?"

"Just to see you, first of all. You're a hard man to find alone."

"I must go back," he said.

Then after a moment: "How is Miranda? Is she safe?"

She didn't answer him. "I have a favor to ask. For old times' sake. Past times in the Ninth Hussars."

They had served together under General Schenck von Schenck. Miranda's father. That's where they'd known each other first. So long ago, it seemed like the beginning of the world.

"Yes?"

"I know you're having trouble with conscriptions, all the Transylvanian battalions. I want to know if I could volunteer, and you could bring me in."

Now suddenly he remembered that old campaign, the sights and sounds conjured to life as if by a few harsh, toneless words. The smell of leather and horses when they were camping in the birch trees above Nova Zagora. Brandy around the fire. The view from the ridge when on horseback he had taken his men down. Not like now, cowering in a hole.

"You're crazy," he said.

Then, because she didn't answer, he went on. "We're not soldiers anymore. We're up against machines. Machines stuck in the mud. You know, like those *Terminator* movies."

It was too tempting not to make a little joke, to bring back something from the other past they shared, when they had been kids together in Berkshire County. And she laughed.

"No," he said again. "You're crazy."

She was laughing. "Please. Don't make this hard. I beg you. Think of that: I'm begging you. Take me as a private soldier under your command."

He understood it must be true—this must be hard for her to say. She had not loved him then, nor did she love him now. She'd been a lieutenant in the old days, Sasha Prochenko on a big white stallion, so dashing and romantic in his forest-green uniform, high boots, fawn-colored pants, so popular with the ladies, his blue eyes flecked with silver. And later at Mamaia Castle on the beach . . .

"No. This is not a place for you. It's not what we need. How could you pass the physical?"

When she said nothing, he continued. "Can you see yourself in a latrine with twenty men?"

That made her pause. "I had not thought you were so cruel."

He looked around. Her voice had changed, and she was closer. "What about your own physical exam?" she asked. "Or were you always Captain Hook?"

Then again: "I am begging you."

"No!" he cried, angry now. Morning had come. There was no time. "Wasn't it your job to stay with Miranda and protect her? Isn't that what we decided, what we agreed on in Cismigiu

Park? I wish that was my job, not to die here in this place. This cesspit."

Now he could see her in the morning sunlight. She stood up on the other side of the wall. She climbed over between the tumbled stones. Always the dandy. Civilian clothes—her pants perfectly creased. She carried a silver-headed cane.

She had a way that both attracted and repulsed him. But he had seen no women for many months, and his heart lifted when he saw her. She was too exotic for mere beauty—her yellow hair under the slouch hat, the soft body hair that made her exposed skin seem to glow, the proud expression and strong features in which her animal nature, now, seemed to predominate. But the sharp, musky smell had disappeared. He was used to it already.

Though she was dressed as a man, and in spite of the dog or wolf that lurked inside of her, she looked more girlish or womanly than she ever had in Berkshire County. Her hair was longer now, curling down below her ears. "It doesn't seem so bad," she said, looking around at the quiet orchard, the guns on the hillside raising their muzzles to the sky.

"It's a beautiful sight," she persisted. "You'd better go. A girl can dream."

But now Peter wanted to stay a moment longer. "Promise me you'll go back to her. This is not the place for you. The Condesa de Rougemont—in Bucharest we had no choice except for her to take Miranda in. But do you remember her on the Hoosick riverbank? Young woman then, old lady now—the place stank of magic."

Andromeda gave him a blank look. She didn't remember. How could she remember? "I don't trust her," he went on. "No matter what Madame de Graz says. I wish I could—no . . . leave a message at the hospital. Will you do that? There's a corporal of the Fifty-third Light Infantry over in those trees. He's got a broken leg. And tell me," he continued. "What does this say?"

He thrust the envelope of hieroglyphs into her gloved hand. She didn't need to squint to read it. "This is a shopping list. Small arms."

"Sure," said Peter. "Is that all?"

"No, it's not all. Chiselet—do you remember Chiselet?"

She smiled, then went on. "You weren't yourself. Neither was I. But I saw those lead canisters in the baggage car. That's what they're talking about here."

Peter shrugged. Andromeda raised the paper to her nose and sniffed it. "They must have been blown up in the explosion," she said, "except for one. An Abyssinian in a gray suit. He crawled out to die south of the tracks. I took the suit, his money, and his watch. But I left the canister two hundred meters in the marsh—a dead oak tree. You could see from the embankment. Everything else was to the north."

Peter scratched his right forearm where the leather cuff chafed. He had his own memories of that day and the wreck of the Hephaestion. From there he'd gone to Mogosoaia, where he'd found Miranda Popescu. "Tell me," he said, though by now it was too late to listen, "how is everyone in Stanesti-Jui? How is she?"

He spoke the name of the village like a charm. It was impossible to send a letter, though he had written many, or else the same one over and over. "Tell me, is she safe?"

Andromeda smiled, cruel in her turn, he thought. Her teeth were sharp and numerous. "You'd better go." And then after a moment: "In any case, I've been in Bucharest."

"Don't tell me you haven't seen her!" Peter said. "Promise me you'll watch over her—is that too much to ask, while I am here? Inez de Rougemont—I saw her on the Hoosick River, dressed in Gypsy clothes. Since then I've told myself that was not real. Madame de Graz had vouched for her, her oldest friend. She talks about her in her letters, but how can I be sure? Promise me you'll go there now."

For a moment there was no irony or slyness in her face. But she was as he remembered her—his old comrade in arms.

"Give her this," he said. He unbuttoned the first buttons of his tunic, then took from an inside pocket the letter he rewrote every fourth day or so, whenever they pulled his platoon from the front line. He kept it over his heart, a piece of superstition. " 'I have a rendezvous with Death,' " he quoted fiercely. "It's lucky I learned that one, isn't it?"

It had been a favorite poem of his mother's in Berkshire

County, a battle poem from the First World War. Now he said it for effect, something Sasha Prochenko might be expected to understand.

Jealous, he supposed, she smiled at him. "It's true—you are the lucky one. I often think about what happened in Chiselet."

Standing in front of him, she took hold of his collar, brushed her fingers against his silver captain's bars. She held his letter in her other hand, along with the hieroglyphic message, which she'd refolded carefully, replaced in its envelope. "No, give it back," Peter said. "I changed my mind—it is not good for me to write to her. That's not what I promised to her father. I said I would protect her, not . . ."

His voice dribbled away. Andromeda supplied the rest. ". . . Care for her? It's not the worst thing."

Was she teasing him? Peter turned his head. He stood looking out over the field. "Madame de Graz told me not to write to her. She told me it was dangerous, because I was a wanted man. She told me the police were looking for me. I haven't seen any proof."

"I'll take your letter," said Andromeda.

"No—I don't want that," Peter said. He reached out for the two envelopes and she came to him. She tucked them into the inside pocket of his uniform. She patted him over his heart, buttoned him up.

Though he was uncomfortable to feel her so close, he did not step away or knock her hands away. He had refused her, after all, rejected her. Her animal scent came back to him, and he could smell the liquor on her breath.

He turned back toward the trench. It was only a couple of minutes later, after she was gone, that he realized she had picked his pocket, taken both envelopes—the letter to Miranda and the pages of hieroglyphs. She'd left him with nothing.